More Praise for
IN THE IMAGE

"In this beautiful first novel, twenty-five-year-old Dara Horn meets you like a torch-bearer in the dark entryway of a mysterious castle, and you follow her into a fascinating labyrinth without looking back. . . . *In the Image* is not merely a striking success as a whole but a technical tour de force [that] has a strange, compelling, romantic fascination."
—David Gelernter, *Commentary*

"Richly imagined. . . . Leora never loses her tourist's eye, and her slightly skewed point of view gives *In the Image* both its poignancy and its wonderfully deadpan humor. . . . [An] intricate web of miracles, coincidences and accidents of fate." —*New York Times Book Review*

"Powerful. . . . In prose that flows like water, Horn tells [a] spiritual odyssey and coming-of-age story . . . with a sure hand and a keen eye for historic detail. A lively, compelling read, *In the Image* not only underscores Jewish identity in America, but more universally, gives suffering meaning and, in the end, hope." —*Seattle Times*

"A stunning example of how to thread the warp of Jewish history into the woof of contemporary American Jewish life. A riveting tale, one that explores a Jewish past as skillfully as it measures the Jewish present. *In the Image* unfolds (and then folds together) its interlocked stories in an accessible way. With this work Dara Horn joins an already impressive gallery of young American Jewish writers." —*Hadassah*

"Simultaneously earthy and sublime, Dara Horn's *In the Image* practically glows with compassionate human warmth and compelling intellectual fervor. Moving deftly from a mundane American suburb (which she wondrously imbues with moral substance) to a portrait of European civility on the verge of barbarity, to a mystical realm where the theologically ineffable becomes surprisingly palpable, it may be the most ambitious and accomplished first novel I have ever read."
—Melvin Jules Bukiet, author of *Strange Fire*

"Impressive . . . remarkable. . . . All of the characters struggle for those gemlike qualities of passion, brilliance, clarity, fire. . . . [Their] worlds intersect in lovely, sometimes heartbreaking ways, as the characters struggle with their memories, their dreams. . . . Horn weaves complex and unforgettable images with strands of sacred text. . . . Memory and identity are at the core of this beautifully written novel, which demands—and rewards—the reader's close attention." —*New Orleans Times-Picayune*

"Riveting—compulsive reading, authoritative from the first sentence. A fine book from a powerful new imagination. Her prose: modest, lucid, and allusive, and ready to knock you down with its strength of perception."
—*PaknTreger*

"*In the Image* is a novel teeming with wisdom—wisdom of Jewish history, theology, and culture, and teeming also with the more quiet, more elusive, wisdom of the human heart. It is a novel full of earned empathy for her characters, both young and old, male and female, religious and secular. I left the novel spellbound by the breadth of Dara Horn's imagination and the generosity of her vision."
—Andrew Furman, author of
*Contemporary Jewish American Writers
and the Multicultural Dilemma*

"[A] fascinating first novel by Dara Horn . . . incredibly poignant . . . with audacious appropriation of lines and themes from Jewish texts. . . . It takes a writer with great self-confidence to pull off this sort of work. . . . [Horn] is a true talent and one of the more promising young American Jewish novelists of the new century." —*Jerusalem Post*

"A novel as deeply felt as it is audacious. *In the Image* is a religious inquiry, a love story, a primer on what to look for when choosing a diamond, an exploration of the dangers and possibilities that lie in the never-reposeful past, a century-long chronicle of the Jewish experience in America, a poetic meditation on the power of images, and a score of other things, all of them connected with a great and satisfying ingenuity in an absorbing narrative that is told with moral passion, vigor, humor, and an unflagging fascination with the coincidences, miseries, grotesqueries, and triumphs of life." —Richard Snow, *American Heritage Magazine*

"An enchanting, introspective and emotionally charged debut. A warmth of appreciation of Jewish culture and heritage, and eloquent use of recurring motifs." —*Publishers Weekly*, starred review

"In this exceptional first novel, Horn deploys rare imaginative gifts to probe the most complex of spiritual themes. Poignant and profound, a novel that invites careful re-reading." —*Booklist*, starred review

"[An] unsettling, otherworldly novel." —*Boston Globe*

"*In the Image* is a gripping story told with learning and passion. It does not just use Jewish sources, it breathes them, and breathes into them the breath of life. Here are fascinating characters who think, who learn, whose lives unfold and whose souls grow."
—Rabbi David Wolpe, Sinai Temple;
coauthor of *Making Loss Matter* and author of *Why Be Jewish?*

"*In the Image* is one of those rare first novels that feels so accomplished you believe the author has been writing for decades already. It is a novel that seems flooded with godly light. Dara Horn's characters—especially Leora, whose journeys lie at the narrative center of the book—become our friends, our relatives. The novel's movements across borders and boundaries are revelatory."
—Jay Parini, author of *The Apprentice Lover*

"Horn creates small worlds, beautifully detailed and textured, that ultimately fit together." —*Jewish Woman*

"With Leora in particular, the author has created a woman of depth and complexity whose emotions and reactions often resonate with accuracy. Even those characters embodying the worst of human nature are compelling." —*Library Journal*

"An ebullient and vibrant new voice." —*Jewish Week*

"A tender and touching story of vanished worlds and recovered lives, where life is framed both in miniature and with an abiding faith in God's grand, often random, design, and where love and loss coexist on both the written page and in the human heart."
—Thane Rosenbaum, author of *The Golems of Gotham*

IN THE IMAGE

IN THE IMAGE

A NOVEL

DARA HORN

W. W. NORTON & COMPANY

NEW YORK LONDON

Copyright © 2002 by Dara Horn

All rights reserved
Printed in the United States of America
First published as a Norton paperback 2003

For information about permission to reproduce selections from this book,
write to Permissions, W. W. Norton & Company, Inc., 500 Fifth Avenue,
New York, NY 10110

Manufacturing by the Haddon Craftsmen, Inc.
Book design by JAM Design
Production manager: Andrew Marasia

Library of Congress Cataloging-in-Publication Data
Horn, Dara.
In the image : a novel / by Dara Horn.
p. cm.
ISBN 0-393-05106-4
1. Jews—New York (State)—New York—Fiction. 2. New York (N.Y.)—Fiction.
3. Jewish families—Fiction. 4. Jewish women—Fiction. I. Title.
PS3608.04945 I6 2002
813'.6—dc21   2002023575
ISBN 0-393-32526-1 pbk.

W. W. Norton & Company, Inc., 500 Fifth Avenue, New York, N.Y. 10110
www.wwnorton.com

W. W. Norton & Company Ltd., Castle House, 75/76 Wells Street,
London W1T 3QT

1 2 3 4 5 6 7 8 9 0

For my parents,
Susan and Matthew Horn,
who took me all over the world,
and for my husband,
Brendan Schulman,
who took me home.

CONTENTS

IN THE IMAGE

CHAPTER 1

TOURISTS

ACCIDENTS OF FATE are rarely fatal accidents, but once in a while they are. Two accidents of fate occurred in Leora's life before she turned seventeen. First, her friend Naomi Landsmann, walking home from their high school on a bright, cold winter afternoon, dropped her glove while crossing a street, bent down to pick it up, and was run over by a car whose newly licensed driver never bothered to look back. And second, eleven months after Naomi's death, Naomi's grandfather Bill Landsmann, spotting Leora's name in the local paper, tried and failed to become Leora's friend.

Bill Landsmann was a tourist. He didn't look like a tourist—no loud-printed shirt, no sunglasses, no healthy tan. In fact, he didn't look much like the type to go anywhere. He was an old man, somewhere in his six-ties or seventies, with a completely white-haired head and a fragile, almost waiflike body that made it particularly hard to picture him lounging on a beach or trekking through the tundra. He had arms like thin reeds and legs like baby tree trunks, and it looked as if a wave or a gust of wind could easily knock him down. Nothing would make Bill Landsmann stand out in a crowd of old men of the skinny variety except perhaps his voice, which was the only clue to the casual observer that he had been anywhere at all. Bill Landsmann spoke with a pronounced German accent, not a harsh one but a refined one, adjusting his pronunciation of *r*'s to suit the word and the occasion, the kind of German accent that might at one time have suggested elegance and culture. There was, however, one other clue to the fact that he had been around. When he looked at things, he didn't see them as other people do. Most people register what they see, however unconsciously, as part of a continuum of time and space, each place and moment melting into the next like sand castles dissolving underwater. But when Bill Landsmann looked around, he saw the world separated into frames, as if his eye were a camera and he were cropping out rectangles of the world, blinking an eye and trapping a moment on the film of his retina. And it showed in the way he glanced at things.

Leora was a tourist too—or, to be precise, she had recently become one. After Naomi's death Leora stopped talking to people. She had never been particularly friendly, and Naomi had been one of her only friends. After Naomi died, Leora stopped speaking and instead simply looked at things, examining her surroundings as if she were a visitor, someone passing through on a long journey. Objects and people, barely distinguishable from each other, froze before her eyes in little panels: students laughing in a school hallway, a fish swimming in an aquarium, her parents, her brother, a bowl of soup in front of her, a pile of old snow by the side of a road.

In the hopes of pulling her out of her silence, Leora's parents had taken her and her brother on a long summer vacation, a tour of several cities in Europe, parts of North Africa, and some of the Middle East. They were thrilled when Leora seemed interested in what she saw, and that fall Leora even won a local essay contest with an entry she had written during their trip, something about Jewish historical sites in Spain. Her parents congratulated themselves, privately declaring her cured. But in fact the trip had only made things worse. Leora had immersed herself in hundreds of years of history, in thousands of miles of places and faces that required nothing more of her than that she click the shutter.

The town paper printed an article about her prizewinning essay on an inside page where all of the other articles were either announcements concerning the local senior citizens' group or obituaries. And that was where Bill Landsmann spotted her, a wandering youth among the ruins, and tracked her down.

"I think we have very similar interests," he told her in his delicate accent over the phone. He introduced himself as Naomi's grandfather, explained that he had met her at a few of Naomi's birthday parties, said that Naomi had spoken of her, often. Leora remembered Naomi mentioning him: a strange man, retired, an amateur photographer who had been around the world. Beyond that Leora remembered nothing about him. "We both are interested in Jewish history, and we both like to travel. Would you like to come visit me? With your parents, they are invited too. I could show you some slides from my travels."

Leora said yes, she would be happy to see the slides. That was her first mistake concerning Bill Landsmann.

"IT'S KIND of strange that Naomi's grandfather would be so interested in Leora, isn't it?" Leora's mother asked.

The family had leased the station wagon a few months before—for some reason, buying a car didn't seem worthwhile anymore—but it still had the New Car Smell. Leora sat in the back, perched on the edge of the hard vinyl seat, and she felt like she was four years old, being discussed by her parents in spelled-out words they thought she didn't understand.

"All old people are interested in Leora these days," her father said, "since she was featured on the Old People page."

"Ha, ha, Dad, very funny," Leora muttered from the backseat. Her parents ignored her. Leora suddenly thought of their summer trip, where in many places they had hired a driver and a guide who would sit in the front, turn backward to face Leora's family in the rear of the car or the van, and lecture to them about the passing buildings—or, in places that didn't have passing buildings, then passing mud huts, passing trees, passing cliffs, passing baboons. For a moment, it seemed to Leora as if her mother were the guide and her father the driver in some strange foreign country, and she felt that confused curiosity that had often comforted her last summer in strange countries, wondering where, exactly, these people were taking her.

"Well, whatever. So he's an old guy, and he reads the Old People page. And he travels a lot. Maybe he just wants to meet someone else in town who likes to travel," her father offered.

"I think there's a little more to it than that," Leora's mother answered. "I mean, think about this guy. His granddaughter dies, his son picks up

and moves to California with the daughter-in-law and grandsons" —
true, Leora thought; it was frightening how quickly Naomi's parents
and little brothers had moved away after she died — "and now what's he
supposed to do with himself? I think he's really just looking for someone to talk to," she said, then paused, as if she had said more than she
intended to.

Leora tried to catch her mother's expression in the rearview mirror,
but it was too dark to see anything. She sat back and looked out of the
car, peering into the uncovered windows of passing houses to catch
glimpses of interiors, decorations, furniture. Houses had interested her
ever since she was a child, when she had kept a dollhouse. Not some
sort of horrible pink plastic contraption, but a real dollhouse — an exact
miniature replica of a three-story town house, complete with painted
clapboard siding, a shingled roof, and furnishings of 1890s-style
grandeur. But Leora could hardly think of it as her dollhouse, because
really it was both hers and Naomi's. When Leora acquired the empty
shell of a dollhouse as a birthday gift long ago, Naomi had been
enchanted by it. They built up the house together, laying down the
grout for the hexagonal floor tiles in the kitchen, putting up the outra-
geous paisley wallpaper that resembled the pattern Naomi's mother
wouldn't let her get for her real room, setting the nonfunctional grandfather clocks past their own bedtimes, arguing for weeks over the names
of each of the little dolls. One day Naomi's parents saw her interest and
asked if she too would like a dollhouse. But Naomi said no. She already
had a dollhouse: Leora's. The dollhouse remained in Leora's bedroom
long after they had grown too old for it, but after Naomi's death Leora
couldn't bear looking at it anymore. She hauled it down underground
to the basement and buried it under boxes of her brother's old toys.

The car turned onto Algonquin Drive. Their town was divided into
sections where all the street names matched a certain theme, and
Algonquin Drive was in the "Indian Section," or, as Leora's somewhat
pretentious teacher at the high school liked to call it, the "indigenous
people's section." Bill Landsmann was indigenous to Algonquin Drive.
Leora's father slowed the car to a crawl, searching among the dimly lit
house numbers for 413. When they found it, a tiny house with thick
curtains drawn over the windows, and walked up to ring the doorbell,
Bill Landsmann had already opened the door for them. Leora did recognize him, once she saw him again. In his narrow lips and his thin-

ness, he resembled Naomi. His left hand was pressed against the door-post, while his right hand, a road map of red and blue arteries and veins glowing through the pale skin, dangled from a perilously thin wrist that looked as though it might tear like paper if he were to offer his hand to them to shake it. He didn't.

"Welcome, welcome!" he announced in the stilted, accented voice Leora remembered from his phone call. "Wonderful to have you. Come in, come in, and I will show you my slides."

When the three of them had entered, Leora noticed that Bill Landsmann's entire house had the New Car Smell. In fact, the vast majority of objects in his house appeared to have been made out of pine paneling and vinyl. They passed through the hallway, devoid of any decoration, and went into the living room. Leora walked behind Bill Landsmann, her parents following behind her, keeping her eye on the back of his white-haired head as if it were a sort of beacon, a torch lead-ing them to their destination. But it was Bill Landsmann's voice that sig-naled them to stop: "Please, have a seat."

Leora and her parents sat down on a hard burgundy vinyl couch. Aside from the couch, the room was furnished with three chairs, a cof-fee table, a rug, and an ancient, wood-encased television set, bestudded with giant dials. Leora was relieved to note, after a quick glance around the room, that no portraits of family members were displayed anywhere. But the strangest part of the room, the part that made it seem as if the three of them had landed in something that wasn't quite a living room at all, was the wall of bookshelves. The shelves, covering an entire long wall of the room, were filled with row upon row of black cardboard boxes, each exactly the same size, distinguishable from one another only by the bright yellow numbers painted, with a perfection that must have required a stencil, on their sides. The numbers went well into the hundreds. Along the right side of the shelves was a small hook, and a black vinyl notebook was hanging from it, suspended by a thick red cord. The bottom shelf was devoted to a complete set of the *Encyclopaedia Judaica*.

"Wow, I see you've got everything catalogued here. What are all those?" Leora's mother asked, looking at the bookshelves.

Bill Landsmann looked at her as if to answer her question, but he didn't. "It is wonderful to have you," he repeated. "I thought we might have something in common. I have visited seventy-two countries,

with a special eye to Jewish history. Oh"—he stopped and looked up
as a tall woman entered the room—"and this is Anna, my wife." To
Leora, Anna also looked vaguely familiar, a burgundy-headed woman
whose hair matched the couch. Leora's father stood up to shake
Anna's hand, but she only smiled at them, a wide and gracious smile,
and hurried to the other side of the room, where she opened the door
to a small closet. She took out a screen, the kind Leora remembered
using to watch filmstrips in elementary school, and set it up against
the window.

"Today I will show you some slides of many various places in the
world," Bill Landsmann continued. "I have arranged these particular
slides so that they show the story of the Bible, displayed in pictures and
works of art." Anna went back to the closet, this time emerging with a
folding chair and a music stand, which she arranged on the far side of
the room, opposite the screen. Then she went back into the closet a
third time. Leora began to think of this as a sort of magic act, like a
magician pulling random objects out of a black hat.

Anna came out of the closet with an ordinary slide projector. She
placed it on an end table near the folding chair and plugged it in, com-
pleting the magic act before disappearing into another room.

Meanwhile Leora had forgotten entirely about Bill Landsmann,
who had not said a word since Anna had reappeared. Now she noticed
that he had wandered over to the bookshelves. He was holding the
dangling black notebook, and Leora watched as he leafed through it
for a moment, squinting though his thick glasses. Then he looked up
at the bookshelf and stood on his tiptoes. It seemed, in Leora's eyes, as
if something were stretching him from floor to ceiling, his waist nar-
rowing in the center like a taut rubber band. He selected box number
seventeen. Once he had brought it down, he pried it open to reveal a
loaded slide carousel, which he placed on the projector. He then
removed a pile of typed onionskin sheets from inside the box, placed
them on the music stand, and turned on a flashlight. The lights in the
room went out.

"I would like to welcome you on a tour around the world," Bill
Landsmann announced, reading from the script on the music stand, "a
tour on which you will see the many sites of the Hebrew Bible, appear-
ing in images around the world. We will begin with Genesis, with the
story of the creation." And so the story began, formless and void, in the

darkness on the face of the deep, and the voice of Bill Landsmann hovered over the waters.

The "tour around the world," taken from the comfort of the vinyl couch, went on for hours. Leora recognized Ghiberti's reliefs from the Baptistery doors in Florence, illustrating the Binding of Isaac; in the slide, Abraham stood arched over his son on a mountaintop as the hand of an angel reached out to stop him, a moment frozen twice, first on the bronze relief and then in Bill Landsmann's slide. "And Abraham saw the mountain from afar, and the two of them walked on together," Bill Landsmann quoted from Genesis, reading from his script. He blinked a picture of an archaeological site below where the ancient Temple once stood in Jerusalem, but in the slide you couldn't see the mosque on the mountain or even the tourists visiting the site, just the rubble of fallen stones as Bill Landsmann read another line: "How the city sits alone, desolate, she that was once full of people, how like a widow!" He showed a slide of goats gathering in a flock alongside a cliff, a picture taken somewhere in central Asia, where one goat had a red cord tied around its horns. "This goat is the scapegoat," Bill Landsmann read aloud, following along with his finger on his script. "We learn about the scapegoat in the Book of Leviticus. The high priest ties a red string around the goat's horns, just like this, and then the goat is pushed off a cliff, to atone for the sins of the people. I myself am a *cohen*, a descendant of the high priest." Poor goat, Leora thought. She imagined Bill Landsmann as the high priest, arranging for the goat to be pushed off a cliff. But before she knew it, they had abandoned the goat to its fate and snapped to the next white-framed slide, and the next, and the next.

The concept was brilliant, in a way: the Bible on film, its greatest moments recorded in stop-action photography, with Bill Landsmann's elegant stage voice reading off relevant verses from his well-rehearsed script. But somewhere around Deutoronomy Leora found herself experiencing a particular sensation familiar from the last eleven months, a hollow nausea in the back of her throat. Naomi had been an artist, in secret. While watching the parade of slides, Leora remembered against her will how Naomi would sometimes allow her to look at her drawings: perfect replicas in gray and white of paintings by Vermeer and Rembrandt, or, on rare occasions, an original work of her own. Naomi loved to tell Leora about the histories and contexts of the paintings she had copied, the tiny framed world of seventeenth-century Amsterdam and places like it. Leora had suspected this was a sham on Naomi's part, that Naomi was in fact copying other people's paintings simply to avoid talking about her own work. But now, listening to Bill Landsmann's voice, Leora felt as if she were going blind. The tour continued, even reaching the infamous waters of Babylon, where the exiles of Israel apparently laid down and wept in a giant pile of deciduous leaves ("Of course, this is not actually the river in Babylon—it is a stream at East Mountain Reservation, right here in our own town. But it always makes me think of the river in Babylon"), and by then Leora could no longer see anything clearly, no matter how hard she looked. When the lights came on, her eyes screamed shut against the brilliant light, like a newborn baby's. Bill Landsmann offered them all coffee, which Anna promptly brought out without a word.

"So you're not originally from New Jersey, are you?" Leora's father asked, stifling a yawn. It was getting late.

"Oh no. I was born in Vienna," Bill Landsmann replied, though he was paying more attention at the moment to getting the slide carousel back into its old box.

"Really?" Leora's mother asked, and Leora and her parents glanced at each other. Being as old as Bill Landsmann was, being a Jew, and being born in Vienna seemed to demand an explanation. Here was a man, Leora thought briefly, who shouldn't be alive.

But no explanation came. "Hm," Leora's mother murmured, giving him a few more seconds to fill in the blank. He didn't. There was an awkward silence until Anna returned, heading for the screen to put it back into the closet.

"And are you from Europe as well?" Leora's father asked, lobbing his question toward Anna.

Bill Landsmann answered for her as she closed up the screen and ducked into the closet again. "No, Anna, she is a real American. She has been here her whole life." Leora revised her earlier take on things. Bill Landsmann was the magician here, the master of the conversational sleight-of-hand. Anna was merely his assistant.

"Yes, I've been here my whole life, born and bred," Anna announced as she emerged from the closet, opening her mouth at last, then reverting back to that gracious smile of hers. Her voice proved her words true, however. It was completely accent-free. As she collected the coffee cups, she turned briefly to Leora, fidgeting with the spoons for a moment to keep Leora from noticing her eyes, which, Leora noticed, were glued to the floor. "You should know," Anna stuttered softly, "that Naomi talked about you all the time. She really loved you," she finished, on a high note that accidentally squeaked as it made its way out of her mouth. Leora looked up at her, but Anna was already on her way back to the kitchen. It was the only time Naomi's name was mentioned that night.

In the car on the way home, Leora's parents reflected, as they often had after passing buildings or mud huts or cliffs or baboons in other countries, that the evening had been "interesting, really interesting." But not as interesting as all the other things they had to do in their lives, apparently, since Leora was the only one who went back.

LEORA'S SECOND mistake concerning Bill Landsmann was that she went back to visit him again. He had called her up to tell her that she had left her sweater at his house, and then he asked her to come over to pick it up and to see a few more slides. Leora didn't want to go. She'd had that hollow nauseous feeling less and less in recent months, but the thought of returning to Bill Landsmann's house prompted it again. Yet Bill Landsmann cornered her on the phone, letting her choose when she would like to come, and Leora couldn't summon up an excuse. She agreed to stop by.

The bumper of the car with the New Car Smell smashed into the fire hydrant in front of Bill Landsmann's house. Leora backed up the car, moved it forward, turned the wheel, tried again. The fire hydrant still seemed to exert a certain magnetic pull on the bumper. She had only had her license for three weeks, after months of refusing to even try to learn how to drive, after Naomi. "Shit!"

"Hello, Leora!" a voice suddenly called. Leora turned off the engine and turned around to see Bill Landsmann standing on his front lawn, hands on his hips, smiling. As he opened the car door for her, she wondered how long he had been waiting there.

"Would you like to see my yard? Let me show you the river," he announced.

"Uh, sure," Leora answered, bewildered. The river? Before she could ask what he meant, he was marching up the lawn, his arms curling behind the small of his back. She trailed behind him, watching the back of his white-haired head again as she followed along, like following a tour guide in another country.

In the yard behind the house was a little river. More like a sewage outlet, really, a stream that came rushing with tremendous force out of a wide pipe poking out of a nearby hill. Still, it was big enough to swim in, though probably not to drown in.

"See, the current is strong now, because of the storm last week," Bill Landsmann announced, gesturing toward the rising waters. "I was just watching it now, while I was waiting for you. We have concerns sometimes with flooding here, because of this stream, but so far we have been lucky—for thirty years we have been lucky." So he had lived in their town for thirty years, Leora thought, almost twice as long as she had. Yet he still seemed more of a stranger than she.

Leora blinked, suddenly seeing the two of them from the outside: an old man and a young girl standing in a yard alongside a roaring little stream. Maybe they were grandfather and granddaughter, or teacher and student? Who could tell, out of context? Bill Landsmann had paused for a moment too, beside the stream, and Leora wondered for a moment what he was thinking, or what he was seeing. Then he suddenly turned around and walked back into the house, Leora following behind him.

This time the slide show was about the Jewish community in India, which according to Bill Landsmann (and, when Leora later checked it out for herself, according to the *Encyclopaedia Judaica* as well) had been living on the Indian subcontinent for twenty-two centuries, beginning when a group of Jewish merchants were shipwrecked near the city of Kochin. The community was documented by medieval Jewish travelers, Bill Landsmann told her, voyaging merchants who kept records of Jewish populations around the world as they traveled. Leora supposed that he saw himself as their heir.

"Who do you travel with on these trips?" she asked Bill Landsmann when he finally turned the lights back on. In all the slides he had shown her, she had never noticed any pictures of him. "With your wife?"

"Oh no," Bill Landsmann laughed. "My wife, she travels with me sometimes, but really she does not like to travel. So I usually travel on my own." He picked up the slide carousel and began putting it away, and Leora noticed a certain tenderness he had when he handled the slides, as if he were caressing a family heirloom, something he had inherited from someone long dead.

"On your own? That's crazy! Don't you get lonely?"

"Oh no," he said again. "I think people can see more when they travel by themselves. I always find it much easier to see what I want to see when I travel alone. I am having an operation in a few weeks, and after that I would like to start planning my next travels."

"Where to?" Leora asked, though she had begun to feel uneasy. There was something strange, almost obscene, she felt, about sitting with Naomi's grandfather and not discussing Naomi, yet it was clear that neither of them wanted to be the first to mention her. The name hung in the air over every word they spoke, almost like a smell.

"Birobidzhan, I think," he said. "That is a part of Russia now, near the Manchurian border. When Stalin was there, he made this place into a Soviet Jewish state. Near China, can you believe it? But it is true. That was a Jewish state."

"Really," Leora said with finality, no longer hiding her discomfort. The smell was beginning to cloud her nostrils, smothering her. She looked at the shelves of slides and stood up. "I should go now, Mr. Landsmann," she said quickly, half afraid that he would try to make her stay. "I wish you the best of luck with your operation."

But Bill Landsmann didn't put up a fight. "I will see you soon!" he said, and escorted her to the door, not without remembering to return her sweater to her as she left—the ostensible reason for his invitation. Leora herself had completely forgotten about the sweater; if he hadn't brought it out to her, she never would have asked. As Bill Landsmann watched her climb into her car and drive away, Leora had a feeling that he already knew when she would be back.

IT DIDN'T take long for Leora to realize that Bill Landsmann was stealing things from her to get her to come back to his house. Each time, it seemed, she "left something behind," meriting a phone call and another invitation to look at a few more slides. First he stole her sweater, then her hat, and once even her wallet. The first few times she didn't mind, finding herself vaguely fascinated by slides of the Jewish communities of Bukhara, Singapore, China, Turkey, Morocco, Ethiopia, Curaçao, Brazil, and Turkmenistan. Some of them haunted her dreams, like the close-up photograph of a shriveled man's face, crowned with a multicolored embroidered hat whose threads hung loose around his ears, his eyes screwed into an angry squint, wincing at the lens. Yet each time, even during the carousels that featured little more than goat after goat, she was somewhat intrigued, not only by the fact that Jews lived in all these places but also by the fact that Bill Landsmann had bothered to seek them out and learn about their lives. But after she had heard more of Bill Landsmann's scripts, it occurred to her that he was in fact casting her in the script. He had begun punctuating nearly all of the captions he read to her with little comments, and had begun punctuating each of those with a superfluous "yes?":

"This synagogue has a floor made of sand, to remind people of wandering in the desert, yes?"

"And this synagogue is built sunken into the ground, because it was not allowed to be taller than the mosques, but this way it could still have a high ceiling, yes?"

"This tribe eats nothing but goat milk and goat meat, but never together, yes?"

The "yes?" at the end of almost every sentence, almost always a sentence to which Leora had nothing to add, had begun to sound to her like a stage manager's cue, prompting her to smile or laugh or nod or frown, as if she were playing the part of someone else. And then she understood why Bill Landsmann never talked about Naomi. He wanted Leora to be Naomi.

One day she was home alone when the phone rang: "Hello, may I please speak to Leora?"

She stifled a groan. There was no way out this time; she had answered the phone. "You already are, Mr. Landsmann," she told him. "How are you? Was the operation all right?"

"Ah, ah, the operation. Yes, it was very nice. Very nice." Leora had never thought that an operation could be described as "nice." Bill Landsmann continued, launching into detail. "I have for a long time had a problem with my stomach that I needed to have fixed, and this certainly makes it difficult to travel. But now it should be easier to carry things when I travel, because that was very difficult with my previous problem. I don't like to stay sitting around at home, yes?" he concluded with a little chuckle.

Leora laughed to be polite. After a loaded pause, Bill Landsmann continued. "Anyway, I wanted to tell you that you left your gloves here at the house. Perhaps you can come back to pick them up sometime, and then I could show you some slides I have now of the Jews of Birobidzhan. I have many pictures of the—"

Leora cleared her throat and made a decision. "You know, I hate to tell you this, Mr. Landsmann, but I really don't think I need to see any more of your slides."

"What?" Bill Landsmann croaked into the phone.

"Well, I mean I think I've seen just about everything I want to see."

Bill Landsmann's voice began to quiver. "But I still have many things to show you! And actually, the main thing is that you left your gloves here. You must come to pick them up. And then you can look at some things I would like to show you, yes? You can take the gloves and I—"

"You can keep the gloves, Mr. Landsmann," Leora interrupted, her voice getting louder. "I'll buy you ten pairs of gloves, if you want them. You know what? Why don't I get you a gift certificate to the army-navy store? Then you could buy a whole truckload of gloves, and we could send them all to the Jews of Birobidzhan. Or why don't we buy you some stock in a glove company? Or how about in some insurance company that covers petty larceny? How about that?" By now Leora was almost shouting, talking faster than she was thinking. And then the words flew out of her: "I'm not Naomi, Mr. Landsmann! I'm not going to be her, no matter how many slides you show me!"

Bill Landsmann was so shocked that he actually stopped talking. Leora could almost feel the silence on the phone. And then he hung up.

A STRANGE THING happened to Leora after she blew up at Bill Landsmann: she started to wonder where he was. When she stopped hearing from him, it occurred to her that she would never find out if something had happened to him, or where his next "travels" would be. She never would have dreamed that such a thing would bother her, but his absence began to weigh on her brain. She began driving by his house occasionally, taking a wide detour when she was returning home in the afternoons or evenings. (Months earlier, she used to drive by Naomi's old house, but now a new family had moved in. New and improved, with all its children intact.) Most people in her town liked to leave their curtains open, Leora had noticed on these dark evening or late afternoon drives. At night you could peer into their houses and examine their furniture, or see people talking together and imagine what they were talking about, guessing, based on the angle of a gesticulating arm, whether they were joking with each other, or worrying aloud, or getting into a fight. The Landsmanns, however, chose to keep their curtains closed at all times. Was anyone home? Was Bill Landsmann sitting in his darkened living room admiring his slides of the Jews of Birobidzhan? Did he even look at his slides when no one else was around? Or had he taken off for Uzbekistan, or Zimbabwe, or some other distant corner of the earth to track down their fellow Jews? She was thinking about him on the day she wandered into the phone booth at the high school, which was how they came to meet again.

Nobody makes glass phone booths anymore, Leora knew, but they still had one at the high school, the old glass kind where you can see who's talking from the outside but can't hear what they're saying. Inside it was an old rotary pay phone and a thick municipal telephone directory. They used to play a game with this phone booth, she and Naomi. There was another pay phone outside, about fifty yards away and plainly visible from the booth through the school's glass front doors, and one day Naomi figured out how to make calls from one phone to the other. After that, they had made a little system of it. Naomi walked home from school each day, while Leora took the bus. Normally you couldn't see the school bus coming unless you were outside the school, where nobody wanted to wait on cold winter days. To spare Leora the cold, Naomi devised a method. After each school day ended, Leora would wait in the phone booth, and Naomi would call her as she began her walk home, giving her advance notice on whether the bus had arrived. It wasn't practical in the least, but that wasn't the point. The point was the thrill of the anticipatory moment, the delight of the wait inside the soundproof booth, the long-distance smile when the phone would ring and Leora would know it was for her. Lately, Leora had gotten in the habit of using the school's side door, avoiding the phone booth entirely. Besides, she wasn't interested in games anymore. Leora had always been a good student, but after Naomi died, schoolwork had become an obsession. She plunged into history books, memorized chemistry equations, could name the capital and describe the type of government of nearly any country in the world; she became class valedictorian. By spring of her senior year, she had been admitted to every college she applied to, with an application essay about how her travels had given her a broad new perspective on life, eyes with which to see the world.

On the afternoon in question, however, before going home for the day, Leora had needed to drop off a form at the school nurse's office, which was near the school's front door, next to the phone booth. As Leora emerged from the office, she paused for a moment, looking at the phone booth. Not thinking, just looking. Still only looking, not thinking, she took a few steps toward the phone booth and opened its door.

She stepped into the phone booth and closed the door behind her, sitting down on its pathetic little ledge of a seat. Now she could see all the students milling around the front hall, heading for the buses, but she couldn't hear what they were saying, and none of them even noticed her. It occurred to her that this might be what it would be like to come to a new country without knowing the language, looking at people all around you and not being able to understand them, and they not noticing you at all, as if you didn't exist. Once, years earlier, searching for something in the dictionary, Leora's eye had come to rest, by accident, on the word "translate." One of its definitions, she remembered as she sat in the soundproof booth, was "to bring over to the afterlife, without causing death."

Leora stared at the phone's receiver out of habit, waiting for it to ring, but then she looked away. Stupid, she thought. Searching for a distraction, she picked up the phone book, which was hanging next to the phone on a thick red cord. She opened it, letting its heavy piles of pages heap up on her lap, and soon she found herself flipping through the *L*'s. There were four Landsmanns in the area, she noted, but only one of them, "LANDSMANN W," lived at "413 Algonquin Dr." Naomi's family, under her father "LANDSMANN B," was also still listed, even though her parents and two younger brothers had already moved away. The town would have to wait until the new directory came out, Leora observed, before Naomi would officially be considered dead. She scanned the names of the other Landsmanns, Landsmans, Lansmans, Lanzmans, and Lanzmanns on the page, wondering if any of them had ever met each other, or even heard of each other. It seemed likely that they had seen each other's names before, and perhaps even been mistaken for one another, receiving one another's packages and phone calls. But beyond their names, did they know anything about each other at all? Probably not, Leora thought.

That was when the phone rang.

Leora looked at the receiver and felt herself turn pale. The phone book slid off her lap like a man on a gallows when the floor falls below him, slipping into thin air and dangling, strangling on its thick red cord. When the phone rang a second time, Leora cowered in the corner of the booth, alarmed by the sound, as if the sound alone were a hand reaching out to slam her head against the wall. On the third ring, she shook her head again and again, trying to think straight, telling herself that it wasn't what she thought it was, that it must be something else. On the fourth ring, she swallowed, asking herself: If it really wasn't what she thought it was, then why should she answer it? But then, shaking her head again, she asked herself: If it really wasn't what she thought it was, then why *shouldn't* she answer it?

After five rings, she picked up the phone.

"Hello?"

"Hello, Leora! Your school day is over, yes?"

"*Mr. Landsmann?*" She almost dropped the receiver.

He laughed. "You recognized my voice!"

"Mr. Landsmann, where are you? How did you call me? How did you know I was here?"

"Relax," he said. "Look outside, see?"

Slowly, Leora turned around in the booth until she could see outside the school's glass front doors. About fifty yards down across the school's front lawn, surrounded by piles of fresh-cut grass, a figure whom she could only assume was Bill Landsmann stood next to the other pay phone, waving at her. This still left several things unexplained, but Leora was too stunned to think about them.

"Listen, Leora, do you have maybe a few minutes? I would like to show you something. Not at my house—somewhere else."

The thought of Bill Landsmann existing somewhere outside of his collection of slides intrigued her, though she didn't want to admit it. She began breathing again. "You mean now?" she asked.

He coughed. The wind was blowing outside, and it was becoming difficult to understand him. Leora wished he would just hang up the phone and come inside. But he didn't. "Yes, now, or perhaps later also. If we go later, you can come back to my house too, and I can show you some more of my sli—"

She cut him off. "Actually, now would be just fine," she said. "I have to go home in an hour, though." Nothing too tedious could really happen in only an hour, Leora reasoned, particularly if there were no slides involved. And besides, there was something compelling about it. For the first time, she was being invited to join Bill Landsmann on his travels.

"Good, then," Bill Landsmann said. "Why don't you come outside, and we will go for a little walk."

THEY WALKED about half a mile together, mostly uphill. Leora saw that they were walking toward East Mountain, the town nature reservation. As she moved along at Bill Landsmann's side, she looked at everything discretely, as if each scene that appeared before her eyes were unrelated to the one before: the newly grown, uncallused leaves blossoming above her head; the few fallen fresh leaves beneath her feet; the tiny, dirty, soaked child's glove that lay by the side of the road. Bill Landsmann, who had been looking at the ground, spotted that glove on the ground too—she saw his eyes darting to it—and Leora wondered if he felt the same way she did, a certain sadness too deep and delicate even to name, when he saw a child's glove abandoned in the street. But Bill Landsmann didn't dwell on the glove. Instead he suddenly looked up and into the distance, as if he could see the place from afar. And the two of them walked on together.

"This place we are going," he said, clearing his throat, "reminds me of the Jewish cemetery in Prague. You have been there?"

Cemetery? They were going to a cemetery? "To Prague? Yes, I was there last summer with my family," Leora answered stiffly. "It was beautiful. Are we going to a cemetery?"

"Yes, very beautiful," Bill Landsmann said thoughtfully. He was listening very selectively. Perhaps, Leora thought, his mind was on that glove after all. "You know, in Prague, in the Middle Ages, the Jews were not allowed to bury their dead except in a very small piece of land by the river. So the cemetery is—"

"I know," Leora interrupted. "I—"

"—only this one small piece of land. But they had to use this one very small piece of land for six hundred years, so they buried their dead on top of each other, and put their gravestones all on top."

"I know. I was—"

"This cemetery in Prague, even today, it is fifteen feet above the street level, because everyone was buried only in this tiny cemetery. They still managed to fit everyone."

"I know."

"Oh, you were there?"

Bill Landsmann continued talking about the cemetery in Prague, but Leora stopped listening to him. Instead she began thinking again about that lost glove, about where the other glove might be, about the child who had lost it, about whether somehow, in some alternative life, all the lost gloves in the world might be reunited with their owners, and with the other halves of their pairs, so there would no longer be sad and lonely child's gloves abandoned on the streets. And the two of them, Leora and Bill Landsmann, walked on together.

"See, it is like the cemetery in Prague, because it is high off the ground," Bill Landsmann said.

They had arrived at a spot near the top of East Mountain, after walking for what felt like a long time alongside a little stream—a stream Leora recognized from the waters-of-Babylon sequence in Bill Landsmann's first slide show. Now they were in a tiny clearing in the woods that was about the size of his living room. Leora looked around. Considering all of Bill Landsmann's travel experience, this choice of destination seemed disappointing at best. There was nothing but a patch of grass, soaked through with puddles, and a little park bench. Leora was about to turn around and demand to know why he had taken her there when she noticed a rectangular island of dark brown stone among the puddles at her feet, with an inscription on it:

NADAV
5660–5707

it read in Hebrew across the top. Below that, it read in English:

NADAV LANDSMANN
1899–1946

Leora glanced at Bill Landsmann, who was looking down at the plaque, his attention, for once, completely fixed. "My father," he said. "He is buried here."

An immense puddle covered most of the area below the plaque, a rectangular puddle, almost the shape of the grave. Full fathom five thy father lies, Leora thought. Of his bones are coral made. She peered into the puddle and saw Bill Landsmann's glasses and white hair looking back, interrupted by a wafting leaf. Bill Landsmann had sunk into a deep silence, which Leora found irritating. It hardly seemed noteworthy to her that Bill Landsmann's father should be dead.

Bill Landsmann sat down on the bench, and Leora sat down beside him, not saying anything. Searching for something to do during that silence, she found herself staring at the Hebrew name on the stone. Nadav. It looked bare and empty, and then Leora realized that the name was incomplete. Usually, on tombstones, a person's Hebrew name is given with his father's name as well, as in "Nadav son of X." But here there was no X, apparently. Then Leora examined the English dates on Nadav Landsmann's grave and tried to do the math in her head. 1899–1946. That would make him—fifty-seven? No, forty-seven. It seemed like a young age to die. But if Nadav Landsmann were still alive, Leora thought, he would have been remarkably old, like one of those shriveled central Asian women in Bill Landsmann's slides. He was Naomi's great-grandfather, after all. Leora watched the leaves in the water for a few moments before daring to say anything. And when she did speak, her voice sounded strange, at least to her own ears.

"Why is he buried over here?" Leora asked. "This isn't near any cemetery, is it?"

She was somewhat curious, but mostly she was just making conversation, to keep from drowning in that guilty silence. That was her last mistake concerning Bill Landsmann: avoiding guilty silences. Because when Bill Landsmann spoke, he said, "A suicide cannot be buried in a Jewish cemetery, even if he is a Jew. That is Jewish law."

Now Leora was really struck silent, the sort of bottomless silence that only comes from being afraid to ask questions. But as she felt herself falling into that silent ocean, deeper than the fifty years between them, she suddenly decided to blurt out two words:

"What happened?"

Bill Landsmann shrugged, not looking at her. After what seemed like an eternity, he declared, "Perhaps we can just say that he did not like to travel." He still didn't turn to face her. "I thought I might tell Naomi about him, someday. My son named Naomi after him, even though I didn't want him to. But I never did tell Naomi about him. I thought that you might—" And then, although Leora barely noticed it at first, Bill Landsmann started crying—silently, staring down at the ground and pinching his eyes shut, shuddering with a pulse that shook his small, hunched back.

Leora watched him as he tried to obscure his face in the collar of his jacket. And then, suddenly and shudderingly, she once again saw herself and Bill Landsmann as if from the outside: a young girl in a black coat sitting on a bench, a white-haired man in a dark jacket seated beside her, his elbows resting on his knees, his head in his hands, staring down at nothing. The stone wasn't visible from this perspective, just the shimmer of the puddle between fallen fresh leaves and blades of pale green grass. Above the two people seated on the bench hovered a canopy of fresh leaves, high above, and the blue sky etched a delicate pattern between them. The man trembled, the girl shifted uncomfortably, the wind blew a loose blade of grass onto the girl's coat, and in Leora's disembodied observation she crouched down, framed the composition, and blinked, trapping it forever on the slide film of her retina.

"Sometimes I wonder if he is really dead," Bill Landsmann said. "He is not really buried, not in a cemetery, yes? So maybe he is still alive somewhere. You never really know about these things, I believe." He trembled. "I am sorry, so sorry," he said, still shaking, rubbing his nose with his hand. Leora didn't say a word.

"Here is your coat," he said, suddenly rising from the bench, and as he stood up, Leora felt as if he had tipped some sort of fragile balance within her. Behind the bench was a thicket of brambles. On top of the thicket a coat was resting, folded and neatly placed between the thorns. Leora immediately realized that it wasn't her coat. It resembled a coat that she owned, it was true, but this one wasn't hers. When she turned it over in her hands, she recognized it. It had been Naomi's.

She looked up at Bill Landsmann, trying to find the words to question it, but he silenced her with a wave of his hand. "Take it. It is yours."

Leora took the coat in one hand, and Bill Landsmann's hand in the other. And then he sent her home.

A FEW DAYS LATER, Bill Landsmann went back to his father's grave. Leora knew this because she saw an article in the town newspaper whose headline was SENIOR FOUND SLEEPING AT EAST MOUNTAIN RESERVATION. As a high school senior, she naturally took interest, failing to notice that the article was printed on the Old People page.

Senior citizen and Algonquin Drive resident William Landsmann was discovered sleeping on the ground near Columbus Rock at East Mountain Reservation early Tuesday morning by Peter Downing, a township police officer who was patrolling the area.

When Mr. Downing discovered him, Mr.Landsmann was lying facedown alongside Babble Brook, a small river that flows through the eastern side of the reservation. After failing to display a permit, Mr. Landsmann was questioned by Mr. Downing and asked to take a Breathalyzer test. Mr. Landsmann showed no blood alcohol content but was unable to explain satisfactorily his reasons for sleeping in the reservation. He received a fine according to municipal regulations.

"When I asked him what he was doing there, he told me that he was just passing through," Mr. Downing said. "I didn't find that very convincing, since he was lying on the ground, but I didn't have any real reason not to believe him."

Mary Beth Parker, the chief administrative officer for East Mountain Reservation, reports that while the reservation has had problems with vagrancy in the past, this case was very unusual. "Most of the time it'll be a bunch of kids, or someone who's intoxicated, or a homeless person who somehow wandered off the beaten track, so to speak," she said. "But this was an older gentleman who wasn't at all drunk, and he has a home."

Individuals must obtain a permit in order to camp at the reservation.

SOMETIMES WHEN Leora drives around her town in the evenings, she looks into the windows of people's houses, not because she expects to see anything interesting, but just because she wants to see. The houses line up in the dark like wrapped glass boxes, their brass numbers embossed on their sides like Bill Landsmann's boxes of slide carousels, their white-framed windows glowing like slides under warm gold light. As she drives by, she tries to look at as many of these little panels as possible. Most of the time, all she sees are curtains, or the bracing slats of a venetian blind. ("Here are the original venetian blinds, you see, in

Venice. This picture is of the Jewish ghetto in Venice, the first ghetto in the history of the world.") But sometimes, when she passes by at just the right moment, the windows are completely naked, and she can stare though the glass at the framed pictures on the walls inside and wonder if anyone is home. Occasionally her question is answered, and she looks into a white-framed window to see a family eating dinner, or an old man playing with a grandchild, or a father and son sitting on a couch, maybe watching television or getting into a fight.

And sometimes, but only sometimes, when the curtains are actually open, Leora sees a woman sitting by herself in a house that was once full of people. How she sits alone, desolate, like a widow, waiting for someone to come home.

CHAPTER 2

IN THE VALLEY
OF DISCARDED NAMES

WHEN THINGS happen gradually, even a tourist's eye snapping pictures in the brain cannot fix them in place. And so Leora, several years later, was the last person to notice the cat getting bigger.

The cat was, for lack of a better term, a breaking-up gift, something to keep her company in what were supposed to be the long and lonely nights after Jason. And the cat might have done that if Leora and Jason's had been a normal teenage romance, if Leora had been capable of such a thing—that is, if Leora were an ordinary girl, to whom ordinary things happened, if she were the sort of girl who laughed and cried and poured out her heart to her friends. But Leora didn't have any friends. And besides, by the time Jason gave her the cat, a big gray cub of a kitten with strange curled-in ears that she had never seen on any other pet, Jason himself might as well have fallen down to the bottom of the ocean, like a diver plunging into the depths of the water, forgetting to save enough air for the return trip.

At the beginning, of course, Jason did seem like the sort of person who should have found himself an ordinary girl, the kind of girl who laughed and cried with her friends over him. He was tall, well built, blue-eyed, shiny-smiled—good-looking in a bland, conventional sense, and with that appearance went all the traits of a man who wouldn't normally have been attracted to a woman like Leora, who had far more brains than looks. Jason was what ordinary teenagers would call a "good guy"—not a "great guy" but a "good guy"—just another varsity soccer player, Jason was, still out with his fellow Argonauts in search of a girl in a golden fleece. Or in search of anything, really, since Jason really wasn't anything yet. Naomi had had a theory about this. Young people, she once told Leora, are like blind heaps of clay, formless, and in that formlessness lies an infinite number of possibilities. Some seize that wet potential in their hands, sculpting shapes never seen before. Others, bewildered by choice, simply pour themselves into a mold. Still others are afraid to commit to even the slightest dent, mercilessly kneading and unkneading every last piece, dreading the moment when they will inevitably harden.

At the time, Leora had been enchanted by this brilliant way of seeing oneself, unfixed, unfinished. But more than that, Leora was enchanted by Naomi herself, the girl still short of seventeen who in spite of her age, or perhaps because of it, seemed to speak like a divine voice emerging from a whirlwind. Later, like nearly everything Naomi ever said, this theory seemed somehow prescient, as if Naomi had known all along that she would always remain unfinished, forever damp and yielding, shaped and changed by the slightest touch from Leora's memory. But after Jason, Leora had to revise Naomi's theory. Some people who had been so gently sculpted before, Leora added, are suddenly squashed—or squash themselves—into something new, throwing themselves into the kiln by force to harden themselves forever. And Leora knew it wasn't her place to judge that choice.

JASON AND LEORA were technically still teenagers when they met, on line for computer repairs in college—both of them clinging to nineteen at a time when Leora still felt crushed by each of her birthdays, uncertain of whether she deserved them. What drew her to him, at first, was nothing more than the sudden awkwardness that overcame him when she asked him a very simple question:

"Where are you from?"

Jason hooked his thumbs into the belt loops of his jeans and shifted his weight from one foot to another, his soccer-victory grin melting off his face as his eyes shifted somewhat to the right. It's an old ploy, this sleight-of-eye, the glance to the side as if suddenly someone far more interesting than the person asking the question has appeared on the scene. Leora recognized it. And when he named the New Jersey town where he was from, she knew why he had done it. For many people, the question "Where are you from?" is a conversation-starter, a curtain drawn open on a lighted window. Leora's college roommate could keep people entertained for hours with stories about her home on a ranch in Wyoming, as could her classmate from the center of Barcelona and her upstairs neighbor from a rural town in Vermont. But for people like Jason and Leora, denizens of an undeclared Jewish state, the question "Where are you from?" was a dead end. They weren't from anywhere special. Or from anywhere at all.

But Leora, watching the sleight of his eyes, surprised him. "I know where that is," she said.

Jason shrugged, impatient. "There's no reason for you to have heard of it," he mumbled, his eyes shifting again.

Leora didn't blink. "Except that I live there. Or the next town over, anyway."

Jason's eyes snapped back. "Really? Where?"

She named her street, and began describing where it was, awkwardly shifting her feet just as Jason had. But this time Jason's feet were planted on the floor as he blurted, "I know exactly where that is! That's my street!"

In a few seconds they realized that they lived about three blocks away from each other, on a street with no more than twenty houses on it. But those twenty houses sat along the town line, placing Leora and Jason in different towns, different school systems, different lives. Squinting at him, Leora tried to decide whether he looked familiar, if she could match his face with that of one of the skateboarding boys from the neighborhood. But the truth was that she couldn't.

"Have you ever been to the East Mountain Zoo?" Jason asked.

It wasn't exactly what Leora was expecting him to say, and perhaps that should have been an early hint that nothing would be what was expected. But Leora didn't take the hint. The East Mountain Zoo was a popular spot for children in their area. Leora wondered whether he had somehow recognized her from there, even though she hadn't been there for at least ten years. "Sure, when I was little. Why?"

Jason smiled. "My dad runs it."

"Really?"

Jason grinned even more proudly, but Leora wasn't about to flatter him, even by accident. In total seriousness, she asked, "Does that mean he's the one who walks through the cages with a giant broom?"

Jason struggled not to scowl at her. "No, it means he's the one who acquires the animals for the zoo."

"But where do the animals come from?" Leora asked. Somehow this question seemed to have more potential than the one about where Jason came from.

"From animal dealers," Jason said. He shifted awkwardly again, but this time for a different reason. "Hey, next time you're home," he offered, as if afraid of the answer, "would you like to come to the East Mountain Zoo with me?"

To Leora's own surprise she agreed.

LEORA LIKED JASON, but it wasn't until a conversation they had much later that it occurred to her to love him. They were sitting at a cafeteria table on a day in early March, one of those horrible days when spring seems so close that you can almost taste it, but dirty snow and bitter winds drag the entire week back down into the winter it came from. As usual, Jason had equipped his lunch tray with five full glasses of preternaturally green Gatorade, which, he claimed, the soccer coach had prescribed for the whole team, even though the soccer season was long over. Leora sat across the table from him, the glowing translucent glasses forming a sort of barricade between them until he picked one up and drained its contents, putting the empty glass back in line like a breach in the green fortress wall. As he poured the fluorescent beverage down his throat, Leora asked him a question, an even more boring one this time than "Where are you from?"

"What are you doing this summer?"

Jason's eyes, previously focused on the Gatorade, flicked up to hers as he plunked the empty glass back down on the tray. "Actually, I already have a summer job," he said.

"Lucky you! What is it?"

Jason picked up the second glass of Gatorade, studying it as if it contained the answers to life's greatest questions. "I have this thing I do every summer. You're probably going to laugh at me, but I have to explain to you why I do it."

"Okay," she answered.

Jason sipped the Gatorade. "It's a community service thing."

"Well, that's cool, isn't it?" Leora asked, mainly just to keep him talking.

"No, actually this job is a very uncool thing to do."

Leora blushed, feeling like she had just made a joke about Mother's Day to someone whose mother had died. Jason was the closest thing she had had to a friend in years, but he still made her feel awkward sometimes, as if she were a stranger who barely knew him. She tried to defend herself. "But I know lots of people who get involved in public service stuff. They all love it."

"Sure, they all love it," Jason parroted, putting down the paper napkin he had begun shredding. "That's because all they do is play with kids all day." He picked up the second glass of Gatorade again and drained it.

Leora watched the Gatorade flow out of the glass, wondering if it retained its bilious color once it was inside Jason's stomach. "What do you mean?" she asked.

"Think about it. Practically every public service program around here is made for kids."

She considered for a moment. It was true. There certainly were a lot of tutoring programs. And after-school activities. And don't-do-drugs projects. And big-brother, big-sister pairings. And play groups. And reading classes. Even safe-sex dramas. She tried hard to think of a public service activity people on campus did that didn't involve children. Other than the soup kitchen, nothing came to mind.

Jason watched her, then smiled in triumph. "See, everything they have is for kids. Or if it's not for kids, then it's something like a homeless shelter, where they're not really helping people as much as just giving them relief. But what about, say, old people?"

"Old people?" Bill Landsmann's living room floated through Leora's mind.

But Bill Landsmann's living room wasn't what Jason had in mind at all. "I mean old people in nursing homes," Jason continued. "See, nobody wants to work at a nursing home, because they feel like it's hopeless. With kids, at least they can feel like they'll somehow turn those kids into adults who don't need their help anymore. But with old people, no one is interested. Actually, it's not even that no one is interested. It's that they're afraid."

"Afraid of what?" Leora asked.

"Have you ever been to a nursing home?"

"Sure."

"Well, how did you feel about it?"

Leora thought of her great-great-aunt Rose, who had been languishing in a nursing home for at least twenty years. Rose harassed Leora's parents by telephone every day, always reminding them that she had big plans to die any minute—a threat she still hadn't made good on, despite the deaths in the interim of three other relatives who had inherited her before Leora's parents did. When Leora and her family went to visit her, Rose would more often than not take whatever food or magazines or gifts they had brought her and theatrically dump them all over the floor, raving that everyone—the staff, the doctors, the woman across the hall, Leora's family, the latest TV talk show host—was plotting to kill her. (It occurred to Leora on one of these visits that this claim was in fact Rose's way of flattering herself, trying to convince herself that she was worthy of being killed.) The halls in the nursing home, reeking of urine, were lined with wheelchairs occupied by pale, bony, drool-covered men and women, waiting to die. Leora glanced at the glowing green glasses of Gatorade and felt vaguely nauseous. "It's not somewhere I'd want to be for any longer than I absolutely had to be there," she admitted.

"That's how everyone feels about it," Jason said, picking up Gatorade number three. "And the difficult part isn't that these people are so close to dying, either. Because if you were visiting an intensive care unit in a hospital, you wouldn't feel that way. It would be scary, sure, but there would be a sort of drama to it. You could visit the patients there and think to yourself, Oh my God, this twenty-five-year-old with cancer could be me, and therefore my visit was Worthwhile, because I learned something Meaningful."

She winced, but Jason didn't notice. He paused for a moment to consume his third glass of Gatorade, then continued. "In a nursing home, there's no drama. It's not like it's a twist of fate or anything. There's just this awful . . . normalness. The upsetting part isn't that the people there are dying. It's that they're alone. Their spouses and friends are dead. Their children are busy with their own lives. They have people who *take* care of them, bringing them their food and medicine and all that, but they don't have anyone who cares *for* them. I want to care for them."

Leora sat back, stunned. Somehow she had expected this little speech to end the way it always did with people their age—that is, with Jason announcing that "someone" had to do something about it, and therefore he had found himself a summer job stuffing envelopes for the American Association of Retired Persons. But actually working in a nursing home? She stuttered, "Are you kidding me?"

Jason shook his head, glancing down at the fourth glass of Gatorade before picking it up and pouring it down his throat, almost without swallowing. "No. That's what I do every summer. I volunteer at the Beth Israel Nursing Home. My parents think I'm crazy. I tell them that it will help me get into medical school, but the only reason I want to go to medical school at all is so that I'll have some skills and get paid for this kind of thing in the future. It's actually just about old people." Jason used part of the shredded napkin to wipe off his green mustache, twisting the rest of it into little tubes.

"Wow, Jason, you really are a *mentsh*."

Jason looked up from his tray, puzzled. "What's a *mentsh*?"

Leora smiled. "You mean you've been working in a Jewish nursing home all these years and you've never picked up any Yiddish?"

Jason's fingers wandered back to the shredded napkin, twitching. "Well, you see, my family's Jewish, but just barely, and—I mean, we don't go to synagogue or anything, so—"

"*Mentsh* means 'person,' literally, but it's used to mean a really good person. Someone who shows the world, through his actions, what it really *means* to be a person."

"And that's me?" Jason asked. Gatorade number five on deck. Slurped. Done.

Leora grinned at him. "Well, I think so."

Jason snorted. "Nah, I'm no *mentsh*. I just like old people."

"And don't you have to go to the bathroom after all that Gatorade?"

"No."

That was when she knew she was in love.

ONCE SHE KNEW of Jason's interest in "old people," Leora often thought of telling him about Bill Landsmann—who, whatever else he was, was certainly an old person, though she doubted the old people Jason visited in his nursing home had recently gone trekking in Birobidzhan. But telling Jason about Bill Landsmann would require telling Jason about Naomi, which was something else Leora often thought of doing. It occurred to Leora that Jason might even have heard of her, from one of the articles in the local paper, maybe, or perhaps through a friend who had attended the memorial service, where, Leora remembered, people who had barely known Naomi had blathered on and on about the terrible tragedy, the life cut short, such potential, such promise—just as they had done the last time some kid in the school died. Ultimately, though, she decided against mentioning it to Jason. Talking about Naomi would mean dragging him along with her to some strange new country, and Leora couldn't be sure he would survive the trip. That wasn't the only reason she couldn't talk about Naomi. Naomi, now sixteen for all eternity, had often flirted with boys, and had teased boys, and there had been boys who had worshiped her from afar, and she had known it. But she had never liked any of them enough to offer them her heart, or even her little finger. As a result, each of Leora's firsts with Jason—their first kiss, their first long kiss, their first caresses over clothes, their first caresses under clothes, each incremental step on their road together—left Naomi further behind in Leora's memory, made her seem more and more like a little child in the distance, reaching for a dropped glove in the road. It was only when Jason began persuading her, pressing her, pushing her, pinning her, that Leora found herself wishing she hadn't left Naomi behind. When the long, frightening night came when Leora lay trapped beneath Jason's spent, slumped weight, thinking that she might cry, she might have, if Naomi had been alive. But because Naomi wasn't, Leora set it all aside and tried to fall asleep next to Jason, turning away from him while fighting off nightmares, staring at a square of moonlight on the ceiling above the window which reminded her of a blank panel from one of Bill Landsmann's slide carousels. It was the week before Passover. The following week, home for spring vacation, she went with Jason to the East Mountain Zoo.

The East Mountain Zoo was not much of a zoo, as zoos go. No elephants, for example, and Leora was glad for that—at least Jason's father had realized that there was no room in New Jersey for elephants. No giraffes either, or hippos or whales. But it did have a respectable aviary, a fair-sized marine exhibit with several kinds of otters and seals, and a large petting pen with enough sheep and goats for a biblical sacrifice routine. (Every family in Leora's town had a picture on the piano at home of one of their children at about the age of five, petting a goat in the East Mountain Zoo.) There were even two little mountain lions there—"ocelots," according to the label on the exhibit—yawning their way through boring days as they stretched in the shade in their glassed-in fiberglass forest. When Leora walked through the East Mountain

Zoo holding hands with Jason, she felt as if the two of them were part of the exhibit, baby animals whose mature form was not yet clear, tiny cubs not yet grown into lions, little birds in their eggs still waiting to hatch. What sort of animals would they turn out to be?

That day was shining, an almost unnaturally gleaming spring day at the East Mountain Zoo, the kind of day when bare arms emerge for the first time from their winter hibernation in deep long sleeves. Leora and Jason were watching the seal show. Mugsy and Mango, sea lions extra-ordinaire, sailed through the air in perfect formation to the predictable delight of the crowd, and the appearance of Sammy, the "true seal" who, like all true seals—as opposed to the sea lions—was a fat round tube of a beast who could barely do anything more than swim and wriggle himself onto a rock, received the usual number of laughs as the zookeeper coaxed him out of the water to tease him, showing all the things that Sammy couldn't do. Yet Sammy the Seal bore it like a humble martyr, ignoring the crowd as he waddled his way onto the demonstration rock and sometimes not even accepting the sardines thrown his way as reparations. Sammy knew who he was, Leora thought, and she followed him with her eyes through the glass sides of the tank as he dove into the water, soaring, with a grace the sea lions would never have, beneath its depths.

About halfway through the seal show, Leora noticed that Jason wasn't paying any attention to Mugsy and Mango, or even to Sammy under the waterline. Nor was he looking at his feet or off into space, as he might have been if he were just distracted. No, Jason was clearly looking, staring even, at the crowd around him, with the same fascination they were directing toward Mugsy and Mango. Leora glanced around and realized what he was looking at. With the exception of the two of them and about ten others, all of the people at the seal show that afternoon were Hassidim.

They all looked different from each other, of course, and the crowd didn't seem like the seas of black hats that sometimes appear in movies or news broadcasts about certain neighborhoods in Jerusalem or Brooklyn. But that was because of the women and the kids, who broke up the black-hat ocean into a saturation of lakes, each surrounded by its lakefront property of wives and children. The women all either had their hair hidden under kerchiefs or hats or had thick, shiny straight hair, often with elaborate bangs—wigs, Leora realized. They wore long-sleeved shirts despite the brilliant sun, and long skirts that stopped short over sneakers or sandals. But what fascinated Leora were the children. Judging by the number of children running and screaming and banging on the glass in front of Sammy's tired face, she estimated that the child-to-couple ratio was somewhere around five to one. Each of the women—weary, worn-out, wrung-out women, although many of them couldn't have been much older than Leora herself—clutched the handles of at least one stroller, more often a twin-style two-seater, and sometimes even a giant wagon with seats for four or five. The mothers were yelling at their children, as mothers at the East Mountain Zoo always did. But the names they were yelling were different.

"Shloymie, come back here!"

"Mendie, stop hitting Shloymie!"

"Gitl, if you don't stop teasing Freydl right this minute, we are never coming back to this zoo ever again!"

Occasionally, a few of the mothers would even yell at their children in Yiddish. Leora had studied a year's worth of Yiddish during her first year of college under the guise of fulfilling a foreign-language requirement; she sensed there was something larger at work in her choice, something dating back to her family's vacation in Europe, or perhaps to Bill Landsmann's living room, although she had avoided thinking very much about what that something might be. The Yiddish she had studied was European Yiddish, academic Yiddish, the Yiddish that Jewish writers once used to free themselves from the religiousness of Hebrew, to prove that they were modern men. But the Yiddish of these mothers was the language of ultraorthodox American Jews, a hybrid of dialects that they used to avoid speaking Gentile English while saving holy Hebrew for only sacred things. Leora couldn't understand them. But she assumed that they were saying something like "Yankl, if you try to climb into that seal tank one more time, you'll be lucky if you make it home with both legs."

Yet Jason stared and stared, as if it were not the flying sea lions but the Hassidim on display. Leora began squeezing his hand to get his attention, but even then he only turned around about once out of every three or four times. Only after Mugsy and Mango had performed their final twists through the air, to the joy of the people in the crowd—who, Leora wondered, might perhaps have seen themselves, somehow, in those fish out of water—did Jason pull Leora off to the side as the families dispersed to the other exhibits with a breathless "Did you see that?"

"See what?" Leora asked, pretending nonchalance.

"Come on," Jason snorted. "You're telling me you didn't notice that today the East Mountain Zoo suddenly moved to Brooklyn?"

Leora sighed. In the course of their time together, Leora had become something of Jason's tutor in reply to his occasional Jewish questions, a post she didn't particularly enjoy. But she did have an answer. Today, she told him, was one of the middle days of Passover, a time when Jewish schools were closed for vacation. So perhaps these parents felt it was a nice day to take their children to the zoo.

"Oh, okay," Jason said, stepping back. "Well, I'm glad it's not a permanent massive Jewish invasion of the zoo."

Leora stiffened and dropped his hand. "What are you, some kind of anti-Semite?"

Jason rolled his eyes. "Yeah, I'm a self-hating Jew. Or maybe a Jew-hating self, more accurately, since I don't hate myself particularly, just other Jews."

Leora watched him as he turned away from her. "I just mean you seem really uncomfortable around religious Jews, that's all," she offered lamely.

Jason leaned against the seal tank and blew on its surface. A wall of greenish water filled with bubbles and sardine bits pressed against the glass. Little waves of water rushed away from him, cowering before his breath. For a moment it seemed to Leora that if Jason blew hard enough, he could blow half of the tank's water away, clearing an empty space for himself to step inside, high and dry. But then Sammy poked his head up through the opaque green waves, interrupting Jason's ripples with his own concentric circles on the water's surface and reminding her that the tank was much deeper than it appeared to be.

Sammy's disappearance back beneath the water's depths seemed to prompt Jason to speak. "I guess I just don't understand how I'm supposed to feel about them," he said, in a voice that sounded resigned. "I mean, I see one of these guys on a bus with a hat and a nice long beard, and I know I'm supposed to be thinking to myself, Yes, you are my brother, we stood at Mount Sinai together. Or something like that. But it doesn't work that way. Instead I just think to myself, Why are you dressed like you're Amish?"

Leora opened her mouth to begin her Jewish tutor's speech, about how Hassidic dress derived from the style of seventeenth-century Polish nobles, about the code of dress for modesty that explained the long skirts and sleeves, but impatience had grabbed Jason by the neck. "And why," he asked, his voice suddenly rising to a throaty gurgle, "do they make me feel, since I'm Jewish and they're Jewish, but I'm not Super-Duper Jew like they are, that everything I'm doing in my life is totally wrong?"

Leora stared at him for a minute, and behind his jittery blue eyes she thought for a moment that she could actually see the undried clay of the person who was Jason, being pulled and stretched and hammered until it almost fractured in two. She took his hands in hers. "Jason, you've donated your vital organs, including your heart and your brain, to a Jewish nursing home. Believe me, you're not doing anything wrong."

Jason's jittering eyes paused and looked at hers, as if plunging into cleansing waters. And then he kissed her for so long that the Hassidim had to try not to stare.

MOST OF THE TIME, the clay that forms a young person's life is kneaded and prodded slowly, gradually, by him and by others, until a shape is coaxed out of it, and it is only after many years, long after the clay has hardened, that one can go back and trace the polished surface, searching for the fingerprints of those who helped to mold it long ago. But sometimes, often by accident, a dent will be made so deep, in clay just beginning to dry, that no amount of prodding will cover it up again. Something like that happened to Jason one summer afternoon a few months later, and Leora knew it when he met her after their summer jobs had finished for the day, back at the East Mountain Zoo.

When she met him at the zoo's entrance, Leora knew that something was wrong. During that summer, meeting at the zoo each day in the late, hazy summer afternoons, they had developed a routine, a daily argument about which animals to visit first. Hogs or hedgehogs? This time, though, Jason, not even stopping to smile, announced, "Let's go look at the ocelots," and breezed his way into the zoo. She had to race to catch up with him.

Leora pretended not to notice that anything had changed. She followed Jason through the zoo, which by now had begun to feel like a sort of home for the two of them, until they reached the ocelots—an exhibit,

Jason had told her, that had just been installed the previous year, with animals on loan from a larger zoo in New York. Jason sat down on a bench at the far end of the exhibit, staring into space. Leora sat down next to him, but Jason ignored her. On the other occasions when they had visited the ocelots, the animals, who were nocturnal according to the explanatory plaque, were almost always asleep. But this time one of the ocelots had just emerged from the shady brush. Leora watched as it climbed out of the scrubby foliage and began walking across the exhibit's tall grass. Its coat was beautiful, dark yellow and gray and glowing with white spots, like a leopard's spots, on its graceful back. The ocelot walked, one foot in front of another in a sort of musical harmony, across the exhibit and then settled down onto a log with its front legs first, stretching its whole furry body out in the sun, its eyes focused on some point in the distance. It looked so peaceful and gentle as it lay on the rock, in such perfect agreement with the world, that Leora almost wished she could climb over the glass barrier and walk up to it, leaning over to pet its silky, graceful back. But then the ocelot suddenly raised its head, squinted its eyes shut, and reared back its head to drop its jaw in a horrifying yawn, revealing long fangs that glinted in the sunlight.

Jason didn't seem to notice. Instead he leaned forward, resting his elbows on his knees and staring at the label on the exhibit, as if the root of his problem had something to do with the Growth and Development of the Endangered South American Ocelot. Leora inched her hand toward his, but some time passed before he took it. After a few moments he dropped his eyes to the ground. "Remember Mr. Rosenthal, who I was visiting at work?" he asked. "He died today."

Leora felt very hot all of a sudden, but she didn't say anything.

Jason snorted. "I know you're thinking it's no big deal, since it's a nursing home and everything."

"No I'm not," Leora said. Which was a lie, since that was precisely what she was thinking. Old dead people didn't impress her very much. She suddenly pictured herself sitting on that bench in the East Mountain Reservation, next to Bill Landsmann, above his dead father. Suicides, she remembered, cannot be buried in a Jewish cemetery. That is Jewish law.

Jason snorted again. He had a habit of snorting whenever he didn't like what he thought someone else was thinking. Everyone else on the soccer team did the same thing. "But that's not what's bothering me," he said. "What's really bothering me is a story this man told me about a month ago."

"What story?" Leora asked. In truth, she was just relieved that there was something for the two of them to talk about other than a dead man in the nursing home. But that was her mistake.

Mr. Rosenthal, as Jason explained it, was a very old man—old even for a nursing home, though no one seemed able to tell quite how old he was. Nor was Mr. Rosenthal himself a particularly reliable source for that kind of information, since Mr. Rosenthal was, as Jason put it, "a little out of it." He could express logical thoughts, but by the time Jason began visiting him, he was having trouble recognizing people, even people like Jason whom he saw every single day. One day about a month ago, Jason walked into his room just as he did every day, sat down, and said hello. But instead of greeting Jason as he usually did, Mr. Rosenthal looked at Jason as if someone had turned on a new switch in his brain. He propped himself up a bit in his bed, smiled a giant smile, and said, with his heavy Yiddish accent, "Good morning, Marcus! Why have you not earlier come to visit?"

It took Jason some time, but soon he realized that Mr. Rosenthal thought he was his grandson, or maybe even his great-grandson, a young man named Marcus who, according to the nurses on the hall, hadn't been back to visit ever since he had had a tremendous screaming fight with Mr. Rosenthal three years earlier, the subject of which no one on the staff could remember. But Mr. Rosenthal seemed to have forgotten about all that by now. No matter how many times Jason tried to correct him, according to Mr. Rosenthal he was Marcus, and Mr. Rosenthal had never been happier to see him. After a while Jason started playing along.

"So, Marcus, how are you these days?" Mr. Rosenthal asked. "You are still playing all those sports and games?" The real Marcus, apparently, was just as athletic as Jason was. Unwilling to guess at the real Marcus's activities, Jason answered that he was still playing soccer, and in fact had been made assistant varsity captain for next year's soccer season.

Jason had thought this sort of thing would please Mr. Rosenthal. Most people in the nursing home, Jason had found, loved nothing more than to be given something to brag about concerning their descendants. But Mr. Rosenthal surprised him. Instead of grinning and congratulating him, Mr. Rosenthal suddenly sprang all the way up in bed in a near fury, grabbing Jason by the arm with his shaky, thin hand and refusing to let go. His smile had vanished. "Marcus, listen to me," he said in a tone of utmost urgency. "I want you to be a deep-sea diver."

Jason sat there, not stunned. He had seen a lot of things like this in his years at the nursing home, and he knew the best way to handle it was to take it for what it was. "Sure, I'll consider it," Jason said, taking Mr. Rosenthal's other hand in his, gently, kindly.

But Mr. Rosenthal wasn't interested in gentle and kind. "Listen to me, Marcus," he said in almost a fierce whisper. By now he was clutching Jason's arm in a vise grip. (Funny, Leora thought to herself as she listened to the story, how both babies and old people have such unbelievably tight grips with their hands. On the edges of life, everyone is afraid to let go.) "Deep-sea divers, they go and get things back from the bottom of the ocean, don't they?"

Hearing Mr. Rosenthal's question, Jason stared at him, bewildered, and nodded, though his knowledge of marine exploration was based mainly on a television special he had once watched about Jacques Cousteau.

"Then forget all this soccer garbage," Mr. Rosenthal whispered furiously, "because *that* is what I want you to be. A deep-sea diver."

Their conversation paused there. Jason had felt awkward, he told Leora, as he didn't usually feel with the old people. Most of the time, he would walk into one of their rooms and just talk with them, for hours. Many of them were so starved for conversation that they could talk about almost anything, for what seemed like days on end. Others didn't like to talk, and preferred to listen to Jason talk, or just to sit with him in silence. Yet it was rare that someone like Mr. Rosenthal, who liked to talk, would suddenly stop. To prod him to continue, Jason asked him, why deep-sea diving? He suspected that the whole deep-sea diving business would turn out to be some sort of delusion, the kind of thing that had been happening more and more often with Mr. Rosenthal. But to Jason's surprise, Mr. Rosenthal actually answered him.

Mr. Rosenthal told "Marcus" that he had come to America when he was just Marcus's age—which of course meant nothing to Jason, since he had no idea how old the real Marcus was, let alone how old Mr. Rosenthal thought the real Marcus was, but Jason was twenty-one, so he began to think of Marcus, and of Mr. Rosenthal when he came to America, as a pair of twenty-one-year-olds, not unlike himself. Then

Mr. Rosenthal began babbling on and on about the journey to America, about how you had to cross two borders with forged papers just to get to Bremen, which was a town in Germany where your ship to England was docked, and then the ship took you to Liverpool, where you boarded another ship, this time to America, and then about how horrible it was in steerage class at the bottom of the ship, how you and all the other Jews were packed in by the hundreds, piled on top of each other like packages, and the ship kept rolling and everyone kept vomiting and there was no ventilation and the whole place smelled like shit and vomit for two weeks and you couldn't even walk three steps without tripping over some screaming little child.

After two weeks in this pit, Mr. Rosenthal finally reached the Promised Land, and he and all the other Jews on the ship crawled out of their steerage hellhole to go up on the deck and see New York Harbor, the place of their dreams. They crowded over to the side of the deck as the ship pulled in right under the Statue of Liberty, and Mr. Rosenthal was as awestruck as everyone else. But then Mr. Rosenthal noticed that the other Jews on the deck weren't just looking at the Statue of Liberty. Instead they were actually pushing up to the edge of the deck, as if they were looking at something in the water. Mr. Rosenthal pushed in a little closer, and then he saw why they were all gathered on the side. They were throwing their tefillin overboard. Because tefillin were something for the Old World, and here in the New World they didn't need them anymore.

"And that is why I want you to be a deep-sea diver," Mr. Rosenthal told Jason. "I want you to dive down to the bottom of New York Harbor and bring those cast-off tefillin back up to the land." Then he collapsed on the nursing home bed.

Jason called for the nurse, but when she came, it turned out that his alarm was for naught—Mr. Rosenthal had just fallen asleep. Jason left and later returned, trying to get Mr. Rosenthal to talk to him again. But Mr. Rosenthal, usually quite animated, refused to say a word. The following day, Jason returned to Mr. Rosenthal's room and found that Mr. Rosenthal had disappeared. When Jason asked about him, he learned that Mr. Rosenthal had had a major stroke the night before and was now in a coma on a respirator. Jason hadn't thought about the story again until today, when Mr. Rosenthal, at the age of no one knew what, abandoned this earth.

Leora looked at Jason, captivated. "That's an amazing story," she stuttered. Then she looked away, embarrassed that she couldn't think of anything more to say about it. An image flashed through her mind of Naomi's memorial service with all its stupid speeches. A terrible tragedy, a devastating moment. Such potential, such promise. "An amazing story," she sneered at herself. What a pointless thing to say.

Jason sat back on the bench, finally looking up from his twitching, nervous fingers. Sitting there, more quiet than she had ever seen him, Jason had never looked more beautiful to Leora. She knew the moment was wrong, but she wanted to kiss him.

"There's only one part of it that I didn't understand," he said, a tinge of hesitancy in his voice, and she waited for whatever he might say next. "Maybe this is a stupid question, but what are tefillin?"

Leora the Jewish tutor didn't know whether or not to laugh at him. How could he have missed the punch line of the story? But she loved him, and was patient. "Do you know what the Shema is?" she asked.

"Sure," he snorted, "that prayer that talks about God being one."

Relieved to have one less thing to explain, Leora told him that the Shema goes on to say that you should love God in everything you do, and that you should bind these words as a sign on your arm and let them be frontlets between your eyes. Tefillin are a set of two little black boxes connected to leather straps, she told him, and each of the boxes has those words of the Shema written on parchments inside it. During prayer, Jewish men actually bind these boxes to themselves, one on the arm and the other on the forehead, between the eyes. Her father had them, she said. He had put them on every day during the year after her grandfather died.

Jason was astounded. "Your *dad*? Really? Stock analyst by day, arm-binder by night?"

"Well, they're only worn in the morning, actually," Leora mumbled, resisting what might have become a whirlwind of questions. She still wanted to kiss him. "So are you going to do what he told you?"

"Do what?" Jason asked.

"You know, become a deep-sea diver and rescue the tefillin."

Jason, apparently cured of his melancholy, rolled his bright blue eyes almost to the back of his head as he stood up and took her hand. "Stop being cheesy," he told her. "Let's go watch the seal show again."

In the back of the crowd for the seal show, she found her chance to kiss him.

WHEN THE school year started again, Leora and Jason went their separate ways: she to the college newspaper office, and he to the soccer
field. Leora had joined the newspaper staff on her parents' advice—her
parents, of course, were always checking on her progress, monitoring
her to make certain she was normal, which she wasn't—and she had
found it suited her. She liked the rhythm of it, the busyness of it, the
requirement to fill space with news when there wasn't always news to
fill it with. At one point a few years earlier, when Leora was still only
rarely talking, her mother would often try prodding her to talk. When
Leora insisted she had nothing to say, her mother would answer, "That
doesn't seem to stop anybody else." At the newspaper, Leora was
assigned something to say each day, thus obviating the need to say anything that she really meant. It was a pleasant arrangement, in Leora's
eyes. And it worked outside of the newspaper too. When people asked
her what she did at school, the newspaper gave her something to say,
something to be, without having to think about who she was. She
worked at the newspaper.

Soccer might easily have been to Jason what the newspaper was to
Leora—a label, whether a real one or not. But since Jason was a normal,
ordinary person, he actually believed in it, mistaking the label for himself. During the season, he spent so many hours of each day on the field
that he could scarcely imagine himself otherwise. And other people
believed in the label too, reinforcing it, encouraging it. If someone mentioned his name on campus, it was almost always followed by the words
"You know Jason—that tall guy on the soccer team?" Soccer was who he
was. But all of that ended in September of Leora and Jason's senior year,
when Jason got his foot caught in an unnoticed animal hole on the field
while pivoting for a pass, tore a ligament, and fractured three different
bones in his foot and leg. Jason's college soccer career was over. And so
was Jason as everyone knew him, including Jason himself.

At first Jason pretended that nothing had happened, or at least nothing of consequence. He still limped his way over to the soccer field on
most days to meet the team after practice. On most nights, he also still
went to dinner with his teammates, bringing Leora along with him, and
Leora noticed that he seemed almost energized by their little jokes
about his leg, how they would pat him on the back and call him
"Stump."

Yet ordinary twenty-one-year-olds forget things easily; thoughts and even people slip out of their minds like things dropped over the deck of an ocean liner. Very little time passed before his teammates began to forget about the Stump. On the team, he was surprised to learn, he was replaced as assistant captain almost immediately, his skills easily substituted, his talents forgotten. He had been interchangeable all along. And he was forgotten in other ways as well. Sometimes Jason would arrive at the team's usual cafeteria table to find that it was empty, no one having told him about extended practice that day or about a trip to a restaurant for a teammate's birthday. Other times he would limp his way over to the locker room after practice, only to find that he could barely even follow the team's conversations anymore. How could he join in their laughs about the idiot who missed such an obvious goal at an away game, or their gossip about the freshman he had barely met, or their impersonations of the new assistant coach he hardly knew? Even off the field, when he and his teammates sat around their long cafeteria table together, he began to notice more and more jokes he didn't get, references to people he had never met, mentions of parties to which they had forgotten to invite him. Jason began to feel as if he didn't exist. As if he had never existed.

Jason changed. His body began drooping, his muscles withering and loosening on his limbs like damp clumps of clay sliding off an unsturdy armature. At first Leora attributed it to his leg, to a lack of exercise. But then she noticed that his face had begun drooping too. His jaw began going slack more often—he would stare into space for a moment, and soon his mouth would fall open, as if nothing were holding him together. His eyes sagged in his face. Even his hairline began to migrate backward, little by little. And as he sank into the depths, he called out and was rescued.

One evening—and it is often evening when these things happen, that time wedged between being clearly one moment and clearly another, where people sometimes get stuck—when Leora couldn't meet him for dinner, Jason went to the campus Jewish student center, sat down at a table at random, and met someone named Moyshie. Leora knew Moyshie, vaguely. He lived a few floors below her in the dormitory, on a floor low enough so that he would never need to use the elevator, since Moyshie would not use electricity on the Jewish sabbath. Jason and Moyshie hit it off, to both Jason's and Moyshie's surprise. By a curious accident of fate—if one believes such things are accidental, for Leora wasn't so sure anymore—Moyshie knew a tremendous amount about soccer, had made himself into a veritable walking encyclopedia of soccer-fan statistics on the various international teams, and watched the World Cup with religious fervor. It wasn't long before Jason got to know Moyshie's friends: Avi, Ari, Shmulie, Yossie. They became Jason's new soccer team. And that meant he had to start practicing.

Jason began joining Leora at the Jewish student center, where she had always gone for Friday night dinners while he ate with his team-mates, meeting her later for a movie. At first Leora was thrilled, stunned to find herself no longer an abandoned woman on Friday nights, no longer needing to hide the fact that she had a boyfriend, or to answer embarrassing questions about where he was if he wasn't with her. But then Moyshie began meeting with Jason on Saturday afternoons, coaching him with the help of a translated Talmud. And not long after that, based on Moyshie's coaching, Jason stopped watching rented movies with Leora on Friday nights.

That mattered. In Leora's house in New Jersey, twenty houses away from Jason's, her family had a special Friday night dinner every week in honor of the sabbath. They lit and recited blessings over candles, sang the prayers over wine and bread, and sat down together for hours at the table, singing songs in honor of the day and then reciting the Grace after Meals, all in Hebrew—exactly like in those old Jewish folktales, except with climate control and less cholesterol. And those evenings always gave Leora the same feeling she got from those folktales too. On Friday nights, the windows of Leora's family's house turned themselves inside out, so that when you tried to look out of them, you could see nothing but black mirrors of the candlelight in the room's gentle dim-ness, as if nothing outside had ever existed, as if nothing were gradually changing as things normally did.

But another element of the specialness of Friday nights at Leora's family's house, the part that doesn't appear in those old Jewish folktales, was the weekly rented movie. It isn't easy to explain, because there's no metaphor for it—no God creating the world and then sitting back to watch home videos, no Sabbath Queen riding down out of the sunset to deliver the latest Hollywood release. And the story one is supposed to read on the Jewish sabbath isn't in any movie—it's the weekly portion of the Torah, which Leora's family went to synagogue to hear every

Saturday morning. But since her family never went out on Friday
nights, in honor of the sabbath, and since Leora's brother refused to
spend time reading anything that he didn't absolutely have to read in
order to graduate from high school (which meant, strictly speaking, no
reading at all), and since Leora's parents loved movies, and since that's
what people do on weekends in little glowing houses in little New
Jersey towns, every Friday night after they had finished reciting the
Grace after Meals, Leora's family would get up from the table, clear
away the dishes, go into the living room, and watch a rented movie.

They didn't watch action movies on Friday nights, or romantic
comedies, or murder mysteries. (They rented plenty of those, but they
watched them on Sunday nights. And on Saturday nights they went to
the multiplex to see some more.) No, Friday nights were reserved for
Important Films: movies that, according to Leora's parents, would
teach them something about the Human Condition. (Leora's mother
was very big on the Human Condition.) A season's Friday night viewing
might include, for instance, *Gandhi*, *Spartacus*, *Exodus*, *A Man for All
Seasons*, *Chariots of Fire*, *Doctor Zhivago*, *Casablanca*, *Ben Hur*, *The
Last Emperor*, *Out of Africa*, and at least three films starring Charlton
Heston. (Not *The Ten Commandments*, though—that one they saved
for Passover.) To Leora, this was the sabbath eve—prayer, food, song,
and epic films. Sometimes these sanctified evenings ended in disastrous
sacrilege, like the costume Leora's brother wore for at least five
Halloweens: a bald cap, tiny round glasses, a white loincloth, a wooden
staff, and an Indian accent in which he would say, "Hello, I am the
Mahatma—Oh God, I've been shot!" before dropping dead. But most
of the time, Friday nights would end with a rewinding of the video and
a recapping of the sacred. There was a certain sweetness to the stories
even in the sappiest of these films, an earnestness, an honesty. You
would go to bed dreaming about them, though you might not understand what they really meant for many years—that is, whether it was the
film that had that earnestness and honesty or whether it was you—and
that absence of knowing stirred you, filled you with a feeling of potential, of possibility. Leora had brought the habit with her to college, and
even when Jason was eating dinner with his teammates on Friday nights
he would still meet her halfway, joining her for the weekly rented
movie. But after signing on with his new team, Jason stopped attending.
Instead he would lounge for hours in Moyshie's room downstairs and

even drag Leora along with him, talking about sports into the early morning hours just like the old team used to do. Except that Friday nights used to be Leora's sacred night with Jason, her night of refuge from the team. Now the team wouldn't go away.

Winter passed, and spring, with each passing day dilating like the pupil of an eye, letting in more and more light. Graduation was approaching. Leora had found herself a job at a magazine in New York and planned to live at home and commute to the city until she had saved enough money to live on her own, but Jason had put off his plans for medical school in order to spend a year at a rabbinical academy in Israel. No surprise, by then. By midwinter Jason had started wearing a yarmulke all the time. He had stopped eating in the cafeteria, instead cramming his tiny student refrigerator with specially labeled kosher food. He would make little comments to Leora if she arrived at the Jewish student center wearing a skirt that fell above her knees. And it didn't take long before, in public at least, Jason stopped holding her hand.

During that year, Leora had kept a framed picture of the two of them on her desk. In the picture, they were standing in the East Mountain Zoo, his arm draped around her neck and shoulder, a baseball cap on his head which cast a shadow over his face in the bright sunlight. They stood posed in front of the goat petting pen, and little goats were nosing their way between the bars around their knees, hoping for food. Jason had his mouth open slightly, and Leora knew it was because he had been shouting at the person taking the picture—a young woman, Leora remembered, a mother with a child walking beside her and a baby in a stroller, a woman with limp brown hair and bags under her eyes who seemed to be wandering through the zoo in a daze, answering the older child's questions in a distracted voice and looking around one glance at a time, as if she were a refugee from another life, uncertain as to how she had ended up there, in the East Mountain Zoo. She had taken Jason's camera with the same distracted air, ignoring the child tugging at her jacket, and he had shouted at her to move her finger away from the lens. It wasn't a very good picture. Yet in the shadows between the bars of the petting pen, under the noses of the little goats, in Jason's half-open mouth, and in her own squinting smile, Leora could sense an air of longing. It was as if the picture had been taken years ago, of people who had since grown old.

One night, a warm night that spring not long before graduation, Jason knocked on Leora's door. When she let him in, he wore a pained expression on his face, under the yarmulke that seemed to be sliding toward the front of his head. Leora glanced at the picture on her desk, where Jason's face was partly obscured by the shadow of the baseball cap. She could scarcely believe how different a person could look, through nothing more than a choice of hats. The people in the picture looked like strangers to her, a young couple she had barely met — just a boy and a girl grinning in a zoo, who had asked her to take their picture.

Jason didn't bother to sit down. Instead he said, still standing in front of the door he had closed behind him, "I think we need to talk."

Leora stood up, her knees trembling, trying her best to keep her voice cool. "Well, in that case, we can skip the rest of the conversation," she told him, "because I'm twenty-one years old and I know that whenever someone says he 'needs to talk,' what he's really saying is that he wants to end it. So let's just say our goodbyes and get it over with, okay?"

Jason looked startled, but he didn't know what to say other than to recite the script he had prepared for the evening. So he went on with the show. "I don't want you to have any hurt feelings about this, or to feel bad about yourself or anything like that. I think you're a wonderful person and I really do love you. It's just that I realize that you are not the woman who is going to be my wife."

Leora stepped back and sucked in her breath. She wanted to lunge at him, grab him, pound on his chest, shout at him that this wasn't how things were supposed to happen. Men were supposed to reject you, of course, but they weren't supposed to bring up the subject of marriage. They were supposed to be completely ignorant on the subject, almost unaware that it even existed, and you were supposed to clue them in with great subtlety — leaving diamond brochures in their underwear drawers, for example — until they at long last got the hint. And none of this was supposed to happen until you were at least twenty-eight. Men were not supposed to reject you at the age of twenty-one because they realized you weren't going to be their wife.

She stood in front of him, feeling her lips beginning to tremble. But she pressed them together, swallowing before she spoke. "Because I'm not going to be your wife," she said evenly.

"Yes, that's right," Jason answered, almost with eagerness, relieved that he didn't have to explain it any further. His yarmulke was slowly migrating forward on his head, Leora noticed, and she wondered how long it would take before his yarmulke and his hairline finally met. "So I don't think we should see each other anymore."

Then Leora shouted. "Well, you're just fucking full of surprises, aren't you?" Jason stared at her, stunned. She continued. "What the hell happened to you, Jason? When did you ever ask me if I wanted to be your wife? When did you ever even *care* if I wanted to be your wife? Don't you think you could have discussed it with me, if that's what you had in mind? God, am I stupid. I thought you were my boyfriend. I didn't realize that I was dating the Lubavitcher rebbe."

Jason may have answered her, but Leora didn't hear him. She asked him to leave, and he did. If Leora had been an ordinary girl, she might have called her friends and cried for hours and hours over Jason. Instead she fought back her tears and waited until she was sure he had left the building. Then she left the building herself and walked and walked, not knowing where she was walking, and not really caring, either. Her feet, well trained from the previous few weeks when she was studying for exams, took her to the university library. She opened the door and went inside. Some of the tables and desks were draped with lounging students in baseball hats, the unlucky few who still had exams left to take. She went into the reference room and began walking in slow circles along its edges, reading the titles on the bindings of all the different reference books. Circling the room this way was almost like circumnavigating the globe, watching the languages change from shelf to shelf. What she noticed most of all were the encyclopedias, entire encyclopedias for entire countries and religions and cultures she had never even thought about—at least, not since she was in high school. Suddenly she spotted a series that looked familiar. Pausing for a moment by the bookshelf, she selected a few heavy volumes from the shelves, carrying them with her in a colossal stack, and sat down with them at one of the reference room tables.

The tables were long and flat, made out of a solid, heavy wood, and sitting at them always made Leora feel as if whatever she was doing there had suddenly taken on a great importance, as if she were a medieval scholar copying out a book in the days before printing presses. Remembering the last time she had taken a tour around the world, she opened the printed volumes she had pulled from the shelves and began reading all the entries in the *Encyclopaedia Judaica* about the expulsion

of the Jews from Spain in 1492, the same year Christopher Columbus
discovered America, as she tried not to think of how much she wanted
to talk to Naomi.

MANY MONTHS LATER, Leora was the last person to notice the cat
getting bigger. Jason had given her the cat, which she named Sammy
after the "true seal" at the East Mountain Zoo, at the very end of the
summer after graduation, stopping by her house in New Jersey as if for
a final farewell before he left for Israel. At the time, Sammy was the size
of a fairly large kitten, and Leora had assumed that he was already several months old. But as the weeks and months passed and he continued
growing ever larger, Leora soon began to suspect that he really was a
newborn at the beginning, and that he was just a damn big cat. At first
she noticed nothing unusual. Sammy may have had an impressive
appetite, but he was just a kitten and he needed his food to grow.
Leora's family went out of their way not to say anything about it at first,
to avoid reminding her of Jason, and their silence fueled her ignorance.
But as the months passed by, even her parents began to make little comments to her about Sammy's size.

"Don't you think Sammy's getting kind of big for a normal cat?" her
father would ask as he and her mother sat reading the newspaper on a
Sunday evening.

"No, he's just growing," Leora retorted, glancing up from her book
and then looking down again, pulling the book closer to her face. "He's
probably full grown by now."

"But that's what we all thought a month ago," her mother said. "I
don't know much about cats, but I know a cat isn't supposed to be the
size of a dog."

"He's not the size of a dog. He's the size of a cat."

"You can believe whatever you want. I'm just telling you, this is not
normal," her mother said. "Look at him. He's practically the same
height as the coffee table." Sammy was walking past the coffee table,
and as much as Leora didn't want to admit it as she peered over the
edge of her book, it was a little alarming to see his spotted fur moving
level with, or higher than, the tabletop. But soon he slumped down on
the floor so that it was impossible to tell how big he was. And the doubts
continued.

After seeing something on the news about the American Association of Retired Persons, Leora's seventeen-year-old brother began referring to Sammy as "the Gray Panther."

"I see the Gray Panther has inhaled his dinner again," he would smirk.

"Yeah, well, you eat that way too, so I wouldn't talk."

"Pretty soon you're going to have to give that thing whole carcasses to eat. Want me to go to the butcher and bring home an entire cow?"

"Cats don't eat beef, only fish and chicken," Leora spat back, not bothering to look up from her book. She was wrong about that, of course, but she didn't see any reason why her brother should be right about anything.

"I bet the Gray Panther could skeletonize a cow in fifteen seconds if he wanted to."

"Shut up." Leora was getting tired of living at home.

But soon she couldn't help wondering if they were right. By January the Gray Panther was eating so much that Leora could hardly keep up with the cat food supply—not because of the price, but because she didn't have time to go to the supermarket every day. She needed to start buying in bulk. And so she embarked on a journey to the promised land of groceries, the paradise of price, where huddled masses yearning to breathe free of halitosis went to stock their shelves with mouthwash and where the wretched refuse of the teeming shore could purchase lifetime supplies of garbage bags, where the tempest-tossed could replace the barbecues lost in the season's hurricanes, and where giant fluorescent lamps stood raised and gleaming beside the golden door. She bought herself a membership at Costco.

Costcos should never be located in a city proper, nor in itty-bitty "towns." No, Costcos are the landmarks of those great American inventions, overbuilt suburban highways, the local strip malls where everything is so gigantic that all the stores have names that end in "co" or "plex" or "Max" or "City"—OfficeMax, Petco, Funplex, Cineplex, Computer City, Party City, Appliance City, like the lost city of Atlantis, waiting for the lucky exploring shopper to stumble upon the riches hidden within.

You need a membership card to get through Costco's garage-style doors with your giant shopping cart, after abandoning your car amid the brigade of minivans. Once you are inside Costco—and it almost seems inaccurate to say "inside Costco," since the place is like an airplane hangar and "inside" encompasses at least a cubic mile—the racks of merchandise tower twenty-five feet tall, forming cavernous canyons of barbecues, lawn mowers, shirts, toothpaste, meats, frozen foods, giant pies, giant cookies, giant fruits, giant filing cabinets, service for seventeen, wrapping paper, flowerpots, stationery, potato chips, bedding, bed frames, diamond rings, flu shots, computers, socks, electronic keyboards, washing machines, eyeglasses, medications, lawn furniture, candy bars, thirty-foot-wide trampolines. But at eye level lies the ultimate American wondergarden of families, their giant shopping carts piled high with children—Waspy families whispering to each other over piles of vegetables, overdressed Jewish families swinging their handbags across cartloads of diet soda, trailer-trash families brandishing their rat-tailed hair behind carts filled with fish sticks, Hassidic families sweating in their long sleeves, black families with children in braids, Asian families with tiny parents dragging huge lawn chairs, Indian families with mothers wrapped in saris, Italian families with daughters sporting feathered bangs, Hispanic families with earringed sons lugging barbecues behind them—all playing bumper cars by accident as they steer around in endless circles, lining up for free samples, loading up their shopping carts like Oregon Trail pioneers supplying their covered wagons as they prepare to conquer the frontier, the parents gazing up at the towering ceilings of low low prices, bewildered and captivated forever by this place they call America.

One evening in early spring, Leora was wandering through this wonderland, hauling several giant bags of Catco Multimax Foodplex, when she fell upon the matzoh aisle. Towering before her eyes on her left stood a seven-foot-high castle built entirely of giant green and orange boxes of Manischewitz matzoh. It crossed her mind that Passover was fast approaching. Perhaps she should buy a few boxes of matzoh for her mother. As Leora tried to slow down her cat-food-laden forklift of a cart, however, its weight made it slide forward until it slammed into the matzoh tower. Several boxes of matzoh tumbled down from the tower into the cart of a Hassidic man and woman, whose cart had meanwhile slammed into hers under the rain of matzoh boxes.

"I'm so sorry," Leora said, though she smiled to herself at the symmetry of it, at the idea that the matzoh had fallen into the cart of someone who might actually want it. Feigning nonchalance, she immediately started picking up the boxes out of their cart, deliberately not lifting her head on the off chance that the man and woman might somehow interpret it as a slight. As she straightened up to put the boxes back on top of the matzoh tower, she indulged a glance at the man and was surprised to see that he was staring right at her. Suddenly she dropped the matzoh. It was Jason.

"Hi, Leora," he said with a smile. "How are you?"

He had gotten thinner, she noticed. His neck, once thickly set with muscles, had slimmed down to become a much looser link between his head and his body, like a young, sturdy branch of a slightly twisted tree. Between the sides of his black cloak, his white-shirted stomach seemed narrow and gaunt, his dark belt fastened on its tightest notch to hold up his black pants. His hands were thin and pale. And his face was nearly covered by a mustache, beard, and sidelocks, the hairs long and bristly from years of shaving. But something had returned to him that Leora hadn't seen since he broke his leg a year and a half earlier. Without the weight of his old muscles, he seemed lighter somehow, less burdened, his shoulders straighter, his head more erect. And his black hat and dark suit made him look as if he were wearing a costume, as if he might at any moment pull the beard off his face to show off his shiny soccer-victory grin.

The woman standing next to him wore a long skirt down to her ankles and a long-sleeved shirt with a high collar; her hair was completely covered by a tightly fitting hat. But there was something that distinguished her from the women Leora had seen at the East Mountain Zoo, and Leora couldn't quite put her finger on it. She glanced again at the woman's clothing, searching for some difference. But soon she saw that it wasn't the clothes that set this woman apart from the women at the zoo. It was her face. Unlike those women, she didn't look tired or flustered or exhausted. She only looked young.

"Hi," Leora stuttered.

"It's great to see you again." Jason grinned at her, and then motioned toward the woman. "I don't think you've ever met Rivka, my wife."

Leora's jaw dropped for a second. The memory flitted through her mind of the only other time she had ever heard Jason use that word: "I realize you are not the woman who is going to be my wife." It took all of the muscles in her face to force a smile. "Wow, congratulations! When did you get married?"

"Two months ago," Rivka replied. She had a low, mature-sounding voice, which secretly disappointed Leora. A normal American accent. "We got married in Jerusalem. We just came back to the States a few weeks ago, actually."

Leora always hated it when people referred to America as "the States." As if the whole place were some ad hoc collection of random entities that just happen to be side by side, a bunch of unrelated stores on a crowded street. How could Rivka, Leora thought, who had clearly grown up here, stand here in Costco and pretend not to get it? America was no cluttered, crooked little thousand-year-old street with fifty different stores each sell-ing its own kind of unpasteurized goat cheese. No, America was Big, New, Open 24 Hours, Cost-Effective, Buy It in Bulk, Bulk, Bulk! America was Members Only, Anyone Can Join, the Land of the Free and the Home of the Brave! What was this bullshit about coming back to "the States"?

"How exciting!" Leora said. And then, turning to Jason: "So what are you up to these days—besides being married, I mean?" She laughed a forced laugh at her own little joke, trying to convince herself that she meant it as a joke.

But Jason didn't even smile. "Working on Forty-seventh Street in New York," he said into his beard. "Rivka's father owns a diamond busi-ness there."

"Oh. Well, that's something new," Leora answered. And it took all of her strength to stop herself from saying what she was dying to say: What about medical school? What about the old people? What about—Jason?

Rivka suddenly turned to him, tugging on his sleeve. "Come on, Yehudah, we need to go now."

"Okay," he said. "It was good seeing you," he told Leora, with the sort of smile he usually reserved for strangers in the nursing home. "Give my best wishes to your family." And then Rivka dragged him away, lead-ing him beside the still waters of Poland Spring.

Yehudah?

WHEN LEORA was very little, long before she knew any of the Landsmanns, she and her mother were cleaning out a closet together in their house, and her mother came across a brown, beat-up piece of paper at the bottom of a box filled with outdated children's clothes. It was a story her mother had written for her first-grade class, in 1953, some forgettable composition that probably required her to use certain spelling words. But at the time, Leora wasn't interested at all in the content, or even in the strange browning ink that came from a dipped pen nib (can anyone believe now that people wrote like that in school, that late?). No, what interested Leora was the name in the corner of the page.

"This story's not yours," she told her mother, in her smart-ass seven-year-old voice.

Her mother looked up in surprise, which gave Leora a secret thrill. "What do you mean?" she asked.

"Well, I mean that's not you," Leora answered. "It's by someone named Ellen, like you, but the last name is different. So it's by some other girl who's also called Ellen, but not you." Leora smiled, triumphant.

Her mother looked at Leora and leaned back a bit, opening her eyes wide, as she always did when she was telling Leora something she needed to know. "Ah," she said, "well, it may not seem like that's me, but it is. That used to be my last name, but I changed my last name when Daddy and I got married. Most women change their names when they get married."

"Really?"

"Yes."

If Leora had been a different kind of child, a fairness-minded child, she might have asked all of the obvious questions. Like why didn't Daddy also change his name, or why didn't Daddy change his name instead of her changing hers, or why did anyone's name need to be changed at all? But that didn't interest Leora. She wasn't a fairness-minded child, and she rarely cared when other people used her toys. Instead she was a conservation-minded child, the kind of child who never allows her parents to throw anything of hers away, no matter how useless or ugly. Things to Leora had lives of their own, little lives, created for a purpose, and she couldn't bear to throw out anything. Old toys would gather dust in her bedroom, untouched for years.

And so she asked a question that her mother surely didn't expect: "So if you aren't using that name anymore, then who is?"

Her mother paused a moment and thought. "No one, I guess," she said, avoiding Leora's stare. "My sisters had that name, but now they're married. And Grandma and Grandpa had that name their whole lives. But you're right, no one uses it now. If Grandpa had had brothers, they would have used it, but he only had sisters, no brothers."

"So what happened to that name?"

"Well, that sounds like a good idea for a story, doesn't it?" her mother said. That was what she always said when Leora asked her questions that she couldn't or didn't want to answer. Then, with a look of extreme distraction: "Come on, let's finish putting these things away."

Leora never wrote the story, of course. But while she lay in bed at night trying to fall asleep, she thought about it, for days. What had happened to all those names? Perhaps there was a place somewhere where all the unused names were gathered, a giant dried-out desert valley where the names, shriveled and lifeless, lay at the bottom.

As the years passed, Leora met more married women, more immigrants, went to more museums. Slowly there gathered in the Valley of Discarded Names hundreds, even thousands more: Rogarshevsky thrown away in favor of Rosenthal, Rosenthal thrown away in favor of Ross. Ross tossed out for Steinberg (a marriage), Steinberg cast away for O'Brien (a second marriage). Liu discarded for Lou. Anand Gupta for Andrew Gordon. Natalya for Natalie. Wilhelm for Bill. Jesus for Jeff. All those names discarded, only written, not spoken, like the name in the corner of her mother's composition, sitting at the bottom of the valley like untouched bones. "Come on, Yehudah," Rivka had said. Leora knew that Yehudah was a dried-out name, one that Jason had found at the bottom of that valley and that he wanted to speak back to life. But she couldn't help seeing all the greeting cards he had written her, stacked up in the bottom of her closet, and the essays he had written for medical schools about care for the elderly, filed away in some office somewhere, fluttering down into that valley with his signatures.

Back home, Leora was looking at the cat again. Sammy by then was about three feet long, with big round ears and ever-growing teeth. She sat down on the couch and began flipping through her magazine, which, she had discovered, is one of the most boring things you can do if you work at a magazine, because you've already read everything before the magazine comes out. Sammy climbed up on the couch beside Leora in a single stretch of his disturbingly long legs, but that seemed normal by then. He settled down on the cushion next to hers, and he looked so quiet and soft that she couldn't resist stroking his back with its little white spots. As she touched him, he raised his head a bit, stretched open his mouth, and yawned, showing off his giant fangs glinting in the afternoon light. That was when she recognized him. He was an ocelot.

   When Leora brought her ocelot to the East Mountain Zoo the next day, the zoo's staff was overjoyed. Ocelots, they informed her, were an endangered species, with fewer than a thousand animals living through-out the world. Their numbers had declined mainly through poaching, though many ocelots had also been captured illegally for the pet trade. When Leora gave her best guess as to how one of these rare specimens had ended up living in her house, she was told that Jason's father no longer worked at the East Mountain Zoo, and in fact hadn't for at least a year. No one could explain how Jason might have gotten it. And Leora, with her tourist's eye that could only see things at specific moments, couldn't explain it either.

CHAPTER 3

BARBARIANS AT THE GATES

BEFORE HER DEATH, Naomi had dragged Bill Landsmann to enough Holocaust movies that he knew exactly what would happen in them. His son and daughter-in-law knew better than to take him to such things. But Naomi, forgivably naive, really seemed to think that these movies would help her get to know him better, better than she could get to know him through his slide shows—as if something in one of these films would inspire him to describe for her some forgotten image, something from his "past." By the time Naomi died, he knew all the movies by heart.

These movies always started with a music box. That was because music boxes were in a class with organ-grinders, clowns, carousels, and calliopes—all those forcibly happy, vaguely European things that children are supposed to love, but which really only exist to make adults feel sorry for children, who have no choice but to die or grow up. And as Bill Landsmann noticed, these Holocaust movies always opened with a child, specifically a little boy—blond and adorable, of course, and generally played by some European child actor named Lukasz.

The boy starts out the film in his charming European-looking home, a beautiful oak-paneled apartment decked with lace, dark velvet curtains, and Royal Copenhagen china, not to mention the obligatory silver menorah prominently displayed on the mantel where the Christmas stockings would have been, to prove to the non-Jewish moviegoer that these people are just like everybody else, see, except that they really like candles.

As the camera pans around the apartment, the little boy Lukasz—"David" in the script—scampers in with carousel-worthy delight, stage left. He pauses for a moment, looking around to see if anyone has noticed him, and then he climbs up on a deep red Victorian ladies' chair, dangling his arms over its back, tiny silver key in hand, to reach the Music Box on the table behind it. The camera zooms in on his little, adorable fingers as they twist the key in the lock and open the Music Box. Then, note by note, the music begins to seep out of the Box: a soft melody, slow and perfectly rhythmic, each little plucked bell-shaped droplet of sound falling in neat order on the audience's ears. It doesn't matter what the tune is, really. (The stage directions, Bill Landsmann imagines, suggest "an old Jewish melody," but due to a careless individual in the audio department, the tune turns out to be "Edelweiss." Bill Landsmann guesses that the director was quite angry about this but kept it in the end, mired in more pressing problems involving Lukasz's contract.)

The camera turns slowly now, keeping pace with the slowing music. At last it comes around to the boy's hands again, which he plunges into the Box's riches (and here, Bill Landsmann thinks, the director must have hesitated—not too much gold, he must have told the props people, because there's this thing about Jews and gold, you see, so go easy on the gold), a child's riches of trinkets and tiny toys. The boy's enchanted face is reflected in the Music Box's mirror behind the turning ballerina figurine, and he handles, with a delicacy only children victimized in movies have, each of the treasures in turn: a charm bracelet with tiny silver sailboats, a locket with a sepia photograph of a woman inside it, a necklace with a Star of David (as if you had to ask), and, lastly, a magnificent diamond ring. The boy takes the ring in his little fingers, fascinated. He kneels on the seat of the chair he was standing on and pretends to propose to the ballerina figurine, who continues spinning as the music continues. Suddenly the boy is lifted, in his kneeling position, right out of his seat. Luckily, the culprit turns out to be his mother, who sweeps him away in an armload of laughter and kisses. (At this point Bill Landsmann would feel Naomi's eyes on his profile in the darkened theater, checking for crying or cringing. He would ignore her.)

Of course, the entire point is that this charming apartment is doomed to destruction—that's what makes it so charming. A few scenes in, the Bad Guys break down the charming door, smash the Royal Copenhagen china, steal the mother's diamond ring, knock the Music Box to the floor (the music stops abruptly), and take the boy's mother away with them while the boy watches the whole scene from under a bed. Later it turns out that there are also papers in the Music Box, letters of permission and forged identity cards that his mother had been hoarding in a hidden drawer, and the boy and his father use them to escape. Many years later, at the end of the film, the boy comes back as an Old Man and opens the Music Box once more to find the locket, with the picture of his mother inside it. By the time the credits started rolling, Naomi would be in tears.

Under the guise of a school project, Naomi had once "interviewed" Bill Landsmann, and he had given her all the stupid details of his life. Born in Vienna, no brothers or sisters. Left Vienna with his father for Amsterdam, then left Amsterdam for America. His mother remained behind in a hospital and apparently died. There was nothing in his story to thrill the American moviegoer, no tattooed numbers on anyone's arms. But the real story, the real movie of Bill Landsmann's life, would have disappointed Naomi—and Leora too, and every other person Naomi knew—more than she or anyone else could have imagined. And that was why, instead, he showed people nothing but slides.

Recast it. The lead will be played not by a cute seven-year-old child but by an underdeveloped, antisocial twelve-year-old boy—himself, that is—with sick thoughts about girls and an archipelago of pimples clinging to the left corner of his mouth. The role of the Bad Guy will be played by a Jew, details to follow. Strike the set. No more plush apartments; instead build a set of two nearly empty rooms, furnished with nothing but a desk, a little table, two chairs, and some mattresses on the floor. And rewrite the script so that what was lost is what was really lost—not the city apartments, not the music boxes, not the Royal Copenhagen china, not all the things that can easily be replaced in some other country a few decades later, but a language, a literature, a held hand, an entire world lived and breathed in the image of God. This is the movie Naomi never saw, because Bill Landsmann never showed her.

IN THE OPENING CREDITS of this imaginary film, Wilhelm Landsmann—or Bill Landsmann, in the subtitles—has just landed in Amsterdam. Shipwrecked, if you will, or, more accurately, land-wrecked. Of course, "just" doesn't really mean much at this point. How long has it been since the wreckage? A few months? A few years? It scarcely matters. He will always feel as if he has just arrived. Wilhelm has "just" become Willem, the second of three names—the third being Bill—that he will use in a period of less than five years.

His Dutch is abysmal. "His" Dutch. A European way of speaking, he decides years later, claiming languages as one's own, as if each person owned a little piece of German or French or Dutch, or a great big piece, and some languages have more to go around than others. In school he slowly picks up Dutch, but Dutch doesn't pick him up in return—he can understand all the insults the other children whisper at him, but he doesn't speak back. German is his, or at least was his. But now he has stopped speaking German, and as a result of "his" Dutch not really being his, he speaks nothing at all. Instead he wanders around the city of Amsterdam, silently creeping around its streets and wishing he could somehow run away and go home.

All of Amsterdam reminds Willem of a rat trap. Crooked little streets, crooked little buildings with hidden dead ends at every turn. You walk home from school, a terrible place—although it is Montessori, and therefore a Very Good School—where each classroom is stacked on top of another and where they put the new kid, right after he arrives and despite the supposed "open classroom" philosophy, in a seat at the back of the room. (Willem didn't remain in that school. Kicked out by Montessori, he had to go to the Jewish school, and at the new school, speaking German was not only discouraged but expressly forbidden. By some quirk of fate, however, he found himself assigned to a seat at the back of the room even there. Someone always has to sit at the back of the room.)

The school is cramped, like everywhere in Amsterdam, so much so that Willem sometimes wonders if putting children in it is actually a waste of space—the floor level is always jammed, but since children are small, Willem thinks, they might have split each of the building's sto-ries in two instead of having six feet of empty air above the children's heads, thus doubling the building's floor space without altering its height. Perhaps that would inconvenience a few teachers, but what of it? These are the things that Willem thinks about all day at school as he stares up at the ceiling, trying his best not to learn any more Dutch even by accident. Anyway, the extra air in the classroom doesn't help the fact that Willem sits in class each day jammed between his desk and the back wall and tormented on both sides by boys—Peter and Jan, they are called—who take advantage of the open education model to spit at him whenever the teacher turns around.

But then the whole city is like some ridiculous maze designed by a cruel psychologist who waits, watching you, testing you to see if you might take a wrong turn and receive an electric shock. You leave the school each day and walk home along the canals, where the big flatboats—reveling in their flatness in this upright, vertical city—seem to be grinning idiotic grins at you just like the boys in school. The boats, after all, are in the right place, while Amsterdam itself, a city built on seventeenth-century pilings of stone, is ever sinking into the sea where it belongs, and the boats themselves seem to know it as they chug their joyous way out to the North Sea. Meanwhile you are stuck on dry land, confined to the narrow streets, some of them walled in by crooked buildings, others open on one side to the freezing canals with cruel grinning boats, and all of them jammed with black bicycles ridden by old ladies in long frumpy skirts madly ringing their bicycle bells. Amsterdam belongs to these frumpy women, and you are forever jumping out of their way.

After you dodge the bicycles, though, you still have to negotiate your way through the tiny little streets, their corners, lampposts, and buildings occasionally marked with the city's seal—a badge shape with three simple letters in a vertical column: "XXX." At the Montessori School, before he was expelled, Willem learned that these three X's stood for the three trials of Amsterdam: flood, fire, and plague. Those X's glare at him at every interval as he wanders in circles around the city looking for a way out, as if to say, Not here, not now, not ever—and if you try to stand still, I'll knee you in the groin.

And if the streets aren't enough to make you feel like a suffocating rat, there is always home. Willem's building in Amsterdam is a canal house, one of the strangled town houses gasping for air along the city's riverstreets. The canal houses each stand about four stories high, but are rarely more than thirty feet wide, with their side walls rubbing each other as they sink deeper and deeper into the city's soft false ground, leaning forward and backward like poorly trained soldiers falling out of line. Inside, the apartments are so cramped that each building has a giant hook protruding from its elaborate gables. These hooks are for pulleys, used for roping up furniture that won't fit through the narrow staircases and hauling it in through the windows.

The hooks stab at the thick blue air during the most oppressive moment of the day. It isn't exactly sunset, especially not in the winter months, but the moment right after sunset—the moment when the day has just disappeared forever, leaving behind a few ragged leaves and scattered regrets. The sky seeps like watery blue ink behind the buildings, but it's not the sky that smothers Willem. It's the lights. Along the brick walls at that moment, windows begin to light up like little slide panels, glowing white-framed pictures with tiny people in them, or yellow squares blurred by casually drawn shades. Each window is its own separate could-have-been, a place he might have lived, a person he might have known, a scene he somehow missed. Instead he walks home through the blue ink, a lost merchant sailing across an uncharted open sea.

And then, at the door of the apartment itself, the test becomes a true challenge, just like a test on a rat who chooses one path for cheese and another for an electric shock. A choice of going in or not going in, of listening at the door to hear whether some anonymous moaning woman might be behind it, and if there is, of waiting in the suffocating hallway behind a corner, sometimes for hours, until you hear the clicking of shoes and laughter—and smell the perfume that smells nothing like how your mother used to smell, your mother who, you remember, used to smell only of coffee, or sometimes of fresh bread, but never of perfume—passing through the building's front door. One time, when Willem first arrived in Amsterdam, he walked into the apartment to find his father and a young woman sitting on the mattress on the floor, still clothed, and he passed through the room to get to his tiny bedroom on the other side. For this his father refused to serve him meals for a week. From then on Willem made a habit of sitting on the grimy tilted floor in the corridor, listening and waiting, torn between an aching curiosity to overhear as much as possible and the wave of nausea when he actually did. Only once in the countless hours of sitting in the corridor did he ever hear mention of himself. The door to his bedroom must have been left open, Willem realized, and the woman asked his

father, in Dutch, if his son was living with him. Willem's father laughed
and answered that Willem had been sent to boarding school in
Switzerland. Willem wished he had. But by then the doors were almost
all closed. The world was becoming a dark and grimy apartment
vestibule, and Willem could do nothing but sit and wait in it.

WILLEM'S FATHER Nadav Landsmann had shell shock, from the
war. He had even received a copy of an army-issued letter from a doctor stating that he had undergone psychological damage on the front, a
letter he kept hidden in a drawer out of some sick refusal to throw it
away, even though he went to great lengths to make sure no one ever
heard about it, including his wife.

Nonetheless, there was something of his illness in the very fact that
he kept the letter at all. One day when Wilhelm—back when he was
Wilhelm, an old-fashioned name even then—was about eight or nine
years old, he discovered the key to the locked drawer in his father's desk.
First checking on tiptoe to be sure that no adult was nearby, Wilhelm
scampered into his father's study in their old apartment in Vienna. He
climbed up on a chair to better reach the drawer, an old wooden desk
drawer crisscrossed with scrape marks, as if someone had been scratch-
ing to get into it. Wilhelm inserted the key into the lock with a fervor
he could taste and turned it in slow restrained ecstasy, and was
astounded and thrilled when the drawer burst forth, gaping and beautiful. Papers mostly, but ah, secret papers! No school compositions, these!
Letters on official printed stationery, some of them, from places with
unreadably long names. Long lists of numbers, more complicated than
a web of tangled shoelaces, with return addresses in Switzerland.
Telegrams, written in incoherent stunted sentences. And long brown-
inked letters in Hebrew script—Yiddish, Wilhelm knew—written in a
shaky hand. Wilhelm plunged his hands into the pile of treasures and
pulled one out at random. A gem: a crisp yellowing sheet, typed and
printed on letterhead with a giant seal of the Austro-Hungarian Empire,
a horrifyingly dark, feathery eagle clutching clawfuls of spears. Wilhelm
savored that picture as if it were a portrait of his mother, committing its
every detail to memory. But quickly, so that he could move on to the
text. And on he read:

Our diagnosis of Private Nadav Landsmann's psychological state reflects that Private Landsmann is experiencing sustained mental trauma of the type broadly termed "shell shock." The condition varies in its effect on patients. Some may require lifelong hospitalization; others experience little disturbance in their civilian lives. In Private Landsmann's case, the illness may express itself, among other symptoms, in continuous nervous behavior verging on paranoia, in sudden or violent fits of temper, in obsessive or compulsive neurotic tendencies, or in the repression of normal emotional response. Further analysis will be necessary to determine the extent and nature of Private Landsmann's disorder.

Wilhelm Landsmann was blessed with a photographic memory, and he quickly filed all the hard words away in his mind like a spy memorizing a secret code, to hunt them down later in the dictionary. Thrilled to the very bone, he continued reading: "Recommended treatment may worsen the—"

Suddenly a giant hand dropped down from the heavens, smashing the letter down into the drawer and slamming the drawer shut. But the magic drawer wouldn't quite close, since Wilhelm's fingers, unaware, were blocking it. And when the hand noticed the reason why the drawer wasn't closing, slamming it once more wasn't enough—the hand slammed it again, and again, and again, and again like cannon fire, faster and faster, harder and harder, deliberately catching Wilhelm's tiny fingers over and over, crushing them again and again until they jumped out of the drawer like animals narrowly escaping a trap.

The shell shock was thus the easy way to explain why Nadav shattered Wilhelm's mother's entire set of Royal Copenhagen china one evening when he returned from work and didn't like what she served him for dinner, or why he tore up one of Wilhelm's compositions for school—the one about explorers in the New World—because Wilhelm had left his shoes on the floor, or why he still managed to convince nearly every woman he met, with little more than a smile and a flattering remark, that he was the one thing they needed to make their lives complete—and why, from time to time, he completed them. But only selfless people keep their illnesses to themselves. Others pass them along. Which is why it was Wilhelm's mother who wound up in a mental institution and first on the list of the doomed.

Like many undeserving people, however, Nadav had done extremely well in life, at least on paper. He was a handsome man with a Clark Gable mustache and truly captivating eyes—bright blue, though they had a certain hard edge to them that could almost cut you. Powerful eyes. After the war and a few long years of academic catch-up, he had managed to enter the university in Vienna, where he studied modern history, and after university he opened a successful business in upmarket cashmere sweaters. Much later in the game, to add insult to injury, he won the Viennese lottery. The papers, not yet propaganda machines but getting there, heralded his victory in headlines on their inside pages: RICH JEW TAKES VIENNA'S MONEY. Nadav was not interviewed for these articles, but someone who had known him from the university was on the masthead of one of the papers and had suggested this interesting angle on the usual lottery-winner story. It was still early. No one had stopped Nadav from winning the lottery. But he realized when he saw the headlines that the best thing to do with Vienna's money was to ship it out of Vienna, so on the advice of a friend in the business, he opened a branch shop in Amsterdam. He had studied some Dutch in university, inspired by a beautiful woman from Amsterdam with whom he had promptly fallen in love. (She went back to Holland and married a minister and he never saw her again. But she left him with Dutch.) Still, when he came to work one morning in Vienna to find the windows of his main store smashed, he stuck it out.

"Barbarians at the gates," Nadav muttered at the dinner table that evening. "We'll see how long we can stave them off." He had recently finished reading yet another book about his latest obsession, the fall of the Roman Empire.

"What are barbarians?" Wilhelm asked, in a moment of extraordinary bravery. He had heard his father use the word before, distinctly remembered it, but when? Where? He regretted his question as soon as he asked it. Why hadn't he just waited until later, and looked it up in the dictionary?

Nadav snarled. "People like you, you idiot, who know so little that their vocabulary doesn't even include descriptions of themselves."

Out of hopeful habit Wilhelm looked to his mother for rescue, but she just sat there staring at her food, stirring it absently as if she were eating alone. In less than a year she would be gone, but she might as well have been gone already. Wilhelm copied her movements, hiding from his father's face. His father pushed his plate away and left the room, and his mother wordlessly got up and began clearing the table, as if nothing had happened. This was always how things went.

Later Wilhelm took out the dictionary. The dictionary—an immense volume, not a children's book, with thousands upon thousands of words—was without question his favorite book. He liked reading just about anything, though most of the books he wanted to read were still too hard for him. But the dictionary! He could sit for hours flipping through its pages, reading the definitions, the etymologies, the sample sentences that made each word seem like the cornerstone of a giant house of speech. Everything in it was necessary, yet nothing was excluded. A perfect economy. By an early age, Wilhelm was convinced that every known fact about the world was included in the dictionary. Why ask people questions when the answers were all right here?

Wilhelm opened the dictionary with care, taking his time as he turned the pages. After all, half the fun lay in the words discovered en route to the destination, the stones kicked up on the path to reveal the diamond mines beneath. Since the word *Barbar* was in the *B*'s, he turned right to the beginning, glancing at the opening lines of the preface before he plunged into the words themselves. "Language," it read,

> is a people's most essential common bond, the one true voice of a nation. Yet the core of language lies not in a dictionary such as this, but rather in the living voice. Through the shared words they speak and hear every day, the people of a nation constantly acknowledge the lives and goals they share, their common destiny.

Idiots, Wilhelm thought once he had deciphered the text, stopping on some of the dictionary's back pages along the way to do so. They don't even like their own book. To the words, then. He passed by a picture of a man playing an accordion, squeezing his eyes closed as if to better hear his own music. In the same section he found another picture, this time of a rat-like animal with long strange thumbs, its arms and legs spread out in all directions as if flattened by a truck. The caption read, "Opossum mouse, *Acrobates pygmaeus*." The definition of *Acrobates pygmaeus*, listed under its Latin name, read, "A genus of marsupial animals found in Australasia, including the opossum mouse, which flies with the aid of its phalanges." This, naturally, meant that Wilhelm had to look up *Phalangen*, on the way to which he detoured to *Penis*, which was disappointing—"The male sexual organ; in mammals it is also the organ through which urine is expelled." *Phalangen*, meanwhile, had something to do with fingers. Staring at his own fingers, he found himself wondering whether there might be some people in the world who could use their fingers to fly, like the *Acrobates pygmaeus*. Wouldn't that be neat? Enough flying around now, though. He rushed back to the front of the book, this time directly to

Bar.bar

No picture. Immediately Wilhelm felt somewhat disappointed, since he had been half hoping that he might find a picture of someone resembling himself. In the wake of this letdown, the long series of derivations and grammatical details following the word bored him. Onward he read:

> 1. Etymologically, a foreigner; a person whose language and customs differ from the speaker's.

Interesting, but not helpful, Wilhelm thought within the confines of his extremely meticulous schoolboy's brain. The people who had smashed the windows were Austrians, after all, and Wilhelm was Austrian too. And they and he and his father all spoke German. So far, Wilhelm was not a barbarian.

> 2. Historically, a: a person who is not a Greek; b: a person living outside of the Roman Empire and its civilization; c: a person outside of Christian civilization.

Here things got muddier. Wilhelm ran down the list. Indeed he wasn't a Greek, so that made him a barbarian according to 2a. But his father wasn't Greek either, so who was he to go around calling other people barbarians when he was one himself? That couldn't be right. As for 2b, well, in school they had learned about the Romans, who had lived a long time ago, in Italy. So Wilhelm certainly lived outside of the Roman Empire, and so did the people who had smashed the windows. But again, so did his father. Maybe his father was a barbarian after all.

Definition 2c made Wilhelm's throat hollow with nausea for a moment. It made him a barbarian, that was certain. But if it made him a barbarian, then it also made his father a barbarian. And it made the people who had smashed the windows not barbarians at all. So—and here Wilhelm's brain worked out the mathematics of it—if he was a barbarian, and the window-smashers were barbarians, but his father was *not* a barbarian, then definition 2c couldn't be what his father meant. Hence Wilhelm was still not a barbarian. Wilhelm suspected that something wasn't quite right about his calculation here, but he forged on nonetheless.

3. A rude, wild, uncivilized person.

Wilhelm sighed. The dictionary really did include everything. But luckily, something lingered below the definitions:

Note: The Greek word originally referred to speech, and it is possible that the word itself represents an attempt to imitate inscrutable foreign speech.

So the word was actually meant to sound as silly as it did? "Bar, bar, bar, bar," Wilhelm repeated to himself as he closed the dictionary, barbling his words as he went to bed.

The barbarians couldn't be staved off for long. Soon Nadav fled to Amsterdam, leaving Wilhelm's mother checked into her institution and thereby finding himself forced to take Wilhelm with him. Secretly, Nadav was dreaming of meeting that young Dutch woman again, of finding her abandoned by her husband, splashing in the water of the canals pleading for rescue, so that he could dive in and pull her up to dry land. He never would find her, but he kept looking for her, in the face of every woman he met strolling through the streets of Amsterdam, while his son barbled away at school, unable or unwilling to speak Dutch. Which brings us to the day in question. Roll film.

IT IS a Saturday afternoon, and Willem's father isn't home. He is sure to return shortly, though, as he usually does, to spend the afternoon in the company of yet another woman, which is always Willem's cue to leave before he guesses they might arrive. But for now the place is his. As usual, Willem sits at the small table in his father's bedroom, deciphering a textbook with his German-Dutch dictionary by his side. Biology is getting boring, though, and Willem has already skipped ahead in the book to the parts about human reproduction. He is secretly hoping for a school lesson on the subject, and he begins fantasizing about live demonstrations in class. Engrossed in his fantasies but restrained by the possibility of hearing his father's key turning in the lock at any moment, Willem sits at the table and stares across the room, dreaming. But then he notices that something on the other side of the room looks slightly amiss. Scanning the nearly empty room, he immediately determines what is wrong. The secret drawer of his father's desk—a different desk from the one left behind in Vienna, a smaller, dirtier one, but with a secret drawer nonetheless—has been left open.

Willem waits a moment, listening carefully in the silence. No one is out in the hallway, of that he is certain. Taking care not to make a sound, Willem pushes away from the little table and stands up, scampering across the room and deftly pulling open the drawer. It is almost too good to be true. There, lying right on top of the pile, is the letter with Private Landsmann's diagnosis. Willem hasn't seen it since they were in Vienna, but he barely needs to read it again. He practically knows it by heart.

The temptation is too great. Willem pulls out the letter, places it right in the middle of the empty desk, and closes the drawer. Then, knowing precisely what he is doing, he returns to the table, picks up his biology book, and retreats to his tiny bedroom, closing the door behind him.

In less than half an hour, he hears his father come in the door, talking with gusto to a laughing woman who steps into the apartment with a click of heels that makes Willem's heart flutter. Willem hears the door close and the echoes of playful kisses as he draws her further into the room. And then they both stop short.

"What's this?" he hears her say in Dutch with a giggle. "Is someone writing you love letters? You remember I can read German, don't you?" Willem stands up, leaning against his tiny window and still holding his biology book. He would cross the room to the door to hear better, but he is afraid of making a sound. He hears his father jump, lunge across the desk, and grab the letter from her hands with a laugh and a stuttered joke, but the words sound as if they are falling apart in his mouth.

Willem smiles. It is almost as if, Willem thinks with stunted pleasure, his father has forgotten how to speak Dutch.

"I've just remembered," the woman says, far too loudly, "I have an appointment this afternoon. I'm sorry, but I really need to go now."

Willem's father stutters his protests, but he seems unable to find the right words. Soon his protests degenerate into begging, then into shouts, but there is nothing, nothing, he can do. The door to the apartment squeaks open, then slams shut.

There is a moment of silence, heavier than the thud of a club against a wall, and Willem's heart pounds so loudly that he wonders if it might be overheard. Then the door to Willem's room clicks open.

Willem remains in the same position he was in before, standing with his back to his tiny window, staring at his book. The apartment is silent. Willem feels his father's glare on him, but he doesn't look up to meet it. His father waits. Willem still doesn't look up. Then, without any warning, something crashes into Willem's chest and knocks him to the ground, smashing the window on the way. Willem sprawls on the floor, his limbs spread like the fingers of a flying phalanger, hearing himself squeal as he sucks at the air. As he opens his eyes amid the rain of broken glass, his pimpled cheek pressed against the floorboards, he sees his dictionary lying on the floor beside him, drowning in shattered glass. His father has thrown the dictionary at him.

Before Willem even regains his breath, his father grabs him by the shirt, lifts him off the ground, hauls him out the door and down the hall, and literally throws him out of the house, kicking him down the steps before slamming the door and locking it.

And so we find our hero, Wilhelm alias Willem, jacketless and freezing and flung out of his house, swung to the sidewalk against a lamppost that has just missed his groin. After a few minutes, he crawls back up the steps and bangs weakly on the door. No response.

WILLEM HATES Amsterdam on principle, but there is something sort of gentle about it. The city is a maze, but at least it is a maze lined with small and interesting things. Bakeries, mostly. And chocolate stores. And candy shops. At the moment, though, the thought of food makes him feel sick and disgusting. He needs to throw things, to smash windows—not that he has the guts to actually do it, of course. Instead he gets up, slowly, and begins walking. He passes one block, then another. And another. And twelve or thirteen more. He turns a corner, then another one, then a few more, wanders even further, for what feels like days, then hurries along a canal. And suddenly, as if rising from the depths of the sea, a giant edifice appears before him. Like all good citizens of Amsterdam, Willem recognizes it immediately. The Rijksmuseum.

The Rijksmuseum, his teacher at Montessori once told their class, is the oldest museum in Europe. The Louvre and other museums may occupy older buildings, but those buildings were originally built as palaces, or train stations. The Rijksmuseum was the first building actually built for the sole purpose of housing a public museum. "In other countries, art was something reserved for the wealthy, for nobles and royalty, and it remained that way for a very long time," his teacher had said, facing the class and thereby giving Willem a short respite from the spitballs. "Here in Holland, though, we realized earlier than anywhere else that the fine and decorative arts should not be partitioned off for the upper classes. They are our national treasures. And that means that everyone in the nation shares these treasures of our kingdom, including all of you."

Willem raises his head until the back of his skull touches his neck as he stands before the giant edifice. The walls are brick, carved and sculpted, ornamented at every turn with arched glass windows and circular rosettes. It looks like a Gothic cathedral, or a towering palace, or a great train station. Funny how train stations look like cathedrals or palaces sometimes, Willem muses, when people don't even live in them—like shrines to the art of passing through. Willem is dazzled by the building's beauty. His feet take him closer to the great entry gate, drawing him step by absentminded step toward its magnificence. And then he bangs his shins against a makeshift sign on a sandwich board just outside the museum's gate. Stunned into alertness, he steps back and reads it, a hand-painted sign that probably wasn't official at all, that might well have been put up by hooligans just that day:

WELCOME TO THE RIJKSMUSEUM
No dogs or Jews allowed

Our hero stands motionless, staring at the sign, a barbarian at the gates. But he doesn't stand there long. Self-conscious twelve-year-olds—particularly underdeveloped twelve-year-old boys, the sort of twelve-year-olds that older people too often mistake for ten-year-olds, and justifiably so—always know not to stand around looking at something, because then someone nearby will notice you looking at it and use it to make fun of you. That's what happens with girls, anyhow. Not that Willem has any ability to talk to girls. It would have been hard in German. When he tries to speak Dutch, even the Jewish girls at his new school avoid looking twice at him. They flounce their little skirts, crossing and uncrossing their knees in front of his very eyes, deliberately almost. Like a slow torture. One girl, Jopie, has tortured him especially of late. Shining blond hair, glowing green eyes, perfect hands, and a hint of a slope beneath her blouse. She isn't Jewish, but her father is, and so she ended up at Willem's school. Late at night, he dreams about her popping out from around a corner in the city, dragging him into an alleyway, and stripping off her clothes in front of him. Meanwhile the boys at the Jewish school still throw spitballs at him whenever he dares step near her. In the daytime, he opens his mouth in her presence and finds it filled with heavy parchment, the words he wants to say written on scrolls under his tongue, in a forgotten language.

Willem walks back to the canal, turning away from the museum casually, glancing at the people on the streets and trying to act as if he were just a curious visitor, a tourist perhaps, just looking to see what this magnificent building is called. The part about dogs was also of interest to him. But the part about Jews? Of course not. As he turns in his attempt at casualness, he is almost hit by a bicycle. The old woman on it, dressed in a long paisley skirt like a school librarian, spins her head around like a witch to shriek evil spells at him in Dutch. His eyes focus on the street in front of him, and he ventures over to the water's edge to peer into the canal. It's a clear day, the sort of day so bright that it's practically insulting to complain of the cold, but he can't help burning with cold. A cruel day. His reflection looks back at him, his left cheek shimmering red from being scraped against the floorboards and his ears sticking out wildly from underneath his messy brown hair. Ears, he had read in his biology textbook, are one of only two parts of the body that continue growing throughout one's life. Unfortunately the other part was the nose. Being Jewish was a double curse. He examines his face, more with his bare fingertips than in the reflection—which, he notes with pleasure, is not quite detailed enough to pick up the little island

chain of pimples alongside his mouth. No facial hair yet, although as
he glances at the canal, he imagines that he can see a bit of a shadow
on his upper lip, until a duck splashes into the water and makes his
image disappear.

He pictures his father's dark mustache and rubs his own upper lip,
suddenly tasting something bitter. But then he remembers something
he noticed in his reflection before the duck landed. He waits until the
ripples in the water dissipate and peers down at himself again. In the
canal's waters, he looks like a dark young man, unhatted and unjack-
eted. But this young man seems much more ordinary than Willem has
felt in the past few months, much more like every other young man on
the streets around him. It takes a moment for him to realize why.
Without his jacket, he no longer has his yellow star.

The image of this starless self enchants him. It is as if his reflection,
plunged into the canal in the duck's wake, has emerged renewed from
cleansing waters. Purified and anointed, he rises up and examines himself in the canal again. Suddenly he looks older, taller, more handsome.
The people on bicycles riding behind him seem to turn their heads
toward him in admiration, smiling and singing Dutch greetings, at least
in the world reflected on the skin of the canal. He has become a grown
man of Amsterdam, a lord of the city. He spins around and faces the
street, smiling with confidence verging on arrogance. The city is his!

Across the street towers the monolith itself, the Rijksmuseum.
Willem knows what to do. He marches right across the street without
even bothering to look both ways for screeching bicycles. Let them
cower before him! In an instant his lordship stands at the sign beside
the golden door.

WELCOME TO THE RIJKSMUSEUM. Willem reads the words again and
hears them as if they were spoken by his old teacher at the Montessori
School, whom he imagines standing at the museum's gate, grinning
and shaking his hand. "Welcome to the Rijksmuseum, my dear
Willem! Your national treasures await you!" Willem pulls open the
museum's heavy door like a bishop entering his own cathedral. A gust
of heated air blows in his face, inflating his thin sweater and shirt on his
skinny shoulders into flowing regal robes as he closes the door behind
him.

Willem stands in line to enter the museum, posture perfect, head
erect. He has urgent business to attend to; his national treasures await.

The only problem, he suddenly realizes with embarrassment, is that his wallet and his yellow star travel together—one on the breast of his jacket, the other in its left-hand pocket. He has no money for admission. With shaking hands he searches the pockets of his pants. Not a single coin.

Bit by bit the line moves forward, and now the people directly in front of him have reached the ticket counter. In front of Willem is a large group, a family—a couple in their thirties, a father already balding and a mother with hair so blond it is almost white, both quite tall. They lean against the ticket counter, frowning and exhausted, while their—how many? Willem counts them—six children whine, play, and harass one another behind them. The youngest looks about three, a little blond girl with chubby legs bulging like rolls of dough between her red pinafore and her sagging white socks, and the oldest, a boy with dark hair and glasses swinging one of the younger boys around by the arm, about eleven. A girl of about five hides between her mother's legs, peeking out from under her skirt. Suddenly Willem has an idea.

"Two adults and six children," the exhausted father recites. Willem edges closer to the children in question, who are far too busy hitting each other to notice him. The little girl has concealed herself completely underneath her mother's skirt.

Willem waits, his breath held, as the ticket cashier leans forward over the counter, lowering his glasses and pointing with his finger as if tapping buttons on an invisible typewriter as he identifies each child. "One, two, three, four, five, six," he announces, handing the tickets to the father. The parents sigh with relief as the man behind the counter leans over to move the velvet rope, allowing them in. And Willem, whom the ticket cashier has counted as their mute fourth son, slinks in behind them.

WILLEM DOES not know what to expect of the Rijksmuseum. At first he is vastly disappointed. From the outset, as he wanders through the maze of endless galleries, it doesn't seem that different from the museums he once toured with his school back in Vienna. Lots of paintings of Jesus, mostly. Jesus as a baby, looking like a wrinkled, hairless old man shrunk to baby size. Jesus as a young man, with shining rays coming out of his head as people gather around him. But of course, mostly Jesus dying on the cross, moaning and bloody, jeered at by an ugly crowd and crowned with the letters "INRI"—a Latin abbreviation, Willem remembers having read somewhere, for "Jesus of Nazareth, King of the Jews." Willem walks by these paintings quickly. Then he turns a corner and enters what seems like a labyrinth of thousands of rooms filled with paintings just of fruit. It is amazing, he muses, how many ways one can arrange fruit in a bowl.

As the rooms full of fruit continue, however, Willem notices the galleries slowly being infiltrated by non-fruit, non-Jesus paintings. Portraits, mostly. Not much nudity, to Willem's disappointment. Instead the portraits show people sitting in dark rooms, their faces looking almost incandescent, as if light were not shining on them but coming from within them. Willem stares for a moment in fascination at a small painting of an old man, seated in an empty shadowed landscape, pressing his delicate white-bearded head against his palm. The title of the painting is given in Dutch: "blah blah Jeremiah blah blah blah," a wordy title that Willem doesn't feel like deciphering. The old man looks as if something tragic has happened to him, but what? Maybe his parents died, Willem thinks to himself, but then dismisses the idea. The man is old, after all, too old to mourn his own parents. But clearly he is upset about something. What?

The painting unsettles Willem. He tears himself away from it and moves on to another gallery, one filled again with those self-illuminating portraits of people in darkened rooms, most of them holding books or quill pens. There is almost always writing of some kind involved. In one painting a young woman who appears pregnant is holding a letter, looking anxious. Or more than anxious. Devastated, more like. Willem finds himself feeling sorry for her. But it's a comforting kind of sadness, like hugging someone who has fallen down or visiting a stranger in the hospital. Her problem, not his.

Countless fruit-lined rooms later, Willem comes upon a gallery with a sign beside its entrance. Suspicious of all signs now, he only glances at it, but the glance is enough to make him pause in his tracks.

POPPENHUIZEN

"*Poppenhuizen*"? A delicious word. Willem tastes it on his tongue, lets it dissolve in his throat like cotton candy. *Poppenhuizen*. Dollhouses?

At first Willem hesitates. Dollhouses are for girls, he thinks. Why would they be in a museum? Toys of old nobles, probably. There is a long explanatory plaque in Dutch, but Willem doesn't have the energy to try to read it—he catches only a vague date in numerals, "17th to 18th century." At any rate, he considers, the *Poppenhuizen* have clearly been classified as national treasures. Willem does a quick mental calculation. If one of his classmates should by chance walk by and spot him in the dollhouse gallery, he will never hear the end of it. But then he realizes something else. In this vault of national treasures, he has found a perfect sanctuary from the children at his new school, if that sign is really true. *No dogs or Jews allowed.* It probably wasn't official anyway, that sign, though. Nonetheless, Willem steps inside.

The dollhouses aren't really dollhouses, to Willem's vague disappointment. He was expecting miniature homes, shrunken bricks, tiny windows he could peek into. Instead, inside the gallery's glass cases stand elegant cabinets, each about three or four feet high, with polished speckled wooden doors flung open behind the display windows. The cabinets are divided into square compartments, a perfect grid.

But inside these cube-shaped spaces are outrageously beautiful miniature rooms. Parlors, bedrooms, kitchens, storage rooms, music rooms, nursery rooms, making each cabinet into a perfect replica of the interior of an elegant old-fashioned canal house. Here, for instance, is a sitting room. The windows against the cabinet's back wall are draped with perfect tiny velvet curtains, tied back with tiny golden braided ropes. Between the windows stand the fireplace, a marble mantelpiece, and then bookshelves, lined with row upon row of tiny, leather-bound volumes. Do they have real words inside them? There is no way to tell from Willem's side of the glass. In the dining room the tiny banquet table is set for a grand dinner. Each place is set with delicate blue and white china, complete with dinner plates, soup bowls, wine goblets, and tiny coffee cups. The cutlery is silver, and the ends of each tiny utensil are engraved with someone's monogram. Silver bowls of fruit, just like the ones in the museum portraits, sit in the middle of the table, their rims engraved with initials and dates. On the mantelpiece are silver candelabra. Ivory inlaid end tables stand like sentinels in the corners, holding tiny jewelry boxes. Upstairs, canopy beds with perfectly arranged pillows lie waiting for someone's miniature dreams.

Willem presses his nose against the glass until he almost feels as if he lives in one of the rooms. Suddenly he wishes that he could shrink,

shrink, shrink down until he was the right size to fit in one of those vel-vet-covered chairs. Then he could step into one of the houses and run through all of it—sitting on all of the plush sofas, eating off the blue and white china with the silver forks, sitting by the fireplace and reading all of the tiny books on the tiny shelves, undisturbed. Or searching for keys in secret places, and then opening the house's countless secret drawers. Suddenly Willem notices something moving inside the room and shudders in fright. In a moment, though, he realizes that what has moved are his own eyes—his face is reflected in the gilt-framed mirror above the fireplace.

The real problem with Willem's plan to shrink himself down into the tiny rooms, of course, is that they are already occupied. Each of the houses is populated by little dolls, dressed in strange costumes, as if they are going out to a masquerade. But then Willem understands that the dolls are a few centuries behind the times. The men wear black trape-zoidal hats and shoes with big metal buckles on them, dark enough to blend into the upholstery except for their starched white collars. The women wear little white covers over their hair, and big dresses with lace bodices.

Yet there aren't quite enough dolls around. Each house seems occu-pied only by a few dolls each, perhaps four or five at most. But the bed-rooms can accommodate more than that, and the banquet tables are set for many more. There must be more people living in these houses, Willem thinks, who are simply off on a journey somewhere. After all, these are the seventeenth and eighteenth centuries, which means that Dutch people have places to go. Willem thinks of the merchants of the house going off on their ships to—where?

To India, of course, cruising off on voyages for the Dutch East India Company, or to Indonesia or the South Pacific—the "Dutch East Indies," they had learned at school—or to Dutch Guiana in South America, or to Curaçao or St. Maarten in the Caribbean, all within the world of the great Dutch mercantile empire. (In the past, everyone con-quered the world for fifteen minutes.) Willem imagines a giant ship with white billowing sails pulling alongside the shore of some distant tropical island, greeted by naked natives in hollowed-out log canoes. He pictures the topless women for a moment, garlanded with flowers above their completely revealed breasts, reveling in the thought. It is as if he is there, touching them. And India—here Willem even conjures up the smell, and his eyelids droop as he takes a deep drag of incense, blown out of some sort of exotic pipe as dark women—also topless, he muses—make offerings to their gods. Willem pictures a shipwreck on an Indian coast, the poor Western merchants lost in a land they never intended to explore, thousands of miles from home. It is easy to picture the scene during daylight hours, Willem thinks. But what if such a shipwreck had happened at night? What if they had washed up on this mysterious shore under a black velvet window shade drawn over the sky, feeling for each other's hands and faces in the thick wet night, crawling onto dry sand without knowing who might be waiting for them on land at daybreak? Was that humid blind man's beach the farthest anyone could possibly be from a warm little glowing Dutch house?

Perhaps more likely, Willem thinks to himself, the dollhouse people would have gone to New Amsterdam, the Netherlands' greatest loss. And here Willem's fantasies run wild. He knows English from school in Vienna, reads his English-German dictionary with passion, lust almost—he knows English better than Dutch, even though he doesn't often hear it spoken. But somehow when he'd stare at the map on the wall back at the Montessori School, he always found his eye wandering across the Atlantic, right to left as if reading a sentence out of the Hebrew Bible. Vienna was indiscernible on the world map from his exile at the back of the room; Amsterdam sank into a muddy delta of borderlines and riverlines, practically lost beneath the sea. But New York! Somehow Willem feels drawn to New York, his mind's eye climbing up the metal skyscrapers he has seen in photographs, crawling through the cavernous canyons of streets. The slightest thought of it enchants him—the buildings so tall, the sidewalks so wide, the streets laid out in perfect rectangles so that no one could ever get lost or disappear into them, the blocks of buildings divided into neat columns and rows like a case of eggs. What fools the Dutch were to lose that little island, that case of gleaming eggs, brimming with people's eager lives always just about to hatch! The dot on the map with its loud black letters in Dutch, NIEUW-YORK, stood out like a stout peg on a coatrack, waiting for something—someone?—to hang on it. Would the dollhouse people go there, building themselves new glowing box houses for a new world?

No, Willem decides. He knows where they have gone. To the Barbary Coast, attacked by barbarian pirates, never to return. Some of them don't even make it that far. They leave Amsterdam and are appre-hended by bandits, their throats slit before they reach Hamburg or even the Amsterdam city limits, their bleeding bodies left to freeze, staining the ice red on the side of the snowy road. Outside of this perfect little house, this glowing fed and heated sanctuary, barbarians were scratch-ing at the gates, held off by nothing more than thin, wavy windowpanes of imported glass!

"Young man, you mustn't touch the glass. You could get shocked, you know."

The voice makes Willem jump. He has plunged so deep into his bar-barian dreams that he didn't even notice the museum guard creeping up on him, uniformed in black, nightstick in hand. The guard is a fat man, with thick hands and a stomach lurching over his wide leather belt. His bald head peeks out from under his cap, crowning a pink face with bright blue eyes. He is breathing through his mouth, panting almost. As he lowers his face to Willem's height, Willem can detect a vague smell of fish on his breath. Instinctively Willem steps away from him, moving his nose just slightly away from the glass. The guard is jok-ing about the glass being electrified, but Willem doesn't know that. Still, he feels a need to disobey this smelly man's orders at all costs. These are his national treasures!

Deliberately not looking at the guard and staying as close to the glass as possible, Willem focuses his stare on the dollhouse lavatory. In the split second after inhaling the sardine breath, Willem has decided that he will force himself to look at the dollhouse, even though he knows he can't stand looking at something while being watched. It reminds him of his father's constant lurking around the empty apartment, where Willem can't even open his bedroom door without eliciting insults. But to his surprise, Willem finds that the lavatory, which he had barely noticed before, is actually one of the most intriguing rooms in the house. On second glance, he sees that it is more of a storeroom than a lavatory. There isn't any plumbing, of course—this is, after all, the sev-enteenth or eighteenth century—but there are basins, basins upon basins, wide basins for washing, dented basins for shaving, round basins serving as noble urinals, all made of that blue and white china. Even the chamber pots are beautiful. All that water partitioned off, con-trolled, brought within the house's hallowed halls on condition that it stay within those basins. The house could flood, of course, if the water seeped in from the man-made ground. It probably did flood, in fact, since flooding was one of those three X's on the city seal. But within this room, one is safe from water's ravages. Thinking about all that water gives Willem a sudden urge to urinate. He pushes the idea out of his mind.

"You like those dollhouses, do you? I've never seen a boy who liked the dollhouses," the guard says, his voice curling up around the word "liked" in a way that reminds Willem of a tiny worm creeping unexpectedly out of a piece of fruit. Willem understands every word of the guard's Dutch. He feels his face going red, and a brief tremor between his legs. He opens his mouth for a second to answer and notices that his lips have dried together, fused by not talking. In an instant, though, he closes his mouth again. A horrible thought crosses his mind: Even if he wants to speak, he can't. Not just because his Dutch is awful but because his Dutch is awful in a particular way. If the guard hears his accent, Willem calculates, the game is up. WELCOME TO THE RIJKSMUSEUM: *No dogs or Jews allowed.* Was the sign outside the museum official, or was it not? Willem swallows, cornered by the guard's smiling stare. He looks at him and nods, then turns back to face the dollhouse. Better to seem like a girl than a Jew.

"Well, a boy who likes dollhouses. You know, I actually like them myself. It's amazing how much detailed work goes into them. The craftsmanship is equal to a lot of the better paintings in the museum, I think. Certainly better than all those still lifes of fruit bowls. If you ask me, they're undervalued as works of art."

Poor man, Willem thinks to himself. He glances at the man's left hand and sees no wedding band, only a set of sweaty fingers. Does he have a wife, Willem wonders? Children? Friends? Or had he been condemned to walk the earth in solitude, speaking only to old women on bicycles and stringy boys who sneak into museums? Willem shudders without meaning to, shifting his weight back and forth from one foot to the other. A little dance almost.

"Cold? We've been having horrible weather lately, haven't we? All this rain. I don't understand why people would spend the one nice day this week in a museum." The guard sniggers, a repulsive little noise. Willem shakes his head and leans his nose toward the glass once more, suddenly thinking again of how noses are one of only two parts of the human body that continue growing throughout one's life. Of all the things to keep growing. He glances at the miniature chamber pots again, wishing that the guard would go away. No such luck. Meanwhile the man has inspired him. He begins thinking about rain, about pouring watery rain, water flowing in and out of the chamber pots, water seeping through the dollhouse foundation, rain drowning out his reflection in the canal. Willem begins tapping his feet on the ground, more and more loudly. Something makes him impatient, makes him want to end this encounter as soon as possible. But what?

"Do you have to go to the toilet?"

Willem shakes his head no. But even the head-shaking goes on too long, becoming part of his little bladder-dance. He tries to stop tapping his feet and comes within instants of wetting his pants. Instead he pounds the floor again. The guard laughs at him and stoops down, an embarrassing stoop, to Willem's eye level.

"Well, you might not like talking, but you still manage to get your thoughts across, don't you! Look, I have to go to the john myself. Let's go together, all right? The route is too confusing for you to find it by yourself from here anyway."

And the two of them walk on together, until, halfway there, alarm bells go off inside Willem's brain.

THE URINAL. Suddenly, as they hurry through room upon fruit-filled room, Willem's entire future seems to be pending between his legs. In some ways, of course, it is a familiar feeling. After all, Willem is twelve years old, and at this point more and more of his thoughts seem to have their origins there. But this time there is real danger in it. In America, Bill will think to himself years later, people all look different, until you take off their clothes and discover that they are really all the same. In Europe, people all look the same until you take off their clothes and discover that they are different, irreparably different, differences scarred into their flesh. He can't very well run away now, though. Besides, he has to go.

Just before they reach the men's room, a woman in her early twenties struts through the corridor, her skirt hugging her hips and swishing around her calves as she swings each leg in front of the other. Willem notices. The guard nudges Willem, muttering down at him. "A knockout, isn't she."

Willem nods and quickly looks to the floor. The last thing he needs at this point is to start fantasizing about some girl. The guard leads him into the men's room and the door swings shut behind them. No one else is there.

"You got a girlfriend yet?" the guard asks with a smile, his voice bubbling like a city fountain.

Willem feels his face turning red. He pictures Jopie and shakes his head. No.

The guard steps up to one of the urinals, unbuttons his pants, and starts babbling.

"It's rough at your age. It gets better, you'll see. I remember when I was about your age—well, a few years older really, when I was more of a man, if you know what I mean—and I fell so horribly in love with this girl. Her name was Lies, and wow, was she a knockout. Big on top, big on the bottom, slim in the middle, unbelievable. My sole purpose in life was to see her naked. I had a friend who lived across the street from her, and he had a little spyglass. I used to go over to his house with a bunch of other guys and we'd try to see whether she was home, just waiting for her to show up in the window. And she'd show up all right. The thing is, she knew we were there. She'd lean over by the window and start slowly opening her shirt, like she was really going to take her clothes off right in front of us, but then, right when she got to about the third button, she'd pull the shades. Right then! Just to drive us nuts! Peter got her in the end, but boy, I would have killed for her."

Willem swallows, picturing the Peter who used to spit at him at Montessori. Peters always spit at people, Willem thinks to himself. It figures that the ones who treat you like dirt end up with the girl.

He steps toward a urinal, two down from the guard's, and opens his pants, terrified. A shameful lump of tortured flesh emerges, used for lewd thoughts at Jopie's expense, late at night after his father's women have gone home. In Willem's new school, they teach the Bible—sort of like in his old school at Montessori, actually, except this Bible is only about half the size. Most of the time Willem passes school time staring at the ceiling, or flipping through textbooks to find interesting pictures in chapters the class hasn't reached yet. The Bible the class uses doesn't have any illustrations—Willem has checked. But once as he was flipping through looking for one, a line in the Dutch translation caught his eye, in something called the Book of Job. The line was so strange that he copied it into his notebook, and he was sure he had mistranslated it as he converted it into German in his head. But that evening he checked in the dictionaries and found that the verse really did mean what he thought it meant: "After my skin has been thus destroyed, then from my flesh I shall see God."

The line was strange enough to make him turn to the beginning of the Book of Job to see if something there might explain it. He found no explanation, but what he did find—even though he had to translate it word by word, until he was spending almost all of his waiting time in the hallway working on it—swallowed him whole. Job, it seemed, was the name of a man who was "simple and upright, and feared God and shunned evil," a happy man, apparently, with happy children and prosperous flocks, who always thanked God for what he had. Then one day someone called "the adversary" (Willem wasn't quite sure about that part, suspecting something funny in the Bible's footnotes, yet he continued nonetheless) asked God, teasing him almost, whether all Job's good faith wasn't something of a sham, since, after all, Job didn't have much to complain about. God decided to let the adversary play with Job a bit, and this was where things started to get interesting. First, all of Job's flocks were stolen, and his children killed, through various disasters. Job, however, took this rather well, continuing his praise of God despite their deaths. Then Job was stricken with some sort of skin disease. The details here eluded Willem's dictionary skills, but it seemed that Job ended up sitting in a pit and scraping himself with a broken plate (and here Willem winced, remembering his mother's china smashed on the floor in Vienna). Three friends came to visit Job at that point, but as Willem read their names—So-and-so the Something-ite, Somebody-else the Somewhere-else-ite, Somebody-else the Nowhere-ite—he suspected that they weren't really Job's friends at all, but rather just some sort of emissaries, reporting their own boring points of view on why Job deserved all this hard luck. It was only then that Job rose up and cursed his God.

Willem found himself feeling proud of Job for this, and the so-called friends and their preachy arguments against the poor guy were making Willem angry. But then came the best part, when God answered Job "out of the whirlwind," roaring at him: "Where were you when I laid the foundations of the earth?" Where indeed, Willem wondered as he crouched in the hallway, where the house's sinking foundation made the floor slant down to the canal. But Willem never got to read the rest of God's answer to Job, because that night his father, furious with the woman who had just left the apartment before Willem came in, took Willem's book and threw it in the building's furnace.

At the urinal, Willem looks down at himself, at the purplish scar where his skin had been destroyed at his circumcision when he was eight days old. He thinks of Jopie and his face burns. He wraps his fingers around it further down than usual, trying to seem casual as he does his best to conceal himself, just in case the guard should glance to the side and notice something missing. *No dogs or Jews allowed.* Probably the sign wasn't even official at all, he thinks to himself, trying to steady his trembling fingers. The guard, however, is standing at his urinal whistling something, and doesn't take much interest in Willem. When Willem has arranged his fingers as best he can, he relaxes and begins to urinate. But then, as he glances down at his strangely intertwined fingers, one thumb on top of the other, he suddenly remembers something that happened at his grandmother's house long ago. And as he empties his bladder he feels himself about to cry.

Willem doesn't know where his grandmother's house was, but he knows it was far away, very far away—so far away that he and his father and his mother had to take a train at night to get there, in a special sleeping car in which he and his mother shared a bed. (Where was his father during the night train ride? Willem thinks hard but cannot remember.) It was scary riding a train at night, but also thrilling, like being in a boat on an open ocean. The porters would knock on their cabin door to ask if they needed anything, and his mother would smile and say no, nothing, thank you, in her public voice that sounded clear and whole, like a single tap of a spoon on a wineglass. And then the door would close and they would be alone together in their clean and glowing room, a box of light whizzing through an endless sea of darkness. His mother would hold him and play games with him, drawing pictures with him in a notebook until it was time to go to sleep. Then they would climb into bed, a funny bed with stiff white sheets and too many blankets, and his mother would turn out the lights, falling asleep almost instantly, as if she existed only for him during the day and then, secretly at night, returned to another world. But Wilhelm had no past, no other world to return to. His only world was the one inside the glowing sleeping car. And so he would press his nose to the windowpane and stare out into the darkness, where he immediately saw that the train wasn't actually going anywhere—he could feel it moving, sure, but outside the window was nothing but a blanket of blackness, a deep and heavy curtain drawn over the entire world. He would stare at that dark curtain until it terrified him, and then he would wake up his mother and tell her that he had had a bad dream. Each time she believed him.

His grandmother's house was also scary at night, but only on the outside. Outside the house—he had sneaked outside once while his mother was busy with something else, enjoying the brief moment before she noticed he was missing and raced outside to find him—he could hear the clopping of the neighbor's milk goat circling the tree where it had been tied when the fence was broken, and some other animals rustling about in their sleep, and he glanced back at the house, where he could see his grandmother standing at the stove by the lit-up window with a look of distraction on her face as she cooked. It was his grandmother's house, not his grandfather's. Wilhelm had never met his grandfather, and neither had Wilhelm's father—he had died before Wilhelm's father was born. His grandmother stood alone, framed in the window. Through the adjacent window, Wilhelm could see his father talking to her, frowning, pacing back and forth. It was strange, this view. Wilhelm knew it was one room, but if he hadn't been inside before, he wouldn't have realized it. It could have been just two little panels, a diptych, photographs framed side by side, not even related at all.

But inside the house it was cozy and warm and small and safe. Wilhelm's mother sat on the crooked wooden floor with him after dinner as he drew on blank pieces of paper with charcoal pencils his grandmother had given him. He had found some leaves during the day, and his mother taught him how to make leaf rubbings, laying the leaves on the floor (Wilhelm had wondered whether this offended the floor's dead wooden planks, but the leaves were from plants, not trees) and pressing against them with paper, scratching his pencils—gently now—back and forth and back and forth and back and forth across the paper until a leaf would emerge, magically, as if he had conjured it into being. Later, when he had made too many leaf pictures, he tried to trace his hand on the page. But it kept slipping off the paper, and soon his mother took his hand and gently pressed it down on the page for him, laying each of her fingers on top of each of his as he moved his pencil around their stack of hands, her thumb on his thumb. Her hand was warm and soft, and he felt, in each of his fingers where his touched hers, as if some gentle and beautiful current were flowing from her fingers to his. His pencil skipped, tracing her fingers instead of his own and catching their silhouettes on the paper. "See, now you're making an image of your own hand, but you're also making an image of mine," she said.

"Her image is yours and yours is hers anyway, you should know, because all men are made in the image of God," his grandmother suddenly said from her chair. Wilhelm's grandmother spoke in a funny way that you could only understand after you got used to listening to her, and sometimes not even then, with all the wrong vowels and weird words and phrases, as if she were reading from some strange old book. (Yiddish, that was.)

Wilhelm's father growled in German. "Mother, can't you stop filling the child's head with this barbarian trash?"

His grandmother snapped her head up and looked at Wilhelm's father. "Listen, young man, when you go back to your precious city, you can fill his head with whatever nonsense you want. But when I'm in this house I say what I mean." Wilhelm's grandmother was the only person who could talk back to his father and win his silence. And silent he remained until they returned to Vienna.

But now Willem stands at the urinal, holding himself with one thumb on top of the other, wondering whether or not he is made in the image of God. Is he even a man yet? No, that much is clear. And what God would stand at a urinal, an intruder in a house of treasures not his own, hiding his sex in his hands because he was afraid a stupid guard would see that he had the Covenant sealed into his flesh? Will any girl ever want him, with his skin destroyed? From his flesh, will he ever see God? Right now all he sees is his mother's face, and as the guard finishes and turns away, Willem squints to keep his tears from sliding down into the urinal's drain. If I ever get up the courage to talk to Jopie, he realizes, or to kiss her, or to kiss any girl at all, or to ask a girl to marry me, my mother will never know it. In that moment, he suddenly understands that he will never see his mother again.

THE WALK home from the museum is much too short. The city has grown dark. All around him, lights begin to flicker on in the houses lining the canals, illuminating the rooms inside them like little slide panels of distant lands. When Willem arrives at his own house, he sees that the light inside his apartment is also glowing. Inside, his father sits at his desk, writing on a piece of paper. His father raises his head for a moment, as if hearing something outside, but then returns to his writing. From his side of the window, he cannot see out. Willem rings the bell and pounds on the door, but there is no answer. His father knows he is there, Willem is sure, but that hardly matters. Willem is forced to watch and wait.

And so Willem watches. It is almost like a silent film. His father writes intently, squinting his eyes and furrowing his brows, pausing frequently, as if after every word. Willem is puzzled. On most days when he notices his father working at his desk—before ducking into his room again, before his father notices him noticing—he is amazed at how quickly his father writes. But now his father is sitting like a schoolboy, struggling to move his pen, his teeth clenching his lower lip, frightened. Like Willem.

The silent film continues as Willem's father puts down the pen to read through the page he has just written, slowly, moving his lips. After what feels like years, he lifts the page off the table, folds it carefully, and slides it into an envelope. And then the silent movie ends: Willem's father stands up and walks away. A moment later, he lets Willem in.

They do not speak to each other. Once they are both inside the apartment, Willem's father turns his back to Willem and returns to his desk. But Willem has noticed something new in the house. Sitting on the table are five envelopes, each addressed, in his father's handwriting, to America.

Willem has noticed stacks of letters like these in the house two or three times before, but his father has always snatched them away before Willem could get a good look at them. But this time, glancing again at his father's back, Willem reaches for them as silently as possible and flips through the little pile. Five letters, yes, all going to America. Three to New York, and two to somewhere he has never heard of: New Jersey. But the names on the letters intrigue him even more. They are strange names, weird names, names like the ones he remembers hearing at his grandmother's house, long ago. Moyshe. Shmuel. Freydl. And all five of them seem to have the same last name, even though the addresses are all different. But they are also all American. Willem's father has

written it in giant letters on each of them: "U.S.A." Who are these people? How does his father know them? Willem knows better than to ask
questions. Instead he places the letters back on the table exactly as they
were and slinks into his bedroom, shutting the door behind him.

He had been hungry before, and tired, and cold. But now, lying on
his mattress on the floor, he can think of nothing but those letters. In
Willem's dreams, the names on the envelopes come to life, five people
dancing in a circle in some giant American house, and Willem dances
in the center. Between their shouts of laughter, Willem hears the
sounds of someone pounding on the door. It is his father, but they
refuse to let him in.

As AN old man, Bill Landsmann doesn't like movies. He prefers slides,
leaving context to the imagination, writing his own script. Instead of a
movie, Bill Landsmann might have presented, to anyone who wanted
to see it, a single image: his father sitting in the window writing a letter,
framed only by possibility, unaware that this moment was already
buried under so many other moments that came after it—unaware, sitting behind the thin pane of glass, that he was drowning in all the
choices that would ultimately destroy him.

CHAPTER 4

THE MISSING LINK

THREE YEARS after Jason, on Amsterdam Avenue, Leora finally found the tefillin.

Work had become the focus of Leora's life, and she excelled at it. She had mastered her own journalistic method after a single conversation, which had taken place when she was twenty years old, at her college's newspaper office. She had come in a bit late that evening, and when she arrived, the office was buzzing as it hardly ever did. Most of the time, the paper ran front-page stories about things as pressing as the retirement of a dean. But that night several phones were ringing at once, editors and reporters were shouting into them, and computer printers were spitting out pages and pages of type. Leora stood at the door utterly confused, like a lost foreign exchange student trying to decide whether she had entered the right room. Jessica, one of the senior editors who would later be hired by a major metropolitan daily, saw her and jumped to the entrance.

"Why didn't you get here earlier? We've got a big story today," Jessica told her. "It's going to be a really exciting night."

"Why, what's going on?" Leora asked.

"Some junior named Joe Solovey killed himself. They found his body on the train tracks downtown," Jessica swooned, breathless.

Joe Solovey lived on the floor above Leora in the dormitory. He

wanted to be an opera singer, and Leora had often heard him through
the ceiling, singing his scales. In those scales, Leora could almost hear
a physical movement, as if Joe Solovey's voice were in fact Joe Solovey
himself, scaling the face of some imagined cliff, climbing higher and
higher until at last he could slap a hand on the ledge above—but just
when he had reached that height, he would tumble down again in a
cascade of pitches, sliding all the way back to the bottom. To Leora it
seemed as though she were overhearing a battle of the will, a striving
and a struggling, always ending in defeat, yet resumed nonetheless,
every time. Joe Solovey was a man unable to complete his work, yet
never free to desist from it. They weren't friends at all, she and Joe
Solovey, but they knew each other's names. She had chatted with him
in the laundry room once. He had performed, in front of a pile of mis-
matched socks, an impressively accurate impersonation of Leora's
roommate, mimicking her intonations with his well-trained voice.
Leora had laughed and told him he was destined for the stage.

"Come on in, we've got lots to do!" Jessica bubbled.

Jessica turned away before Leora, still stunned, could scream what
she wanted to scream in Jessica's face: *You disgust me, you sicken me,
you barbarian!*

Instead Leora rushed to the bathroom, where she locked herself in a
stall for twenty minutes, sitting on the toilet seat with her pants still on,
trying to cry. She couldn't. All she could do was imagine that puddle-cov-
ered grave in the East Mountain Reservation, and wonder whether Joe
Solovey's family was Jewish, and hope that if they were, they would find
some technicality so that they wouldn't have to bury him alone somewhere in the woods. But no matter how hard she tried, she couldn't cry.

In the weeks that followed, in the afternoon silences when the ceiling
no longer sang Joe Solovey's scales, Leora decided that the barbarian
way was the right way—or if not the right way, then at least the best way.
It was much better, much more pleasant, much more possible, to look at
such events as just that: events, incidents, an "exciting night," a "big
story." She decided that after graduation, she wanted to be a journalist.

It worked. And it wasn't just as a reporter that Leora excelled, as
might easily have been the case. No, Leora had also mastered the feature story, the human interest story, the sort of story that parents clipped
out of magazines and mailed to their grown children. She had an eye
for detail, could paint the perfect gut-wrenching image, knew just

where to place a heart-stopping quote. She was praised for her work, even receiving the occasional letter to the editor drooling over her "moving" stories, her "sensitivity." It was easy, being a barbarian. You could take over the whole world if you wanted to.

Outside of work, however, Leora had failed to take over the world, or even to try. Instead, not wanting to attract the attention of any more off-kilter individuals—such as seventy-year-old kleptomaniacs obsessed with central Asian Jews, or twenty-one-year-old born-agains with a penchant for capturing endangered species—she tried something she had never tried before: being normal, or at least ordinary, or at the bare minimum, mediocre. It wasn't so difficult, once she put her mind to it. The lives of most people her age, she determined, could be parceled out into various predictable segments—predictability, of course, being the key factor in being ordinary. An ordinary person, she theorized, was one who could easily divide her life into groups of years so predictable that they could almost be named after different types of cheese. The cheddar cheese years, for a start, during which life is something encased in shrink-wrapped packages decorated with superheroes in brown paper bags, opened only at assigned moments of freedom, when freedom is a burden that forces you to decide where you belong—at the lunch table with the cool kids, or with the nerds? Then there are the mozzarella years, quick years when life comes delivered in a box to your door, as hot and fresh as if you had made it yourself, and you enjoy it in tremendous quantities, and dozens of others eat with you. Much later, some people enter the years of Brie or Camembert, life served in cultured slices, or brought out only for important guests. But in between come the Parmesan years: years when life comes out just a dash at a time, not a thing-in-itself but something to season the unseasoned seasons as you eat through them alone. One could argue that she was assigning too much meaning to cheese. But that's what life felt like to Leora, as she made herself spaghetti each night in her apartment on West Ninety-second Street and Amsterdam Avenue, her little carved-out point in the coordinate plane of New York.

The big secret of the city of New York is that no matter how much they may try to hide it, white-collar New Yorkers in Manhattan are all out-of-towners. Municipal records show that only twelve people were actually born and raised in Manhattan during the last twenty-five years, and of those, nine are now studio executives in California and the remaining three are pursuing independent research in former Soviet republics. Leora lived in an apartment with two other out-of-towners named Lauren and Melanie, boring people who always answered questions with questions: "I went to SUNY Binghamton? I majored in psychology?" Their jobs were so boring that Leora couldn't even remember what they did. She vaguely remembered Lauren telling her, tossing her voice up at the end of each sentence, "I keep track of Web sites? For our clients?" Melanie technically did something involving fund-raising, but judging by the number of forwarded e-mail jokes she sent Leora every day from her office account, it seemed unlikely that she ever did any work. Of course, Lauren and Melanie were not the only people Leora lived with on Amsterdam Avenue. During the past three years, she had traded in a roommate at a rate of at least one every nine months as various roommates—all of whom might as well have been named Lauren or Melanie—left to move in with their boyfriends. Survival rates on Amsterdam Avenue were shockingly low.

Leora and Lauren and Melanie slept on futons, ate off of hard plastic picnic plates, hung their posters on the walls using poster gum, and lived their evenings by the light of halogen lamps. They recycled their newspapers, deleted their answering machine messages, and rarely were in the apartment at the same time. They each bought their own food and never even considered consolidating their shopping, preferring somehow the three half gallons of orange juice that clogged up the refrigerator each week. Every woman for herself. Only Lauren bothered to clean the bathroom. There were a few pots and pans, hauled in by various parents on various move-in days and duly bequeathed to the apartment at large upon move-out, but only the spaghetti pot received any kind of regular use. The vast majority of their drinking glasses were mugs embossed with the names of insurance companies. It was as if all of them had signed a secret unwritten lease stipulating that it wasn't worth buying real forks or getting things framed or having real beds, that this wasn't real life but rather some kind of dress rehearsal for it, that they wouldn't be there long. In the meantime, months and seasons and years passed, five different Laurens and Melanies had cycled through the place, and Leora was still eating Parmesan cheese.

Of course, Leora had people to talk to beyond the many permutations of Laurens and Melanies. There were people at work, for instance—an ever-changing stream of Erics and Jeffs, with survival

rates similar to Amsterdam's. And then there were the people she knew
from her synagogue, where she had never actually bothered to pay the
membership dues since, after all, she didn't plan on staying there very
long. The synagogue was a little stricter and more traditional than she
would have liked it to be, but she continued attending nonetheless,
because almost no one under the age of thirty-five attended the more
liberal ones. The people from the synagogue—Rebeccas and Debbies,
mainly—were a slightly different breed from the Laurens and Melanies.
The Laurens and Melanies liked to spend their Friday nights at bars,
looking for men. The Rebeccas and Debbies liked to spend their Friday
nights at a sabbath dinner table in a friend's apartment, looking for
men. As Leora took turns spending her Friday evenings one way or the
other—either at a bar with the Melanies or at a sabbath dinner with the
Debbies—she saw that there really wasn't very much difference
between the two evenings. The Melanies were looking for live-in
boyfriends. The Debbies were looking for live-in husbands. The con-
tenders for these positions in both groups consisted mainly of twenty-
five-year-olds who tried to impress you by naming the companies they
worked for, expecting you to care. One group turned their halogen
lamps on and off on Friday nights while the other turned their halogen
lamps on and off using programmable timers. A technicality.
Conversation in both situations revolved around gossip and TV. For
both groups, Friday night was the night to relax, enjoy life, and track
down one's soul mate, the big night Out. But nobody ever wanted to
spend the evening simply thinking or dreaming, to make it the big night
In. No matter how hard she looked, Leora couldn't find anyone willing
to follow up a sabbath dinner with a screening of *Gandhi*. And so, more
and more often, she began staying in by herself on Friday nights, and
sometimes Saturday nights and Sunday nights as well. After a while she
didn't mind anymore.

The one redeeming feature of the apartment was a simple brass chandelier suspended over the apartment's only table. Sometimes, if she was
working on a story for her magazine but didn't want to have to sit in her
cubicle late at night, she would come home and set up her little computer on the table, typing into the dark under the moonlight of the
chandelier. The chandelier had a shiny globe at its base, and if she
glanced up at it from her seat, she could see her own reflection on its
round surface as if looking through the wrong lens of a telescope. She

noticed that she was shrinking deeper and deeper into the apartment, whose walls in the reflection curled in around her like a white wooden frame soaked in water until there was a bend in the wood. Sometimes, when the story she was working on proved particularly dull, she would reach up to the chandelier and give it a little spin. The fake electric candles on its crown would twirl around like a carousel, projecting shadows on the walls that would stoop and spin, lengthening out of control so that the carousel horses grew to hideously large proportions and then shrank to frighteningly small ones, their giant horse-mouths laughing at the poor imaginary children riding them, forced to grow and shrink with them.

Leora knew that she was supposed to be in the prime of her life, delighting in every turn of events, rejoicing in all the new people she would meet with each new Melanie who signed the lease. But in the time she had lived within that twisted white frame of walls, she had suddenly become older. Her face was hardening into a portrait, a chemical combination of lights and darks trapped on an old-fashioned slide film and cast in the shadow behind her on the apartment's curling white walls. She became a projection.

And then, one Monday morning in the darkest days of her third winter on Amsterdam Avenue, she finally found the tefillin.

ALTHOUGH THE PLACE was only a few blocks away from her apartment, Leora only happened to go there on an assignment related to work. There had been a wire story entitled "Missing Link Found in New York Shop," and her magazine sent her to check it out. It seemed that recently, a mysterious man had made a sale to the owner of a curio shop on Amsterdam Avenue. The man, a mere messenger disposing of a deceased collector's estate, gave no indication that his wares—largely a series of human and animal bones—were anything out of the ordinary, and the store kept few records of the materials' source. But when a scientist from the nearby Museum of Natural History stopped inside while shopping for a friend's birthday gift, he noticed that one of the skulls on the store's shelves, a generic-looking extinct primate skull to the casual observer, did not fit into any of the extant categories of evolutionary man.

Without actually buying the skull, which lay far beyond his price

range, the man brought a team of paleobiologists to the store. The ensu-
ing examination confirmed his suspicions. The skull did not match that
of any existing animal, or even any known extinct one. It resembled, in
various ways, both *Homo erectus* and *Homo sapiens*, had some traits of
Java man and others of Peking man and others of Neanderthal man, but
it wasn't any one thing or the other—it was somewhere, disturbingly, in
between. The skull was the only trace of a vast period in human history,
or human prehistory, or prehuman prehistory, the sole remains of a lost
fifty thousand years, and it had randomly turned up in New York. Its
owner, who probably had never had a name in his lifetime—probably
one of the last people in prehuman prehistory to have no name what-
soever—was labeled "Amsterdam Avenue man." Or, for short, the missing link.

The store where the skull had appeared was called "Random
Accessories." With a name like that, Leora felt, it had no excuse not to
be called "Random Access" or, better yet, "Random Excess." Store
names like "Random Accessories" were the sort of thing Leora found
insulting in daily life. She had always wanted, for instance, to open a
maternity shop for the sole purpose of naming it "Great Expectations."
Instead she found herself forced to walk through a city filled with maternity stores with names like "Expecting Great Things." A maze of unful-
filled possibilities and missed opportunities catalogued by street
number.

However, when she arranged her interview at Random Accessories,
she was relieved to learn that it was owned and operated by a man
named Rick Random. Mr. Random was finishing up an interview with
someone else when Leora arrived at his shop, so she started to look
around the store—taking notes, technically, but mainly just killing
time. After a few minutes, though, she was engrossed, or, to speak the
language of skulls and jaws, swallowed whole.

Mr. Random had assembled a fascinating collection of items that
were once remarkably useful, to the point where a person from a hundred years ago might have walked into Random Accessories to find
something like the opposite of Costco—a store selling many of life's
necessities, but in small quantities and at astronomically high prices. A
washboard, priced at $150, waited for takers. Butter churns crowded
one corner. In another, sewing machines—which the U.S. Department
of Commerce, Leora had mentioned in a recent article, had now

reclassified from "apparel" to "recreation"—stood in silence, wondering if anyone would ever again press down on their creaky treadles and breathe them back to life.

What was most engrossing at first were the bones, which also, she supposed, fit into the category of things that once were useful. It seemed that it was scarcely unusual for strangers to deliver unmarked skeleton parts to Mr. Random's door, since a large percentage of his inventory appeared to be made up of bones. Human bones, animal bones, bones that looked like they could scarcely be from anything but giant animals long extinct. Sharp-toothed skulls of cats, assembled together with rib cages large enough to accommodate a trapped rat.

But mostly there were skulls of people, sitting in long rows like a nightmarish display from the Cambodian killing fields, grinning from earhole to earhole. As Leora stood there staring at the rows of human skulls, she began to notice that she wasn't watching them as much as they were watching her. The grins disturbed her most of all. How strange, she thought, that one needs to be alive in order to frown. She turned away from their eyeholes and came across a shelf with a yellowed paper pamphlet.

ATTENTION, ATTENTION!!!!
NEW YORK IS SINKING INTO THE ATLANTIC!

The typeface, a narrow bold block print that unmistakably dated it in the same way that the Times New Roman typeface would one day date Leora's magazine, trapped a sadness between its serifs, the same sadness trapped in the sickly yellow-green of photographs and films from thirty years ago. The diamond-shaped decorations on the tall letters jutted out like bony knees, misplaced hips on an old man who hobbles along with swooping uneven steps, too gnarled to run. Of course, it wasn't so much the typeface as the words that sank into a hollow space in her gut. ATTENTION, ATTENTION!!!! they screamed. Caught between the double *T*'s languished a time when saying "Attention!" was enough to get someone's attention.

She turned the yellowed pamphlet's page, its corners crumbling in her hand like the city's dissolving cornerstones. The pamphlet described, in painful detail, how the weight of newly built "skyscrapers" of seven stories or more was crushing the island of Manhattan at an alarming rate. Various scientists estimated that in less than three years, New York City would be lost beneath the sea. All residents were advised to sell their property—the pamphlet didn't mention who the hapless buyers might be—and flee to New Jersey before it was too late. As she scanned the text, Leora remembered learning at some point about this particular nineteenth-century hoax. People had believed it, and those who could afford it had hurried to New Jersey, leaving the wretched refuse of the city's teeming shores to sink into the sea. The tempest-tossed, however, too poor to think of leaving, saved their flight to New Jersey for later generations, when their descendants abandoned the city's dark streets for even darker ones, darkened by trees instead of char-latans and thieves. As she slid the pamphlet back onto its shelf, though, she saw something that caught her own attention on the shelf just alongside it: a painted tin dollhouse.

Not very many visitors to the shop would recognize this particular Random Accessory as something more than a child's toy, but Leora's years of checking random facts for her magazine had trained her well in trivialities. For a story about the patent office, she had once had to spend several hours in the patent division of the New York Public Library, researching patents for, of all things, mousetraps. One can barely fathom the sheer variety of patented mousetraps produced in America over the past hundred years—it was as if the country had gone through the plague. The familiar snap-trap and a variety of glue-based traps had certainly endured, but what stayed in Leora's mind were those traps that seemed constructed less for the mouse's elimination than for the trap-setter's entertainment. A glass or clear plastic ball, for instance, which the mouse entered through a delicate door that could only be opened from the outside, would force the mouse to travel around the room as it scurried inside the ball searching for a way out. This was among the "humanitarian" traps, where the idea was to release the mouse into a nearby field. (Of course, this presumed that one lived in a place that had "nearby fields.") Another, less humanitarian trap kept the mouse running for several cycles on a sort of treadmill before sev-ering its head.

But the most elaborate of all, and the one that stood in front of her in Random Accessories, was the "mouse house." This painted miniature house with an open back, designed to resemble a child's dollhouse sur-rounded by a water-filled trough, lured the doomed vermin with a trail of food that led it through each room and up three flights of stairs until it reached the rooftop. There, the mouse's weight triggered an electric shock that sent its mangled corpse tumbling into the waters below. Leora looked at this trap with its unfurnished dollhouse rooms and felt her chest constrict.

"You a reporter?"

Leora jumped. The voice had been just over her shoulder, almost inside her ear. When she turned around, she saw Mr. Random already moving away from her so that they could sit down behind the store's front desk. She moved away from the mouse house, awash with relief.

Mr. Random was a fat man in his late fifties who didn't think too deeply about things and was a better person because of it. Leora asked him all the expected questions about the skull—which sat on the table in front of them, grinning its unnerving prehistoric grin—and he answered them with the wonder of a man so unaccustomed to awe that he has no words for it, other than the words he would use to describe that amazing play in last year's Super Bowl.

"It's just incredible, don't you think? I mean, you got this guy, who's hell knows how old, dead for zillions of years, and then somebody digs him up somewhere, probably not even on purpose, and then he turns up in my shop. I mean, what are the odds?" The interview yielded no surprises; it was one of those articles where the key wasn't in the information uncovered, but in finding a way to show the reader that it mattered—a way to make the reader say, as Mr. Random had, "It's just incredible, don't you think?" That was Leora's specialty. Before she even arrived at the store, she had already written the story in her mind, interspersing little lines between the facts: A *passing glimpse, through empty eyeholes, into the recesses of history. An accident of fate, unearthing buried treasures of forgotten time.* And so on, up to the word limit. Once trimmed of excess words, it would be even better. A *glimpse of history. Accidents of fate. Forgotten time.*

After she had asked all her questions, Leora saw that another reporter had come into the shop, armed with his own tape recorder and notebook. She thanked Mr. Random and began to leave the store. But on her way out, she saw something on a shelf near the door that stopped her in her tracks: two dried-out little boxes wound up in bundles of matching leather straps. Tefillin.

She stood in front of the shelf, first just admiring them and then, glancing over her shoulder to make sure that Mr. Random wouldn't notice, taking them in her hands. Tefillin, she realized, had now been classified as a Random Accessory.

But these tefillin were more random than most. They were extremely old. The leather flaked onto her hands. One of the boxes, the one meant for binding on one's arm, was cracked open so badly that the parchment inside was exposed. Taking the leather straps between her fingers, she unwound the box and pried it open just a bit more, until the parchment inside fell onto the shelf. Still holding the box in one hand, she unrolled the tiny parchment on the metal shelf and began to read the Hebrew words she had read thousands of times before, hand-written in the usual script:

> *Hear O Israel, the Lord our God, the Lord is One.*

Something had happened in the world during the last three or four millennia, she thought to herself. The number of gods had declined steeply, the sort of decline that would bother people if it were happening to ocelots or spotted owls, but which didn't seem to concern anyone when it happened to gods. Long ago, there were dozens of gods, hundreds even. But at this point the number was hovering somewhere between zero and one. Was it possible that by now that number had shrunk even below one, not quite to zero, but perhaps somewhere just below a half? Leora continued reading the words from the Bible that she had read in synagogue countless times before:

> *Love the Lord your God with all your heart, and with all your soul, and*
> *with all your might. And these words which I command you this day shall*
> *be on your heart. You shall teach them to your children. You shall speak*
> *of them when you sit in your house and when you walk on the road, when*
> *you lie down and when you rise up. You shall bind them as a sign upon*
> *your hand, and they shall be frontlets between your eyes. And you shall*
> *write them on the doorposts of your house and on your gates.*

She thought of Jason for a moment and winced, remembering his voice: "Your *dad*? Stock analyst by day, arm-binder by night?" Jason probably had four children by now, she thought. Did he ever visit the

East Mountain Zoo or Beth Israel Nursing Home? Did he even visit his parents anymore? Yes, she decided, he must have been visiting his parents that time when she saw him in Costco. For all she knew, maybe he had even persuaded them to join him on his spiritual journey. Or maybe not. "It's sad," her brother used to joke, "how simple things can tear a family apart. A hungry pack of wolves, for instance." Trying to ignore the Jason in her brain, she noticed there was another paragraph on the parchment, just below. She kept reading, even though the passage was once again familiar, letting her eyes roll over it like a music box cylinder plucking its notes.

> *And if you listen to my commandments that I command to you today, to love the Lord your God and to serve him with all your heart and with all your soul, then I will give the land rain in its proper season, early rain and late rain, and you will harvest your grain and wine and oil. I will give grass in the fields for your cattle, and you will eat and be satisfied. Take care, lest your heart be deceived and you turn away and serve other gods and worship them. For then the anger of the Lord will be kindled against you, and he will stop up the heavens and there will be no rain; the earth will not yield its produce, and you will soon disappear from the good land which the Lord gives you. Therefore, put my words upon your heart . . .*

And then Leora stopped reading. This, she realized with a jolt, was the problem. The commandments were conditional! "If you listen to my commandments," God had promised, "then I will give the land rain . . . you will eat and be satisfied. . . ." It was an "if . . . then" statement like those she had studied in math class back in high school. (If it had been taught earlier in her high school career, then she would never have remembered it. But she had learned it during her senior year, when she had poured her whole life into books, and as a result she had mastered it.) *If P, then Q*, as the textbook had put it. According to the rules of logic she had memorized, if this statement was valid, then its complete reversal was also true: *If not Q, then not P.* So if people *weren't* eating and being satisfied, for instance, or having rain in its proper season, then that meant they *hadn't* listened to the commandments. Likewise, following along in the paragraph, if people *didn't* see their rain and crops disappear, then that meant they *hadn't* forsaken God—all of which seemed clearly false. Surely there were people who listened to the commandments and still found themselves going hungry—not to mention others who ignored the commandments and watched all their dreams come true. She thought of Mr. Rosenthal, the dead man from Jason's nursing home. If people really had thrown their tefillin overboard on their way to America, people who had been starving to death in Europe and probably still starved in New York, perhaps it wasn't just because tefillin were archaic. Maybe it was because tefillin were wrong.

"Excuse me, miss, but you can't just handle the merchandise like that."

Mr. Random made Leora jump for the second time that day. She released the little scroll on the shelf, just catching it before it curled up and rolled over the edge to the floor. Mr. Random stood right over her shoulder. The rest of the store was empty except for the woman at the front desk, yawning over a newspaper. At first Leora thought she was reading it, but then she began using it to wrap a set of large plastic fish. Leora mumbled an apology, her face growing hot.

"Are you interested in these?" Mr. Random asked, pointing to the tefillin as Leora struggled to slide the parchment back into the damaged box. "They're priced at $500. It's some Jewish thing, I forget what, but I could look it up in the back for you if you're interested. I heard that new ones are worth half that or more, so I've upped my price for an antique. Interested?"

Leora felt her face getting warm. "Not at that price, no." She paused for a moment, unsure whether to continue. "This has nothing to do with the article," she said, "but can I ask you where you found these?"

Mr. Random laughed. "Oh, I'm never the one who finds the stuff. People just bring it to me, you know. Like I told you before, how it happened with that skull. It just happens, you know."

"Oh," she said, looking at the cracked leather straps on the shelf. The store, she thought briefly, was something like a train station for oddities. The store proprietor, the equivalent of a master ticket agent, could tell you exactly where each item was going after it passed through the gates, but he couldn't for the life of him tell you where a single one of them had come from. It was somewhat amazing, actually, that both Random Accessories and the rail companies were able to stay in business without having any idea where their customers were coming from. Then again, Leora supposed, you can always count on the need to travel, and the need to throw things away.

"This item, here, though, I've got a good guess on," he said, picking up one of the boxes from the set of tefillin. Taking one of its leather straps in his hands, he pinched it between his brown-stained fingers and pulled at it from both sides. The leather began to crack almost immediately under the slightest strain, an audible snapping of lacquer that Leora could almost feel.

"See this? This here is water damage," Mr. Random proclaimed. "Saltwater damage. Know how I know that?"

Leora shook her head, not in response but in disbelief. Mr. Rosenthal from the nursing home, she thought. Could it have been true?

Thinking she had answered him, Mr. Random continued, smiling. "Easy. You probably think I'm some kind of specialist or something, right? Nah. I don't know nothing about forensics. But that's where my supplier found them. In the ocean. Believe that?"

Leora swallowed. "How?"

"That's the hard part. Hard for him, not for me. My brother's kid Tony, he's a real young guy, like you, and he's in utilities. Takes classes at night, business school. Real hardworking kid. Anyways, he's working for this company that's in charge of cleaning up the harbor downtown. Real nasty work, dredging, basically just pulling up trash all day long. It's amazing how much trash they've got down there. Anyways, most of what they pull up is so disgusting you can't even look at it. Sometimes they find bodies. I don't know how he managed it, but they dredged up some of these leather things here and he spotted them and pulled them out—cleaned them up and gave them to me. Later I had them checked out, and seems like they're about a hundred years old."

"They were at the bottom of the harbor?" Leora asked. She still didn't believe it.

"Not only that, but according to Tony there were *tons* of them down there. You'd figure they'd disintegrate, but he found a bunch of them that were caught under some kind of metal casing—that must've covered them up enough so you got what you see here. According to him, the place must've been like an underwater graveyard of thousands of these things. Most of them were completely disintegrated, even under the casing, but he found one or two like these that must have been totally caught inside another case that got tossed over right then with them. Weird, huh? The bottom of the ocean, it's like going back in time. I found out later from a friend that it's some kind of Jewish thing, like I said, I forget what right now but I've got it written down. It'd make an interesting story for your paper."

"Sure," she said, astounded.

"Tony, see, he knows I'm in the business, so he's always on the look-out for this stuff. A real good kid. You interested?"

"Yes, definitely," she said, meaning in the tefillin.

Mr. Random smiled. "Good, I'll give you his number! You available this Friday night? I know he doesn't have class then."

Unfortunately for Tony Random, Leora had a date on Friday with her VCR.

Two days later, Leora was doing a perfunctory fact-check on an article at her magazine that mentioned, in an off-the-cuff kind of way, the philosopher Benedict Spinoza. Her job consisted of looking up Benedict Spinoza in an online biographical encyclopedia to make sure his name had been spelled correctly. The name was familiar, but she didn't know much about him. Once she started reading the Spinoza entry in the encyclopedia, though, she was hooked.

Benedict Spinoza, seventeenth-century Dutch rationalist philosopher, grew up in Amsterdam in a religious Jewish family. His family, like many of the Jewish families in seventeenth-century Amsterdam, was descended from the Jewish community that had been expelled from Spain in 1492. As a child, Spinoza showed himself to be a marvel in his religious studies. But he was a little too smart for his teachers, and soon he began doubting most of the major premises of everything he had learned—that the Torah was written by God, for instance, or that God meted out reward and punishment, or, after a while, that God had any kind of relationship with his creations at all. Before he had even expressed these ideas in the written works that would give him a place among the most important philosophers of the Western world, he was formally excommunicated by the Amsterdam Jewish community as a heretic. Spinoza moved to The Hague and spent the remainder of his days grinding lenses for a living while writing works of philosophy, turning down an offer to chair the philosophy department at the University of Heidelberg because he preferred to spend his days in quiet research. No Jew was allowed to speak to or engage with him again for the rest of his life.

Spinoza believed in God, but the God he believed in resembled the God of the Hebrews only in passing. He deduced that the entire universe was formed from one type of matter, which one could call God, and through a series of logical statements he determined that this meant that all of God's creations, and in fact the entire world, was simply an extension of God. This meant that God couldn't interact with his creatures, so to speak, since God and his creatures were one and the same. To this day the Amsterdam Jewish community, tiny as it is, refuses to have anything to do with Spinoza's memory.

Spinoza enchanted Leora as if he had offered her a magic potion, poured from its bottle for the first time in centuries. If God was not only everywhere, Leora reasoned along with him, but also everything and everyone, then there was no need for all the nonsense about reward and punishment and destiny and divine plans. The world remained alive, inhabited, pulsing and breathing, yet there were no loose ends anymore. If people got killed crossing the street, or if they took their own lives, or if cats turned into lions, you could still believe in God, but you didn't have to blame God for anything. Everything was simply one, the hems of the world stitched complete.

As it happened, a few weeks after her obsession with Spinoza began, Leora went to visit a cousin at Columbia University and saw a poster on a bulletin board there:

IS GOD MATTER? OR *DOES* GOD MATTER?
A CONFERENCE
ON THE LIFE, WORK, AND INFLUENCE OF
BENEDICT SPINOZA

She looked at the poster carefully, examining its angle and placement as if she had put it up herself, and for a moment she wondered if she had. "Is God matter? *Does* God matter?" She could have thought of that. Looking at it more closely, she noticed that the poster was very old, one of those announcements that seem to get caught on the corners of bulletin boards and completely forgotten. The deadline for the call for papers had passed almost six months earlier. At the bottom of the poster, Leora noticed the date and location of the conference: in January, less than a month away, in Amsterdam. Leora stared at the poster and found herself seized by a certain passion that she hadn't experienced since she moved to New York. The word "Amsterdam," italicized near the bottom of the page, seemed to waver back and forth, like a swaying finger beckoning her, asking her, If not now, when? And so she copied down the addresses and contact numbers at the bottom of the poster and decided to go to Amsterdam.

LEORA KNEW from the start that there was no way she could afford to pay for the trip herself. She also knew that she couldn't afford to take time off from work. The only solution was to get the magazine to send her there. But why in the world would an American magazine send a reporter to Amsterdam, a place with no wars, no terrorists, no crime, no newly created high-tech virtual universe, and almost no publicly traded cultural identity beyond a fondness for hot chocolate?

At the editorial meeting the following week, Leora told the editors that she had a great idea for a story: drugs.

"Wasn't that on the cover of some magazine last year, the whole 'drugs in Amsterdam' thing? I seem to remember an article called 'Europe Just Says Maybe,'" the deputy section editor Suzanne said, after Leora had poured out all her preliminary research to explain why this story was timely and essential: a violent demonstration in California a month ago, related to legalizing marijuana; a bill pending in Congress for limited legalization for medicinal purposes; a large-scale study just published in Europe about the relative health risks of hallucinogenic drugs; the messy arrest of a drug smuggler the previous week which had led to the killing of a customs agent in Miami—all the boring garbage she had slogged through in the papers and on the wires to dredge up what she needed, in the same way that a normal person might poke around his bank account or push around his frequent flier miles to pay for a vacation. Leora suspected that Suzanne, who was in her forties and hardly wrote any stories herself, was jealous of her, as one of the magazine's rising stars. She began to wonder if she might be able to devise some way to remain a rising star in perpetuity.

"Of course," Leora said, trying her best to be ingratiating. "But this would be more of a personal look. Following around weekend drug users for the day, for instance. I know you're going to say it's been done before, but I feel like there's been something missing from the other stories, don't you?" Not that Leora had spent much time reading such stories looking for brilliant insights. Her own interest in other people's magazine feature stories had diminished lately; they had become something she associated with work. Even reading the newspaper had begun to feel like a chore. When she wasn't at work, the only part of the newspaper she ever read was the weekly food section, pretending that she might someday cook something that didn't involve tomato sauce.

"Why, what's missing from those stories?" Suzanne asked.

"Well, all they talk about is how these people are using drugs casually, the way we would use alcohol—as a way to relax, or to escape from reality. But since some of the drugs we're talking about are so much more potent, it might be worth looking at what kind of reality they're trying to escape from. I mean, it's not like this is Pakistan or something. These people aren't homeless, they aren't starving, and they aren't even poor. And it's also not like they're all young and rebellious. These are people in their teens and twenties, but also in their thirties, forties, fifties. What can't they get from reality that they need to get from drugs?"

"And do you have people lined up to interview for this kind of thing?" Eric asked. Eric was the executive editor, a man about Suzanne's age, but with three children at home, finger-painted masterpieces taped to his office door, and no chip on his shoulder. He was easy to impress.

"Of course," Leora said, proud that the final portion of her research—which had consisted of four e-mail messages to pothead acquaintances who had sneaked into Europe through various fellowships—was at last bearing fruit. Anyway, she reasoned, there was no shortage of potheads in the world. And there was certainly no shortage of potheads dumb enough to want their names published in a magazine. But Leora also knew that the real appeal of her idea had nothing to do with the details of her pitch and everything to do with the research she had conducted, subtly, on Eric himself. During the last few months, she had been paying close attention in the editorial meetings to what sorts of ideas caught Eric's attention. Little by little, she had noticed that he was hungry, desperate even, for stories that would interest young people. At some point the circulation department must have informed him that if he didn't start attracting younger readers now, in thirty years his entire subscriber base would be dead. And what better

way to addict young people to his magazine than to start publishing stories about drugs, other than to include free samples?

"Great, then," Eric said. "Go to Amsterdam."

Suzanne turned around, shocked. "Can't we just send a stringer?"

To Leora's delight, Eric waved her off. "Nah, if Leora has people she
can talk to, then it's better that way." Suzanne stared at him in disbelief,
but Eric just ended the meeting. Leora put on a grin, though she was
just as shocked as Suzanne was. It's amazing how easy it is to fool people, Leora thought. You just have to be willing to make the effort.

"Have fun," Jeff, another reporter, called to her as she left the room.
"Bring us back some pot!"

Drugs it was, then, and she was off. It later occurred to Leora that
most normal individuals would have tried her scheme the other way
around—that is, they would have found someone to pay their expenses
to attend the conference on Spinoza for the purpose of getting access to
a marijuana supermarket. Unfortunately, if she had suggested a story
about Spinoza, no one would have been interested.

LEORA CERTAINLY had nothing to worry about in Amsterdam in
terms of her story, since, from her worm's-eye view of the city, it was
tough to find someone in Amsterdam who *wasn't* a recreational drug
user. Practically every taxi driver tried to sell her Ecstasy. Following easy
leads, starting with the people she knew and then spinning off to more
and more of their drug-addicted friends, she went to midnight raves and
watched as people swallowed and inhaled and injected themselves with
incredible combinations of elements. The people Leora interviewed
were old, young, male, female, employed and unemployed, educated
and uneducated, Dutch people and visitors and recent immigrants, but
they all had one thing in common. When she asked them what mattered most to them, none of them could answer her. Instead they
twisted her question into a question of identity, telling her that only the
drugs allowed them to be who they really were. "If you ask me, everyone has an inner high, just fighting to get out," one forty-five-year-old
told her with a cotton-mouthed smile.

In his words, and in almost all of the words she collected in Amsterdam
in her notebooks and tapes, Leora heard an unmistakable echo of grief.
One or two of the people she interviewed broke down crying right on the

tape. Others spoke in cocky tones, whether in English or through inter-
preters, convinced that they had discovered the elixir of happiness in the
chemical of the day. But even among them Leora detected a defensive-
ness, a sloppy slurring of feelings. Behind every self-satisfied phrase, she
sensed, lurked a drunken mother, a lover who had wandered off, a half-
forgotten child from an ill-thought-out marriage, an abandoned spouse,
a dead friend, a father with a flying belt landing on someone's back—or,
at least, a casting about, a floundering, a profound failure in life or in
love. Yet Leora had no desire to think about these things. Fortunately she
was able to write them down without thinking about them, guiding her
stray thoughts toward her readers as if she herself were nothing more
than one of the city's dug-out canals, channeling waters out to the open
sea. In the early morning hours in her hotel room, she would lay in bed
trying to sleep off the evening's smells, closing her eyes as if drawing a
deep and heavy curtain over the entire world.

   During her afternoons in Amsterdam, after mornings spent entombed
in the sleep of the dead, she went to the lectures at the Spinoza conference. But at the conference, Leora found herself wondering why she
had come at all. She tried out as many lectures as she could, jumping
from metaphysics to philology to sociology to theology faster than she
had taken in the psychopharmacology at the previous night's drug raves.
A woman from the Sorbonne elucidated Spinoza's idea of divine matter,
explaining it so well that you could hardly imagine the universe existing
in any other way. An old man from Tel Aviv explained how Spinoza's
ideas on biblical criticism were almost identical to some of the most can-
onized of Jewish commentators; his idea that the Book of Job was a non-
Jewish book translated into Hebrew, for example, was shared by the
medieval Jewish commentator Ibn Ezra. Someone from California
tracked the influence of Spinoza's work on the other philosophers of the
day, until it seemed that no one except Spinoza had ever had a thought
of his own. All of Amsterdam, during Leora's brief visit there, swung like
a pendulum between daytime and nighttime, each side filled with its
own kind of believers. The people at the conference spoke with the same
self-assured smiles as the people she interviewed in the evenings, with an
expected reverence for their subject, painfully conscious of each word
they chose to defend their beliefs, whether for or against the philosopher. They had faith in the importance of Spinoza the way Leora's nighttime addicts had faith in drugs.

The very last lecture Leora attended, however, made her think twice. The lecture, given by a man from Columbia, was entitled "Spinoza and the Amsterdam Jewish Community: Who Rejected Whom?" The Jewish community in Holland at the time, the man argued, had a warped perception of what Judaism was. Forced underground by the Spanish Inquisition a century earlier before fleeing from Spain to Amsterdam, they had had only limited contact with Jewish learning and had developed their own form of Judaism where one's beliefs were more important than one's actions—a style of religion that had more to do with Christianity than with Judaism. But as descendants of people who had been forcibly converted to Christianity, they were also very sensitive about their Jewishness, and fiercely loyal to it. Combining their distorted view of Judaism with their weak position as a small community compelled to report to secular Amsterdam authorities, the Jewish community in Amsterdam at the time used excommunication more as a way to keep the community in line than to truly kick people out. Most people who were excommunicated during this period—and there were many—applied to the community to be readmitted, and nearly all of them were. Spinoza, however, chose not to do this. In effect, Spinoza excommunicated himself.

On her second-to-last day in Amsterdam, the conference was over, but Leora still had dates with the potheads that evening and the next. After she woke up at about noon—allowing herself to sleep off the exhaustion from the previous night's ecstasy parties—she asked the concierge at the hotel what might be a good thing to see on her first free afternoon in Amsterdam. He recommended the Rijksmuseum.

THE RIJKSMUSEUM looks like a magnificent cathedral, a towering carved edifice rising out of the canals. Inside, Leora stumbled about in a daze from room to room, until, as if carried off by a gentle, unexpected tide of rising waters, she wandered into a gallery filled with paintings by Rembrandt.

The light in his paintings, of which the Rijksmuseum was blessed with an impressive number, made every scene look like a tiny refraction through a windowpane, a panel of glowing faces within the darkness of shiny golden frames. Rembrandt, Leora read on one of the translated museum plaques, had used models from Amsterdam's Jewish quarter for many of his paintings, because he believed that they more closely resembled the characters in his biblical scenes. (For some reason, though, Leora noticed while looking at a portrait of Rembrandt's son, he had not been able to resist naming his own child Titus—the name of the Roman emperor who had destroyed Jerusalem and sent the Jews into exile in Europe, thus providing the artist with his models.) Her favorite was a small painting, of profound depths of detail, called *The Prophet Jeremiah Mourning over the Destruction of Jerusalem*. A weighty title, not at all fitting for the delicate pain of that painting, the darkness encroaching on the timid patch of light, the pressure of the prophet's cheek against his palm, the shrouded eyes with their white brows that quivered as they fought back tears, the thin veins stretching beneath the translucent, baggy skin of the single bare foot.

Leora almost wanted to leave the museum after seeing that painting, because she knew that after that painting there couldn't possibly be anything more for her to see in Amsterdam. She wandered through the galleries, searching for the exit. But then she found herself stopping short in front of another tiny painting, this one by Vermeer, called *Woman in Blue Reading a Letter*.

The woman in question stood in profile, staring at a letter that she held above what looked like a pregnant belly. You couldn't see what was written in the letter, of course; that was for the woman's eyes alone. But clearly it had upset her. It must have been from the baby's father, saying that he wouldn't marry her, or maybe a notice that the baby's father had died. Or maybe it wasn't a letter she had received, but a letter she was about to send. A letter to the baby's father? To her parents? To her husband? To her lover? Leora had never thought before about how frightening it must be to be pregnant—if the woman was indeed pregnant; or was it just her dress?—to be part of something that required two parties but in the end only came down to you.

Something else bothered her about this painting, though, besides its uncertain pregnant woman. There was something about this painting—and, in fact, many of the others—that felt familiar to her, as if she were peering into a window she had peered into many times before, though she couldn't determine where or when. As she stared at the pregnant-looking woman, the image grew more and more familiar, and she struggled to remember where she had seen these paintings last. The ones she had seen had been black and white, she remembered, not the vivid color panels in front of her now—reproductions in a sketchbook? Out of habit, she pulled out her notebook and began squinting at the painting's label, taking notes.

Suddenly she felt the air between herself and the painting getting hotter. Someone was standing next to her. She avoided looking at the person and continued scribbling in her notebook, jamming three lines of text between each pair of ruled notebook lines. As she was about to walk away, though, she indulged in a glance over her shoulder to see who had been standing next to her.

It was a man, and as she paused before leaving, she noticed that he too looked familiar. A young man, in his late twenties or early thirties, his thick black hair close-cropped to his head with a receding hairline that actually flattered his square-shaped forehead. He wore round glasses with black frames. Leora thought perhaps she had met him at one of the drug gatherings, but something seemed American about him, a lack of pretense in his gaze. He was a little too awkward to be a pothead; too square. Then she realized who he was. He was the man who had given the last lecture, the one about Spinoza excommunicating himself. She glanced at him again to make sure it was him. But before she could turn her head away, he caught her glance and spoke.

"Excuse me, you were at the conference, right?"

Leora wondered whether she had left something in the room where he gave his speech, or if there were some other reason he had recognized her. She didn't know why, but his voice made her nervous. Her fingers trembled slightly as she shuffled her notebook closed. "Yes," she answered, "and you were the one who gave that lecture about excommunication, but I don't remember your name."

"Jake." He shook her hand. He had nice fingers, she noticed; gentle, long and thin.

"I'm Leora."

He smiled at her. His teeth had tiny spaces between them, which made her wonder whether he might be European. But his accent was American. "Are you a graduate student?" he asked.

She fumbled for an answer. "No, um, I'm, well, I'm a reporter for a magazine in New York, and I'm actually doing a story about drugs, unrelated to the whole Spinoza thing, but I saw a sign and I thought I'd stop by." That was true, more or less. "I really liked your lecture."

"Thanks," he said, a little too enthusiastically. Leora wondered if anyone had ever complimented him on his lectures before. Clearly this should have been the end of the conversation, but neither of them moved. It was like some kind of cowboy standoff, each wondering when the other would draw. Close up, and without his suit and tie, Jake looked different from how he had looked during the lecture, much younger. There was something very fresh about his face, as if he were really a thirteen-year-old boy trapped in a body closer to thirty. Leora wanted to say something, but nothing came to mind.

"Is this your first time in Amsterdam?" she heard her own voice ask.

She watched Jake's face relax, his mouth starting to smile. He seemed as relieved as she was to have something to say. "Actually I've been here lots of times. My mother was Dutch. One of those Dutch Jews who hated Spinoza, I guess."

Leora scanned his clothing. A tucked-in, button-down flannel shirt, far too tucked-in, over rather eighties-ish unfaded jeans with yellowish-orange stitching on the pockets. Clearly he wasn't living with a woman, unless it was his mother. But he had mentioned his mother in the past tense, or so it had seemed. Jake, she thought to herself, making the sort of random association that might seem profound to someone taking drugs, was a certain kind of name: the name of a kid in a children's movie whose mother had died. Not any particular movie, of course. It was just a generic name for a motherless child in a sappy movie or TV show, in the same way that all children of divorced parents on TV shows have bowl haircuts. An industry standard. To her shock, though, she suddenly heard herself speak:

"I was just wondering: did your mother die when you were a child?"

After it came out of her mouth, Leora couldn't believe she had actually said it. She wanted to crawl into a hole and die.

Jake turned bright red, an effect that in a strange way became him. His face matched the red pattern on his shirt. He choked and spit out his answer, softly: "Yes, she died when I was thirteen."

He didn't ask her how she had known, and she didn't apologize—not for the question, and not for his mother's death. Suddenly she was reminded of sitting with Bill Landsmann next to his father's grave, of discovering someone else who had a hole in his heart, gaping like an open window. Was that really seven years ago? She felt uncomfortable for a moment, as if she had to go to the bathroom. The feeling passed.

"You're a professor at Columbia, right?" She remembered reading that on the lecture list, though he looked a bit young to be a professor.

"Assistant professor," Jake said, the color draining slowly from his face.

Leora felt herself reaching for another inappropriate question, even though she knew she shouldn't. "Does it ever bother you," she asked him, "that no more than six people in the entire world actually care about anything you write?" Once again, she could scarcely believe she had said it, but she took a sort of sick pleasure in anticipating the shocked look on his face.

She never got it. Instead, without even pausing, he rebutted: "Does it ever bother you that no one in the entire world actually cares about anything you write for more than six days?"

Leora swallowed and stepped back. Suddenly this encounter had changed from an exchange with a stranger to something entirely different. She thought of walking away, but felt as if she were rooted to the ground. Instead she changed the subject.

"What did you think of the conference?" she asked after enough seconds had passed.

Jake smiled, once more relieved. "It was fun, as things involving Spinoza go. People presented stuff pretty well. As for Spinoza's ideas, though, between you and me I think it's a cheap way out."

Leora was thoroughly confused. "A cheap way out of what?"

"Well, let's say you're dissatisfied with your life, for good reasons. Things aren't turning out for you the way you wanted or expected them to. There's a war, you get a disease, your dog dies, whatever."

Or your mother dies when you're thirteen, she thought. But for once she kept her mouth shut. He continued.

"A traditionally minded person would have good grounds to reject religion at this point. God promises to take care of us. Then he doesn't. The logical conclusion is that either God has betrayed us, or God never existed in the first place. The easier choice, of course, is to forget about God altogether."

"So how is Spinoza a cheap way out?"

Jake cleared his throat. Nervous, she thought. Like before giving a speech. Except that when he gave his speech at the conference, he hadn't seemed nervous at all. "Because he makes it possible to believe in a God that isn't really God. If the whole universe is this God-substance and we're all part of that substance, then we're all part of God.

But that's not a meaningful conception of God, because then there isn't any connection between God and his creations. The whole reason people want to believe in God is because they want to believe that the world isn't indifferent to their presence." His delivery was a little formal, but cute, Leora thought. His ears were almost perfect.

"I think it's cheap," he continued, "because it makes it easy to dismiss the fact that people don't always get what they deserve. It's almost as cheap as saying that it all just balances out in the afterlife. But just because life doesn't work the way you want it to doesn't mean that what happens in the world is completely random. The times when people really do interact with God are exactly those times when life doesn't work out fairly, and that's when people can really feel God's presence in the world—if they're willing to take on that kind of thing, I mean." He cleared his throat. "That's what I think, anyway. But this isn't really my field, to tell you the truth. I'm a historian, not a philosopher. My specialty is dead people."

There was a pause between them then, only slightly less awkward than the first. Leora wondered if Jake was speaking from personal experience. She decided not to ask him. Meanwhile he stuffed his hands into his pockets. He thought a moment, as if deciding whether or not to say what was on his mind. "Okay, you guessed right about me, so now I'm going to guess right about you," he announced. "I'm going to show you something that I know you're going to like. Come." And then, before she could stop him, he started walking away.

She raced to catch up with him. They began wandering through what seemed like hundreds of galleries, most of them filled with paintings of Jesus, followed by an endless series of rooms filled with paintings just of fruit. Row upon row of fruit, so much fruit that she began to marvel at all the different ways one could arrange fruit in a bowl. But before she knew it, they had entered a separate gallery, and standing in front of her was a dollhouse.

It wasn't a dollhouse really; not in the sense of a miniature building. Instead it was sort of like a cabinet, divided into little cubic spaces, and inside of each of those spaces were the most spectacular miniature rooms imaginable. Set tables with engraved silverware arranged alongside blue and white china. Windows covered with velvet drapes fringed with silk and lace. Little canopy beds with down comforters; a kitchen with a fireplace stove and copper pots hanging from its ceiling. Book-lined shelves and upholstered chairs. And dolls dressed like Pilgrims at a Thanksgiving dinner, sitting down at their banquet tables in their high black hats and silver-buckled shoes.

Leora looked at the dollhouse, trembling, silent. Many seconds passed before she was able to speak. When she could, she turned back to Jake, swallowing first to keep her voice clear, and said, "I used to have a dollhouse."

Jake touched her hand. An even stronger shudder went through her, but then she saw what he was doing—flipping through her notebook. "I thought you might have had a dollhouse," he said. "See, this is how I guessed." He planted his finger on an ink-filled page. "Look how tiny your handwriting is."

He was right. In the notebook, words were crammed at least three lines to every notebook rule. Leora was still a conservation-minded person, and she liked to take down as much as possible, even if it meant shrinking the words.

She turned back to the dollhouse, glancing at each room as if counting them, numbering the dolls. One of the dolls, a girl, was seated in a chair opposite a miniature painting. Leora looked at the girl looking at the painting, and then suddenly, after so many years, stopped looking.

She turned to Jake again, who had noticed that it wasn't a game anymore. He was biting his lip slightly, searching her face. At last she spoke, struggling to hold her voice steady. "My friend—her name was Naomi—my friend Naomi and I had a dollhouse, once. We shared it. Naomi—she—Naomi died, but—well, I—I said before that I used to have a dollhouse, as if it were just my dollhouse, but the truth is, it wasn't just mine, it was Naomi's too. And I said before that I used to have a dollhouse, as if I didn't have it anymore, but the truth is, I still have that dollhouse, somewhere. I put it away after Naomi died." It was the first time that she had said Naomi's name aloud in seven years.

Jake didn't apologize. She had been afraid that he might. Instead he waited a moment and then reached into his pocket, taking out a scrap of paper and a pen. "I'm flying back home tonight," he said as he leaned the paper against the glass, and Leora saw that he was writing his name and address on it. "When are you going back to New York?"

"The day after tomorrow," she answered. He continued scribbling. But as she watched him scratching against the glass, she decided: no. She didn't want it to happen that way, with silly phone calls and then some stupid coffee date, followed by lunch, followed by dinner, followed by heartache. But was there another way to do it? She glanced back at the dollhouse, where, in one corner of a study, she saw a pile of yellowing pamphlets, gathering dust. Attention, attention! she thought. And suddenly, she knew what to do.

"I'm not going to give you my address," she said.

Jake's hand, until then scribbling furiously, stopped short. He looked up at her as if she had stabbed him in the chest. "Why not?"

"Because I've thought of a better idea," she answered. "Look, there aren't very many Leoras in the world, or at least not in journalism anyway. And I'll tell you about an article I wrote, for an extra easy clue. You could go to your library and look it up if you really wanted to track me down. But if you want to see me again, I've got a puzzle for you."

Jake's expression slowly changed to a smile. "Puzzle?"

"Okay, here it is," she said, working out the details in her mind before speaking. "A few weeks ago, I wrote an article for my magazine about bones—about the skull of some guy who lived thousands and thousands of years ago. He's supposed to be the missing link or whatever, and he just turned up in this weird gift shop in New York, as if he'd risen from the dead or something."

As she spoke, Jake's eyes seemed to light up, as if he somehow knew exactly what she was talking about. He seemed about to speak. But when she paused for him to say something, all he said was, "Like in Ezekiel. You know, dry bones?"

Leora looked at him blankly. Jake searched her face for something, some level of recognition. She had none to offer him, but she was too embarrassed to admit it. They stood in silence until he continued.

"There's a passage in the Book of Ezekiel where the prophet Ezekiel has a vision. He sees this valley, filled with old dry bones. So God says to him, okay, Zeke, do the prophecy thing with these bones—tell them that I'm going to give them flesh and make them breathe again. So Ezekiel prophesies to this valley of dried-out bones. Then there's this giant noise, and the valley starts shaking, and then the bones start fusing together, and their flesh grows back onto them, and the winds blow breath back into them, and then they stand up in the valley, ready to walk."

Jake's hands kept waving in the air as he talked, as if he couldn't tell a story without acting it out. Leora thought of Naomi, allowed herself to think of Naomi, glanced back at the dollhouse, and remembered

Naomi—who, as a child, had never been able to talk about their doll-house without teasing her fingers through the air, as if tracing her vision for their house on the skin of the sky. She looked at Jake again and saw that his hands moved more sloppily, more openly, not at all like Naomi's. And Naomi, at that moment, for the first time in seven years, felt to her like an old friend, not only a dead friend but just someone she had once loved, and still loved, and missed, yes, but—

"I'm interrupting," Jake muttered, his hands suddenly falling back to his sides like a puppet whose puppeteer had wandered away. "You were saying something about a store with bones."

She cleared her throat, trying to remember. "Yes, the bones," she stuttered, pausing for a moment to make sure she had the details straight. "I want you to find the store where I saw those bones, and meet me there the day after I get back—let's say around five in the afternoon, before it closes. But not just anywhere in the store. It's a small place, but I want you to find the thing in that store that interested me the most. I'll give you a hint—it wasn't the bones. All right?"

Jake shook her hand for the second time. "Thursday at five in your magical hiding place. See you then," he said. And then he left.

No three days of Leora's entire life ever passed more slowly than those three days. She spent her last afternoon in Amsterdam wandering the canals in a daze, feeling the ground sinking underneath her. On the flight home she didn't sleep, or listen to her interview tapes, or read through her notes, or even read a book. Instead she watched the in-flight movie screen for hours without bothering to put on the headphones. Back at her apartment, she ducked into her room before Lauren or Melanie could ask her about her trip and left a message on her parents' answering machine telling them that she was going to bed so they shouldn't call her back. Then she lay on her futon all night, staring at the ceiling with its peeling paint.

At work the following day she acted like a zombie, ignoring routine tasks and failing to show up for the daily section meeting, thus subjecting herself to a barrage of jokes from Jeff about all the pot she must have smoked up in Amsterdam. When he asked her about her trip, she fended off his questions with claims of jet lag until he left her alone. She sat at her desk waiting for time to pass, surfing the Web until she had tracked down everything she could find about Jake. She found his last name on the conference's site, and then she hunted further. He was listed as an assistant professor at Columbia, and he had his syllabus posted for one of the courses he was teaching—something about the history of modern Jewish thought. She also found a review in one of the academic journals of some book he had helped edit. Address searches showed that he lived about twelve blocks away from her. She flipped through the newspaper aimlessly as the hours dragged on. At twenty minutes to five, she told Suzanne that she needed to sleep off her jet lag, grabbed her coat, and ran for the subway.

When she got to Random Accessories, Jake wasn't there. She considered waiting for him inside, but she didn't want him to take her by surprise. She waited and waited, leaning against the doorpost in the cold until twenty minutes past five, when she was so cold that she had to go indoors. She positioned herself so that her face was framed right in the window where several primate-type skulls sat on display, along with about ten newspaper articles elucidating the store's claim to fame. (Amsterdam Avenue man himself had since been relocated to the Museum of Natural History—at great profit to Mr. Random—for further testing.) Half past five came, then five-forty, as she stood displayed in the store window like an exhibit. People walking down the street couldn't help staring at her; perhaps she was the missing link. At five forty-five she read the backwards figures on the glass door and saw that the store would close at six. In a panic she abandoned her post at the window and stepped over to the shelf where she had seen the tefillin a few weeks earlier. But to her astonishment, the tefillin had disappeared.

She began scouring the store. She looked behind the pamphlets, between the sewing machines, inside the rooms of the mouse house, even underneath the skulls. There was no mistake about it. The tefillin were gone.

Leora walked up to the woman at the cashier's desk, who had clearly noticed her earlier but had chosen to ignore her. The woman was once again engrossed in wrapping a set of plastic fish in newspaper. Stuck-on pieces of masking tape elongated each of her fingers, like claws gone limp. After a few moments, she finally looked up. "Yeah?"

"Excuse me, I was wondering about a piece of merchandise I saw here a few weeks ago, and I can't seem to find it now. Is there a storage room where it might be?"

The woman's lips smacked together, making a popping sound. Leora realized she was chewing gum. "We don't keep no back inventory. Probably moved."

"Moved?" Leora asked. Not that tefillin walking off by themselves would be all that strange, she thought to herself, considering where else they had been.

"Yeah, as in, moved. M-O-V-E-D. Sold."

"*Sold?*" Leora asked. Her voice squeaked.

"That's what I'm telling you," the woman said, cracking her gum again. "This ain't brain surgery."

Leora thought for a moment of the scientists at the Museum of Natural History cracking open the missing-link skull, as if they might find a missing-link brain inside it. "See, but you don't understand, this isn't the type of thing someone would buy," Leora stuttered, confusing even herself.

The woman looked unimpressed. She peeled a piece of masking tape off her ring finger. "What're you looking for?"

Leora felt herself turning red; she wanted to leave Random Accessories as soon as possible. It had all been a mistake. "They're — tefillin. Like, uh —"

"Filling? Filling for what?"

Leora wanted to go bang her head against the wall. "Forget it," she said. And she left.

LEORA WALKED back to her apartment, a walk that seemed much longer than its seven blocks. The city had grown dark. All around her, lights began to flicker on in the apartment buildings lining the deep streets, illuminating the rooms inside them like little slide panels of distant lands. Her own building seemed empty and gray. Inside the grimy, empty apartment vestibule, dirt collected as usual between the bathroomlike tiles on the floors and walls in front of the broken elevator. She was heading for the stairs, thanking the Laurens and Melanies of days gone by for choosing a second-floor apartment, when she realized that she hadn't checked the mail that morning. Leora, Lauren, and Melanie shared an oversized mailbox in the building's vestibule, and it had become Leora's job to bring in the mail, much as Lauren had fallen into bathroom-cleaning. (Melanie did next to nothing, but Leora didn't care enough to complain.)

Leora turned the key in the mailbox lock, and the door burst open as usual under a tidal wave of envelopes. She scooped the pile out, letting the three glossy catalogues slip to the floor. Credit card bills, mostly. A few promotional letters; piles of coupons; something from the SUNY Binghamton Alumni Association. Leora discovered that she May Already Have Won Ten Million Dollars, or perhaps Lauren or Melanie Had Already Won, since they had all been blessed with copies of the same letter. And then, a thick padded overnight mail envelope, bulging. For her.

Leora dropped the rest of the mail, littering the vestibule with a blizzard of notices with their Important Information Enclosed and ripped open the overstuffed envelope, forgetting entirely to check the return address. Inside were wads of plastic bubble wrap, alongside of which she found an index card. She took it out and read its unfamiliar flattened handwriting:

> *Leora, I'm sorry I can't make it today. Hope this makes up for it—Jake.*
> *P.S. The Mouse House was out of my price range.*

Below that was a line written in smooth Hebrew script:

> *Ezekiel, Chapter 37, verses 13–14:*
> *. . . as I opened your graves, O my people, and brought you up out of them, I shall put my spirit in you and you shall live . . .*

Inside the bubble wrap, she found the tefillin.

CHAPTER 5

Go Bang Your Head
Against the Wall

THE NIGHT before her wedding, Naomi's great-great-grandmother Leah had a dream. Leah dreamt that her family had written to her grandmother to tell her about the wedding, and her grandmother, despite the horror and length and expense and absurdity of the journey—first the trip to the port, which could take weeks in itself, and then in steerage class to New York Harbor—had miraculously decided to come. To surprise them, in effect, since sending a letter to warn them would have taken too long.

So Leah's grandmother made the journey in the hull of a ship, handling her nausea like royalty in front of the other vomiting immigrants, and sailed into New York. The immigration officers at Ellis Island couldn't believe that someone had come to America all the way from a town south of Kiev just to attend her granddaughter's wedding, but in the dream Leah's grandmother convinced them, and found her way to Manhattan and finally to Orchard Street, where she could hardly believe what she saw. Giant buildings rising out of the street, as huge as palaces in her eyes, row upon row of them, an endless canyon carved from cliffs of brick and iron. She found 99 Orchard Street and opened the door. Then she climbed up the stairs, glowing orange from the new gaslights, to Leah's apartment, bewildered by the building's many stories, the identical doors that appeared at every turn. She lifted her tiny wrinkled hand and banged on Leah's door. No one answered. She banged again. No response.

The reason no one answered, of course, was that they were all at work. But "at work" didn't mean anything to Leah's grandmother, who even in 1898, the year of Leah's wedding, had never heard of a world where people went somewhere to go to work, and certainly not a world where everyone in an entire family did so, where at least one person out of seven or eight or nine wasn't working inside the house or tending the little vegetable patch in the yard nearby, where there weren't at least a few children plucking chickens in the house even if their parents had gone to a market fair, a world where it was possible — normal, even — for a home to remain empty all day long. And so Leah's grandmother banged and banged and banged on Leah's door, for hours and hours. After the entire day had passed, she gave up, walked out of the building, returned to New York Harbor, and got on a ship going back to Europe. Leah ran after her, but her grandmother never turned around.

Leah remembered that night of dreams as she lay in bed at 99 Orchard Street many months later, in the same bed where she had dreamed those dreams the night before her wedding — a narrow iron cot in the kitchen of her family's three-room apartment, shared with her ten-year-old sister Freydl, who this time, just like on that night before the wedding, snored at the top of her lungs through the entire night while grinding her heels into Leah's calves and thumping her head against the wall, almost as if on purpose. "Frances," they called her in English at school. Their parents slept in a bedroom about five feet away. Leah's three younger brothers slept in the living room under the same blanket, their heads on the sofa and their legs balanced on crates. During most months there were also a series of boarders who would take turns sleeping either on the floor or on a row of boxes next to the boys on the sofa, men in their twenties and thirties who worked hours so long that the family only saw them asleep. Only Leah's older sister Rachel had escaped the apartment, but even she had not made it out of 99. She and her husband lay right on the other side of the ceiling above Leah's head, trying to make a baby as they had been trying for the past three years. The great tragedy of Rachel's twenty-one years of life was that she could not become pregnant.

It was about five in the morning, almost time to get up for work. Leah felt her stomach lurch in the darkness of the windowless room. She kicked at Freydl to free herself from the cot, swung her pale legs onto the filthy floor, and rushed to the deep metal sink with its water bucket, in which she promptly threw up. As she had done almost every morning for the past three weeks.

LEAH WAS just barely seventeen years old, pretty, but not exceptionally so. Her face was a little too round, her shoulders a little too low, but she had a tall, lithe figure and a brilliant smile, when she showed it. Her height made her awkward, and she walked everywhere with her shoulders slightly stooped, straining to look down at other people's faces. She also had a small dimple in her chin which gave her no end of torment from the other girls in her old town, who told her that if you had a dimple in your chin, it meant your husband would die young. ("Don't listen to these stupid people," her mother told her. "You need them like a hole in your head.") And she had blue eyes—blinding blue eyes, so bright that they practically overwhelmed her face. They were her most beautiful feature, but she had hated them ever since she was about ten years old, when a boy a year younger than she, a puny little thing squirming around his mother's seat in the women's section of the synagogue in their old town, told her she had "Cossack eyes."

"No I don't," Leah had insisted, thinking he just meant she was a tough little lady, which she wasn't.

"You do too. My uncle told me. You were born nine months after the pogrom, stupid. Didn't you ever notice that everybody in your whole family has brown eyes except you?"

At that point the boy's mother slapped him across the face. But after many weeks, Leah had asked her mother, timidly, choosing the moment with great care, about her blue eyes. Her mother, heaving a load of laundry out of a water barrel, simply said, "Don't listen to these stupid people. People who have nothing better to do than tell stories should go bang their heads against the wall." Seven years later they moved to America, where nobody looked at you long enough to notice what color your eyes were.

LEAH HAD heard a lot of things about New York—mostly, she realized later, from people who had never been there—but what no one had told her was that New York was a city filled with clocks. Clocks were ticking everywhere, patrolling high atop colossal buildings like watchmen guarding the city, posted on every wall like wardens guarding the rooms, shackling people's pockets with their chains. You didn't begin work at sunup, but at six o'clock. You didn't end at sundown, but at eight o'clock, or nine o'clock, or half past nine. In the factory, Leah had to stitch three seams per minute. Per minute. Per minute.

Another thing no one had told Leah was that everything in New York came in wrappers. Candies wrapped in paper, walls wrapped in wallpaper and paint, expensive things in shops wrapped in packages, hatboxes, shoe boxes, all sorts of crates and boxes everywhere lining the streets, which were in turn wrapped in layer upon layer of cobblestones and pavement. As if people were afraid to touch things. Bread came in paper sacks, medicines in bottles wrapped with sticky printed labels pasted on them. No one lived just behind a door—even the dankest slum apartments were wrapped within other homes, carefully embedded in a series of stoops, front doors, second doors, vestibules, hallways, foyers. Even soap came in a box. To Leah, sometimes the entire city seemed like a child's game, a series of blocks fitted one inside another like a puzzle, and you went to open one box only to find another box inside it, and then another, and then another, and you got more and more excited about what must be within the innermost box, the very center of the world, the holy of holies, but when you at last reached the final box, you would open it to discover that it was empty—someone had opened it before you, taken out the contents, and discarded them, leaving you with nothing but a pile of empty boxes.

As she stumbled through streets, failing to speak English, Leah realized she had also never been told that in America the only thing that anyone cared about was *how*. Not *why*—that never interested people anywhere, really, unless something horrible had happened. Not *where*, either, and certainly not *who*. *When* mattered, as did *what*, but mostly *how*. Carriages raced along the mathematical streets, trains rumbled along their tracks, and new buildings rose up as if emerging from the sea, planting their iron feet on that narrow slip of land that barely held their weight. But no one seemed to care where people were going on those trains, or who would live in those buildings, or even what went on in them. In Europe, people built houses so they could live in them, then hired carriages to take them from one place to another. Here, though, the only thing that mattered was how the house would be built, how you would move in, how you would move out. Leah's parents, bludgeoned on all sides by clocks and boxes and wrappers and four younger children who spoke incomprehensible English after only six months in town, had stopped asking who or why or where and now asked only how: how they would make a living, how they would feed the children, and, of course, how they would find a husband for Leah. It didn't much matter who.

Leah knew that it had been inscribed on a time sheet somewhere that it was better to be here than there, that there were more minutes here than there, a better life, a longer life, parceled out in a pretty wrapper and counted out minute by minute. But each time she looked at the clock above the assembly line, that clock that sometimes didn't seem to move at all from one glance to the next, she thought of what she would have been doing at that moment over there—the stream where she sometimes waded on heavy summer days, the thick oozing ground in the nearby forest where she used to slide around in circles when she was supposed to be collecting firewood, the moment on clear winter evenings when she would find an excuse to step outside after dark and tilt her head back to a sheltering canopy of stars. Leah wanted a life made up not of minutes, but of moments.

Every Friday night before dinner in New York—the only meal that the family managed to eat together in New York, with all of them working different shifts—ritually, immediately after reciting the blessing over bread, Leah's mother would add, "And thank God we're out of that horrible place." Leah's little brothers had gotten in the habit of reciting the line with her, mimicking her exasperated sigh and following up the routine with vulgar jokes in English that their mother couldn't understand. When they had finished their act, their mother would spit back at them: "You idiots can go bang your heads against the wall. That place is filled with dead Jews. Every inch of that entire continent is soaked with blood. Have you ever noticed that you never hear about people in America killing Jews?"

No, Leah later thought to herself, you never hear about people in America killing Jews. In America, Jews, so accustomed to being killed, take matters into their own hands and kill themselves.

LEAH HAD seen David twice before their wedding. He was a cousin of her sister's husband, a handsome boy fresh off the boat and thoroughly confused about why he had bothered to come at all. The first time they met was at Rachel's brother-in-law's wedding, where he impressed all the male guests at the groom's prewedding table with his commentary on the Talmud's marital laws. After the wedding he became the talk of the town. No one so young and learned, at least no one they knew, had ever come to their neighborhood before. Usually, only the lesser students from the Jewish academies in Europe abandoned their studies to come to the land of silk and money across the sea; it often seemed that American Jews emerged straight from the bottom of the European Jewish barrel, the people who hadn't managed to make it and therefore were better off running away. In a town of ignoramuses, David was a gem. And he knew it. Though he couldn't speak a word of English, his Yiddish and Hebrew illuminated the squalid block like an unearthly light in an old dark painting.

David and Leah first met at the wedding reception, where the groom introduced them in the vague area near the back of the room where men and women hesitantly mingled with each other, the dancing, of course, being divided by gender. David congratulated her on being related to the groom.

Leah twitched nervously. She was not accustomed to speaking to men alone, and the groom had been distracted by another guest, leaving the two of them an island unto themselves in the noisy room. "I heard you spoke brilliantly earlier," she said.

David was accustomed to receiving compliments, but he had not been trained to say thank you. "I see people have a lot to learn around here," he proclaimed, glancing to the side as though someone far more interesting had appeared behind her. Then he looked at her, as if suddenly noticing that she was still there. "What's your name again?"

"Leah," she answered, smiling until her face ached.

"Ah, Leah," he murmured, letting what Leah assumed was a scholarly expression settle over his clean and handsome face. "Leah and her sister Rachel. In the Book of Genesis, Rachel is the wife of Jacob that everyone remembers, the one he waited and worked for for fourteen years, having been tricked into marrying her older sister Leah before he could add Rachel as his second wife, the one he really loved. But who was Leah really? Rachel barely had any children, a measly two. But

Leah had six children, including Judah, the direct ancestor of King
David and King Solomon and, someday, the Messiah. Rachel may have
been beautiful, and there are always beautiful people who steal the
show. But Leah stayed devoted to Jacob to the last, without even the
support of his love. Think of what it says in the Book of Proverbs—
'Grace is false, and beauty is vain, but a woman who fears God, she
should be praised.' Leah, not Rachel, she's the one for me." He grinned
at her.

Leah smiled again and blushed. Something about his little lesson
made her feel uneasy, but with the wedding musicians blaring in her
ears she couldn't pinpoint what. It wasn't just the suggestion that she
wasn't beautiful, but something else. Still, she clearly couldn't add anything to what must have just been an example of his scholarly commentary, though everything he said had been easy stuff, straight from
the bible—things that a woman could understand. Besides his supposed genius, there was something appealing about David. He had a
way of speaking that made you draw closer to him, a way of stepping
back in order to make you step toward him, a way of teasing the air in
front of him with his fingers until you found yourself wishing he would
run his fingers along your arms. Desire, that was. Leah's older sister had
whispered it in Leah's ear.

The second time Leah and David met was at a sabbath dinner at
Leah's family's apartment, where he had been invited after her parents
decided that the two would make a good match. The match was struck
almost before they sat down.

"I will treat her only as a woman should be treated," David stated at
the dinner table, after awing Leah's parents with an esoteric discourse
on the legal obligations of the Jewish priestly class. Her parents were
impressed.

"You can tell a fool by his face and a wise one by his eyes," Leah's
father said after David had left. Leah winced when she heard it, thinking of her own eyes, but when her parents asked her if she wanted to
make the match, she thought of those teasing fingers and said yes.

THE NIGHT before their wedding, Leah was plagued by dreams, first
the one about her grandmother, and then still others. Asymptotic
dreams, dreams where she tried again and again to do something, com-

ing closer and closer to doing it but never quite accomplishing it. In one dream, she was in the factory stitching seams on the fingers of a glove. First she stitched up the side of the glove and formed the little finger, then the ring finger, and so on. But after a few minutes at three seams per minute, she realized that the glove was a never-ending glove. Each time she sewed a finger and moved on to the next finger, it seemed like she was just one finger away from the thumb, but the thumb never came, just more and more and more fingers, one after another.

In frustration she woke up, then fell back to sleep to find herself trying to open a box tied with twine. She kept winding the strings in and out of each other, trying to undo the knots, but somehow with each loop of the twine she managed to tie yet another knot, and another. Soon the knots began to form knots, and after a while Leah found her fingers and then her hands and arms bound to the box, until she couldn't move anymore. When she woke up from that dream, sweating so much that Freydl's feet slid off hers, she fell asleep again to find herself feeding Freydl's cat, the one she had left behind with neighbors in their old town. She fed the cat its usual food, but it kept purring at her for more food, and more and more. After a while it began growing uncontrollably. Leah kept feeding it more, in the hope that it would be satisfied at last and stop, but it simply couldn't get enough. The cat grew and grew until suddenly Leah looked up from the cat's dish to find herself standing before a lion. That time she woke up with a scream. Freydl was such a deep sleeper that she didn't even notice.

At her wedding, just before the ceremony, Leah sat enthroned on a chair, flanked by her mother and her older sister as the wedding guests danced and sang all around her, waiting for the groom and his party to come in to cover her with her veil for the wedding ceremony. David danced in surrounded by the male guests, who nearly carried him as he approached his bride. Leah gazed at him as if he were a prince at a royal parade. A broad grin covered his face as he lowered her veil, and in his smile she felt a fire burning.

As she began to make the seven circuits around the groom under the wedding canopy, she noticed him watching her, his black eyes following her as she walked slowly around him for the first time. Something thick and heavy filled the narrow space between him and her. The air grew furry under the wedding canopy, its strange fibers tickling her face under her veil. She found it difficult to breathe. On the second circuit, she felt his eyes on her again, but she avoided his gaze. Every bride is nervous, she thought to herself, hearing the words as if someone else were saying them.

On the third circuit, she permitted herself to look back at him, turning her head slightly as she passed in front of him to meet his gaze. Her veil was heavy, but through it she could see his eyes rolling over her body, his jaw drooping slightly as his thick red lips pressed together to hold in his tongue. His black eyes lingered over her legs, her hips, her stomach, then came to rest on her breasts. Leah watched him staring at her breasts and felt the floor giving way beneath her feet. She stepped backward in horror, then remembered where she needed to go and stepped forward, hurrying past him to complete the circuit, holding her breath until she was behind him. At his back, she sucked in thin, desperate breaths. On the fourth circuit, Leah looked at him again. This time he was smiling, shining his smile on the rabbi before aiming it at Leah. But when the smile hit Leah, she slunk back terrified. His eyes looked in her direction, but it was as if she were a window frame: he looked straight through her, smiling at some imaginary person behind her as if she did not exist.

Leah swallowed and made herself into a bar of iron. She completed the rest of the circuits without thinking and then stood at his right. As the ceremony hurried along, she tried to listen to the wedding blessings, but her mind kept wandering back to the previous night's dreams, of her grandmother and the knots and the ever-growing cat. When the ceremony ended, the newlyweds were escorted to a tiny room to spend the first few minutes of their married life together before the reception commenced.

The door clicked closed behind them, leaving the air in the room thicker and heavier on Leah's reddened cheeks. As she stood alone for the first time with her new husband, she trembled, unable to think of anything to say. Luckily, David didn't seem to want to talk. Instead he took her face in his hands and drew her toward him. Leah closed her eyes in anticipation, unsure of what to expect. What she expected least, though, was what happened next: in that instant, David tightened his grip on her face and slammed her head against the wall until she reeled to the floor.

"Now you know who's the husband and who's the wife around here," he announced when she regained consciousness.

Leah lay where she had fallen in the corner of the room, trembling as a driven leaf, her skull pierced with pain. When she opened her eyes, her veil had fallen back over her face. Through the fabric, she saw him standing over her, leaning in between dark patches that clouded her vision. Then he pounced.

He grabbed her ankles and pulled her forward, her dress catching on the floorboards so that her pale legs were exposed. Then he scooted up on the floor and smashed the heel of his hand over her veiled forehead between her eyes, slamming her head against the wall again and again and again as he slid his other hand up toward the insides of her thighs, where no one had ever touched her before. When she started to scream, he shifted the heel of his hand down to her mouth, pressing the veil up against her lips, and kept slamming. For the sake of the couple's modesty, the little music troupe had stationed itself just outside the door. No one outside heard a thing.

Suddenly David jumped up, hoisting her off the ground before taking her wrists in his hands and pulling her to the door. When he opened it, the guests greeted them with open arms, the men carrying David off to dance with them and the women moving in on Leah. But Leah pushed her way to her parents first. Everyone was smiling, thrilled, excited. Only her mother noticed that Leah wasn't smiling.

"What happened?" her mother demanded, motioning to Leah's sisters that they should distract the other guests. Leah started crying and wouldn't stop until her parents had pushed everyone away. Then she showed them the swelling on the back of her head and started babbling that he had hit her, that he had slammed her against the wall, that he—

"But why in the world would he do that? He's a scholar, a genius! How could he do such a thing?" Leah's mother shouted over the music.

"I don't know, he's a lunatic! Ask him! Why are you asking me!" Leah screamed. Some of the guests nearby turned around to look. Her father glanced over his shoulder with a smile, waving them away. Her mother pushed her hand against Leah's mouth, which made Leah nauseous. She drooled in her mother's hand.

"Listen, Leah," her father said, "just forget about this, all right? Forget this boy. Let's just dance a little, eat a little, let everybody enjoy themselves today, but you're coming home with us tonight, understand?"

"And then I'm going to start saving money to buy a ticket back home," Leah announced when her mother released her hand, her voice shaking as she tried to keep it firm. "I won't stay here! You can't keep me here!"

Leah's parents knew it was the wrong time to protest. They pulled Leah back out into the crowd, where the women danced around the bride in circles for hours and hours without noticing the redness in her eyes.

When the case finally came before the rabbinic court—after three months of Leah's father hounding David to give her a divorce, and three months of David refusing—Leah heard what the witnesses her father had tracked down reported, and she nearly threw up on the spot. If David was such a brilliant and successful scholar, Leah's father demanded, why had he left Europe at all? According to three different witnesses from David's hometown and the town where he had studied, David's scholarship was the real thing. Everyone had known him as the town prodigy. Once he had left home, he had become the genius of the rabbinic academy. The only problem was that, in one of the houses where he ate his meals in the town where the academy was, he had beaten the host family's youngest daughter so severely that the girl could no longer walk or move her arms. It was little more than a miracle that she hadn't died. After the incident, he was expelled from the academy and returned to his hometown, where his relatives shipped him off to America as soon as possible. By the force of the court and under threat of excommunication, David granted his wife Leah a divorce.

On her wedding night, Leah lay in her iron cot with Freydl again, crying until daybreak as Freydl, in her violent sleep, thumped her head against the wall.

The day after her wedding, Leah went back to the factory as usual.

ALL DAY Leah sat at her sewing machine, hemming skirt after skirt after skirt, glancing now and then at the clock ticking on the factory wall. Sometimes it seemed to her that the hands of the clock were moving backward—she could have sworn that the clock had read ten o'clock at her last glance, but when she looked up later, it was only half past nine. As the minutes ticked by, minute by minute, she began to feel as if she were not sewing the skirts, but rather that they were sewing her. It was as if the sewing machine needle were moving back and forth along her arms, stitching them together and then encasing her whole body in seams until she was ready to be folded up and shipped and bought and worn by some other woman who, in some distant time, would profit from life more than she had. By the time the sky outside the factory's few windows had dimmed to a deep blue, she felt like she was dead.

When the streetlights came on outside and the factory clerk turned up the indoor gaslamps, the factory's few windows turned inside out. All Leah could see in those windows when she glanced up was the reflection of the inside of the factory, the dozen or so other machine girls stitching like a row of dolls in a puppet theater. There was no world outside, just more and more girls sitting in rows at their machines, stitching. When at last the clocks tolled the end of the final shift, the little rows of machine dolls got up in unison, filed past the factory clerk who recorded their hours worked, and left. But Leah didn't move. Awakened from her trance by the silence of the sewing machines around her, she put her head down on her own sewing machine table—her head that was now covered with a kerchief, now that she was married, a head covering she would have to wear for the rest of her life, whether she stayed married or not—and started to sob.

Silent sobs, mainly. Years of sharing bedrooms and beds had trained her well at concealing and controlling crying. By the age of seventeen, she had reduced it to a series of shudders, an almost imperceptible quivering and a covered face. This time it mattered less, since she had the factory to herself. Leah cried and cried until she forgot what she was crying about, which was of course the purpose of crying in the first place. And then, out of nowhere, she heard a whisper hanging in the air in front of her.

"Leah?"

With a start, Leah pulled her head up. Sitting in front of her was Aaron, the factory clerk, his dirty white shirtsleeves rolled up over his thin, hairy arms. Out of instinct she looked toward the entrance to make sure the factory door was open. It was, which meant, technically, she wasn't alone with a man in private, a privilege reserved for husbands and wives.

He was a young man, with dark brown eyes and thick dark hair that hung over his forehead like a mop. A few leftover pimples along the cor-

ner of his mouth testified to his youth. She had heard one of the foremen call him Aaron once, and she had remembered his name because
Aaron was also her father's name. It surprised her that he had remembered her name, at first. But when her brain at last settled down, calm-
ing its tumult slowly like water's surface after something drops into it,
she realized why he knew her name: he was in charge of counting off
the workers' hours every single day. He knew everyone by name; it was
part of his job. She wiped her eyes, hoping he hadn't noticed them.

"I saw that you covered your hair today," he said. "Did you get married? I just wanted to say congratulations, if you did." Just hearing him
speaking Yiddish somehow made her feel better, but what he said shook
the settled pool in her brain again.

"Don't congratulate me," she snapped in her mother's conversation-
stopping voice, an ax on a chopping block. "I'm getting a divorce."

Leah thought that would scare the clerk away, but it didn't. He stayed
seated in front of her, his little lips pressed together as if he knew he
shouldn't say anything but wanted to. Normally, Leah would have felt
uncomfortable sitting with a stranger, but a certain harmlessness
seemed to creep from the clerk's little lips with their pimples along the
side. Watching her, he brushed a lock of hair off his forehead in an
unconscious gesture, though it slid back down again without his noticing a moment later. Leah felt like she was sitting with one of her
younger brothers. He didn't say a word until a thick silence had crept
into the room, like water seeping up through the floorboards. Then he
tapped on the water and broke the surface.

"Quick marriage, huh," he chirped at last, shifting in his seat. "You
knew so fast it was a bad match?"

"Some people don't like to waste time before they slam your head
against a wall and knock you unconscious. Perhaps you've never met
such fine individuals." Leah leaned her cheek against her palm and
stared at the sewing machine needle. She wanted to slide her hand
under it and stitch her fingers together, to do anything that would make
the clerk go away and leave her alone.

"No, I've met some people like that," Aaron answered. Leah looked
at him again. He was staring right into her eyes, and she remembered
David's glance at her during the wedding ceremony, how he had looked
right through her. With the clerk, it was the opposite. It was as if, for
him, nothing existed in the entire factory at that moment except her.

"But at least you found out early," he continued. "Just think, you could have spent years with this person. You saved a lot of time this way."

He had gone too far. Leah let her tears run freely, and her words too. "I don't even think there is such a thing as time now," she began babbling, choking back sobs. "Sometimes I look up at the clock on the wall here, and I know that it's been a long time since I last looked, but instead the clock says some time even earlier than the last time. I'll look up and it will say ten o'clock, and then I'll look up much later and it will say nine o'clock. I know it's just a delusion, but I can't help thinking that—"

"It's no delusion," Aaron interrupted. His voice was solid and clear, and it sounded to Leah like a knock on a tree trunk. "They're the ones deluding you. They fix the clock almost every day."

Leah stopped crying. "Fix the clock?" she repeated.

Aaron grinned. "Sure. All the factories around here do it. Haven't you ever noticed? Maybe you haven't, since you're stuck at the machine all day. You probably don't look up much, right?"

"No, not much," Leah said, rubbing her nose with the back of her hand.

"Well, if you did, you would notice that on most days, the foreman calls in to have the clock 'fixed,' like it's being repaired. When they 'fix' it, they just turn the hands back an hour or so."

Leah stared at him, feeling her eyes drying up. "You're joking."

Aaron shook his head. "Happens almost every day," he said. "Sometimes twice."

Leah looked up at the clock on the wall with its giant black hands, then at the clerk's hairy black knuckles, then back at the clock, then burst out laughing. It was the first time she had laughed since she had been in New York.

Aaron laughed along with her, matching her laugh for laugh. "I think you could use a little help," he said while her smile still lingered.

"More like a lot," Leah admitted. "I want to go back home."

"Home? You mean, leave America? Are you crazy?"

"Yes, according to my mother."

"No, you don't want to leave. You just need a fresh start. Maybe I can help you find a new husband for after your divorce," he offered. Leah noticed his ears turning red and realized he hadn't meant to say that last part out loud.

She stopped smiling. "Like who, you?" she asked with a sneer, almost spitting the words at him. She hadn't meant to scare him, but it worked. Aaron shrank back, staring at the floor in front of the machine.

"No, not me," he stammered, then regained his composure. "You need a real American, not some jerk like me who still lives in a boardinghouse. You want someone who can straighten everything out for you."

Leah considered. The clerk had a point.

"Listen, I'll ask around and see if I can find some nice Americans who are looking for a girlfriend. How about if you stay late again tomorrow night, and I'll let you know then? If I find someone, I'll even bring him in to meet you if you'd like. Meanwhile I can help you with your English. That will make life easier like you wouldn't believe. If you learn it well enough, you'll never need any help from anybody at all."

Leah pulled her eyebrows together and shook her head. "I can't stay late unless I'm working overtime. My parents need me at home, or else they need the money."

"I'll put you down for an extra hour then."

Leah stared at him with wide eyes. "You can't do that," she stuttered.

He smiled. "Of course I can. I'm the clerk! Besides, you're already working that extra hour, because of the clock. While they're working on fixing the clock, we'll work on Fixing Leah's Life. What do you think?"

To her own surprise Leah agreed to it.

EVERY NIGHT after the evening shift, Leah stayed at her sewing machine and Aaron came to meet her, propping the factory door open before telling her about boys he knew who might be interested in meeting her. During the second half of the extra hour each night, he began teaching her English. About once a week Aaron brought round what he called "prospectives," young men he'd met through people at his boardinghouse, some of them even American-born, always briefing Leah the night before.

One man was a factory owner. "He's just perfect, Leah," Aaron told her with the boyish thrill he always got from telling Leah about a man. "He's rich, American, and the sweetest man in the world. I'm serious. He even knows how to cook!"

Meeting the man in person, though, was a disappointment. "Ugh, Aaron," she said afterward, "nice, but so *old*! Why is he so old?"

"Well, his wife died a few years ago."

"You didn't tell me that!" Leah shrieked. "Besides, he's too short."

"Too short, too tall, too ugly, too handsome, nothing works for you!" Aaron cried out to Leah's laughter.

"I have a right to be picky, don't I?"

The men paraded by one by one, and Leah began to feel like a princess choosing among the suitors presented by her royal consort. Many months later, Leah's English had improved dramatically and the pool of eligible men had dwindled to the point where some of the "prospectives" didn't even speak English as well as she now did. But sometimes she and Aaron forgot about the suitors and just talked. Aaron's entire family, except for one brother named Hayyim, had died in their town in Galicia in Austro-Hungary during a cholera epidemic. He and Hayyim were left with an elderly aunt who drove them both crazy. Hayyim had married a woman named Sarah just before the epidemic and had already moved in with Sarah's parents, and Aaron, out of work and alone in the world, abandoned his aunt to her gossipy friends and shipped himself off to New York. "Shipped myself, like a letter. That's what it felt like," Aaron told her. That was two years ago. After the letter arrived, though, no one was around to claim it.

After one monthlong dry spell of men, Aaron greeted her at their evening rendezvous with exciting news. "Okay, Leah, this time I have the perfect man for you," Aaron announced.

"If he's anything like the last few, I'm not interested," she said, laughing. It was all a joke to her by now, but she enjoyed it.

Aaron banged his fist on the sewing machine table. "No, nothing like them. This one's completely different, I promise."

"All right, so who is he?"

"Well, he's an immigrant, but he's been here for a while, so he can help you out a little. And his parents are dead, so you won't have any in-laws to worry about!"

"Aaron, don't joke about dead parents, please. You of all people should know that."

Aaron frowned for a moment, then resumed his boyish smile. "Fine, no jokes. Anyway, this guy's no genius—"

"Good, because I've decided I don't like geniuses."

"—but he can handle things like nobody else. I mean, he's a really hard worker. When he got to New York, he started working in a factory, just like you, but now he's already moved up to a desk job. And you'd never guess it, but he's been saving lots of money. He even thinks he might open his own business sometime soon, once he has enough saved up."

"That's the kind of genius I like. What else?"

"Well, best of all," Aaron said, still grinning, "this guy knows how to treat women."

Leah groaned. "Forget it, Aaron. Not one of those."

"No, that's not what I mean! Just the opposite. I mean that he isn't like all those other jerks who think women are just there for them to prop themselves up on. He used to have lots of sisters, whom he really really loved. And he heard a lot of horror stories growing up about men who used to beat up on their wives, and his family wouldn't stand for it. His mother used to take these women into their house to protect them from their husbands, and this guy learned a lot. He's a *mentsh*, Leah."

Leah, slouching before, sat up a bit at the sewing machine table. "So I assume he's amazingly ugly, right?"

Aaron laughed a little, turning just the slightest shade of red. "No, I don't think he's that bad. He's not too tall, but tall enough for you, so I think it's a good match. He's on the thin side, a few pimples but not too many, and he's got brown eyes, and a lot of brown hair that's always falling over his forehead."

"Sort of like yours?" Leah asked.

"Sort of like mine," Aaron said softly, his face growing redder.

"Are you asking me to marry you, Aaron?"

Aaron turned completely red and stared at her blue eyes. "If I did," he answered, "would you say yes?"

"It's so wonderful to meet you, Aaron," Leah's mother gushed as she escorted him into their apartment the following week, using the voice she only used with strangers who were on her good side. Leah had spent the previous hour cleaning her family's entire 325-square-foot dump until it shined. She had told her parents all about Aaron, and they could scarcely believe their luck that Leah had actually found someone for herself. To be precise, they didn't believe their luck. But when Aaron walked in with his funny hair and his wide smile, Leah watched their faces light up like little gas streetlamps.

"Aaron, a lovely name. In fact, that's my name too," Leah's father said, smiling, after the four of them had taken their painstakingly cleaned seats in the little living room where Leah's brothers slept at night. They had already exchanged the usual pleasantries, along with a few facts about where the young man came from and what he did. It was time for business. "What is your family name, Aaron?"

"Cohen," Aaron answered.

"Cohen. And are you really a *cohen*, a member of the priestly class?" Leah's father asked. "One never knows, these days."

Aaron straightened up proudly. "Yes, I am."

Leah's parents glanced at each other. Her father coughed a loud, dull cough and then settled back into his seat, wiping away his smile with the back of his hand. Her mother assumed the same expression, the smile melting off her mouth as she leaned back, chewing on the side of her lower lip. From her seat in the corner of the room, Leah felt something horrible hovering in the air, but she didn't yet realize why.

"Aaron Cohen," Leah's father said slowly, "Leah has told us that you are interested in marrying her. As much as we would love to have you join our family, I'm afraid it will not be possible."

Leah started to open her mouth, but she saw that Aaron was biting his lip to keep from interrupting. She knew that if she started talking, she would start shouting, which would only make things worse. When her father finished, Aaron spoke.

"I understand if you have reservations about me, since you don't know me very well," Aaron said earnestly in his tree-trunk voice, carefully controlling himself. Leah could tell that he had been rehearsing his speech for days. "If you give me some time, I'm sure I could put any fears you might have to rest. If it's money you're worried about, don't be. I'm not a rich man, but I'm a hard worker and I've already moved up in the factory. I live simply and I've been saving my money. I'm thinking of opening up my own store, once I have enough money put away. I know you want Leah to marry someone who cares about religion, and I do. Before I came here, I was a student. I studied the Torah for many years. And I will be good to Leah—that I can promise. If you need more time for me to prove these things to you, I understand."

Leah's father coughed again, a low, rattling cough. Then he spoke. "Aaron Cohen, I do not doubt your integrity. I know from what I have heard from Leah that you are a *mentsh*. I am certain you will be a very good husband for some girl someday. But unfortunately that girl will not be Leah. You should know that Leah is a divorced woman. And a divorced woman cannot marry a member of the priestly class. That is Jewish law. No rabbi will allow that kind of marriage, and neither will we."

As her father spoke, Leah watched Aaron's blood rush to his face. "You—you must be joking," he stammered. Leah knew he was losing it.

Her father didn't move. "Aaron Cohen, unfortunately this is not a joke."

Then Aaron lost it. "But Leah is NOT 'divorced'!" he shouted. "I mean, she is, but—really! She was married for about ten minutes!"

"Three months," Leah's mother interjected, her lips pursed.

"Yes, three months spent living here, waiting for the divorce! Please! That law can't possibly apply to Leah! The only purpose of that law is so that a *cohen* avoids marrying a woman—a woman who—well, a woman who has—"

Leah's father cleared his throat. "Aaron Cohen, there is no way to prove what did or did not happen in that room at Leah's wedding."

Leah felt her stomach heave up, but Aaron was polite to the last. After an appropriate silence, he thanked her parents for their time, wished them the best of luck for all their children, and allowed Leah's father to escort him to the exit. When the door closed behind him, Leah sat posed in her seat like a statue.

"Leah," her mother began. Softly, not in her chopping-block voice this time.

Leah did not move or speak. Her eyes were fixed on the shining floor.

Her mother tried again. "Leah, please don't get so upset over nothing. There are thousands of Jewish boys in New York. I'm sure you can find someone in this giant city who will make you happy. Making a good match, it's not so impossible. I mean, think about it—your father and I didn't even know each other before we got married."

"I tried that already," Leah choked. "Congratulations. I wish you a hundred and twenty years of happiness."

"Leah, I know you're upset, but you don't need to be rude with me."

Leah tried to smirk at her mother, but couldn't. She was struggling not to cry. "I was serious when I told you I'm planning to go home," she announced as firmly as she could. "I'm already saving money for a ticket. I'll go live with Grandma. Anything is better than here."

At that moment Freydl crept into the room, making a beeline for the sofa where one of her rag dolls was sitting propped up on the armrest. Leah's parents ignored Freydl as her mother raised her voice, loud enough for the neighbors to hear.

"So, save the money and go back to that shit-covered country! Leah, you're a lot better off here."

"That's true," Leah's father said in what he hoped was a soothing voice, "so don't be ridiculous. There really are thousands of Jewish boys in New York. Not all of them are like that David, you know. Given the situation, I don't see why you need to marry someone named Cohen."

"But why can't Leah marry him? Who cares what his name is?" Freydl suddenly said. She and her doll both looked up from the sofa, the doll staring at Leah with huge black button eyes.

Leah's mother glared at her. "Freydl, leave us alone. If you have nothing to do, go bang your head against the wall."

Moving as slowly as humanly possible, Freydl picked up her doll, slid down off the sofa, and dragged her feet to the doorway. Just before exiting the room, she suddenly whirled around and screamed in her new, nasal American English, "Stop callin' me Freydl already! My name is Frances, not Freydl!" Then she slammed the door and ran down the stairs and out of the building.

Only Leah had understood her.

THE FOLLOWING EVENING after everyone else had filed out of the factory, Leah remained at her sewing machine as usual. But as soon as all the other workers had left, Leah stood up and marched toward the door. When she got there, Aaron was standing in front of the exit.

"Aaron, please move. I need to go home."

"No."

"Aaron, get out of my way." She pushed toward the door.

He stuck his arms out and blocked the doorway. "No. I have something to show you. It's important. Will you give me just a minute to show you?"

Leah paused. For a moment she felt her blood running faster, until she saw him step back to his desk. He picked up a large piece of paper and walked back with it toward her sewing machine.

"Do you know what this is?" He spread the paper out on one of the sewing machine tables for her to examine, smoothing out its creases and then stepping back to the wall to turn up the flame on the gaslight. As the little blue flame grew and blazed orange, the paper on the table began to glow, a shining white rectangle like a framed picture of pure light. Leah's eyes adjusted, and soon she could make out what was written on it.

It was an inventory sheet from the factory, with lines and columns for bookkeepers to fill out the number of garments produced each day and how many remained in stock. But instead of neatly written lists in English of skirts and petticoats, someone had ignored the column lines altogether, writing instead in a tiny, racing Hebrew script from right to left straight across the columns as if they weren't there, filling the entire page. At the bottom of the page were two signatures in different handwriting: "Abraham son of Elijah" and "Mordechai son of Israel." She tried reading the text itself, but she couldn't understand it. She could tell it was something rabbinic, a Jewish legal text, but since she had the misfortune of being born female, her education had been limited and her reading ability was poor. A few lines down from the top of the page, however, she recognized two names: "Aaron son of Jacob" and "Leah daughter of Aaron." Her heart began fluttering, but she said nothing.

After a long silence, Aaron took a deep breath and spoke. "It's a marriage contract. I copied it out today, after the morning shift. Signed by two witnesses. You know Abe and Mordy, the foremen?"

Leah laughed, a sighing laugh of a woman much older than her seventeen years. "Aaron, this isn't going to work. We can't get married. You can show this to my parents or to ten thousand rabbis, but it still isn't going to work. Forget it, please? Just forget it!"

But then Aaron shook his head, his eyes flashing in the semidarkness as his hands began to flutter in the air. "No, Leah, I figured out how it can work! We don't need your parents or a rabbi or another horrible wedding celebration for you. The wedding canopy, the smashed glass, even the rabbi—all that is just custom, not law." His voice grew louder. "It's true. All you need for a wedding, by Jewish law, is to have a marriage contract signed by two witnesses, and then those witnesses need to watch the groom offering the bride an object of value and hear him recite the marriage formula, and then the witnesses have to see that she willingly accepts. That's all, Leah. Leah, we can have our wedding right now!"

Leah thought for a moment and suddenly felt her stomach lurch. She realized that he was trying to fool her, hoping that she simply wouldn't know that he was wrong. But she knew. "So what if you can make your own wedding?" she said, her voice beginning to shake. "That doesn't change the fact that we can't get married. You're still a *cohen* and I'm still divorced. No one will accept that—not my parents, not my relatives, not your brother in Europe, nobody. There isn't any way around that, and you know it."

She was hoping he would offer her something else, some minor point of law her parents had overlooked, something, anything, that would make everything work. He paused and swallowed, and she saw that he had nothing left to give her. He knew she was right. But then words started running in torrents out of his mouth.

"I know, but I don't care! We can't get married because of some legal technicality? That's absurd! Let's just get married, Leah. We'll run away to California, or Chicago, wherever. No one there will know you were divorced. We'll just be husband and wife!"

Leah paused in the gaslight, imagining herself abandoning her parents and sisters and brothers. The image didn't seem real. But then she imagined abandoning Aaron, coming back to the factory every day and pretending he had meant nothing to her, and that seemed even less real. Leah felt her heart beginning to pound, as if her blood might race to her brain and force her to make a choice. She cloaked herself in sarcasm to conceal her beating heart, asking him, "And what 'object of value' did you have in mind? Another inventory sheet?"

Aaron reached into his pocket and took out something small, metallic. He raised his hand in the air and let the object between his fingers glint in the gaslight. A ring.

"My mother's," Aaron said, "may her memory be a blessing."

Leah stared at his face, which had changed color in the gaslight to a glowing ruddy brown. A drop of sweat was beading on his left temple, just below his thick brown hair, but the skin of his face seemed soft and gleaming, even the leftover pimples on the side of his mouth. She wanted to hold his face, touch it with her fingers, swallow it whole. Instead she said, "Aaron, can we really do this?"

Aaron clenched his thin fingers into hairy fists at his sides. "Of course we can. I've been saving money and I almost have enough for train tickets, for both of us, and you have the money you've been saving to go back to your grandmother, so we could use that too. Leah, I can't keep on living without you, I just can't. I want to marry you, Leah."

"But your plan still doesn't work," she said. It felt to her as if someone else were speaking in her voice, as if she were someone much braver. "Where are your witnesses?"

A little boy's smile crept onto Aaron's face. He turned and walked toward the window and threw it open, showering himself with a cascade of old paint chips as the window slammed against the top of the dirty wooden frame. A cold gust of air blew into the factory. He leaned out the window into the mews, letting in the stench from the outhouses below, and shouted the Hebrew marriage formula: "BEHOLD, YOU ARE SANCTIFIED TO ME WITH THIS RING ACCORDING TO THE LAWS OF MOSES AND ISRAEL!"

He turned around again to Leah, who was laughing so hard she could barely stay standing. "I guess they didn't hear me," he said with a smirk. "Let's try it again. Come over here," he told her. Bewildered, she followed him, and the two of them leaned out the window, once he had gone to the wall again to crank up the gaslight. The light became bright enough to make the windowsill burn white. There was barely enough room on the windowsill for them both. She saw the sleeve of his shirt touching the sleeve of her dress and drew away slightly. After all, they weren't married. Yet.

"Hey, Mordy! Abe!" Aaron shouted. To Leah, he said, "They both live in that building right over there. Convenient, isn't it?"

Aaron leaned on his elbows along the windowsill, holding the ring between his fingers at eye level, as if displaying it to the night sky. This time a light came on across the outhouse alley, about twenty feet away. As the light glowed brighter, a thick man appeared framed in the window, like a painting hanging on a wall. The buildings were close enough together so that soon Leah could make out every feature of his face. It was Abe, the foreman. "You kept me waiting forever!" he yelled back.

"Where's Mordy? Get him," Aaron shouted.

The man craned his head upward, and to Leah it looked as if nothing else existed in the world other than that window across the alley, as if once the man stepped out of that window frame and into the next room, he would disappear forever. The tension in her chest trickled into streams of relief as she saw that Abe didn't leave the window, but instead shouted toward the ceiling, "Hey Mordy, he's there with the girl now, so get over here!" As if out of nowhere, Mordy appeared in the framed window above Abe's head; the two men stood in their windows one above the other, like framed portraits. How strange, Leah thought to herself, to see the big factory foremen, the same ones who yelled at the machine girls all day long, standing in their nightshirts.

"See this ring?" Aaron shouted, jabbing at the air with his clenched fingers. He twisted the ring around his thumb a few times so that they could see it flash in the gaslight.

"Yeah, we see it," Abe shouted back.

"You too, Mordy?" Aaron called out.

The answer hurtled back in Mordy's nasal voice, the voice that had so many times screeched at Leah to get the assembly line moving faster, faster, you lazy broad, we have an inventory to meet, do you want to be sacked? "Yeah, like he told you, we see it! Enough already! We're working the early shift tomorrow, we want to go to sleep!"

"This will only take a minute," Aaron answered, just as loud. Then he turned and whispered to Leah, "Are you ready?"

Leah looked at him, her heart racing. Her lips were trembling so much that she could barely answer. Then suddenly she felt something she had never felt before, a whoosh of hot air that came up between her legs and through her stomach and heart all the way to her head, as if her soul were being burned out of her body and into the night air. She stretched out her hand and said, "Yes."

Aaron straightened his back, drawing a deep breath. Looking straight at Leah, he bellowed into the night: "BEHOLD, YOU ARE SANCTIFIED TO ME WITH THIS RING ACCORDING TO THE LAWS OF MOSES AND ISRAEL!"

He took her hand in his and slid the ring onto her finger. It was the first time, besides that slam of her head against the wall and crawling fingers like worms along her legs, that a man outside her family had ever touched her.

"Congratulations!" Abe shouted across the alley, echoed by Mordy. "May you live a hundred and twenty years together!"

"SHUT UP!" a woman's voice yelled from across the alley, in English. "What the hell are you trying to do, wake up the whole goddamn neighborhood?"

Leah laughed out loud as Aaron pulled the window closed and then suddenly hurried toward the door of the factory. For a moment she thought he wanted to take her somewhere, but then she stopped laughing when she heard him gently close the door, making the factory a private room. The door clicked closed behind him. Stepping toward the place where she was standing, he reached over to the wall and put out the light.

In the darkness he leaned toward her. His hands, soft from six months of working at a desk, reached for her face and then the top of her head, where he pulled off the kerchief covering her hair and began caressing her hair and the back of her head, the place where David had slammed her against the wall. But Leah wasn't one for waiting. She grabbed his whole delicious body in her arms and swallowed it whole, sinking down below the sewing machines to the factory floor, where pools of darkness seeped up through the floorboards like the gentle moisture of the earth.

LEAH HATED her synagogue's women's section. In the men's section, where the people who led the services stood and where the Torah scrolls were read, they prayed with devotion, swaying back and forth furiously in movements that made her think of Aaron. Just looking at them made her lips tremble, burning with their secret, which was more than two months old by now. But in the little balcony where the women had to sit, people barely prayed. Instead the women sat around and gossiped, leafing through the prayer book now and then when the gossip got too vindictive. Worst of all were the children who came with their mothers, little children, some of whom hadn't yet mastered the concept of the outhouse. Leah had been feeling vaguely sick for the past weeks, and sitting in the women's section surrounded by foul-smelling little children only made her feel sicker. But this was what everyone in her family had taken a pay cut for, resigning themselves to jobs in shops that paid lower wages in exchange for letting workers leave for the sabbath. Economically it was foolish, but her parents had insisted. Many people didn't insist, choosing sacrilege over starvation, which was why fewer and fewer people came to the synagogue every Saturday morning.

That week's Torah portion was chapters 9, 10, and 11 of Leviticus. Boring stuff, mostly. Step-by-step instructions, in painful detail, of the sacrifices that Aaron, the high priest, had to offer in the ancient temple—exactly what kind of animals needed to be sacrificed and in what quantities, when to burn the incense, procedures for the burnt offerings. Leah heard all about it from a voice that billowed up from the men's section, some famous rabbi visiting from Europe who was invited to speak after the Torah reading.

The rabbi spent much of his time elaborating on the temple rituals, but then he came to the interesting part. After the complicated sacrifices that Aaron performed, two of Aaron's priestly sons—Nadav and Avihu, crazy names that nobody used anymore—tried it for themselves, their own way. The two of them each took a pan with fire and incense, more or less just as their father had, and offered "a strange fire before the Lord, which he had not commanded them." The Lord, unimpressed by Nadav's and Avihu's creativity, responded to the gift by burning them to death. Aaron and his other children were forbidden from mourning them.

Leah had heard the story before, but had never given much thought to it. Yet this time, surrounded by smelly children, she couldn't get it out of her mind. As he spoke, the rabbi referred to endless commentaries that all seemed to try to clean the story up, claiming that Nadav and Avihu had done something truly wrong, that they had brought profane materials into the holy of holies, that they were worshiping idols, that they were plotting to take over their father's role, that they were drunk—anything to explain what was so "strange" about the fire they had brought in. But when the rabbi repeated the exact text of the story, translating it word by word for the ignorant Americans, Leah noticed that nothing in the text itself suggested that anything was wrong with this supposedly strange fire, other than that it was a gift God hadn't asked for. Leah felt as if she were the one who had been burned. Was thinking for oneself really a capital offense? Or, perhaps, was it possible that the sons of Aaron had committed no crime at all— that instead they themselves had become the real burnt offerings to the Lord?

Suddenly a thought entered Leah's mind, something that hadn't occurred to her before. She stopped listening. Instead she stared at the mothers in the seats around her with their whining children, children upon children upon children, and began counting days in her head. The clocks in New York, Leah knew, were all "fixed." But the clock inside her body wasn't, or at least shouldn't have been. Yet at that moment, surrounded by crying children, she understood that Aaron had fixed it.

A few nights later she became completely certain that she was right. That was the night when she lay in bed remembering her dream about her grandmother. She threw up that morning with a sense of purpose and decided that as soon as she saw Aaron, she would tell him.

WHEN LEAH went to work that morning, Aaron wasn't there. Not typical of him—in fact, Leah couldn't remember Aaron ever being late before. Abe the foreman had to sit at his desk for him, checking the workers in as they entered. As she sat down at her machine and began the day's stitching, she began formulating her speech in her head, how she would break the news to him. Her first move, she decided, would be to tell him that they needed to buy the train tickets for California as soon as possible.

After the morning shift, though, Aaron still hadn't appeared. That was when Abe approached Leah at her sewing machine and asked to speak to her outside. Surprised, Leah stood up and abandoned the machine. She strutted behind Abe's thick back, following him out into the vestibule. Her sewing machine seemed like a single silent island in the factory's raging sea.

Once they were outside, Abe turned to face her and handed her an envelope, the standard kind that were used for all the workers' pay at their factory. "Mordy and I thought you should have this," Abe said to her in a low voice.

Leah took the envelope, which had Aaron's name on its front. Inside it was two weeks' worth of Aaron's pay—three times what Leah earned.

"Why?" Leah asked in her chopping-block voice.

"You mean you haven't heard?" Abe asked, turning pale.

Leah felt the air in the room change color. "Heard?"

Abe stared at the floor. "There was a fire in the boardinghouse on Rivington Street last night. Somebody put a shirt or something over a gaslamp, probably some kid. They managed to get most of the people out of the building, but Aaron was sleeping on the top floor. It was probably the smoke that got him first, but the room burned so badly that he could never have survived it. Luckily when they got him out they could still identify the body."

The body. In Europe, he would have been buried directly in the ground. But since this was America, the land where everything came in a wrapper, they had to bury him inside a wooden box, so that his charred body would never touch the earth again.

THERE WAS no official mourning period, because nearly all of those who would have been official mourners were dead. Except, of course, for Aaron's wife, but no one knew about her besides the factory foremen.

So Leah mourned by herself. She stopped going to work. Instead she tore the sleeves of her shirt and the hem of her own skirt and slept on the floor for a week. She didn't eat anything for three days. On the third day, Leah's mother, paralyzed by regret until then, spoke to her at last.

"Leah, we only want the best for you. I know it doesn't always seem that way, but it's true. We've been very worried about you. And we've been thinking that maybe what's best for you now is to go back home. You could stay with Grandma."

Leah didn't know what to say. Her mother laid her hand against Leah's cheek and asked her, "Do you have money for a ticket?"

Thanks to Aaron's fire, Leah did.

The last dinner at home was the most horrible meal of Leah's life. Everyone had managed to come home for it, even though it wasn't Friday night. But no one spoke, not even her rowdy brothers. Without her mother's blessing over their arrival in America, it felt as if they were eating sacrifices to pagan gods. Only afterward, as Leah packed the last of her things, did Leah's father find the courage to speak.

"Since you're going back, I wanted to give you something," he said. Stepping into his bedroom, he opened a drawer and pulled out a small metal box, and as Leah watched, he straightened up and opened the lid. Inside the box was a set of tefillin.

"These were made for me by the scribe back home—you remember Raphael, the old man?" her father asked.

"Of course," Leah answered.

"Good. Well, he's an excellent scribe, and I don't trust anyone on this side of the ocean to fool with these. Some of the parchments need to be repaired. I'm using my father's set now, so I don't need these at the moment, but I hoped that you might be able to bring them with you so that you can get them fixed and then send them back to me. I'm going to seal the box up with some paraffin so they won't get damaged on the trip over, so don't try to take them out until you get there, all right?"

Leah promised him. But when her ship began sailing out of New York Harbor, a giant empty ocean liner where she had the once-crowded steerage levels almost all to herself, she climbed up on deck to look out at the grimy, burning city. As the ship passed under the Statue of Liberty, she took the box with her father's tefillin and tossed it overboard.

FOR THE REST of the voyage she regretted it, and she cried enough tears to fill the vast ocean with bitterness. But when she finally reached her old town, it turned out that there would have been no one to repair them anyhow. As it happened, a few days before Leah left New York, her grandmother's house had burned to the ground. Raphael the scribe, her neighbor, had died trying to put out the fire. Her grandmother had not been hurt, but she had died shortly thereafter, the neighbors said, of guilt and despair. When Leah arrived at the place where the house had been, the earth was still scorched so badly that even the mud that covered the rest of the town wouldn't stick to it.

Leah avoided lying, at least technically. After an appropriate interval, she sent her parents a letter saying she had met someone and had gotten married—which was true, though it had happened before she left. She told the people in the town that her husband had died in America, which was also true. In the letter, and when she told the people in the town, she even gave herself and her imaginary husband a new family name: Landsman (or, as the government registers would later spell it, Landsmann), a name common enough that no one would question it, but also a word that had meant so much to her family in America and now meant nothing to her—literally, a word for a person who came from the same place as you, from the same hometown. It meant more than that, though, to Leah's family. Meeting a landsman was a kind of relief; you had the deep comfort of knowing that you weren't alone in a city full of strangers. There wouldn't be any more landsmen in her life, Leah realized as she mailed the letter. Even the people in her old hometown, her real landsmen, now seemed like strangers to her.

When the baby was born, a boy, she wanted to name him after Aaron, but since her father Aaron was still living, she couldn't use the name. Instead she named him Nadav, a strange name, not the sort of name anyone had used much in the last three thousand years. When people asked her about it, she told them it had been her dead husband's name, and then they didn't ask any more questions. No one likes to dig up corpses. A few weeks after the baby's circumcision, she went to a nearby town to have the baby's portrait taken, and nine months later she sent her parents the sepia photograph of the newborn baby, who had since grown big enough to crawl and wander away from his mother. When the baby got a little bigger, she picked up with the baby and moved far away, to Galicia in Austro-Hungary, to settle in the town where Aaron's brother Hayyim lived with his wife Sarah and their beautiful children.

Leah had dreamed that she would tell them everything, confiding in unfamiliar faces and ignoring the shame it would bring them. But when she arrived at their house, something stopped her. When she saw his brother's face at the door, a face so familiar, and the face of the young woman beside him, and the faces of the two little girls squeezing in the doorway behind them, and the face of the little boy that the woman was holding in her arms—a child just a few months older than hers, stretching his little hands toward her own child until both babies burst into a chorus of wailing—she threw her story overboard. She introduced herself to them simply as his dead brother's friend, a failure from America looking for work. They welcomed her, pretending to believe her. But the wailing of the two baby boys, and the way the man smiled at Leah and reached for Leah's child to comfort him, and the way the woman tried to draw her own child away, was enough to convince her that they knew—that they assumed the child was Aaron's, and that it was a bastard child, and that now she was spreading his shame, looking for someone to hide all three of them: herself, the baby, and their dead brother's memory. And wasn't that, after all, the truth? That evening, the babies played together. When their mothers tried to separate them, when it was time to go to sleep, they both wailed again, refusing to sleep until they were put to bed side by side.

In the letter she had sent to her parents with the newborn baby's photograph, she wrote that her husband had died in a fire, not long before the baby was born, while traveling in a distant city.

CHAPTER 6

A Long and Dreamless Night

VERY FAR AWAY, Leora once read somewhere, there are two countries, thousands of miles apart, where all of the inhabitants have forgotten how to sleep.

In daylight, they forget their sleeplessness. They do not notice the slight dullness in each other's gazes, the miscounting of transactions, the dreamless fingertips of lazy lovers too tired to explore each other's skin. But as soon as night falls—when the stars lower themselves down on tiny invisible strings until they are suspended just above the highest trees—the people in the two countries begin to wail.

The opening cry sails up from one of the countries and then travels thousands of miles, over mountains and valleys and cities and across the ocean, until it reaches the still, twilight air of the other country, where night is falling. As darkness drifts down, the air begins to vibrate, drumming into the spaces between houses and doorposts and ears. The sky moans. When the people in the second country hear it, they remember their sleeplessness and they too begin wailing, a wail that flies through the air in a fury, like feathers beaten out of unused pillows. They wail all night, children and adults together, old people and young people and babies in a chorus, wailing for the other country to stop wailing, wailing for their own lost sleep. But when the first deadened light of day begins to peek through the darkness, they lower their voices, rub their tired eyes, and return to their ever-waking lives.

Leora remembered this story on one of her own long and dreamless nights—dreamless nights that had started not long after she started seeing Jake, and only a few hours after she realized that she loved him. Not that she had told him. Even now, several sleepless weeks later, she still hadn't told him. But she had thought about telling him each night as she climbed into bed, and as a result she had forgotten how to sleep.

It was torture, not being able to sleep. And what was even more disturbing was the realization of how easy it is to forget how to sleep. Sleeping isn't natural, she thought. Babies have to learn how to sleep through the night, mastering it only after many months of agony. During her nights of sleeplessness, Leora had discovered that sleep is a delicate gift, so delicate that even the slightest thought before bed can knock it out of place, shattering it on the floor below the twisted sheets. Leora would lie in bed, thinking of Jake, and soon thoughts would begin piling on top of each other, one after another, her mind grinding and groaning like the cogs of some unstoppable machine.

Leora's mother had once told Leora that a person remains a child until his parents die. During her sleepless nights since seeing the picture of Jake with his mother, she had begun to see what her mother had meant. On nights when she couldn't sleep, she sometimes went into the living room and read one of Lauren's or Melanie's women's magazines, hoping to bore herself to sleep. When she was younger, she used to assume that these magazines were describing what her life might be like in the near future, when she was just a little bit older than she was while she was reading them. Now, though, she noticed a peculiar pattern: the magazines seemed to be written for children. One billed itself as "the magazine for your years of YOU," years when, according to the "From the Editor" section, "you no longer live with your parents, but you still aren't tied down . . . years when you are free to be YOU." Another, following the theme, had a section called "You, yes, you!" while a third had a similar section, this time called "Me, yes, me!" Leora read these magazines endlessly on her long, sleepless nights, rolling her eyes through the same cycle of articles about shoes, men, sex, men, and shoes, expecting to feel some sort of inspiration from these people who were telling her that she was now a free woman, free to use her time and salary to choose whatever shoes she wanted to fill. But the more she read, the more she felt like a child, her world circumscribed by what she could grab in her tight pudgy fists, the things she could point to and say, "Me, yes, me!" And then she really couldn't sleep.

Jake was past his "years of YOU," and it showed. He was about five years older than Leora and never seemed to think about himself, even by accident. It was obvious, for one thing, that he rarely thought of buying new shoes. He hardly remembered to comb his hair. Not only that, but he also didn't seem to read newspapers or magazines—not even more serious ones. Whenever he met Leora somewhere, on their handful of dates, she always found him reading a book while waiting for her, usually a hardcover one in the generic brown binding of a university library, making it impossible to judge the book by its cover. He seemed completely unaware of current events. Leora always had to explain to him whatever it was she was working on that week for her magazine, as if she were talking to someone who had just landed from another country. Yet he always asked about what she was doing, and listened with rapt interest. One had the feeling, with Jake, that he was immune to trends, suspended in time; that unlike almost anyone else around her age, Jake could have been born in any era, in any place in the world, and would probably have turned out more or less the same.

His tiny one-room apartment, where she had recently been for the very first time, had two walls almost covered with ceiling-high shelves. On one side, the shelves were stuffed with academic books, history books, philosophy books, books in all sorts of languages. On the other wall, they were piled high with notebooks—small spiral notebooks, nearly all identical. But if you looked a little longer—as she had done on the evening before her first sleepless night, her first time in his apartment, when he had invited her over for dinner—you would notice that the peripheral shelves, the highest and lowest shelves just beyond the obvious places to look, were filled almost entirely with cookbooks.

"I see you're a real chef," she had said that evening from her perch by the bookcase, having been forbidden from going near the kitchen while he cooked.

"No, I'm a fake chef," he answered back, stirring something in a frying pan. "Real chefs make things up. I just follow instructions."

She looked again at the cookbooks. There must have been thirty of them. She took one down off the shelf at random: a French cookbook, paperback. It had clearly been well used; it was spattered all over with all sorts of sauces, its pages warped from spills. She opened to a dog-eared page, a chicken recipe, reading it as if it were a story—like many people who cook only spaghetti, she was fascinated by recipes—but soon she noticed something unusual about this recipe. Someone had edited it. Wherever the recipe called for butter, someone—was it Jake's handwriting, or someone else's? the capitalized letters made it hard to tell—had crossed out the word "butter" and written "margarine." She flipped through to some of the other folded pages. In a steak recipe with a light cream sauce, someone had crossed out "cream" and written "non-dairy creamer." She flipped again, assuming she was in the hands of a lactose-intolerant cook. But then she saw a recipe for vegetables with hollandaise sauce, circled with the word "Good!" written next to it. And as she flipped again and again, she saw that the revisions were everywhere, and everywhere consistent—the dairy products were omitted only from the meat recipes, scallops replaced with mushrooms in the bouillabaisse, the chapter on pork obviously untouched. It was the same thing Leora's mother did at home: editing the cookbooks to make them kosher. There were some kosher cookbooks on the shelves too, but those looked much newer. She put the book back quickly as Jake began bringing the food out to the table.

The meal was stupendous, better than any she had had in any restaurant in recent memory. He accepted her compliments with regret, as if he had intended something much better and had cooked this meal almost by accident.

"How did you become so interested in cooking?" she asked him toward dessert. She expected an answer involving some sort of lifelong fascination with food—which would have made sense, considering the bookcase—or a cooking class somewhere, or perhaps a relative who was a chef.

"Necessity," he said. "My mother was the one who used to cook for us, and after she died, my father didn't have time to learn. I decided that I might as well try to have fun with it. The alternative was to spend the next five years subsisting on spaghetti."

"Which is what I've been doing for the past five years," Leora joked, and immediately regretted it. She had wanted him to say more, but she had changed the mood. The conversation trailed off into jokes about food and cooking. But after Jake retreated to the kitchen—she was once again banned from the kitchen while he was cleaning up—she stepped back toward the bookcase again. That was when she noticed, on one of the middle shelves in a space between some history books, a framed picture of a young woman and a little boy.

The woman, a dark-haired, broad-shouldered woman who looked about five or ten years older than Leora, was holding the boy, who looked about seven years old and had a huge head of dark curly hair and brown eyes that seemed to take up half his face. The woman had both arms around the boy, though he was too big to sit on her lap. He was seated next to her on a lime green couch, one arm around her shoulders. The boy grinned in pure earnest, oblivious to the way his arm slung high around the woman's neck made it look like he thought of her as a school friend; the woman, meanwhile, smiled a much more canny smile, but still seemed on the verge of laughing at the boy, almost winking at whoever was behind the camera. It was the woman in the picture that drew Leora's stare. The closeness of their ages—the woman's and Leora's—caught her attention, and the woman's smile, her half wink at the camera, made Leora feel almost as if they were old friends sharing a secret. There seemed to be some sort of promise hidden in the picture, a forecast of future happiness that comes only from being young and loved.

Leora heard the water being turned off at the kitchen sink behind her, the last clean plate clanking into place. Jake turned around to join her where she was standing. He had taken off his glasses for a moment and was cleaning them on the corner of his shirt, unaware that she was watching him. When he looked up, his eyes—which she had never seen unmasked by glasses—were the eyes in the photograph. He turned her to face him and began kissing her, collapsing with her on the sofa across from the bookcase. And since then she hadn't been able to sleep.

Leora reached for her alarm clock, which she had turned around to keep herself from constantly looking at it. She had even switched her clocks around after her last sleepless night, packing up her blindingly bright digital one and instead displaying the little portable clock she used on business trips, whose hands she could barely make out in the dark unless she really tried. It didn't help. The last time she had checked the clock, it had been half past three in the morning. Since then she had squeezed her eyes shut, then forced them open in the hope of exhausting herself, then pulled up the sheets, then pushed down the sheets, then attempted to make a mental list of all her elementary school teachers, then attempted to list all the roommates she

had ever had in her life, starting with summer camp fifteen years earlier, then began panicking about work, where she had three interviews
the next day which she would now have to conduct with less than five
hours of sleep, then forced herself to pretend that her bed was a boat on
the ocean, a boundless ocean with never-ending waves—and then she
gave in and looked at the clock again. She was sure two hours had
passed, at least. When she turned the clock around and saw that it was
only a quarter to four, she felt her sanity slip away and, remembering
that Lauren and Melanie were both out of town, started to wail.

She cried and cried, unable to stop herself and without even knowing why she was crying, except that suddenly everything seemed terrifying—the apartment, her bedroom, the darkness in the room, the
stillness of the air, the bed, the half-shaded window that let in a square
of light like the entrance to a tomb. She wailed into the darkness,
louder and louder, until all the empty space in the room reverberated
with her wailing, jolting the room with waves of sound. She sobbed and
sobbed, wondering if anyone would hear her—and then she realized
that she was hoping someone would. Still wailing, she blundered in the
dark for the phone. As she picked up the receiver, the glowing numbers
on the handset almost blinded her. She hung up. But a few moments
later, her wailing had grown so loud that her throat had begun aching
from her cries. The walls were painted with them. She released a few
more wails, feeling like a wolf howling in the night, then picked up the
phone again and dialed.

After two rings, she heard Jake's voice, which sounded surprisingly
alert. "Hello?" he asked with earnestness, as if he were genuinely curious as to who was on the other end of the line.

"Jake?" she asked, her voice still flying from the wailing.

"Leora?"

"Did I wake you up?" A stupid question to ask at four in the morning,
Leora thought an instant later.

But Jake surprised her. "No, actually," he said, still sounding baffled,
and Leora heard in his voice that he really was awake. "I wasn't sleeping so well, so I just got up and was reading for a while. I wasn't exactly
expecting to hear from anyone. Even the telemarketers usually wait
until sunrise." She could hear the smile on his face. But then his tone
changed to worry, almost panic. "What's wrong?"

"Nothing, really," she tried to say calmly, but she heard her voice crack into another wail. "I just couldn't sleep, that's all. It's stupid. I'm so sorry to call you—I shouldn't have called. I'm just not thinking straight," she blubbered. She wished she hadn't said anything at all, that she had hung up after she heard him say hello.

"It's not stupid," he answered her. His voice didn't sound at all condescending, as she had thought it might. "I had that problem a few years ago."

"Really?"

"Sure," he said. "I couldn't sleep for months. I don't even remember why it happened, now. Something was upsetting me, I guess. But the worst thing about it is the feeling that you're all alone. You're just lying there waiting for hours to pass, and it's like everyone in the world is dead except for you. It's very scary, I remember."

"It is," she heard herself say. But already she felt less scared.

She heard Jake put something down on a table. "Listen, Leora, would it help you if I came over? Just to keep you company, I mean. I think it would have helped me when I couldn't sleep if someone had been with me."

She struggled to speak again. "You don't need to do that," she said, feeling even more embarrassed than before.

"No, seriously," he said. "It's no trouble. Do you think it would help?"

She paused for a moment. "Yes, maybe."

She wanted to die as soon as she said it, but the words had escaped. "Great," Jake said, and his voice betrayed an eagerness unnatural for four in the morning. "I'll be there soon, okay?"

"Okay," she answered. The phone clicked as he hung up. When she heard the click, she released another sob, a long, loud one. She hung up the phone and continued to wail.

SHE WAS still crying when Jake arrived. He took her in his arms until she stopped, escorting her back to her bedroom and sitting down with her on the bed.

"I'm not sure what to do with a person who can't sleep," he said. Leora, comforted by his presence until just then, heard something strange in his tone. He glanced straight ahead before turning to her, as if he were reading his line off the wall across the room. "Do you want a glass of milk or something?" he asked.

"All we have is spaghetti," she spluttered, finally feeling her tears shrink back.

He laughed a little, but in his laugh she noticed it again—a foreignness, as if it wasn't really he who was sitting beside her. "I'm sure there's an all-night grocery store somewhere around here," he murmured, almost to himself. His fingers, resting on her arm, began moving in little circles, doodling on her skin with invisible ink.

"Are you all right?" she asked.

"Sure," he said, lowering his eyes to her arm.

"No you're not."

His fingers stopped moving. "It's nothing. It would only upset you more, and anyway it's not important. I'll tell you some other time, okay?"

She leaned toward him. "Jake, I'm up. I'm never going to fall asleep tonight."

He began tracing circles on the bed with his fingers, barely stopping before saying, "On my way over here, I saw someone die."

Leora felt herself choke. "What are you talking about?"

He completed the circle he was tracing before speaking again, keeping his eyes away from her. "I was walking over here, and about two blocks away from my place, on the corner, there was a fire truck and an ambulance," he said, finally looking up. "It was one of those crappy old buildings, about five stories tall with a rusty old fire escape. Well, the ladder was up to the top floor of this building. It's weird—you have this mental picture of a fire from movies, with windows belching flames and everything, but it wasn't anything like that. To me, it didn't look like anything. They didn't even have the sirens on.

"But then I saw one of the firefighters coming out of the window, and he had this person over his shoulder. He's carrying this guy all the way down the ladder, and I stopped walking and I just stood there, staring. But I got what was coming to me, because when they finally brought this guy down to the bottom, I was close enough to see his face—and he was all covered with ashy smoke, so I couldn't be sure, but I swear I knew this guy. Then I realized that he was one of the clerks in this store where I buy my groceries. A really young guy—it was probably his after-school job. I think he was even at the counter when I went in there a few days ago. And then the next thing I see is that they're putting him on this stretcher, but suddenly all the people who had been running around before by the ambulance aren't running anymore, and everyone sort of steps back, and then they're just really slowly loading him into the ambulance, and—it makes me sick to think I actually did this, but I even took a few steps forward so that I could be sure that he was dead."

Leora watched as his wandering gaze finally landed on her face. She reached around him, propping a pillow behind his back. "That's not sick, Jake, that's normal. Everybody stops to look at accidents. Haven't you ever been stuck in traffic because of people slowing down to watch?"

"No, this wasn't like that, Leora. This was something else, and I figured out what it was. While I was walking here, I remembered that my mother once told me a story about someone in her family who died just like that, in a fire—but a really long time ago, I mean, at the turn of the century. Her grandmother had some uncle who died in a fire in New York. My mother caught me burning something in the bathroom sink once when I was a kid, and then she yelled at me to stop it, and then she started telling me this old family story about how her great-great-uncle died—about how he was trapped on the top floor of an apartment building and no one could get him out in time, and how it might have even happened because some kid like me was being careless. Then she started going on about how I had better stop playing with matches because someone in our building could get hurt, even if it wasn't me, and I should think really hard about how I could ruin somebody else's life—like if there was a fire and one person died, then really it was like thousands of people died because of all the children and grandchildren they could have had, and even if they already had children, it would totally change their children's lives, and on and on. I found out later that that was the day her doctor told her that she was dying."

Jake suddenly stopped talking. He looked up at Leora and slapped himself on the head. "God, I'm so stupid. Why am I telling you this? I came over here to help you fall asleep," he said.

Leora watched him as he sat up straight, bending toward her, avoiding her eyes again. "There's got to be something better to talk about," he muttered. "I can't think of anything right now. You think of something."

"Okay," Leora said. Jake leaned back on the bed, and before his back had even hit the pillow again, Leora heard herself say, "What was your mother like?"

He looked at her, bewildered. "What do you mean, what was she like?"

Leora swallowed, embarrassed but trapped. "I don't know—what did she do?" she mumbled, letting her voice fade.

Jake sat up a little on the bed. "She was a high school teacher. She taught foreign languages. French, mostly." He paused, and then turned to Leora. "But if you're asking me what she did, I mean what she really did, then she kept notebooks."

Leora felt her embarrassment dissolve. "What do you mean, notebooks?"

He pried his shoes off, lining them up neatly next to the bed before sitting back. "Notebooks. She had these little black notebooks that she'd write everything down in. I think she started doing it when she found out she was going to die. I have all of them, now."

Leora stared at the window across the room. "You mean the ones you have on those shelves at your place?" she asked. He nodded. "I thought those were yours."

"Well, now they are, I guess," he said.

Leora watched the window a few seconds longer before turning to him again. "What did she write in them?"

Jake smiled at her. "You know, it's weird. It was always this big secret when she was alive. She would never show them to anyone, and after she died I still didn't want to look at them. I figured there must be something really profound written in them, or at least something really personal, like a journal or something. My dad gave them to me a few years later, and it turned out they were just lists."

"Lists?"

"Yeah, sort of like 'to-do' lists, except instead they were 'have-done' lists. Lists of all the things that happened to her each day. Some of them are almost clinical—lists of what she ate, things like that. But there isn't much about her being sick. I think she was trying to prove to herself that she was living a normal life, even though she was in the hospital most of the time."

Leora wanted to ask about her illness, but something stopped her. She had embarrassed herself enough, for now. "So what kind of things are on the lists?" she asked instead.

"Oh, all sorts of stuff. Actually, I was surprised, but most of it was about me."

"About you?"

Jake smiled again. "Yeah, me. Like 'Jake has a crush on a girl at school.' Or 'Jake hates writing reports about coral.' Or 'Jake got an A on his essay about explorers in the New World.' The strangest thing is that when I read through those lists, I suddenly remembered all these things that had happened with her and me, little silly things that I didn't even know I remembered. Like that essay about the explorers. I hadn't thought about it in years, but when I saw that on the list, I remembered very clearly writing it at the kitchen table and asking her to read it over for me, to help me with the spelling. And then I remember that I asked her if she thought of herself as an explorer in the New World, and she said yes."

Leora listened with her eyes down, looking at the veins on the back of her own hand. They stood out like little raised ridges on a topo-graphical map, not yet civilized by age into highways and roads. She thought of Bill Landsmann with his veiny hands, an explorer in a new world. "Your mother really recorded your whole life for you," she said.

"That's what I thought too, at first," Jake said, covering her hand with his own, which was already charted with the beginnings of the earliest beaten tracks. "But then I started thinking about all the things that have happened to me since she died, important things, and I realized I don't have any record like that anymore. For a while, I tried to make lists myself, but I couldn't do it. It just felt so pointless."

He coughed, and Leora could hear that it was a fake cough, a noise to hide something he would never say in daylight. "But things don't really disappear, I don't think," he continued. "Maybe you and your own children might forget about something, but if that happens, then someone else's children will find them eventually. I feel that way when I'm doing research—I mean, here I am reading some guy's letters, and maybe his great-grandchildren haven't even heard of him, but I have, and his letters are important to me. I think that's one of the reasons I wanted to be a historian—to find those lost things."

Leora noticed the earnest expression that had settled on his face. It reminded her of the movies she used to watch with her parents, which invariably reached moments like this—moments when you sometimes squirmed in your seat, too embarrassed to take them seriously, yet secretly wishing you could. It had been years since she had seen that expression on anyone, outside of old movies. "So have you found any-thing yet?" she asked.

"Well," he said, suddenly grinning at Leora, "I think I found more things like that in one afternoon at Random Accessories than I ever did at the library. You'll never believe this, but a week before I met you, I had already read your article about that skull."

Leora sat all the way up on the bed. "Really?"

Jake laughed, pushing her back down against the pillows. "This is never going to work, Leora. I was supposed to come here to help you fall asleep!"

She smiled. "It's too late for that, Jake," she said, but as she leaned against the pillows propped up against the wall, she felt, for the first time that night, something like fatigue.

Jake leaned back beside her. "I don't normally read magazines, but I guess I saw it in the dentist's office or something, and I really remembered it," he said. "There was something about that article—I don't know, it wasn't one of those usual gee-whiz science stories. It really made me think."

Leora usually laughed to herself about people who took her articles seriously, but this time she didn't. Instead she asked, "Why didn't you tell me you had seen the article—in the museum, I mean, when I told you to meet me at the store?"

Jake paused a moment before answering. "I know I should have said something, but I didn't want you to think I had been stalking you. It was bad enough that I was following you around the museum."

"You were following me around?"

He leaned back and groaned. "Don't tell me you didn't notice me then, and I just embarrassed myself for nothing."

She smiled. "I didn't notice you then, and you just embarrassed yourself for nothing."

They both laughed, he covering his face with his hands. His perfect ears had turned completely red.

"I saw you at my lecture, in the back of the room," he said a few moments later. "Everyone else was taking notes, but you were looking right at me. I felt like I was having a private conversation with you. I wanted to find you afterwards, but someone else stopped to talk to me, and then I saw you walking away. You were gone before I could catch up."

"I probably had to go interview some drug addict."

"Well, I was kicking myself for the rest of the conference that I let you slip out like that. I couldn't believe it when I saw you at the museum.

Did you know I was right behind you in line at the entrance?"

Leora tried to remember going into the museum. To her surprise, she couldn't remember that moment at all, though it hadn't been so long ago. In fact, she couldn't even remember whether or not there had been many people there that day—or even, now that she tried to think about it, where the ticket booth at the museum had been, or what the museum had looked like on the outside. It was shocking, realizing how things slip from the mind. Or was she simply too tired to remember?

"I came so close to tapping you on the shoulder," he continued. "But then I thought to myself, Let's see what's she's really like, when she's alone. It's really rare that you get a chance to watch someone that way. After you've met someone, you don't very often get to know what they're like when they're alone."

Leora tried to think of people she knew, or had known, and tried to remember if she had ever seen them alone. As she ran through various people in her mind, it occurred to her how little she knew about any of them, even her own family. A deep sadness pressed on her, which she tried her best to shake off. "So what am I like when I'm alone?" she asked.

Jake took an audible breath and said, "You're good at seeing things."

Leora looked at him, then realized she was looking at him, and laughed, feeling foolish.

"No, I mean it," he said. "Not everyone has the same kind of senses. Some people have a really good sense of smell. I think you have an excellent sense of sight."

"I don't wear glasses," she shrugged.

"No, I don't mean looking. I mean seeing. I mean really understanding what you're looking at."

She smiled, embarrassed. For a moment she felt glad that she didn't have a tendency to blush. But then she realized that maybe she did and didn't know it. After all, she hadn't seen herself alone very much either. "How could you tell?" she asked.

Jake bit his lip a little, as if trying to decide what to say. "I watched you looking at the paintings in the museum," he answered. "Most people who go to museums don't really see the paintings. They read the little descriptions that the museum puts on the walls, and then they look at the paintings as if the paintings are puzzles that they have to solve, where they just have to look for the tricks of where the artist put the paint. But not you. You would read the titles, sure, but then you'd look at the paintings for a long time, staring at them up close, then from far away, then up close again. You looked at them as if you were actually looking at the people and places in the paintings, like they were real. You didn't look at the paintings—you looked *into* them. That was obvious about you, even from ten feet away." He stopped talking for a moment, breathed, spoke again. "My mother was like that. She was the only other person I've ever seen look at paintings that way—like she was looking through a window. She was good at seeing things."

"Was she an artist?" Leora asked, imagining sketchbooks lined up beside the notebooks, filled with doodles.

"No," Jake said. "But I'm not sure that artists see things the way I'm talking about. I would guess that an artist would have to think twice when looking at something—first to see it, and then to figure out how to represent it, though maybe real artists just see things once; I don't know. But to see things the way I mean it, you have to really believe in what's in the image, without thinking about it at all—just believing it. It sounds easy, but it takes a certain kind of person to see things like that."

Jake drifted into silence. Leora felt awkward, remembering the dinner at his apartment, his reluctance to accept her compliments. She felt equally reluctant to accept his. She watched him as he turned his eyes away from her, then tried to cover the silence by sliding down further on the bed, until she was lying down on her pillow. From this angle she could see Jake's face only from the bottom, and for a moment she felt as though she were a little child, looking up at a grown-up's face.

"How did she die?" she asked.

Jake cleared his throat. "She had a rare form of cancer. It's not worth explaining, really," he said, and shrugged.

Leora suspected that it was worth explaining, that in the explanation there might be all sorts of other things she might find out, things that Jake thought were junk but that she might consider treasures. She let him breathe for a moment, and then changed the angle of her question slightly. "How did you hear about it when she died? Were you there?"

Jake slid down until he was lying beside her. He kept his face away from her, staring at the ceiling. "I was in the hospital with her," he said after a long pause. "My dad and I were both there together. I made up a reason to leave the room for a minute, because I thought my dad wanted to be with her alone just then. I went to the bathroom, and I got lost a little, walking through all those hallways with all those rooms. When I came back, my dad was standing outside, and he wouldn't let me go back into the room."

He still didn't look at her. But Leora turned to face him, staring at his profile. A strange light seemed to suffuse the area around his face in the dim room, like the faces in old portraits. A long time passed in the slow silence of that light, the two of them lying side by side, and suddenly Leora felt the way she had felt when she had seen that picture in his apartment, the air glowing gently with something yet untouched.

After a long time, Jake broke the silence, shaking off the light around his face with a sudden shake of his head. "What about you—how did you hear about it when your friend died?"

She pursed her lips, astonished that he had remembered. Once the initial surprise had passed, she had to try hard to think of the answer. It had been a long time since she had allowed herself to think about that particular moment—not since it had happened, in fact.

"In school, the day after," she finally said, after a long pause. She noticed that her voice didn't tremble, though she had expected it to. "It was while we were in high school. She got hit by a car. I actually saw the ambulance coming as my bus was pulling out of the parking lot that day, but I had no way of knowing it had to do with her. I even called her that evening—we used to talk every night—but that day she had mentioned something about going out to dinner with her parents, so I didn't think it was strange when she didn't call me back. She died in the hospital that night, but no one thought to tell me. The principal made the announcement over the loudspeaker the next morning, right after the Pledge of Allegiance. He didn't even know how to pronounce her name."

Jake waited a moment before asking her, "What was her name again?"

"Naomi. Naomi Landsmann," Leora answered. This time she was the one watching the ceiling, feeling Jake's eyes on her ear.

"She was a close friend?"

"The best I ever had," Leora said, and though she had never used those words to describe Naomi before, hearing herself say them seemed to make them come true. For a moment, lying on her bed, she thought of telling him more about Naomi, about her drawings, about her way of seeing things, and then about her grandfather and his slides, but the sense of urgency faded. She suddenly knew that she could tell him another time, anytime—maybe tomorrow, maybe the next day, maybe even years from now. The present moment seemed to float above her head, buoyed up by a light and gleaming future. They were both silent for a moment, and Leora closed her eyes. Her bed felt like a boat on the open ocean, caressed by waves.

"You know, I meant to tell you about this weird thing that happened when I went into that antiques store," Jake said many moments later, his head close to hers. She could tell he wanted to keep talking, even if there wasn't much left to say. At first Leora thought it was rude of him to change the subject. Then she realized that he had done so for her sake, to remind her that they were both alive. She smiled, feeling sleepy. "There was this guy there who was talking with the owner behind the counter, and I thought he looked familiar. When I started talking to them, he said he was the owner's nephew, and then I realized that I knew him from elementary school."

"You mean Tony Random?" Leora asked, her voice dull.

She felt Jake jolt beside her. "How do you know Tony?"

Leora laughed, a slow and sleepy laugh. "I don't know him. I just— well, his uncle sort of tried to set me up with him."

"Tony's a jerk. He was probably the biggest bully in the school. I remember one time he was teasing me on the playground, and he had all his little cronies with him. Soon his whole little gang was teasing me and pushing me around, and he basically provoked everybody until they started beating me up. I guess I should give him the benefit of the doubt—I mean, that must have been twenty years ago. Still, I wouldn't date the guy if I were you. People like that don't change much, I don't think."

"You don't have to find me a date, Jake," Leora said slowly, slurring her words. A wave of fatigue had washed over her, lapping at her limbs. "Jake?" she asked weakly. It was as if sleep were water and the room were slowly filling with a rising tide. The soles of her feet were already drowning in it. Then her legs, and then her hands—

"I think it's time for you to go to sleep, Leora," Jake said to her, his voice shrinking into a whisper.

"But I want to—tell—tell you—something." Words were beginning to escape from her mind, scurrying into the tangled sheets.

"What do you want to tell me?" Jake asked, brushing her hair away from her forehead and onto the pillow beside her.

But it was too late then, very late, and too early too. He reached over to the night table and switched off her lamp, expecting the room to fall into total darkness. But instead, as his eyes adjusted, he noticed that the room was beginning to fill with a dim, dull light, dripping softly through the window. "What do you want to tell me, Leora?" Jake asked again, but Leora's eyes were already closed. Her breath flowed in and out in hushed rhythms, like gentle waves on a beach.

Jake lay beside her, his eyes wide open, staring at the small slivered square of light projected on the ceiling from the glowing window. Then he turned to her, watching her, breathing in her hair that was spread on the pillow. He leaned toward her and put his arms around her, sliding one hand under her neck until he had encircled her with his arms, and rested his lips on her ear.

As for Leora, she felt herself drifting, slowly drifting, as if she were on a boat crossing the distance between two countries, off to sleep, dreaming that she was telling him.

CHAPTER 7

THE SAME LONG AND
DREAMLESS NIGHT, ELSEWHERE

D o YOU remember this, Anna?" Bill Landsmann asked.

But it had been a long time, years, since Anna Landsmann had remembered anything. It had started the year after Naomi died. That was the year Anna—sharp, incisive Anna, organized, meticulous Anna, always prepared with whatever word or act the moment demanded—suddenly forgot how to tell time.

It began slowly. That autumn, on the day everyone was supposed to turn the clocks back an hour, Anna did not turn them back. To be fair, Bill didn't remember either that day, having just returned from one of his trips and suffering from his own time-zone confusion, but still the fact remained: the clocks were not turned back. It wasn't until Ben called the house—which was confusing too, in terms of time, now that he had moved to California, what with their always calling Ben too early and his always calling them too late—and mentioned the time that Bill suddenly noticed that they were an hour ahead of where they should have been. When he mentioned it to Anna, she laughed, joking that the two of them were surely ahead of their time and telling him not to bother fixing the clocks himself; she would make the rounds of the house and set them back where they belonged. But the next day he noticed, after seeing another customer's watch in the supermarket, that the clocks still had not been changed. He reminded her, and she laughed again, telling him again that he didn't have to bother, that she would fix the clocks as soon as she had a free moment. She never fixed them. A few weeks later, he looked at her watch, which she had placed on her night table before going to sleep, and he noticed that it was broken. When he mentioned it to Anna, she laughed yet again, joking that her watch wasn't really broken, since it still told the time correctly twice a day. But these jokes were no longer funny, because by then Bill had realized that something was seriously wrong. She had not only forgotten how to read a clock; she also no longer understood what time was for. She had forgotten how to tell time.

Once you forget how to tell time, you realize that telling time is only the beginning, for time is the one thing that binds us to everyone else in the world. Anna started by forgetting how to tell time, and then moved on to forgetting appointments. At first it was simple appointments, with people like the doctor or the hairdresser who were accustomed to being forgotten by patients or clients. It was more difficult with her two best friends, whom she had been meeting for lunch on Tuesdays every week for the past thirty years. The first time she didn't show up, they feared for her life. The second time, they feared for her friendship, assuming that they had insulted her terribly in some way. It was only after the third time that they feared for her mind.

And the loss of time in Anna's mind was only the beginning, for then she moved on to places. One day the following year, it took her an hour to come back from the supermarket, a trip that should have taken ten minutes. She had spent the remaining fifty minutes driving back and forth on Algonquin Drive, suddenly unable to identify which house was hers. It was only when Bill, noticing the car pacing the street, poked his head out the living room window that she remembered where she was—and that wasn't even remembering, really, merely recognition. A few months later, recognition began to fade as well, as she moved on from forgetting places to forgetting faces. It was the peripheral ones that slid from her mind first—first the doctor and the hairdresser, then casual acquaintances, then the children of friends, and finally the friends themselves. She still knew who Bill was, it seemed. But not long after she stopped recognizing faces, she also stopped recognizing people's presence. Bill stopped traveling to be with her, but many times she no longer understood when Bill was in the room. The border of Anna's world continued shrinking until it no longer included the house, or the room she stood in, or even the air she breathed.

"Do you remember this, Anna?"

Bill Landsmann was screening slides for his wife. He was hoping that one of them might trigger some reaction from her—a sign of recognition, a feeling, something. It was like rummaging in a deep and crowded drawer for a lost key.

He had decided he would save the easiest slides for last, staving off disappointment as long as possible. Instead he had started with the obscure ones, ones from the few trips she had taken with him years ago, clicking through the images and feeling refreshed himself by every familiar scene as he tried to remind her of the foreign streets.

"Do you remember this, Anna?"

Anna didn't say anything. She stared at the space straight in front of her—and Bill had cleverly seated her directly in front of the slide screen, so that the fact that she wasn't really watching the slides was less painfully obvious. During the past few years she had gotten much worse. Now she hardly even spoke, except to make almost childlike demands—"I'm hungry," "I'm tired," and, on the increasingly rare occasions when he took her out, "I want to go home." He still spoke to her, all the time. But it was like talking to himself.

After the first few years of her forgetfulness, though, Bill began to think that it didn't really matter if she never answered when he spoke to her. When they were first married, Bill used to pity the older couples he saw in restaurants staring at their food or off into the distance, dining in silence. He saw in those silences what he knew of silence then: the brutality of loneliness. Now, though, as an old man, he smiled at the foolishness of his younger self. Some of those couples may have hated one another, yes. But the silence between old couples, truly old couples—people who are not merely old but have become old together, whose ages are twisted and bound together like interlocking vines— their silences are formed not from absence but from presence, a divine presence filling the space between them. For them, speech is superfluous. They already know everything the other person would say.

Bill still remembered the first time she had read his mind. It was very early, while they were still in high school. He was walking her home, back to her parents' house in Irvington, New Jersey. They were both walking very slowly, and he was dreading the moment they would arrive at the house and he would have to say goodbye for the night, not to mention dreading her curfew, which they had already broken.

Anna's parents weren't fond of him, and they weren't shy about showing it. Their dislike had nothing to do with him and everything to do with his accent. He had been in the country for years by then, but he never succeeded in casting off his accent—he had come a few years too late for that, he knew. Anna's parents were themselves immigrants from Russia, but they had both arrived just a few years shy of the age when one can no longer lose a foreign accent (which, Bill later read, was around the age of eleven) and therefore spoke a brash, ungrammatical dialect they considered to be an English fit for royalty. On the evening they first met the young and still slightly pimpled high school student who came to take their daughter out, they were horrified as soon as he opened his mouth. Anna's little brothers agreed—identical-twin brats who ran through the front yard with pillowcases tied behind their heads pretending to be Superman. (One later became a Clark Kent, a grind at a New Jersey newspaper; the other continued believing he could fly, and was shot down over Korea.) They made fun of his accent from the moment they met him, quickly converting their Superman capes into Dracula robes and bearing their rotten little teeth like fangs, running up the stairs as they shouted with insane glee, "Ah-nah, somevun vants to suck your blood!"

Her parents were more subtle. They simply refused to give him the time of day. When he would come calling for her, her mother would tell him that she was so sorry, Anna wasn't available this afternoon, she was at her piano lesson (she especially loves ragtime, rather old-fashioned but still so charming—though you wouldn't know about that sort of music, would you?), or tutoring the neighbor's child in English composition (I'm sure someone like you must have noticed how beautiful Anna's English is—or perhaps you wouldn't quite appreciate it, would you?), or volunteering at City Hall, since today was Election Day (but I don't suppose you knew today was Election Day, did you?), or, best of all, out on a date with the captain of the football team (but I don't suppose you would know what football is, would you?). When he tracked Anna down in school the following day, he learned that she wasn't half the model of civic virtue her mother made her out to be. In reality, he discovered, she was something of a recluse, and had been sitting in her bedroom listening to records each time he had rung their doorbell. After the third or fourth time he called, he noticed a letter to the editor in the local paper signed by Anna's father, concurring in a qualified manner with a guest editorial entitled "Confronting the Refugee Bloodsuckers."

It wasn't until Bill's father died that they began to warm to him, at last noticing how many times he continued to call, how courteous he was to her parents despite their lack of encouragement, how many times he brought her flowers even when she was out on her imaginary dates with the football team captain, how many times he refused to give up—not to mention noticing that he had no intention of sponging on them, that he had found himself a job, that he was going to college at night, and, more than anything else, that he was now a genuine orphan with no one left to love him in the world, except, of course, for Anna. It is true, Bill Landsmann thought to himself, that you really do remain a child until your parents die. Only then do you suddenly find yourself with recourse to nothing but the most painfully voluntary love.

But the time Anna first read his mind had nothing to do with his thoughts on her parents, which anyone could probably have inferred and which therefore wouldn't have been much evidence of telepathic powers. They were on their deliciously slow walk home, and she was laughing about how her parents acted like prison wardens, letting her out for exercise now and then but always trying to keep her in sight, under lock and key.

"I wish my father were more like a prison warden," Bill said. He had meant it as a joke, sort of, or a lighthearted comment at least. But like many things he said in English when he was almost seventeen, it didn't come out quite the way he wanted—and he felt himself separated from her by a veil of misunderstanding, one that prevented him from knowing how what he had said had sounded to her ears.

She laughed, and he could hear that it was a pitying laugh. But he loved her so much then—yes, already, then—that it would have been completely beyond him to fault her for it. Instead he felt a familiar feeling growing within his stomach, a sick nausea that reminded him of being a twelve-year-old boy and listening to some unknown woman groaning inside his father's room.

"You hate your father, don't you," Anna suddenly said.

He was so stunned that he stopped walking. She didn't stop walking, and he stared at her back until her hand, clutched in his, pulled her around to face him. "What?" he stuttered, wishing he could find the words to express his amazement. It was eerie, having someone read your mind, particularly when that someone was beautiful and you were desperately in love with her.

"I said you hate your father, and I don't think it's right."

He dropped her hand, which didn't make her move any further away from him. He squatted down, untying and retying his left shoe. Anna had met his father, once, when she had made him take her to the candy store where his father worked. He had introduced her to him, and Anna had been extremely gracious. His father had grunted and gone back to trying to fix the broken cash register.

"You do not know about this," he mumbled, hearing more than ever how stilted his words were. He straightened up, regretting that he couldn't go on pretending to tie his shoes forever. "He is a terrible man."

Anna looked at him, with eyes that seemed like those of some gentle animal unaware of its own claws. "What's so terrible about him?" she asked.

"Please, I do not wish to discuss it."

Anna stared at the ground under the streetlamp. She began tracing the cracks in the cement with the toe of her shoe, waiting for an opportunity to say more, unaware that at that particular moment there was nothing on Bill's mind at all except the movement of her foot (ah, that shoe, he thought, that tiny shoe, the tiny foot inside it! If only—but no, not now). Watching her foot, he succeeded in forgetting what they had been talking about, until, with her foot resting between two cracks (ah, that delicate tracing of that delicate foot! Not to mention the leg it so soaringly became, and then—), she said, "I don't know what he did, Bill, but you can't help but feel a little sorry for him, can't you? I mean, before all this, didn't you say he had fought in the first war? And then—"

He cut her off, enraged. "I do not—don't—" (That was right, wasn't it? He could still picture the little English textbook from when he was nine years old, but naturally with the relevant line in the table gone blank—was it "don't"? Or was it "donot," like "cannot"? After five years, he now only forgot the easy things, and then only in moments of utter panic—) "I don't believe that that is important, Anna."

(But was that what he meant? Or should he try again? That was one of the blessings of Anna—she would wait and listen while you tried again. Anna's presence in the world was proof that there was a God.) "Suffering doesn't earn a person the right to make others suffer," he heard himself say.

"But it can explain it a little, can't it?" she offered, suddenly standing still.

"No, I am not sure," Bill said, feeling his body tremble slightly in the dark. "It is often said that we are shaped by our experiences, but I do not—don't—believe that's true. Because we don't choose our experiences, yes? I think we are not shaped by our experiences, but by what we do choose—by the way we *react* to our experiences." (God, what was he saying? And why had she stopped moving that beautiful foot?) "My father has not reacted well. Yes, I hate him for it." His hands were clutched into fists, he noticed after he ran out of words. His body burned. He turned his face away from Anna, ashamed.

Anna watched him; he could feel her eyes on his cheek. She spoke slowly and carefully. "I don't want to say this, Bill," she began, "but—your father might be, well, sick in the mind, don't you think?" She paused a moment, as if uncertain whether to continue, and then said, trying to sound defiant, "It wouldn't be very fair for you to hate him if he were."

Bill Landsmann thought of the letter in his father's desk drawer and flinched. He said, feeling his jaw clench, "There is such a thing as being sick in the mind without being sick in the soul."

He heard Anna swallow, and saw her delicate neck move. They were both silent for a moment until Anna finally spoke again. "But if people are shaped by how they react to their experiences," she asked, "and you react to yours by hating him, then how are you shaping yourself, Bill?"

Bill felt himself turning pale. He watched her feet, though he knew that her toes wouldn't trace the cracks anymore that night. He was terrified to look up, as if she were offering him a priestly blessing, and seeing her blessing him might be fatal. He stared at the sidewalk.

She took his hand. Her fingers were gentle, small and thin, and he felt his own fingers closing around them, caressing them, feeling the warm, beautiful current that flowed from her fingers into his. But suddenly his stomach lurched, as it occurred to him that her fingers held his for the wrong reasons, as if the warm current flowing from them were somehow polluted. He raised his voice and spoke.

"Do you—do you pity me, Anna?"

"What do you mean, pity you?"

He winced, swallowing, searching for words. "Why do you spend time with me, Anna?" he at last let himself say. "Is it because you pity me?"

Anna's hand jumped in his, startled. But then her fingers pressed against his again. She watched him until he looked at her, and when he did, she smiled and said, "Maybe it's because I like you, Bill. Hadn't you ever thought of that?"

No, he had never thought of that. But for the rest of his life, in every moment of tragedy or triumph, even now as he sat on the couch beside this shell of her, screening his slides, he thought of nothing else.

"Do you remember this, Anna?" Bill Landsmann asked.

He had switched to a slide carousel from a less exotic trip, a road trip they had taken around the western states. As the hours went by and Anna still sat silently on the couch, Bill was running low on travel slides that included her. He gazed up at the hundreds of slide carousels on the shelves and realized how many of them had nothing to do with her, containing only slides from distant countries where he had traveled without her. To Bill, this scarcely seemed strange, because in his mind, when he traveled alone, she was always sitting right beside him. He was used to talking to this imaginary Anna, describing for her everything he saw while he was away. When he returned from his first solo journey so many years ago, Anna's homecoming kiss at the airport burned his lips, like an angel searing his pink mouth with a glowing coal. It was as if he had been summoned to prophecy. But prophecy fades, he learned as the years passed—the urge to speak might not fade, but the urge to listen does. Bill Landsmann continued clicking through the carousels, prophesying to her, but Anna could no longer listen.

One Sunday not long ago, he had taken her to an old-age home. It was far away, in Brooklyn, but it had been specially recommended by a doctor as a place for people who couldn't remember things. Just to look, of course, he kept telling himself as he drove with her down the highway toward the city, passing by the exits for the area where he and Anna had lived out their younger days, places that he remembered as gleaming with shiny cars and promise and which now smelled of burning tires, piles of old junk. (Was it the riots thirty years ago that had left them like that? Or were they like that when he lived there, too, except that before, other people's trash had been his treasures?) Then he drove into New York itself, through two boroughs' worth of it. The city, as he saw it out the driver's side window, seemed to be teeming with young people. It was as if there had been some law enacted forbidding anyone over thirty-nine from living there. Some of these young people scarcely looked like people to him, with their bodies wrapped in shiny accessories as if they were clad in armor, tattoos bound as signs upon their arms, weird metallic frontlets between their eyes. But in between these armored youth he also noticed others with frank faces—young people who smiled to themselves, or who walked hand in hand or arm in arm and sang out at the traffic lights as they walked, their eyes giving the world a fresh coat of paint. Bill Landsmann noticed these young men and women and kept driving, thinking, for a split second, of Naomi. He glanced at Anna in the seat next to him, but she seemed to have seen nothing. She stared straight in front of her, her eyes on the road ahead.

When they arrived, he could see why the nursing home had been recommended. The building was new and beautiful, with luscious carpets and manicured interior gardens, and the bulletin boards boasted of all sorts of events and activities for those whose memories could still hold up long enough to take in a concert or a game of cards. But the odd equilibrium that had come over him dissolved as soon as he saw their tour guide for their visit: a young Hassidic man.

Bill hadn't been expecting such a person. In fact, when he spotted him in the reception area, he had assumed that the man was a visitor, and he felt himself jolted when the man actually spoke to him, unable for a few seconds to understand what he was talking about when the man introduced himself as a weekend volunteer. As they began the tour, Bill struggled to ask his questions in a normal, level voice, trying his best to pretend that nothing was unusual—as at the production of *Fiddler on the Roof* he had once seen at a local theater, in which one of the daughters was played by a black actress. You just had to get used to it, he told himself; that's all. And it wasn't so hard to get used to, he discovered, especially since this particular young man seemed so modern in his speech and gestures, using the same sort of slang his grandsons used on the phone—so different from other Hassidim whom Bill had encountered in his life, whose slangless English betrayed their youthful years spent free from television.

But something about this man still unnerved him. His fresh young face, framed by sidelocks, reminded Bill of someone, though it took him until almost the end of their visit to realize who. Near the end of the tour, the young man looked Bill straight in the face, mid-word, a slightly unpleasant expression lingering around his mouth. It was his father, Bill realized, the way his father had looked in a picture he remembered seeing at his grandmother's house—how long ago, even he could not remember.

In the picture, which Bill had discovered in a drawer as he helped his grandmother put some things away, his father must have been about thirteen years old. It was a portrait, but not a very good one. His father's light-colored eyes glanced off to the side of the camera, his thin mouth caught in a laughing smile that Bill had never seen on him in real life. But what had stunned Bill (or Wilhelm, as he was then) was his father's hair, which framed the thin face of the portrait in long, scraggly side-locks. For a moment, he had felt an unexplained revulsion welling up in his stomach.

He hadn't even recognized the person in the picture as his father, at first. And even when he recognized his father's eyes, the curls in front of the boy's ears still made him doubt his identity. Yet the boy was his father; the more he stared at the picture, the less possible it became to doubt it. He even asked his grandmother, and she confirmed it, smiling and saying something about what a beautiful child his father had been. And this fascinated him, and then disturbed him, especially when they returned to Vienna and he noticed again the cartoons in some of the newspapers, more and more of which featured characters with his father's old haircut. Only after many years did Bill realize that the revulsion he had felt when he saw his father's photograph had come from those cartoons. Or, as he thought about it even more years later, not precisely from those cartoons, but from the way he himself, even as a child, had chosen to react to them: his decision, on a level he wasn't even aware of, to believe in those images instead of the image of his father, who wore a smile in the picture that Bill Landsmann never saw again.

The remainder of the tour was almost unbearable. Anna, who did not know where she was but somehow knew that it was not their house, began asking Bill to take her home, over and over again, at intervals that shrank from every few minutes to every few seconds, making it impossible for their guide to speak. When it became obvious to her that the two of them were trying to ignore her, she suddenly flew into a rage, picking up a small glass vase of flowers from a hallway table and throwing it at the Hassidic man, drenching his black pants from the knees down and shattering the vase on the floor. Bill apologized repeatedly as the man stooped to pick up the larger shards of broken glass. Then he turned and pulled Anna away, raced back to the car, and drove all the way back to New Jersey without looking in any direction but straight ahead.

"DO YOU remember this, Anna?" Bill Landsmann asked.

He had moved on to the family slides now, the sacred series that recorded the scenes she should most remember. He put on the slide carousel labeled "Ben, age six," and clicked to the first slide. But what Bill then saw projected onscreen stopped him cold—not because of the slide itself, but because of the slide behind it, the one that shined through it against his retina, between his pupil and his mind, glowing through the blank patches on the screen.

The slide was not at all exotic, and not a great picture, either. It was of the three of them: he, Anna, and Ben, apparently when Ben was six years old. The picture had been taken at the duck pond in the East Mountain Zoo—a duck pond, Bill had noticed years later when he took Naomi and her brothers there, that had since been filled in to make room for other exhibits, with newer, more exciting animals—and Ben was feeding the ducks. They had visited the duck pond before, and this time they had brought a loaf of bread with them. In the picture, Bill and Anna smiled into the camera, his arm around her shoulder, her hand on Ben's arm. But Ben was far too preoccupied to face the camera. He was pictured in profile, mid-swing, casting a large piece of bread into water that was already filled with crumbs. The zoo had not liked this, Bill remembered, and someone on the staff had pulled them aside immediately afterward to reprimand them for it. But this image, taken by a stranger moments earlier, had survived nonetheless, immortalizing their transgression. In the picture, Ben wore a look of sheer joy visible even in profile as he cast his bread out into the depths, far more thrilled to be throwing bread in the pond than to be feeding the ducks. It was the look on Ben's face as he cast the bread into the water that

drew the image in Bill's mind into focus. The image he suddenly
remembered, frozen in his head and only now beginning to thaw, consisted of himself as a child throwing bread into water, far away and long
ago.

Bill was Wilhelm then, around six years old, and he and his father
and mother were visiting his grandmother for the Jewish New Year. It
was mostly a boring trip, despite his fascination then with anything outside of the Vienna city limits. Much of their visit passed in long, dull
hours in the synagogue—the sort of place they never, ever went to in
Vienna. His father sat near the front with a man called Uncle
Hayyim—who was his father's uncle, or so Wilhelm was told. Uncle
Hayyim was very old, older than Wilhelm's grandmother even. He and
Wilhelm's father sat together in the midst of a sea of men, and
Wilhelm's father's face looked to Wilhelm like an island in a vast dark
ocean, his bare cheeks naked, pale islands in a sea of beards.

Wilhelm, who should have sat with the men, had cried until they let
him stay with his mother and grandmother in a sort of women's gallery,
along with someone called Aunt Sarah, who was older than his grandmother, too, and married to Uncle Hayyim. During the service, which
seemed to last for centuries, Wilhelm made a sort of game out of examining Aunt Sarah and his grandmother at close range, memorizing their
features and gestures and then looking away and quizzing himself to see
if he had gotten it right. By the end of this game, in the sort of strange
insight that only comes when one is six or seven years old, it struck him
that there couldn't be any way that this Aunt Sarah was related to his
grandmother. His grandmother was very tall, even though she was old,
while Sarah was tiny even without the stoop in her back. His grandmother had a wide, round face and a long neck and large blue eyes
sunken into her wrinkles, but Sarah had a sharp nose and dark, almost
black eyes, pinched toward her nose, the whole effect making Wilhelm
think of a black-feathered bird. And besides, Sarah and Wilhelm's
grandmother hated each other—that too was apparent from Wilhelm's
game. Sarah liked to talk during the service, but she never smiled at
Wilhelm's grandmother, even as she joked with the other women
around her. To his grandmother, he noticed, she offered only a sort of
smirk. His grandmother, meanwhile, sat in her seat with a plain perse-
verance, her eyes glued to the prayer book in her lap and her lips list-
lessly mumbling prayers. When Sarah leaned over to say something to

her, she often pretended not to notice until Sarah was practically speaking into her ear. Then she would offer Sarah a plaintive expression, which Wilhelm had seen before on the faces of the nicer girls in the schoolyard in Vienna when a mean girl tried to play with them.

The service dragged on, and even Wilhelm's little game couldn't keep him from drowning in boredom. But Wilhelm was surprised when something very interesting happened after the service was over. Instead of dispersing and going home, everyone who had been in the synagogue walked en masse away from the center of town, toward the river. And there Wilhelm found himself pushed by Uncle Hayyim to the front, by the water's edge.

Now they were all standing on the riverbank, the men and women gathered in clusters by gender. The smaller children, pushed to the front by their parents, scampered back and forth a bit among the women and the men, though most of the littlest ones huddled closer to their mothers, even if they were boys. Wilhelm, standing with his mother and grandmother, looked around at the other children, both in the women's section and in the men's. The girls looked more or less like the girls in the schoolyard in Vienna. But the boys—everyone except Wilhelm—had long locks of hair alongside their ears, like little flaps; some of them, the very smallest ones, had long hair all around, almost like girls. The children stared back at him, then moved away from him. Wilhelm began to feel very hot, despite the cool breeze blowing from the river. Someone had begun passing out little pieces of stale bread, and Aunt Sarah stuck one in Wilhelm's hand.

Wilhelm looked at the bread, grateful. The service had been long, and he was starving. But as he brought it to his mouth, he felt Aunt Sarah smack his hand, making him drop the piece of bread on the riverbank. He looked at the bread in the mud and felt himself about to cry.

His grandmother stooped down to face him, holding his chin in one hand and picking up the bread with the other. "It's not for eating," she said in her funny way of talking, putting the piece of bread back in his hand. "It's supposed to be your sins—everything you did wrong during the past year. We're going to say a prayer now, and then you're going to throw it in the river and ask God to forgive you—to forgive you," she finished in awkward German.

Wilhelm was stunned. He looked at the piece of bread, now half covered with mud, fascinated. But before he had time to think about it, all the women and men began chanting and mumbling, the men with prayer books, most of the women without. Wilhelm's grandmother had a little book, though. She remained stooped by Wilhelm's ear, telling him what they were saying in her funny way of talking, and then his mother bent down too, putting her face between them and turning the funny words back into German.

"Who is God like you, who forgives sin and pardons the transgression of the remnant of his heritage?" his grandmother whispered—"That means God forgives bad things," his mother whispered back, "bad things you did during the year."—"He does not seize his anger forever, for he delights in kindness," his grandmother whispered—"God won't stay mad at you," his mother whispered. "You will again be merciful upon us and subdue our sins, and cast all our sins into the depths of the sea," his grandmother whispered—"God will take the bad things you did and forget about them, and throw them in the water," his mother said. There was a bit more after that, but Wilhelm could barely listen to it. Instead he stared at the children around him, intrigued, unable to believe that they spent every New Year throwing bits of stale bread in a river.

". . . for the earth shall be filled with the knowledge of God, as the waters cover the sea," his grandmother whispered—"Like the waters cover the sea," his mother finished. The riverbank was silent for a moment. "Now try to think of what you did wrong during the year, and then throw the bread in the river," his grandmother told him.

Wilhelm tried to think of what he had done wrong that year, but he couldn't think of anything. Soon people started throwing the bread in the water. From his perch on the river's edge, bread seemed to be raining from the heavens, flying into the river and racing downstream. Certain that he had done something bad during the past year, or even many bad things, and simply couldn't remember what, Wilhelm drew back his hand in a mighty pitch and cast the bread into the river with thrilling abandon, hoping that the bread would remember his bad deeds better than he did and drown itself in guilt in the river. As he followed his piece of bread with his eyes, he watched as it blended with all the other pieces of bread until he couldn't tell which one was his anymore. Some pieces sank below the depths; others were snatched up by birds; the rest floated downstream, far away, and, Wilhelm imagined to himself, out to sea.

The crowd began to mingle and disperse, the adults gravitating toward husbands and wives and the children drawing back from the water's edge, to be scooped up by parents who carried them away. Wilhelm's father and Uncle Hayyim came over to where Wilhelm and Aunt Sarah and his mother and grandmother were standing, but Wilhelm continued staring at the floating bread. Above Wilhelm's head, the grown-ups in the family were talking—at least, all of the grown-ups except for Wilhelm's father, who remained silent. But as Wilhelm traced the paths of the bread in the water with his eyes, his ears, tracing the sounds of the voices above his head, registered his father's name. "Unfortunately, not everything can be cast into the water, Nadav," Aunt Sarah suddenly said.

Wilhelm snapped his eyes up from the river, twisting his head around until he had a full view of Aunt Sarah's nostrils, which were blazing open, her lips protruding from her face. "Some things never go away, Nadav. Even the New Year doesn't atone for sins between one man and another."

"Stop it, Sarah," Wilhelm's grandmother said, her voice quavering but getting louder, her chin, miles high from Wilhelm's perspective, jutting out like a finger pointing at Aunt Sarah's nose. "He didn't do anything, and you know it. Just because you want someone to blame— God, it's been fifteen years, Sarah. Stop it already!"

"That's easy for you to say, with a living son!" Sarah shrieked.

"Sarah, please stop," Hayyim said, grabbing her arm. "Of all times of year—"

"I'll even say it in German—the boy should know it too!" she shouted, pointing at Wilhelm's father and forcing the funny words and vowels out of her voice until she was screaming in stilted German: "He killed my baby! I don't care what they tell me—I know he did! He killed my baby!"

Then Sarah lunged at Wilhelm's father, and her fingernails might have dug right into his father's eyes if Wilhelm's grandmother hadn't grabbed her son from behind and Uncle Hayyim hadn't restrained his raving wife.

What happened after that, even Wilhelm Landsmann's normally watertight memory couldn't precisely recall. Nor did he ever find out what exactly was happening on that riverbank. But he knew that for one of the few times in his life, he had suddenly felt that he was on his father's side—that this woman, whoever she was and whatever she was talking about, was sick in the mind, not just sick in the mind but sick in the soul too, and that his father deserved her claws no more than Wilhelm himself deserved his father's cold cruelty. Suddenly things made sense. A moment later, before his mother and grandmother dragged him away, Wilhelm noticed an extra piece of bread resting on the riverbank. He picked it up and flung it in the river, watching as it hurried out to sea.

BILL GLANCED at the rest of the captions on the list enclosed with the slide carousel called "Ben, age six"—a variorum of "Ben feeding ducks" covered at least five pictures—and decided he couldn't continue with this carousel. Not now. Instead he took that carousel off the slide projector and went back to the shelves to select a newer one, a better one. He consulted his catalogued list of carousels and decided, with an inner shudder, that it was time for the final test. He selected a box from one of the bottom shelves, labeled "Naomi's sixteenth birthday party."

Anna was still sitting on the couch, motionless, her world contained entirely within her skin. He approached her like a high priest approaching the altar, bearing his offering in his hands. "I want to see if you remember this, Anna," he said.

His fingers were trembling slightly, and he had to struggle to remove the carousel from the box. He put it on the projector in a daze, barely seeing it. He didn't want to look at the slides, to be awed or disappointed by how many of them there were on this particular reel. It was enough to do it by touch. He clicked the machine to the first slide.

"Remember, Anna?" Bill Landsmann asked.

He looked up at the slide, unwilling to check the captions, as if he were quizzing himself. The picture was of Anna, smiling at the camera, bringing a glass of soda to a young girl, one of Naomi's friends. It was the same girl, Bill instantly realized, he had found in the paper, the one who came to the house, the one who—but what was her name?

He consulted the list of captions, where, he discovered, he hadn't recorded her name either. All it said was "Anna and Naomi's friend." Terrified by the hole in his own memory, he clicked to the next slide, moving his eyes down the caption list to the next entry, where he had typed "The birthday girl!"

"Do you remember, Anna?" he asked.

After he asked the question, he glanced at Anna, dreading the empty look in her eyes as she faced the screen. But to his shock, he saw her watching the screen, genuinely seeing it, her eyebrows raised above her glasses as she leaned forward on the couch as if she had come back to life. Following her gaze, he turned toward the screen himself.

It was blank.

Bill stared for a moment at the empty screen, feeling like he was staring into a pool of opaque water. The whir of the projector's fan made the blank screen seem to vibrate slightly. There was a mistake, he knew. He must have lined up the slides wrong in the carousel, though he was always careful not to leave gaps. He clicked to the next slide.

Blank.

He clicked again. A picture of himself and Anna came up on the screen, arm in arm, she half laughing. Bill sighed with relief. But when he looked at the list of captions, he saw "Anna and me" listed as slide number four, which was exactly where it was on the carousel. There was no mistake. Slide number three, according to the list, had been "Me and the birthday girl."

He clicked again, to slide number five, listed as "Ben hauls in the presents," and Ben appeared in full force on the screen—a much bigger, older Ben than the one who had been feeding the ducks in the last reel—making a fake grimace under a pile of little wrapped gifts that couldn't have weighed more than a few pounds. Then he clicked to what should have been slide number five, "Anna and Naomi and me."

Blank.

Now Bill leaned over to stare at the slide carousel itself on the machine and saw that it had been pillaged. Nearly half the slides were missing. He counted slides with his fingertips, following along on the caption sheets. Number seven was missing—"Naomi and friends"—as was number eight, "Naomi and friends, again," and number ten, "The birthday girl, with Mom and Dad." Numbers fourteen through eighteen, inclusive—"Make a wish: Candles and cake!"—had vanished without a trace, not to mention numbers twenty-one, twenty-three, twenty-four, and twenty-five, all labeled "The birthday girl opens the gifts!" Bill clicked through the entire carousel like cannon fire, one after another. Every picture of Naomi was gone.

Anna was seated on the couch, leaning forward, a strange smile on her face. Bill glanced over at her and was struck by her expression. He felt her presence in a way he hadn't felt it in a very long time, since her mind had begun to fade. He reached for her hand. But then suddenly something occurred to him.

"Did you do something with these slides, Anna?" he asked.

Anna leaned back against the couch, her eyes still focused on the screen, which by now was blank again. She turned to face Bill. Just when he had decided for sure that she had missed what he had said, she suddenly whispered, "Yes."

Bill stared at her. "What is this, 'yes'?" he asked, his voice rising. He couldn't believe the implications of her answer—first, that she had actually understood his question, and second, that she had touched his slides.

"Yes, I took out the pictures of Naomi," Anna said, her voice piercing the air in the room.

Bill sat stunned on the couch, paralyzed for a moment before roaring, "Why?"

Anna wiped her left eye under her glasses. "I didn't think they belonged there, Bill, with so many other slides on those shelves—with all those slides of strangers from other countries, catalogued like that. I just didn't think it was right."

Her lucidity was jarring. It had been months since she had said something so coherent, so conceptually subtle, so unrelated to basic demands—so similar to the way she used to be. Bill wanted to take her in his arms and fly with her into the sky. Instead he asked, making his voice as gentle as he could, "And what exactly did you do with those slides?"

"I—I don't remember."

"You don't remember?" Suddenly it seemed strange, atypical, even cruel and unjust, for her not to remember something. Bewildered, he asked again, "You don't remember?"

"No . . . no, I—I don't."

A wave of rage rose up from Bill's stomach. He felt himself beginning to shake, violently, fighting to stay seated, to stop himself from lunging at her, from screaming as loud as he could scream: *You killed my baby!*

Instead he clutched the arm of the couch with one hand, shaking, silently begging her to say more, to remember some tiny clue as to what happened to those pictures, or even to just prolong that moment when she had spoken so clearly, a moment of pure transparent light. But the moment proved fleeting. He watched her as she slowly closed up again, a blank expression falling over her face like a curtain. "I'm tired," she suddenly said. "I'm very tired."

Bill glanced at the clock. It was late, later than he had thought it was—or perhaps he too was beginning to lose track of time. They both stood up, and he escorted her to their bedroom, not wanting to find out whether she would be able to make it there without him.

They began to get ready for bed. This, at least, Anna understood. She still remembered how to sleep. As they slipped under the covers, Anna closed her eyes almost immediately. She had forgotten that he was there.

"Anna," he whispered as he turned out the light on his night table, finding her hand in the darkness. It lay limp in his. "Do you remember when you told me not to hate my father?" he asked. He no longer expected answers, but that didn't matter. He already knew what she would say. "I don't hate him, Anna. Not anymore. You should know," he finished. But Anna was already sleeping, her breath spilling out in tide pools on her pillow.

Bill, however, couldn't sleep. He squeezed her hand in the dark, then put his arms around her, watching her dream. And Bill himself dreamed while still awake, dreaming her dreams for her, dreaming of the pictures of Naomi, stored somewhere in the sanctuary of Anna's lost mind.

CHAPTER 8

THE BETTER DEAL

B ACK WHEN the Dutch owned the entire world, fleeing their sinking country to spread their love of miniatures, chocolates, and blue and white china from South America to the South Pacific, they also planted their feet on the ground in southern Africa—ground where, a few hundred years later, a child discovered a "pretty pebble" on the farm of Nicolaas and Diedrick de Beer, leading to private Dutch control of De Beers Consolidated Mines, which would later become the largest diamond mining cartel in the history of the world. Unfortunately, like Dutch control of New Amsterdam, this state of affairs lasted about fifteen minutes, concluding when the de Beers were bought out by British conquering titan Cecil Rhodes and subsequently bought out by German conquering titan Ernest Oppenheimer. No one conquers the world for more than fifteen minutes.

Diamonds are pure carbon, pieces of coal, more or less, buried beneath hundreds of miles of molten rock, emerging one billion to three billion years later as shining stars, like hardened fire. The carbon that forms them comes from the earth's mantle, the layer of molten matter that forms the bulk of the planet. But some diamonds come from organic matter forced into the mantle—that is, the corpses of primeval life, sunk to the bottom of the ocean, forced by earthquakes toward the center of the earth, and pushed up by volcanoes as xenoliths, or foreign rocks, to the earth's surface billions of years later. Others come from meteorites, carbon remnants of the corpses of distant stars. Which is a long and complicated way of saying that, despite all the conquests across the surface of the earth, nothing is ever really lost.

Yet something happens to those pieces of coal under the intense pressures that they withstand beneath the surface of the earth. Buried and trapped for so many years, they emerge only after they have hardened into glowing, impenetrable stones. And then, captured by the mining cartels and gemologists of the world, they are classified and reclassified into smaller and smaller groups, each with its private level of refracting potential and its irreparable dents and flaws—and no one is able to recognize any longer that their source, miles and miles away so many years ago, was more or less the same.

JAKE COULDN'T remember the last time he had been to New York's diamond district on Forty-seventh Street. Actually, that was a lie. He could remember, but chose not to. Whenever that distant moment was, he might as well have been a different person at the time. And it was certainly before they had put up those tacky gateposts at its Fifth Avenue and Sixth Avenue intersections, the ones with the giant plastic diamonds on top of them, or at least he hadn't noticed them the last time. When he saw them, he laughed out loud, then stifled his own laughter as he found himself stared at by dozens of Hassidic Jews dressed in dark suits and black fedoras as they entered the plastic diamond gates.

Mad Hatters, Jake thought as he glanced at the passing Hassidim, remembering the tea party scene from *Alice's Adventures in Wonderland*. He had always found the phrase "Mad Hatter" pretty ridiculous on its own, but once he saw a museum exhibit about labor in the nineteenth century which set him straight about what made hatters mad in the first place. Long ago, hatmakers treated the felt for hats with mercury, and the exposure to mercury caused the hatters to develop neurological problems that sometimes led to insanity. Indulging a cruel thought, Jake wondered if the Mad Hatters of Forty-seventh Street suffered from a similar ailment. Something about black fedoras seemed to send people off the deep end. The Amish, he noted, had the same problem. Despite their fedora-induced risk of madness, however, the Mad Hatters did seem to know a lot about diamonds. For reasons yet unstudied, some amazing percentage of the diamond businesses on Forty-seventh Street were owned by Hassidic Jews—and despite their insanity when it came to things like hats, when it came to jewelry, the businessmen of Forty-seventh Street could not have been more sane.

Once a week for the past month, usually late in the day, Jake had taken the bus down to Forty-seventh Street. At first he had just peered into the display windows, learning the different sizes, different shapes, different settings, so many so similar to one another but no two exactly alike. Trying to guess what style would suit her best, Jake felt like he was searching for Leora herself in a police lineup, unable to rely on eye contact through the one-way glass. It should have been obvious, but it wasn't. Did he really know her well enough to know which one was her? After days of gawking through glass, he dared to set foot in the stores themselves, like a diver plunging into the open ocean after preparing only by staring into an aquarium. Only after many days of studying the treasures at the bottom did he feel ready to bring one of them up to dry land.

Jake opened a door in the tiny slot between two giant, flashing jewelry stores, passed through the metal detector at the entrance, and marched up to the reception counter with confidence. "I have a ten o'clock appointment with Mr. Abramovitch," he told the security guard. On a last-minute impulse before he left his apartment, he had put on a tie.

The guard, a fat man with thick hands and a stomach lurching over his wide leather belt, looked him over. Jake felt better about wearing a tie. He watched as the guard's bald head began peeking out from under his cap, crowning a pink face with bright blue eyes. His name tag read "Peter."

"Mr. Abramovitch went to a trade show today," the guard said. "But his son-in-law can see you."

"Son-in-law?" Jake's stomach shuddered as he clutched his wallet's outline on the outside of his pants pocket. Here, he thought briefly, had begun the classic bait and switch. Then he remembered his telephone conversation with Abramovitch. The diamond dealer had mentioned that he might be out of town this week, but that his son-in-law could see him instead. "He's a great guy," Abramovitch had avowed. "Not a good guy—a great guy. You've got nothing to worry about with him."

"That's right, his son-in-law," the guard answered. "He's been in the business for a while. Is that all right with you?"

Jake glanced at the guard's pink forehead, swallowed, and smiled. No lousy son-in-law was going to stand between him and a diamond. "Sure, no problem."

The security guard motioned for Jake to come around to the back of the desk, tapping out a combination on a keypad to open a vaulted elevator behind him. Then he reached into the elevator to press one of the buttons. Jake stepped in and watched the doors close in front of him.

The elevator began moving upward. But in Jake's stomach it moved downward: down, down, down, down to the depths below the bottom of the ocean, miles and miles and miles beneath the surface of the earth.

A HASSIDIC MAN sat waiting for him at a desk in a small room, behind a table with a black velvet cloth on it, next to a wastebasket filled with torn luggage tags from KLM Royal Dutch Airlines, perhaps since, as Jake vaguely recalled, Amsterdam was a major diamond-cutting center—or was it Antwerp? Antwerp, he decided. Jake felt a sudden warmth at spotting the familiar luggage tags, as if he had just recognized an old friend's picture on a stranger's desk.

The Hassidic man was reading something on a piece of paper, but when he noticed Jake, he immediately stood up. The man looked about Jake's age, or maybe a little younger. He had a bristly beard, surprisingly light in color, and his hairline had already receded beneath his black fedora. When he came out from behind the desk, Jake saw that his eyes were bright blue under the shadow of his hat brim. He took off his hat and laid it on the desk behind him; his head was still covered underneath it by a large black yarmulke. A hat trick, Jake thought. Now the tea party can begin.

"You must be Jake," the Mad Hatter stated carefully, like a man reading from a script. His voice was calm and direct, with no trace of a whine or stutter.

Jake looked at the young man's hat on the desk and gulped. "I'm looking for a round brilliant cut stone, about three-quarter carat, VS2 or SI1, around H or I color class, in the range of four thousand to fifty-five hundred dollars," he announced.

The Mad Hatter laughed. "And I'm Yehudah. Pleased to meet you."

Jake blushed, laughing a nervous laugh and offering Yehudah his sweaty palm. Nothing like starting out on the right foot, he thought to himself.

"So you've found the right girl, huh?" Yehudah asked, shining a mischievous grin that Jake didn't quite expect.

"Yes, I think so," Jake said with a smile, feeling the color draining gently out of his face.

Yehudah raised his eyebrows. "You think so, or you know so?"

Jake paused. The undue familiarity made him uneasy. "Oh no, no, I mean I know so," he stuttered.

"Good, because we're not all that excited about returns around here," Yehudah laughed. The laugh annoyed Jake. It reminded him of the kind of laugh the cool kids used to use to laugh at him in elementary school, though he couldn't picture Yehudah as a cool kid. Jake wondered if there was such a thing as a Hassidic cool kid. Probably not.

Yehudah kept talking. "Don't tell me you think so, tell me you know so. The more people think about this sort of thing, the worse off they are, in my opinion. Because if you have to think about it, then why are you doing it?"

Jake considered for a moment. The Mad Hatter had a point. "Fair enough," he conceded. "But I know so."

Yehudah slapped his hand on the table, making both Jake and the black velvet jump. "Good, we're all set then. Now let's get this straight—you want round brilliant cut, three-quarter carat, VS2 or SI1, H or I color class, from four thousand to fifty-five hundred dollars. Correct?"

Jake was impressed. Perhaps Abramovitch was right after all. "Yes, that's it."

"Great. I'll just go over to the vault and bring out some samples, and we'll see what we can do." Yehudah stood up, cocking his index finger at Jake in another gesture Jake didn't expect. "I'll be right back," he said. "Don't think too much while I'm gone."

Jake smiled and loosened his tie. "Don't worry, I wouldn't think of it."

And the Mad Hatter disappeared.

JAKE'S MOTHER had warned him when he was nine years old about the perils of thinking too much. It was a good thing she had told him then, because she only had thirteen years in which to warn him about these things. Sometimes Jake wondered whether she knew, in some untapped pool beneath conscious knowing, how the clock of her life had been fixed.

"Nobody likes a person who sits around pulling everything apart in his head," she had told him one day in her clipped Netherlands English. He was helping her make dinner in his nine-year-old way, setting the table and chopping peppers (being very careful, of course, not to let the knife slip and cut his finger, not to deprive himself of this rare privilege, rarer and more valuable than buried treasure, of cooking with his mother), while his mother told him stories about one of her old lovers, from before she met Jake's father. Her "lovers." She was allowed to say that because she wasn't American. Americans weren't allowed to have lovers, unless they were describing their extramarital affairs. Instead Americans were stuck playing like children with "girlfriends" and "boyfriends," even if the girls and boys in question were well into their sixties. God forbid you should grow up.

"Some intelligent people think that if they sit there taking apart their problems all day long, they'll eventually see how to solve them. But they're wrong. When you surround yourself with your own thoughts, when you walk around thinking and talking every tiny aspect of life to death, all you're doing is taking all those little pieces of yourself and building a wall around yourself that you'll never come out of," Jake's mother declared, almost with anger. "Thinking too much is selfish."

It took Jake until his first year of college, five years after she died, to see what his mother had meant. In high school, people primped and preened and squealed and shouted whenever they reeled in the boy or girl of the moment. But in college, with the agony of sharing rooms and staying up all night for stupid reasons, love became something burdensome, a heavy and tedious affair. People in college and thereafter didn't talk about love. They talked about "relationships."

"Relationships" were something entirely different from love affairs. Unlike love, which was something light and deep, unquestioned and unconditional, "relationships" involved "work," "struggle," "compromise," "problems," and "issues." Jake's friends, both male and female, loved nothing more than to sit around and talk for hours about the "issues" they needed to "work on" in their "relationships." Relationships weren't fun. They were serious, a full-time job. And Jake watched his

friends building little walls around themselves with each new relationship, so that no one could reach them anymore. They became like
cities under siege, bricked in by their issues and struggles and compromises and by their need to be loved without ever needing to love.

Jake had wasted years of his life on someone like that. Rebecca was
the reason he had been to Forty-seventh Street before. Not that she
came with him, of course. Not that she even knew he was thinking
about it, though if she had known she probably would have left much
sooner. They had been "relating" for almost five years when she told
him she needed "space," time to "think," time to "work things out," and
accepted a fellowship to spend a year in Heidelberg. He cared too
much to risk begging her to stay. In December he came to New York to
visit his father and went to Forty-seventh Street to look at diamond
rings. Just window-shopping, that's all. Just to look. When he stepped
into the subway car on his way back to his father's apartment, he saw
Rebecca and another man wrapped around a subway pole together,
working things out. From then on, he only took the bus.

With Leora, the only thing he ever needed to "work out" were the
solutions to the puzzles she constantly threw at him. Once, on the
anniversary of the day they had met, he had to go to a conference in
California, promising to take her out to celebrate when he returned.
When he arrived at his hotel room that night, he found a slide projector propped up on a chair in the middle of the room, its cord attached
to an outlet by the darkened window and pointing at a large segment of
bare white wall. He called the front desk and told them someone had
left something behind in Room 413.

"Left something behind?" the man at the front desk asked, his accent
vaguely European.

Jake sat on the bed, staring at the slide projector, which was squatting
on the chair and aiming at the wall like a cannon, ready to blow it up.
He noticed that it was loaded. "Yes, a slide projector. There are slides
left in it too. Someone should come and pick it up." Jake swallowed.
"Or I can bring it down myself, if that's better for you."

"Ah yes, the slides," the man laughed. "No, you do not have to return
them here. They are yours."

"Mine?"

"You are in Room 413, yes?"

"Yes, but they're not—"

"They have been sent to you."

"What?" Jake heard himself croak into the phone.

"They were sent here to you, in Room 413," the man intoned. "You can return the slide machine when you finish. But the slides you keep."

Jake hung up the phone and looked at the slide projector, hesitant. Standing up with care, he took a few short steps toward the slide projector, inspecting it. A normal slide projector. It occurred to Jake that he hadn't seen a slide projector in ages, since high school even. Slide projectors were going the way of the gaslight and the treadle sewing machine.

It was January. The city outside had grown dark. Lights were beginning to come on in the buildings outside the hotel room's giant window, little panels of offices and apartments with people glowing in them, leaning over to draw the blinds. He stepped backward, keeping his eyes on the slide projector as if it might wander away, and reached along the wall to turn out the lights in the room. As he fumbled for the light switch, he jumped as he noticed his own figure reflected on the room's giant windowpane. With relief he turned out the lights, setting the slide projector's power switch in his line of sight as his eyes adjusted. Crouching next to the machine, he turned on the power, alarmed by the sudden lion's roar of the projector's fan and the blinding square of white light on the wall, burning like fire. When he pushed the button to change the picture, he found himself kneeling before a giant projection of Vermeer's painting *Woman in Blue Reading a Letter*.

The slides continued, a vast selection of paintings from the Rijksmuseum, tiny scenes and crying prophets. The final slide shone pure white light, with Leora's tiny handwriting inscribed right on the slide film—handwriting that was actually legible when projected to hundreds of times its actual size. All it said was, "Thank you."

With Leora, there was no need for "work," for "issues," for "compromises," or even for a "relationship" at all. Leora was simply a light. And he was a square of slide film, and she shined herself through him and made all the things inside him appear, not as strewn bricks around his feet but as a clear image projected on the screen of his life, something he could point to at last, after so many years of darkness, and say, without thinking, "Here I am."

"HERE I AM," Yehudah heard his own solid voice announce. The customer looked up to see him strutting back into the room, his hands full of black leather pouches with white labels. "There's a whole range of cuts here, so you'll be able to tell the difference."

"Not including the unkindest cut, I hope," Jake smirked.

Yehudah smiled, feeling slightly resentful about not getting the joke. He took out ten different stones and laid them on the black velvet, picking up the last one and fastening it between a pair of jeweler's tongs. "Nothing is more important than the diamond's cut," he said, pulling a large loupe out of his pocket. He felt a deep satisfaction as he laid the loupe down on the table for the client, a satisfaction that wiped away any annoyance he might have felt about jokes he didn't get. The client could say whatever he wanted, but he, Yehudah, was the one in control. He detected within himself a surge of competence, mastery, power. Before he started working here, he hadn't experienced that feeling since scoring his very last goal on the soccer field in college. He had missed it.

"What you mainly want to look for," he continued, driving toward the goal box, "is the height of the stone's crown compared to the depth of the pavilion—that's the bottom part—and also the width of the table, which is the flat part at the top. That's what determines the two most important things for the stone's cut. The first thing is brilliance—how well the stone reflects white light. The second is fire, which is the way the stone divides light into rainbow colors. What you're looking for is a balance of brilliance and fire."

Jake had begun examining the diamonds through the loupe. It was amazing how much you could see when you really looked. Diamonds that appeared exactly alike on the table, once projected through the magnifying lens, resolved into fabulously different shapes, like a row of faces, each one unique. "Brilliance and fire," he repeated. "Wouldn't either one of those be good enough? How about just brilliance, or just fire?"

"No." Yehudah took a pen flashlight out of his pocket and shone it on the stone Jake was holding in the tongs. "Look at this one you've got here. See? Lots of white-light reflection, but not a lot of rainbows in the diamond itself." Jake peered through the loupe. The diamond glowed like a fading lightbulb. Yehudah switched off the penlight. "It ends up looking dull. Compare it to this one," he said, unscrewing the tongs and fastening them onto another stone before shining the light again. "See the colors? Nice, but the light barely reflects. It ends up looking glassy. Most of them have too much brilliance and not enough fire, or too much fire and not enough brilliance. You end up with a lot of low-grade stones that way."

"My own problem is not enough fire," Jake ventured, wondering if the Mad Hatter would catch on.

Yehudah caught on. "And mine is not enough brilliance."

RIVKA, YEHUDAH'S WIFE, had been shocked in their private room on their wedding day when her new husband, touching her for the first time, ever so gently slid his tongue between her lips. She didn't stop him, but despite her efforts not to show her alarm, Yehudah felt it—the stiffening of her lips, the sliding of her mouth to one side, as if she had been expecting something more akin to a kiss on the cheek. That night he peeled off her clothes with shaking fingers, restraining his urge to rip her dress off and plow into her, instead revealing her body bit by bit, as if he were removing the shell of a hard-boiled egg before sinking his teeth into the yolk. He kissed her repeatedly as he lowered himself on top of her, careful not to crush her, keeping her face occupied with kisses, stroking her hair and holding her hands when she yelped in pain, and trying as hard as he possibly could, for the first time in his life, to make love instead of having sex.

She knew that he had had girlfriends before. It was no secret that he hadn't always been religious. But it wasn't until their wedding day that Jason realized that what she probably thought he had done with his old girlfriends was radically different from what had actually occurred. If he had asked her to guess, she might have ventured that he had dared to hold hands with them, or maybe to kiss them goodnight on their parents' doorsteps. Never in three thousand years would she have guessed that of the women her new husband had slept with in his short lifetime, she was number seven.

At least one of them hardly counted, he reasoned, since they were both drunk at the time and he barely remembered her name. But the others had meant something, even if all they had meant was the stupidity of overgrown friendship, of boundaries crossed and sometimes regretted, though usually not regretted at all. Once it was just the stupidity of thinking that a driver's license was a diploma of adulthood, paired with the miracle of having the backseat of a minivan and an empty Costco parking lot in which to prove it. On at least three occasions he had even been in love.

Leora had been one of the three, and she was the only case he regretted. He had made her sleep with him. Not "forced," exactly. He was on the soccer team, not the football team or the boxing team. But "persuaded" would have been too gentle a word. "Pressured" was more like it, though he hated that word too. It reminded him of someone preaching to him in junior high school about drugs. (For all that education against caving in to pressure, he thought to himself, why hadn't anyone ever taught him not to instigate it?) The most accurate word might have been "tricked," though that attempt had been unsuccessful. She was a bit naive, then. She had shared his bed many times, literally sleeping with him whenever she found herself in his room at three in the morning and was too tired to go home. On one such night, in the heat of the moment, he had asked her not to go home that night, to stay with him. He knew what she thought he meant, and he knew what he really meant, and he knew that the two weren't the same, but he just hoped she wouldn't ask him to clarify—and he felt a raw, unchecked power surging through his flesh when she didn't. He already had her pinned to the bed by the time she told him to stop.

He stopped, of course. He wasn't on the football team. But "stopped" was also a misleading word, because in truth that night was only the start of it, the first in a long series of nights of pushing her, bit by bit so she barely noticed him pushing, until having sex remained little more than a technicality. It also didn't help matters that the entire soccer team was monitoring his progress almost as closely as they followed Brazil to the play-offs in last year's World Cup. He had known his teammates longer than he had known her, after all, and unfortunately he was the one person on the team who couldn't lie to save his life. The day he came to the locker room—it was off-season, but a group of them liked to train together regularly all the same, to stay in shape—with the long-awaited news, though, he felt sick to his stomach as soon as he said it. And he felt even more nauseous when the team burst into a chorus of whooping cheers, high-fiving him as if he had scored the ultimate goal, as in fact he had. He stayed a moment in the locker room after they filed into the gym, reeling with nausea and holding his mouth open over the toilet for a while, but nothing came out. That was the problem, he realized as he braced himself against the toilet bowl, his strong hands sliding along the slick porcelain rim. It wasn't going to come out. Everything he had done to her hardened inside him like a lead bullet lodged in his gut.

He slept with her many times after that, but there wasn't a single time he slept with her again that the image didn't flash through his mind of that day in the locker room bracing himself against the toilet, of that ugly thing lodged inside him that he could never remove, of how he could never return to the person he used to be, unburned by selfish fires; that the Jason he had been before had been charred and destroyed forever. He ignored that image for a year, maybe more, until he couldn't ignore it anymore. He began to hate himself. And then he fell into his new world like a diver plunging into living, purifying waters, that animal hole on the soccer field tripping him like a proof of God's presence in the world. Now when he recited his prayers, he sang out loud the words written in the prayer book, his secret vow to God: "Turn us to You and we shall return—renew our days as of old!"

"How old are you?" Jake asked suddenly, looking up from the jeweler's loupe. His own question took him by surprise. Being with Leora had given him some bad habits, not the least of which was the habit of asking strangers obnoxious questions.

Yehudah snorted, feeling attacked. This guy was just a customer, his ten o'clock. What the hell business did he have asking questions that didn't have to do with clarity and cut? "Twenty-nine," he proclaimed, lying upward.

"Me too," Jake replied, lying downward.

Yehudah believed him and snorted again, feeling less ashamed of his real age than vaguely pleased by it. He scanned the customer in front of him. A Jewish guy, of course, but clearly one of these Jews who could care less about Judaism, who probably thought it was some outdated code with nothing of value left in it, the type who hadn't celebrated a single holiday since childhood—a heretic, why not come out and say it? And this guy was also the type, Yehudah deduced, who had been living with his girlfriend for years and years, and sleeping with her for even longer, not even considering marrying her before doing any of the above, never even contemplating letting down his guard until some ridiculous number of years later. God forbid you should trust another person. He felt for a second saddened and even genuinely repulsed, imagining every man he passed on the street repeating the same mistakes that he himself had made, again and again and again. What are these people waiting for, he thought to himself, all their hair to fall out?

"Is that about average, do you think?" Jake asked. It was amazing how similar he had become to Leora.

Yehudah snorted for a third time. This guy was starting to remind him of someone, someone he didn't want to be reminded of. But who?

"Average for what, getting engaged? Probably," Yehudah answered, stroking his beard. "Actually, to be honest, most of the guys we see are a little older than that, more like thirty-two, thirty-three."

Jake detected a note of smugness in Yehudah's voice, which he had somehow expected. That was what bothered him, he realized. Mad Hatters always seemed so smug, as if having no doubts about one's own life were itself the highest virtue. As a scholar, Jake believed, in the deepest sense of believing, that this wasn't true, that doubt itself had the power to be the very agent of truth. He knew that the people who had changed Jewish life for the good hadn't been the ones who didn't question life as it was, but those who did and who therefore demanded better—the brotherless daughters in the Book of Numbers who had demanded their father's inheritance despite their gender, the prophet Jeremiah who had insisted that people pray to God and build houses and plant gardens even in exile, the rabbis who had required that the mother's religion, not the father's, determine whether a child was Jewish so as not to abandon children of rape, the obstinately secular Theodor Herzl, who actually stated, exactly fifty years before the creation of the state of Israel, that there could be a state of Israel in exactly fifty years. Yet despite everything, Mad Hatters still roamed the planet, remnants of a seventeenth-century religious revival in the Carpathian Mountains who somehow felt the need to act smug while selling diamonds to professors of Jewish history. That pissed him off.

But there was something different about Yehudah, Jake thought, something slightly off from your standard Mad Hatter. What was it? He had, of course, looked at Yehudah's ring finger already—as he had been looking at every man's ring finger lately, on the streets, at the university, on the bus. Wide rings, narrow rings, round rings, flat rings, gold, silver, platinum, Jake didn't really care what they were so much as he cared *why* they were. Behind the rings on these legions of unfamiliar men, he thought to himself each time he spied one on the bus, stood legions of women, one woman for each man's ring, tied to each other by tiny invisible strings attaching her ring to his, a web of millions of invisible strings crisscrossing the whole city, the whole country, the whole world. But then he remembered that some religious Jewish men don't wear wedding rings; only the women do.

"Are you married?" Jake asked, glancing at the Mad Hatter's beard. Then he suddenly remembered who he was talking to: Abramovitch's *son-in-law*. God, did he feel dumb.

Yehudah, however, didn't notice the mistake. He snorted again, then used his most offhand voice. "Sure," he replied. His answer made him genuinely proud, as if the man had just asked him whether he had graduated with honors. Still, something about this customer was really getting on his nerves. It was as if the man were judging him, staring at his beard as if he really knew what he was looking at. What he couldn't see, Yehudah thought, was the beauty of the world hidden beneath the black hat resting on the desk behind him—a world where every moment could be considered holy, a world where your sincerity mattered more than where you went to school or how much you were paid, a world where nothing was considered worse than playing recklessly with someone else's heart, a world where people knew who they were and didn't spend years on end deciding it, a world where large numbers of people built entire careers around the academic study of how to be a better person, a world where you didn't need a medical degree to justify spending every Sunday afternoon visiting strangers in a nursing home. How could this customer stare so hard and still manage not to see a single thing?

No glasses, Jake realized. That was what made this guy seem different. He had never seen a Hassidic man before who didn't wear glasses.

"So you know how this all feels, huh," Jake said, smiling a fake smile. Then he panicked for a moment, realizing he might have said the wrong thing again. He glanced at the Mad Hatter's forehead, where beads of sweat were gathering on the crown of his head like droplets of dew on a leaf. His was probably one of those arranged marriages, Jake thought to himself. The guy probably never even kissed a girl before he got married. If he's twenty-nine now, he's probably been married for years on end, with a flock of children too. Still, he thought to himself, there was room for his own comment to make sense—after all, maybe it was just a friendly comment about getting married, not about the ecstasies and agonies of romances or the unbounded, unimagined, unanticipated joy of suddenly, stunningly, being *done*. Jake felt himself beginning to turn red, wondering what Yehudah would say.

But the Mad Hatter showed no signs of alarm. Instead he smiled back. "Oh, sure," he laughed. "You think this is tough? Try buying an engagement ring for a girl whose father owns a diamond business. I mean, we're talking about a girl who's actually going to *recognize* a one-and-a-quarter carat, G-class VS1. That was a nightmare I wouldn't care to repeat."

Jake laughed to be polite. Yehudah, a smile lingering on his lips, lined up the three stones that had been judged best in cut and moved the others aside to form a constellation on the table. Three stars of Orion's belt twinkled in a firmament of black velvet. "Now you'll see what we mean by diamond color," Yehudah said, speaking in his father-in-law's voice: dismissive, professional, like a knife on a chopping block. "Look at these three. Which one's the whitest?"

Jake looked at the three gleaming stones. The diamonds winked at him in turn, identical against the deep black velvet, each whispering at him—choose me, choose me, choose me. First one flashed whitest, then another, then the third. A sudden uneasiness crept into Jake's stomach, as if he were competing in a spelling bee and had just been asked to spell a word he had never heard of. The unpronounceable word barbled in his throat. Still, he didn't look up, staring at the stones, silently begging them for an answer. They laughed.

"You can't tell, can you?" Yehudah asked.

Jake felt himself turning red again. "No."

Yehudah smiled at him. "Neither can I. But now you will." He reached over to the desk behind him, picking up a piece of white card stock folded into the shape of the letter M, and placed the stones in the white paper's crease. As each of the diamonds landed in the crease, Jake watched, fascinated. The three diamonds, winking their identical winks against the black cloth, fell onto the white paper and changed colors as if stripped naked. The first sat tarnished on the paper, throbbing a bruised and tawny color; the second glowed a dim yellow like a dying gas lamp in an old painting. The last one, exposed and revealed, blazed burning white.

"See, you never know, out of context," Yehudah said. "You just have no idea."

Jake looked up from the glittering stones into the Mad Hatter's blue eyes, and agreed.

BEFORE HE met her, Jake used to feel like the butt of that old joke describing a Rhodes Scholar: a bright young man with a brilliant future behind him. Ha ha. She was the first person in years who didn't see him that way. He wanted to fall at her feet.

It was a night when they had come pretty close, a Friday night. Leora's roommates were out of town, and they had spent the evening at her place having their own private sabbath dinner, singing the prayers together before retreating to her room for a screening of the original *Planet of the Apes*. After aping the apes, along with the human among them lost on his own planet, they took off most of their clothes, but not all of them. Jake asked her once more, but Leora still wouldn't sleep with him.

"I'm pretty insulted," he said for the seventh time in what felt like as many months, with more humor than exasperation by now, "that you'll sleep with some random college boyfriend, but not with me."

"You should be flattered," she told him. "It's just that Jason was the kind of boy you sleep with, that's all."

Jake scowled at her. "Oh, so I'm the kind of boy you don't sleep with."

"Yes, that's right," Leora answered.

"You're very Leorable, you know," he said, after a moment of trying to decide whether or not to say what was on his mind. He decided to go for oblique over sentimental.

"What's that?"

"The opposite of adorable."

She threw a pillow at him. He cowered in the corner of the bed, aping the human captured by apes, until they started communicating in ape noises again. Growling the words in her nearly incomprehensible ape voice, she grunted, "Would you put my pajamas on for me, and then I'll send you home? They're in the bottom drawer."

It was a tremendous tease, and she knew it. Jake frowned as he reached over to the drawer where she kept her pajamas, ridiculous flannel pajamas with red and blue checkers, like something a six-year-old would wear. Fighting his own fire with all his might, he turned back around to where she was sitting half-naked on the bed, stretching out her arms for her pajama shirt. He made a face like a crazed alien ape and put the pajama pants on over her head.

Leora started laughing from inside the pants, so hard that he had to pull them back off her head so that she wouldn't suffocate. But when the elastic waist was stretched around the crown of her head, holding her hair back from the face that never failed to fascinate him with its endless mimicking expressions, she looked at him with a gaping smile he had never seen before. Jake saw that smile and knew, as if he had seen her face projected in a giant image on a bare wall with a voice in the background reading a caption, exactly what she was thinking. That thought made him forget about feeling insulted or flattered, made him forget about how much he wanted her, because he suddenly understood that she was going to be his:

Someday, he heard a voice reciting the thought written across her beautiful forehead, you'll be tucking our daughter into bed, and you'll pull her pajama pants over her head and make her laugh so loud, and I'll be standing in the doorway waiting for you to drink in my smile, unable to believe how lucky I am.

"FINDING THE right stone is really a matter of luck," Yehudah said as he lined up the VS2's and SI1's, already chosen from the earlier selections of color, carat, and cut, on the black velvet cloth in front of him. Jake had begun inspecting them through the loupe as he took each of them in the tightened tongs one by one, looking for "inclusions," little spots or blemishes beneath the surface of the stone. Things that people would rather not include. Yehudah twirled a sidelock in his left hand as he spoke. "Sometimes you'll have two stones that are technically the same value and the same number of natural inclusions. But on one of them the flaws will be situated such that some people will notice them right away, while the other will have flaws that you won't notice unless you're trying to find them. If you see flaws that are near the bottom of the stone, nineteen times out of twenty the prongs of the setting are going to hide it. Just luck, really."

Jake examined each stone for what seemed to Yehudah like days on end, plotting each one's inclusions with a pencil on a piece of paper in front of him. Without the loupe, all of them looked more or less perfect. It was when you stared at them through glass, magnified by a factor of ten, that you saw the slight abrasion on the crown, the minor scratch on the side of the pavilion, or, most maddeningly, the inclusions, the inaccessible flaws buried within the depths of the stone, the tiny internal blemishes that distinguished one diamond from another. He left no stone unturned, no facet uninspected, suddenly overcome by a desperate urge to find the perfect gem. Would it somehow, in some way so small that the prongs of the next few years would hide it, be a different marriage if he chose a different stone?

Yehudah sighed, the deep, patient sigh of a man much older than he. "Look," he said, "take your time, but you aren't going to find one in this class with no inclusions. And you know what? It's better that way. If diamonds were all flawless, there would be no way to determine their worth outside of quantity. At least, there would be no way to distinguish them naturally. Not every natural feature is beautiful to the eye, but if it's part of a beautiful thing, you have to take the whole package."

Jake squinted at him, his eyes magnified through the loupe. "Are you trying to tell me not to look? Because I'm going to look," he said. He smiled to let the Mad Hatter know he didn't mean it cruelly. Yet the distrust was still real.

"No, I'm just being honest with you," Yehudah said, leaning forward. "You're picking a flawed stone. And once you buy it, you've got to like all of it. So just be prepared for that."

Jake remembered the first time he met Leora, in the museum, all the horrible questions she had asked him, the nasty way she managed to drive nails right into his heart. She was still petulant now.

He looked again at the diamond below the loupe. There was a small cluster of inclusions near one of the pavilion's facets, invisible to the naked eye, probably impossible to see even with magnification once it was set. But under the magnifying lens, he could see what looked like tiny pieces of soil caught within the stone, like packed-up treasures buried in a closet, reminders of where it had come from. "I'll take this one," he said, laying the tongs down on the table.

THEY HAD been married for over a year when Yehudah finally confronted her about it. He hadn't minded at first. Yehudah knew, like everyone in his new circle knew, that his wife would be pregnant before their first anniversary. To be honest, at first he had dreaded the thought. But then he realized that it was Jason—the remnant of the old Jason—who was dreading it, not Yehudah, the new person he had become. Yehudah, the new Yehudah, wanted children, lots of them, knew that children were the greatest blessing. (The old Jason had known that too, but he wasn't the sort of person who would have admitted it. And certainly not if he had been married less than a year.) And so Yehudah waited for the inevitable. But the months passed—joyfully, days throbbing by as Yehudah remained stunned by the idea of himself as a husband, and even more stunned by this woman who sat in his apartment waiting for him when he came home at night, by her gentle voice that sang out in encouraging him, by her unexpected jokes shared only in private which made him laugh so hard he choked, by the odd change in his own voice when he pronounced the magic words "my wife." It was a long time before he stopped being amazed long enough to start worrying.

The thought first occurred to him one day at work, when a customer, shopping for an engagement ring—most of their clients were retailers, but once in a while they did have people come in on referral, looking for a single stone—had come in carrying a baby. Whose baby was it? A sister's? A friend's? His own, from an ex-wife? From a dead wife? From the woman he would surprise later that week with a diamond ring? Yehudah didn't ask, keeping the conversation carefully clipped. But as he stood on the subway that night, trying not to watch the man and woman his own age who were wrapped together around the subway pole three feet away, he found the question floating in his mouth, words written on a scroll under his tongue in a forgotten language:

"Rivka, do you want to have children?"

It was a ridiculous question. Not if Jason had asked it, but from Yehudah it was like asking whether man had been created in the divine image—something so obvious that no one bothered to think about it. Yet for the past few months Yehudah had begun wondering the unwonderable. Maybe, just maybe, Rivka didn't believe in the divine image, and didn't want to replicate it either. Maybe it was all her fault.

"Rivka, do you want to have children?"

Yehudah started to suspect. He began examining everything Rivka said and did, like a jealous man who believes his wife is sleeping with other men behind his back. He picked up each word that emerged from her mouth, particularly when she jabbered in fluent baby talk to her nieces and nephews, and held it gingerly in his mind like a jeweler holding a loose stone in a pair of tightened tongs, appraising it through the loupe of his brain for the slightest flaw. The tiniest inclusion in her speech or gestures—her strange smile upon hearing about her sister's fourth pregnancy, the intense concentration she suddenly bestowed upon her steaming vegetables when he made some joke about their own future children, the narrowed eyes she used for watching the neighbor's kids waiting for the elevator as if she were their mother—gave him reason to downgrade her to a more flawed, lower class of gem. There was a possibility, one that grew more and more distinct in his mind each day, that he had overvalued her.

After a few weeks of watching and listening to her this way, testing her clarity and cut, Yehudah went on the offensive. He searched the bedroom and bathroom drawers, knowing—in a way that would shock her if she knew—exactly what each of the several things he was looking for looked like. He racked his brain trying to remember where the last six girls had kept these things, hoping against both reality and logic that at least one of them had something in common with Rivka. The medicine cabinet was too obvious. Kim, Liz, and Katie had kept theirs in bedroom drawers, but never the same drawer. Katie hid hers inside a pair of socks, which he in his high school panic had thought too easy to discover. Liz, bolder and with hippie parents who didn't care, kept hers in a drawer full of what she called "important things," the majority of which seemed to be movie ticket stubs. (Movies she had seen with her old boyfriend Chris, mostly. That had pissed him off.) Kim kept hers next to the tampons, or sometimes right on top of her dorm room dresser, her underhanded way of bragging to her roommates. The memory repulsed him.

But Rivka, Yehudah reasoned, would need to be subtle. One day when Rivka was out visiting her sister, Yehudah came home early and turned the entire tiny apartment upside down, looking inside every pocket of every skirt, under every fold of every towel, behind and between the books that crammed their floor-to-ceiling shelves. After she came home, while she cooked, he even checked inside her wallet. Nothing. Yet there were things a doctor could prescribe that he wouldn't even know about, lots of things, things he hadn't even thought about since his high school health class. Perhaps Rivka had hidden secrets, things girls kept not in drawers, but somewhere inside themselves. Maybe even now she was cruising about among their family and friends, smiling her unnerving smile and pretending that nothing was wrong when people asked. Which meant, by implication—Yehudah instantly realized—that there was something wrong with *him*. The thought burned him in horror. Was there? The next day he went in to work and listened intently to Abramovitch talking on the phone at his desk, imagining that his clear, professional voice was actually a fabricated accent, a decoy voice speaking in code, confirming yes, that's right, we are not affiliated with that store, yes, indeed, I have your order right in front of me, while what he really meant was, yes, that's right, you are not what you thought you were—and yes, indeed, I know it.

Yehudah burned all night on the way home, fires of fury consuming him on the subway filled with overheated lovers. The city's grime squirmed along the tracks, fueling his rage like rags stuffed into a burning gaslight. When he reached their apartment, he turned the key in the lock slowly, deliberately, and pushed the door with his fingertips, inching it open. He had to do everything in tiny motions, in inches. Otherwise he would have burst into his own apartment and shouted at the top of his lungs, the way he had once seen a client who represented a big jewelry store burst into the diamond office, raving mad, screaming: "You ripped me off!"

Rivka was in the kitchen, cooking dinner. Something was boiling in a large pot, and she stood at the tiny counter space next to it, her back to him, chopping vegetables. The sound of the water boiling ruffled the air in the apartment, like waves at the seashore caressing dry land. He watched her for a moment from behind, following the imaginary curves of her body with his eyes beneath her long dark skirt. He had dated prettier girls. But there was something solid about Rivka, something stately, a firmness and a density of valor that made her rise above them all, with her feet still on the ground. As if she were a sturdy, unbending column, holding up the sky.

She noticed that he had entered the room. He saw the slight stiffening of her spine, the ripple of movement through the back of her shirt, the thousandth-of-a-second pause at her elbows before the next stroke of the knife. She knew something was wrong; that he saw right away. Still, she stood at the kitchen counter chopping peppers, refusing to turn around.

"Rivka?"

He restrained himself, slightly too much. She continued her chopping, even stepping up the pace of the knife on the cutting board. He
tried again, with less restraint.

"Rivka, I have a question for you."

She still did not turn around, nor even pause in her chopping. The
knife fell with rhythmic regularity, the pace quickening exponentially.
Stepping a bit to the side, Yehudah watched as the blade became a blur
between her hands, beating against the cutting board faster, faster,
faster. And then he asked the question.

"Rivka, do you want to have children?"

The knife kept flying between her fingers, its tempo hurtling forward,
faster, uncontrolled. In a flash the blade fell, and Yehudah, watching at
an angle, saw it land on the side of her finger. She screamed.

"Rivka!"

He leapt to her side as she dropped the knife and grabbed her bleeding hand in his own fist. She bent her head down over the tiny wound,
unworthy of her scream, and they both stood still for a moment staring
at her hand, watching as the little stream of blood slowed to a stop. But
when she looked up, he gasped. Her face, bright red, was crumpled and
streaked with tears—not the tears of a woman who had cut her finger,
but larger tears, older tears. Then she started babbling, a torrent of
words flowing from her mouth like a river swollen and roaring with
waters from a rainstorm, about how she had been ill as a child, not just
ill but fatally ill, how the doctors, dozens of doctors, had told her parents that she would almost certainly die. She didn't die, in the end; she
spent months in and out of the hospital, and to everyone's shock a miracle occurred and she was rescued. But the illness had done its damage:
she escaped with her life, but not with anyone else's. The doctors told
her parents that she would almost definitely never be able to have children. For the past six months, she had been seeing a fertility specialist,
but nothing had worked. She was sorry. So sorry.

Yehudah listened, bewildered. For a moment he couldn't speak at all,
the words he wanted to say caught under his tongue. At last he opened
his lips, seared by the pressure and fire of her voice.

"And you never told me any of this," he said evenly, controlling his
rage. "We've been married all this time and you never told me any of
this."

Rivka avoided his eyes. "No, I never told you."

Yehudah lost it. He shouted at her, in a way he hadn't shouted in years, at the top of his lungs: "Why the hell not?"

Rivka stood facing him, pinching her wounded finger. Even reduced to tears, she looked to him as if she were holding up the sky. "Because I thought—" she began, but quickly resumed choking back sobs.

His imagination completed the sentence for her. I thought you would never find out. I thought I could handle it myself. I thought I shouldn't bother you about it. I thought you didn't want children now anyway.

She tried again. "I thought—"

His imagination kept filling in the blank. I thought you didn't want a pregnant wife. I thought it might get better on its own. I thought it might not get better on its own. I thought you wouldn't care. I thought you would care. I thought it didn't matter.

She paused for a moment, waiting this time for her sobs to subside. He waited with her. When her breathing at last smoothed itself out, she said, with astounding, cutting clarity, "I thought that if I told you, you wouldn't want me anymore."

Yehudah stared at her in shock.

"But Rivka, why would I ever not want you?" he asked. He felt his own voice slicing through the air like a jeweler's precision saw, polishing the unfinished edges and rough deceit out of the space between them until it suddenly emerged, shining, the perfect cut.

"How could I ever not want you, Rivka? Rivka, I love you!"

He had said it before, many times, to many people. But that was the first time he knew what it meant to mean it.

"I MEAN it when I tell you how helpful you've been," Jake said as he took out his checkbook. "I really appreciate your honesty." The chosen one, the yet-unset, stunningly cut, I-color, VS2, .78 carat diamond lay on the table in front of him, ready for him to retrieve it in its clean, simple, shining setting the following week after the check had cleared. In his mind it was already on her finger.

Yehudah passed him a pen. "Well, if you get it appraised somewhere and there's a problem, just let me know. She's going to love it, I'm sure. You've picked a winner."

"I know, thanks to you."

Jake signed his name across the bottom of the check, feeling enno-
bled by the size of the figure above it. As he glanced at his signature, he
felt as if he had just signed a marriage contract, written in fire on a glowing coal buried miles beneath the ground, that Leora would only discover in time after it had turned into the most glorious gem—one
burning with blinding clarity, wed by brilliance and fire.

The two men stood up and shook hands again. Jake left the office,
singing his goodbye to Peter the security guard as he strolled out of the
building. Yehudah went back to the vault, with a lightness in his step as
he began putting away the unwanted stones. And both men smiled to
themselves for the rest of the day, each believing, in the hardened
believing of coal burned solid deep below the surface of the earth, that
he had gotten the better deal.

CHAPTER 9

FLOODGATES

THE DOLLHOUSE PEOPLE are waiting. They have been waiting silently for many years, but only now has their waiting become real, waiting for something in particular rather than simply waiting. They are waiting for Leora to come home.

Being with someone, Jake believes, does not so much resemble a time as it does a place. A moment spent with Leora does not join the moments of his life alongside the other moments, sliding like a bead onto the string of his life and clicking into place next to the moment spent walking to meet her at a restaurant and followed by the moment spent squinting at the sky alone later that evening while trying to make out a star. No, a moment spent with Leora separates itself, refusing to associate with the drab neighborhood of memories around it, walling itself off like an ancient quarter of a city filled with crooked streets, where you don't need to know where you are going because you are already there. Once he dreamed that she had become a tree, her feet rooted deep in the earth and her arms held high, sprouting leaves from the tips of her fingers, her wrists blooming with ripe, sweet fruits. Afraid to pick the fruits, he instead sank his teeth into them while they still dangled from her wrists. Of course, he can never tell this dream to her. Instead he decides to restore her dollhouse.

The idea came to him at work, when he overheard Jim, the departmental assistant, mention that he was going to upstate New York over the weekend for a miniatures show.

"Miniatures?" the student in the office asked. "Do you have a little girl with a dollhouse at home?"

"Don't I wish it were as normal as that," Jim half scowled, half smiled, with a good-natured exasperation that Jake always wished he had himself. "No, it's my wife who's obsessed with it."

"Your *wife*?"

"Yup, thirty-two years old and going on ten!" he laughed. "She's a collector, really. She's got three of these dollhouses, and she's always looking to expand. It's a pretty good hobby when you live in a tiny apartment."

Jake stood up at his desk for a moment, catching a glimpse of the student's half-slackened jaw and lipsticked mouth through the narrow crack in his office's slightly open door. "What does she buy at these shows?" she asked, fascinated. "Furniture?"

"Oh, you wouldn't believe what they have at these shows," Jim answered in an insider's deep tone. "I mean, it isn't just little chairs and tables there. We're talking barbecues, rugs, lawn mowers, molding, tiling, electrical lighting, trampolines. . . ."

Trampolines? Jake thought. Somehow the word illuminated something in his brain. Within the last few weeks, he had seen a trampoline. But where?

Sitting back down at his desk, he pictured the trampoline he had seen. It had been a giant one, about thirty feet across, yet it had been inside some sort of store, with giant stacks of boxes and other giant things alongside it—and then Jake remembered. Costco.

Two weeks earlier, he had been staying with Leora at her parents' house when her mother had sent the two of them on an errand to Costco. Leora was in the driver's seat, scooting her family's car down the sort of overbuilt suburban strip mall that would have made his mother laugh out loud, escorting him through the garage-style doors and into an American wonderland of consumer products that would have made his mother laugh even louder. Jake laughed too, as they passed through each Grand Canyon-sized aisle, but not at the store. He laughed at Leora, who was competing in the Costco triathlon: heaving a truckload of Poland Spring bottles into the cart, racing down the mile-long aisle to get to the front of the free-sample line, scaling the warehouse cliffs to get a case of thirty-two rolls of toilet paper ("Why don't you just take the stuff on the bottom shelf?" he asked, only to be berated, with the accompanying eye roll, "Two-ply, Jake, two-ply!"). Her exuberance in this giant's wonderland enchanted him, all the more so because what he truly knew of her was her tiny side, her obsession not just with miniatures but with the miniature rooms of time itself. She had furnished his hours and days with her voice, decorating them with miniature details that she pointed out to him—a key embedded in the sidewalk, a particular shade of blue sky at a particular moment of twilight, a pocket mirror flashed at him to show him the look on his face—teaching him, at every moment, how to live his life in the present tense.

Jake pictured Leora's dollhouse, which he had seen once, behind Leora's back, in a state of disrepair in her parents' basement, and suddenly he placed himself in the picture. He picked up the phone, reserved a rental car, and set out that Sunday for the miniatures show.

The key to miniature success, Jake realized as he marveled his way through the Costco of dolls that Sunday afternoon, was not just the level of detail but rather the level of *verisimilitude*. For instance, consider one item Jake saw on display, a boxed men's shirt. If the only issue were detail, the miniature-makers would have labored over the box, asking themselves, Does it have the right store's logo on it? But these craftsmen had a different priority in mind. Instead they asked themselves: first, if the shirt is in a box, can the box be opened? If so, is there a real shirt inside—not merely a bit of fabric but a real, tailored miniature shirt, complete with buttons, cuffs, and a real front pocket? If so, can the shirt be removed from the box? And if so, could a doll conceivably wear it? This was the level of reality Jake witnessed at the International Miniatures Show. It was exactly what he was looking for.

First he bought a complete set of the works of Spinoza, all with actual miniature text inside them. Then a small TV—which didn't actually work, to Jake's great regret, though it glowed a blank white at the push of a tiny button—and a VCR that actually accepted miniature non-functional videotapes and spit them back out with the tap of a miniature "Eject" button. Jake purchased tiny fake copies of *Gandhi*, *Chariots of Fire*, and *The Ten Commandments*, among others. He bought a set of silvery candlesticks with miniature white candles in them (although lighting them, the saleswoman warned, was not recommended), a silvery wine goblet, and blue and white china service to go on top of an intricately embroidered white tablecloth. He bought a miniature wooden easel, and then miniature palettes, paintbrushes, and a set of oil paints—real paints, of course, miraculously squeezed into incredibly tiny paint tubes, though only a doll could have the agility to actually apply them with a brush to a canvas.

But Jake wasn't looking for a canvas. Instead he set out for the home utilities section of the show—booths selling miniature hardware, where one could outfit a dollhouse with indoor plumbing, doorknobs, window shades, flagstone porches, and, most importantly, indoor electric lighting. It took some time, but at last, in a booth that exclusively sold miniature light fixtures, Jake found exactly what he needed: a small light panel that could be installed directly on the miniature easel. The perfect size for a slide.

FRANCES WAS only about ten years older than Nadav, which depressed him. To him she was an old, fat, washed-out woman, the sort of person whose presence would have embarrassed him at a party in Vienna. But in her dumpy two-family American house, she was the queen of the castle, and Nadav Landsmann—along with his son Wilhelm, or Bill, as Wilhelm was now called—was her prisoner.

On the night in question, a drab winter evening late in 1946, their little family had assembled around the horrible yellow "breakfast nook" in the blinding linoleum-wrapped kitchen. Only Nadav was eating, forcing down oily chicken soup as Frances, his salvation from the Valley of the Shadow of Death and to whom he owed his eternal gratitude forever and ever in the land of the living, watched him eat. Wilhelm was out, as usual—out with a girl, some American girl he had been going with for a while now, though Nadav still couldn't remember her name. Frances and her husband Joe, a thick, silent man with more fat than brains, weren't eating with him because they were going to a cousin's wedding. Nadav had not been invited, and for that reason he had been looking forward to this particular evening for weeks.

"Make sure you eat all the soup, it's getting cold," Frances chirped. "Look at him, Joe, he's turning into a pile of dried-out bones."

Joe smiled a halfhearted smile, stifling a snort.

Frances snorted. "Didn't anyone ever teach you to eat over there? Look at him, Joe, he's wasting away."

Nadav didn't say anything, but he began slurping the soup a bit faster, as if every mouthful might bring him closer to the moment when Frances and Joe, already dressed for the evening, would leave him alone at last.

He was right. As soon as he reached the bottom of the bowl, Frances stood up, with Joe following her in quick succession, and stepped over to the kitchen counter to pick up her purse—revealing behind it the musty framed sepia portrait of a light-eyed baby, a picture Frances seemed to move from one room to the next so that it was never out of Nadav's sight. Nadav hated it. But this time he grinned slightly when he saw it, leaning his graying mustache against the heel of his hand as Frances bustled around the room for no good reason. It was the beginning of the end.

"We'll be back by midnight at the latest, so don't worry about us. If you want to go to sleep before we come home, that's all right," Frances sang. Joe smiled at her, and Nadav wondered for a moment: did Joe smile because she was so ridiculous, or was he being just as ridiculous as she was? Never underestimate Americans for ridiculousness, he thought to himself. A few seconds later, Frances confirmed his thought by asking:

"Do you think you'll be all right at home by yourself, or should I let the neighbors know you're here?"

Nadav snorted, which, thankfully, Frances took to be an indication of his well-being. Joe opened the door for her, and she sang her goodbyes as she stepped out the door. For a second as the door was closing, she turned back, her lipsticked mouth hanging open.

"Don't forget to wash the dish—" she began, but the door slammed before she could finish. Which was a good thing, because washing dishes wasn't on Nadav's agenda for the evening.

Finally at peace, Nadav remained in his seat in one of Frances's horrible chrome-lined chairs for a moment. He let his eyes rest on the baby portrait and suddenly felt himself sliding into the image, as if he had reverted to being a baby, without a care in the world.

Most of his assets had been left behind or liquidated. The cash had all gone toward bribes, first to get out of Vienna and then out of Amsterdam. He had approached the bribes with bewilderment, as if the lease on his life was running out and the rent had suddenly been jacked up to an exorbitant price, though still within his means. He had never tried very hard to make money, but he had discovered, as a young man, that he was one of those rare people who attracted money without trying to, as a magnet attracts iron. He had had a similar effect on women. When he arrived in America, though, he was shocked to discover that he was not a natural magnet but rather an artificial one, an electromagnet for which someone had slowly, gradually, turned off the power. When he first set foot in Frances's house he knew his magnetic power was lost forever.

It was hard to pinpoint the moment when he became desperate. But if he had to, it would have to have been that evening when, after months of first assuming and then merely hoping that keeping up his friendships in high places would suffice to protect him, or that some mysterious visiting South African woman would fall in love with him and take him away with her, or that those who could pass some sort of written exam in German history would magically be deemed non-Jews, he finally bit the bullet, pulled out his fountain pen, and wrote to his mother's brothers and sisters in the United States.

He had never met any of them before. In fact, he didn't even remember their names. He had to rummage through thousands of pages of documents in the deep drawers of his desk before he managed to find the list his mother had given him about five years earlier with their addresses, on which she hadn't even remembered to include her sisters' new last names. The Dutch sounds of the places on the list surprised him. Stuyvesant. Hoboken. Bronx. He was alone in the bare apartment in Amsterdam that evening, sitting at the cramped, used desk by the window. (Where was Wilhelm that day? Nadav thought hard but couldn't remember.)

"Dear _____," he wrote in a Yiddish he barely remembered, filling in the names only later as he consulted his mother's list of lost siblings. "I apologize for not keeping in touch."

Apologize for not keeping in touch? Since when had he been responsible for keeping in touch? He crossed that out. Even kissing up to save his life wasn't worth a humiliating lie. He tried again.

"Greetings from your European nephew. It has come to my attention that—" That what? That he was cornered against the dikes like a trapped rat? That all his successes meant nothing after all? That his mother, at the age of seventeen, had chosen to destroy her own life along with his?

Nadav, who was accustomed to whipping out pages of company reports in the blink of an eye, spent hours upon hours on these letters, laboring over every word before finally dropping them in the mail.

Months after Nadav sent the letters, though—months during which he continued writing to the five of them repeatedly, always the same letter, again and again—it became obvious that most of his efforts were in vain. From his mother's three younger brothers (and, who knew, presumably their wives and children or even grandchildren by now, probably dozens of people in total, at least one of whom might have had the courtesy to pick up a pen and answer him) he received no reply. No offers of rescue, no letters sent on their nephew's behalf to representatives in Washington, no wiring of emergency funds, no telegrams assuring him that they were even alive. Not even a postcard saying, "Yes, I exist, but sorry, I'm not in the mood." For all Nadav knew, these American relatives were nothing more than products of his mother's imagination. After some time, a bundle of Nadav's letters, the ones he had sent to his mother's older sister Rachel, were returned to sender, stamped "Deceased." He stared at the envelopes, the only evidence he had that any of these people existed, and wondered: Couldn't they have forwarded them to her children? This Rachel woman must have children somewhere. They would probably be Nadav's own age, too—old enough to write back to him, even to do something for him. As the time groaned on with no replies, Nadav began to feel as if it were he, not they, who didn't exist. As if he had never existed.

One day, long after he had given up hope, Nadav received a letter with the return address "Irvington, New Jersey." In a bubbly, babbling Yiddish spiked with random English words like "college" and "retail" that Nadav had to look up in one of Wilhelm's dictionaries, his mother's younger sister Freydl wrote that of course she remembered him, or maybe not "remembered" exactly, since they had never met, but she knew him, or felt like she knew him, because ever since his mother had left home they had talked of nothing else when she was a girl, about how her sister had a baby so far away, and it was such a tragedy how the father had died before the baby was even born, before anyone in the family even met him, and her sister had sent a picture of the baby which in fact she herself now had sitting on her dresser, can you imagine, all these years Nadav's image had been on her dresser and now out of nowhere he was writing to her, she could hardly believe it that here he was all grown up, and with a son too (and here something was crossed out in thick black ink: a reference to his unmentioned wife? Nadav sighed with relief at the small vestige of courtesy that kept Freydl from asking about her), and she was sorry she hadn't written back to him sooner, she knew how urgent the situation was, but her younger daughter just got married and she had been quite distracted, and she didn't have a single second to write until just then, since she had been so busy arranging the food, and the flowers, and the guest lists, and the music, and the daughter's new apartment, but now that it was over she could help him out, she would do whatever she possibly could, and actually it was better that she had waited until the wedding was over because now she could even offer him and his son the room at her house where her daughters had lived, now that the girls were all grown up, it goes so fast, doesn't it, as a father himself he should know what she was talking about, one day they're babies and the next day, well, she even still thought of him too as a baby, since that was all she had of him, that old baby picture, isn't it incredible how the time goes by, but in fact she could even give him a job in the business she and her husband owned, at least until he got up on his own feet again—oh, she could hardly even imagine him standing on two feet, all she could see when she thought of him was that baby, poor little one!—and it would make it much easier for him, moving to a new country and everything, to at least be with the family. She signed the letter, in English characters, "Frances." Underneath her signature, she wrote, in spaced Hebrew letters printed like a child's, "Freydl." In quotation marks.

IT ISN'T easy to restore a house, particularly one that has been neglected for as many years as this one. Chairs and tables with snapped-off legs slump to the dollhouse floor; toys from other realms—cars, robots, extraterrestrials—desecrate the hallways; tiny wineglasses have been smashed. Much rearranging, repairing, and replacing is necessary when things are obscured by a thick layer of dust and forgetfulness, sometimes so much so that the task seems pointless, hopeless. But it can be done. Jake works his way through the house room by room, purging the alien accessories, gathering the scattered pots and books and toys, cleaning the windows, beating the dust out of the rugs, polishing the filth out of the wooden and tile floors, repairing the broken vessels.

Several hours later, after all the impurities have been removed, Jake at last brings in his own offerings. The miniature books he bought are displayed on a shelf in the study, where one of the dolls is now immersed in a reading of Spinoza's *Ethics*. On the top floor, in a room that is half bedroom, half playroom, the TV and VCR have recently been installed, and another doll stands beside the new entertainment unit clutching a copy of a video in his miniature hand. Down in the dining room, two of the dolls are seated at a dinner table laden with a miniature feast. In a bedroom, another doll snuggles down into a luxurious bed, awaiting her miniature dreams.

Outside the house—the real house, that is: Leora's parents' house— rain pours down in vast translucent sheets, curtains of rain, drawn closed over the entire world. As Jake works, the little window near the ceiling in the basement room rattles violently now and then, battered by winds and rains pounding on the panes as if begging to enter the house. After some time, the rains become so strong that a tide of water, trapped in the gutter alongside the house, begins rising a few inches up the windowpane. Through the windowpane, Jake can see what has become a sort of tiny aquarium. Leaves, driven by the winds, dive down into its depths. The sound of the rains wraps the house like a drawn curtain.

The train that Jake took to Leora's parents' house that day was almost empty. Jake, one of the few people in the greater metropolitan area who neither watches the news on TV nor consults any newsy Web sites nor reads the newspaper, failed to notice the warnings for the hurricane arriving that afternoon, predicted to be the worst hurricane to attack the area within the past fifteen years. Jake often suspects that he experiences life quite differently from those around him. Every day as he walks around the city, he sees people with cellular phones welded to their ears and little electronic organizers in their hands. People are always setting a time to meet someone, plotting their course of action for the next fifteen hours, deciding how much money they will need to retire. Jake has no problem with technology. Contrary to what his father accuses him of, he doesn't live in the past. It's just that he lives in the present while everyone around him lives in the future.

Living in the future wouldn't have helped anyone this time, though. A hurricane is one of the few things left on earth that no one can do anything about. And so Jake enjoys the moment, the ruffled sounds of rain making him feel all the more dry and warm and safe inside Leora's parents' basement as he places the dolls in their positions. On the top floor, in one of the bedrooms, he sets up the miniature easel with the light panel, onto which he has glued a slide of Jan Vermeer's *Woman in Blue Reading a Letter*. Beside it, he stands the doll who looks the most like Leora, fixing a palette and paintbrush in her hand. On top of the doll's head, like a crown, he places the diamond ring.

ON THE EVENING Frances and Joe went to their cousin's wedding, Nadav had spent the previous eight hours, as usual, at the "job" Frances had given him, standing behind the counter in her candy store with its blazing awnings screaming the store's name: "Columbus Candies."

"Because we were the first ones in the family to discover America— the greatest discovery in history!" Frances answered when Nadav once asked about the name, her voice shrilling with the nasal enthusiasm of the soap opera actresses who blared out of the radio each day. She gave a considered snort. "You know, I was only ten when we left, but I still knew our town over there was a garbage heap. It's more than forty years ago now, but I still can't believe your mother went back to Europe. You know what I call that? Suicide! She was a suicidal maniac! What in the world she was thinking I'll never know. And that letter we got from some office when we wrote to find out about her, telling us she died of a heart attack! As if we were going to believe that!"

"She did die of a heart attack," Nadav said, his palms becoming damp as he dug his fingernails into them. "I got a telegram from the hospital about it while we were in Amsterdam."

Babbling on in her English-spiked Yiddish, Frances wouldn't give up. "Well, maybe you're used to believing everything they tell you over there, but here in America we call that bullshit. I suppose every Jew in that hospital had their so-called heart attacks on the exact same day. I bet it was just one big heart-attack block party. God, it makes me sick. It's a miracle you and Bill made it home."

"Made it home," Nadav thought to himself as he stood at the cash register in Columbus Candies, with its ridiculous blinding red licorice and diamond rock candy, as if all anyone wanted was to break their teeth on a pile of rocks. Nadav Landsmann's business in Vienna had been worth millions. He had known the names and dates of every

Hapsburg ruler, could identify any Mozart symphony by the first four bars, had memorized the librettos of Wagner's operas just to be on the ball in his box seats. He had read histories of the Congress of Vienna for fun. He had fought for his country while he was still a teenager. He had *killed* Americans! How could she stick him behind the counter of her stupid Columbus candy store and pretend not to get it? What was this bullshit about "making it home"?

As Nadav stood behind the clunky cash register, staring at the clock on the wall and praying for the closing hour, four boys came into the store. Fat American boys, their eyes dilated from too many movie-house cartoons and their cheeks red and bulging from too much candy. Nadav watched them out of the corner of his eye as they filled their fat fists with lollipops and chocolate bars. It occurred to him, as he watched their greedy faces glancing toward the open door, that his position behind the counter made it almost impossible for him to run after them if they decided to make off with the goods. Not that he actually cared.

The boys came up to the register, giggling as they pushed their candy onto the counter as if enjoying some private joke. Nadav rang up the candy carefully, as he still did every time, focusing all his efforts on not hitting the wrong button on the infernal machine.

"Tventy-seeks cents," he pronounced, pausing before he said it to pout out his lips for the *w* sound, and then to position his tongue just behind his upper teeth, making it cling to the roof of his mouth, to trap the air for the *ih* sound in "six" before it escaped.

The boys looked at him, a perfect line of eight vapid eyes, then glanced at each other, tucking their fat chins into their jackets to conceal their furtive grins. Then all four of them suddenly jutted their right arms out in the air in a mock salute. The fattest one reached out with his other arm and swept the candy into his school bag before Nadav could blink. As they raced out of the store, they spun their fat mouths back around at him, each screaming:

"Nazi!"

THERE ARE seven dolls in Leora's dollhouse: a mother, a father, two boys, and three girls. Jake doesn't know their names. But as he positions them, each in a separate corner engaged in a separate task, he gazes at the tiny family with its tiny brothers and sisters and feels a sudden yearning.

Jake doesn't have any brothers or sisters, because his mother died. Not because she died too early, but because she was always so busy dying. When he was six years old, his father told him that she was sick. For the rest of that week, Jake avoided her, shying away from her hugs and kisses because she herself had advised him, back when the flu was going around, to stay away from people who were sick. Also, a boy in his class had recently told him about the plague, which was a disease that killed you and a long time ago somebody with this disease sneezed and half the people in the world died. When he told his mother his concerns, she laughed and said he had nothing to worry about. She didn't have the plague. But later that night he heard her crying in his parents' bedroom, his father whispering to her. After that he stopped talking to the boy at school who had told him about the plague.

Leora's mother—Ellen, as Jake is slowly beginning to call her—also had a mother who had died, Leora once told him. Not when Ellen was a child, but actually in the same year Jake's own mother had died. She had barely been in her sixties. They never talked about it, he and Ellen, but he suspected that it was one of the reasons why she liked him. They shared certain things, he noticed, as motherless people: a stubborn public competence and resourcefulness, a distaste for sharing feelings, a maddening incapacity to take things for granted, a failure to be impressed by people's material achievements, a lack of taste for going to bed angry, an inability to leave anywhere or anyone without first saying goodbye. Last Mother's Day, under false pretenses (an early birthday celebration, a belated thank-you) and without planning it at all, they gave each other gifts. A secret pact.

Jake takes another look at the dollhouse. Everything is ready, it seems. But then he notices the grandfather clock, whose little door to its pendulum—not a working pendulum, Jake sadly notes—is hanging by a single hinge. He takes out the tube of glue he has been using all afternoon and begins rolling up the end, squeezing as hard as he can. Nothing comes out. Glancing at his watch, he panics for a moment, then bounds up the steps.

Ellen steps into the kitchen as he arrives at the top of the stairs. "Need anything?"

"Yes, glue," he answers, holding the empty tube of glue in one hand and the clock in the other. "This one's run out."

Ellen begins rummaging through a nearby drawer. In the rush of quiet between them, Jake feels as if he needs to say something.

"Some storm, huh?" he asks softly, cautiously.

"You know, you're probably the only person in a hundred-mile radius who didn't know that there was going to be a hurricane today," she answers, still rooting through the drawer. "You'll be lucky if Leora's train even makes it here for your little surprise." She turns around, smiling as she hands him the glue.

"I heard about the hurricane," Jake says quickly as he takes the glue, glancing away from her, toward the window. The rain is so thick that the trees outside the house are invisible.

"Yeah, probably after you got on the train to come here," Ellen smirks. "You probably sat down on the train, when the sky outside was practically green and the rain was pouring down in bathtubs, and that's probably when you suddenly thought to yourself, Looks lahk a storm's a-comin' in—yup, I kin feel it in ma' knee."

She rolls her eyes, waiting a few seconds before joining in his laughter. Ellen has that same harsh streak running through her as Leora has, Jake thinks—honest to the point of comedy or pain. If he didn't know better, he might have mistaken it for cruelty.

"You're sure Leora doesn't know I'm going to be here? Nobody told her?" he asks for the third time that day.

Ellen groans. "How many times do I need to say it? Nobody told her anything. As far as she knows, she's just coming home for the weekend."

A tremendous smash of thunder sounds, cracking open the sky outside. Both of them turn their heads toward the window, mesmerized.

"You know what I think is weird?" Ellen asks after the rush of rain returns. "They always go around naming these hurricanes. I mean, it's not like they name earthquakes, or tornadoes, right? Or do they?"

"No, I don't think so," Jake stutters, applying the glue to the clock's tiny door and pressing it shut. All of a sudden, he feels the urge to keep the small talk to a minimum. Down in the basement, the dollhouse people are waiting.

But Ellen wants to talk. "The last one was Irma, so this one must be a man's name with a J—Jeff or Jonathan or something, was it? No, it was a stranger name than that. Maybe Judah or Jeremiah or something? I

remember thinking it was one of those more ethnic names, like Jorge
or something, but I can't remember what the name was right now. Can
you?"

"No," Jake says.

Ellen smiles. "Are you one of those people who's bad with names?"

FRANCES REFUSED to be called Freydl, even when they were speaking in Yiddish. And she always called her husband Joe, even though
there wasn't any real J sound in Yiddish, just so that when she spoke
Yiddish—which was purely for Nadav's benefit, since they spoke to
each other in English, and to Wilhelm too—you could feel the J jump
out at you like a flash of light in the dark. It went without saying that
she called Wilhelm "Bill." At first Nadav had made the effort. At the
beginning of his time with them, he went out of his way to refer to
Wilhelm as Bill, to Freydl as Frances, and to her husband as Joe, with
his best attempt at a J. Recently, though—long after he had at last
begun to feel, well, certainly not comfortable, but at least accustomed
to feeling uncomfortable—he heard Frances talking to Joe in English
behind their bedroom door. (Just the bedroom door itself used to infuriate him, with its vague suggestion of the couple's privacy behind it
while he and Wilhelm shared the children's room. The narrowness of
Nadav's bed alone was enough to make him groan in agony, feeling his
old magnetic power leaking out through the soles of his feet.) They
were talking about him, Nadav could tell, even with his poor grasp of
English. Frances confirmed his suspicions when he heard her say, in a
squawking imitation of his voice and accent, "Beel" and "Zho." That
was when he stopped trying.

Before that, he had tried. One night a few weeks earlier, Frances
invited him to a "social" at her synagogue. "There's a group of new
people there who just came from Europe," she told him, picking a
piece of something out of his hair as if she were his mother and he were
eight years old. The gesture infuriated him, but Frances didn't notice.
"I think you'll have a lot in common with them, being from the same
place and everything," she chirped. The same place, Nadav thought to
himself. What, the same side of the planet? "You'll go, you'll meet people, it'll be fun."

Despite himself, Nadav walked alone to the synagogue's social hall that evening, wondering if she might be right. Perhaps the whole problem was that he spent too much time with Americans—Frances and Joe, for one thing, and all of Frances's stupid women friends who came over to play some stupid Chinese domino game every week, and every child who walked into Columbus Candies whispering to his asinine friends about the Nazi who worked behind the counter. Maybe what he needed was to meet a few people who had concerns other than rock candy. Steeling every sinew of his no longer magnetic body, he pushed open the door to the social hall and forced a smile on his face, ready to socialize.

But the "social," as it immediately appeared to Nadav when he entered the synagogue's social hall, was possibly the most antisocial gathering he had ever attended. The hall—a nauseating American room wrapped in a thick layer of "modern" pine paneling and linoleum—was cavernous, making the twenty or so people in it look like little dolls. But these doll-like people were less like dolls than animals. A table of finger food had been set up in the middle of the hall, and the people were attacking it like a flock of vultures, gorging themselves on everything in sight and filling their pockets with whatever they couldn't cram down their throats. It was only after the food on the table had been entirely inhaled, to the very last crumb, that anyone felt the need to step back from the table and, in halting, stuttered sentences and with averted eyes, to speak.

Nadav ventured toward two women and tried to be friendly. Trying to tone down the German within his Yiddish, he made a few overly cheerful remarks before asking, "Where are you from?"

"Bergen-Belsen."

As Nadav later discovered, prior to his arrival the room had divided into camps: there was a group who knew each other from Bergen-Belsen, another group from Terezin, and a clique of partisan fighters who saw themselves as a sort of upper crust. When the second round of food was brought out, Nadav took advantage of the moment of blind ravenousness to escape into the dark and dirty streets. As he walked back toward Frances's house along the streets lined with their giant telephone poles and giant cars, he thought of his wife in her mental hospital and wondered: Dachau? Auschwitz? Where was she from?

THE GRANDFATHER clock from the dollhouse parlor—and it's clearly a parlor, not a living room or a den, Jake thinks as he walks back down the hall and down the stairs into the basement, clutching the tiny clock—reminds Jake for a moment of a trip to Disney World with his parents when he was a child. The three of them went on what must have been the most boring ride in the entire park: the "Carousel of Progress."

The Carousel of Progress wasn't built for Disney. It was a relic, a left-over ride from the World's Fair in New York in the 1960s. How it had gotten to Florida neither his mother nor his father could explain. They both remembered it, though, just as they remembered that entire World's Fair, in fantastic detail. Jake's mother had taken a job selling chocolate at the Dutch pavilion, a silly summer job to help pay for her studies at a university in New York, on a year abroad. They made her wear a ridiculous paper hat, and Jake's father spotted her from all the way in the back of the chocolate line. It was the wisp of black hair, peek-ing out from under the white paper, that caught his attention even as he jostled for his place in line ten yards away. Black hair. A curl tucked under a hat, as if the people who ran the pavilion had tried to make her hide it, that tiny bit of Spain expelled to Amsterdam five hundred years earlier, but there it was, a single curl of shining black hair. Jake's father must have bought chocolate ten times that afternoon, each time pray-ing that her hat might tip over a bit more as she reached to give him the melting mass (who buys chocolate in the summer?) and reveal just one more lock of that glowing, unearthly hair. When, on his tenth purchase long after the lines had dwindled away, she actually spoke to him, he fainted. But that was only because of the heat.

Jake heard this story as the three of them waited on the eternal line for the Carousel of Progress, his mother laughing, no, that wasn't how it was at all, don't listen to him, Jake, he's making it up, twisting one of the black curls now trimmed to just below her ear. Jake was eight years old then and didn't know whom to believe. He didn't think of it again until he was fourteen, and then he couldn't ask anymore.

After all that buildup, though, the Carousel of Progress was boring as hell. It was a revolving theater that took the audience through four dif-ferent scenes in the same room, each set in a different period but mirac-ulously inhabited by the same unaging family of audio-animatrons. The first scene was the one that the little grandfather clock had reminded him of. It was a log cabin scene, with a robotic, mustached mannequin rocking in a squeaking rocking chair, holding a pipe, and announcing, "HERE we ARE, at the TURN of the CENTURY." Jake hadn't understood what he meant by "turn of the century," but he suspected it had something to do with the grandfather clock whose hands were slowly turning on the cabin's far wall. The clock had ticked through what seemed like years by the time the theater revolved to the next scene, where the cabin had been transformed into a 1920s-style kitchen replete with stray electrical wires, followed by a 1940s one with a clunky television set and everything lined in chrome. The final scene took place in "the present day," but of course "the present day" had just a few Jetsons-style pieces of furniture and a digital clock, recently added, that blinked from 6:18 to 6:24.

But then the ride went haywire and the carousel stopped. At the end of the scene, instead of spinning them to a newer era or even to the exit, the digital clock blinked back from 6:24 to 6:18 and the unaging man started talking again about how wonderful life was now with all its conveniences like commercial airplanes and frozen foods and girls wearing pants, ha ha. People in the audience started getting angry. One man stood up, clearly crazy, and started yelling something about the draft. Jake realized that the other parts of the audience must be getting repeats of the twenties and the forties and the turn of the century. But even if they hadn't gotten stuck between 6:18 and 6:24, they still wouldn't have progressed, Jake registered in his eight-year-old brain, since the ride had only four parts, and if they had turned again, they'd have turned back to the turn of the century. Because in fact the only way to progress on the Carousel of Progress was to jump off of it.

As Jake steps onto the basement floor at the bottom of the stairs, clutching the repaired grandfather clock in his hand, he notices that the carpet seems somewhat damp. No, not somewhat damp—incredibly damp. Soaked. No, more than soaked. Drowned? As he gingerly shifts his weight onto the basement floor, he feels both of his feet sinking into the old carpeting, the water creeping through the sides of his unstylish canvas sneakers and oozing into his socks. The door to the room with the dollhouse must have slammed closed as he left, and Jake feels a certain inexplicable fear seeping up through his socks as he reaches for the doorknob.

He opens the door, and a tidal wave strikes his legs. Water is gushing down in an unchecked waterfall through the burst-open basement window, and the room has become an ocean, flooded seven inches deep. Seven inches of water isn't much of a flood for a house. But for the doll-house, it is a deluge worthy of Noah's Ark, already filling almost all of the ground floor. Chairs, tables, videocassettes, three of the dolls, and the library of Spinoza's works float tempest-tossed amid the watery waves. The doll who had been standing by the easel has fallen out of the second floor into the deluge, where she waves her miniature arms, calling for rescue out of the depths, still wearing the diamond ring crown on her forehead.

Jake grabs the bejeweled doll out of the water and spins around on his own drowning heels, craning his neck toward the top of the stairs and calling out for help. He swallows one word and then shouts:

"ELLEN!"

The word he swallowed was "Mom."

NADAV CONSIDERED jumping off a bridge into New York Harbor, but he dismissed the idea almost at once. First of all, the last thing he wanted was a public spectacle, with all its opportunities for well-meaning people to try to stop him. And second, if no one stopped him, then there would be a chance that Frances and Joe and Wilhelm might think he had simply run away, or, worse, been killed by someone else. He had already bought off that option, thank you. He wanted no ambiguity, no opportunity for someone to claim it had been an accident or to make it a news story that the whole world would read about for six days before forgetting it. He wanted there to be no need for some filmworthy ingratiating note, apologizing and taking full responsibility and bidding them all farewell. Nadav didn't want pity. He didn't want to jump off a bridge. He wanted to jump off the whole screaming foreign planet.

The rope he found, which he had stolen from a street construction site near Columbus Candies—the thought of someone building more candy stores made him want to vomit—needed to be shorter. Much shorter. Hauling the heavy coils of rope into the house in his sagging arms, Nadav struggled to lock the door behind him. Stupid, he thought. As if he really cared if someone sneaked in and robbed the place. Or as if there were anything worth taking among all of Frances's junk. He dragged the rope into the kitchen, put it down on her stupid kitchen table with its stupid "modern" chrome edges that made the place look like a factory, and began rooting through her kitchen drawers for something to cut the rope with.

Any of the instruments he found in the drawers—the chopping knife, the giant kitchen shears, even the cold-meat fork, if adequately sharpened—might have sufficed for his purposes, eliminating the need for the rope altogether. But Nadav had had enough of blood. As a teenager he had decided that he was finished with blood. When he first enlisted he had dreamed of becoming a doctor once peace returned, but that sentiment lasted all of a week of his time in the service. Then, he decided, no more blood. Even years later, the sight of his wife's stained undergarments used to infuriate him, to the point where, when he saw them tucked away in the bathroom, he would sometimes even throw them out before she had had a chance to clean them. A few times he even used a pair of scissors to slice them into shreds. As he clamped the giant shears from Frances's kitchen drawer down on the thick rope, his thin wrist shaking as his fingers strained to squeeze the blades together, he suddenly remembered himself standing in the bathroom of their apartment in Vienna over a marble sink, cutting his wife's bloodied underwear into narrow strips and flushing them one by one down the blue and white china toilet.

It was unclear to him whether he had ever loved her. Actually, that was a lie. It was perfectly clear to him that he had never loved her, but he had also never hated her, and her inability to give him any reason to hate her made him misunderstand his feelings, made him believe that she was in fact all he ever wanted, a woman who wouldn't torment him or betray him, a woman with whom he could live out his days in peace.

They had met only a few months after his beloved Dutch woman had abandoned him forever. Nadav was living in Vienna, where he had become a manager in a small upmarket sweater business, a job that barely paid the rent on his tiny bachelor's apartment. He spent his evenings eating meatless meals alone in his rented room, or occasionally going out with a few friends in search of fresh flesh—trips that invariably ended in a drunken stupor, often with a woman he hadn't really wanted anyway slapping him across his stubble-covered face before running off. Modern women were unbearable. Nadav was despondent, so despondent that his friends after some time began to avoid speaking to him on their girl-hunting expeditions, afraid his bad mood would spread like a bad cold. If he hadn't woken up lying in his own vomit on the floor of his room that particular morning after another girl-hunt gone wrong, Nadav probably wouldn't have even considered taking his mother seriously when he received her letter that day about Bella, a friend-of-a-daughter-of-a-friend-of-hers who had moved with her parents to Vienna when the girl's father struck it rich.

Bella and her parents lived in a massive oak-paneled apartment, far from the part of town where Nadav had rented his closet of a room. When he first visited them there, Bella's mother sat proudly at the table while a servant poured out vats of steaming chicken soup into gleaming blue and white china bowls. Nadav slurped the soup up like a starving man, pouring new life down into his own dried-out bones. Bella's father, a man with elegant glasses whose bulging ears still looked naked in the absence of the sidelocks he had shaved off ten years earlier, droned on and on about the importance of investments in this recovering economy, which was perfect for people who were just starting out, young people like this fine young man, for example, who only stood to gain from all that life had to offer. Bella herself—or, as Nadav's mother had called her, "Beyleh"—a dark-eyed waif of a girl whose hands shook when she moved, was almost silent, a queer silence that held Nadav captive in a way similar to beauty. They were engaged four weeks later, and married five weeks after that. Six weeks thereafter, Nadav used the vast sums of money his father-in-law had given them as their wedding present to buy the sweater business and make plans to expand it. Seven weeks later, he spent a month of afternoons lying on the desk in his new private office with one of the salesgirls. If Bella knew, she didn't say anything.

He had received the telegram from his wife's mental institution while he was in Amsterdam too, telling him how she had *expired unexpectedly comma complications from drug treatment stop condolences stop.* "Expired." By then he didn't have the strength to suspect what Frances would surely have assumed was the real story: an unexpected lethal-injection block party, or perhaps an unexpected complication from being forced into a room filled with poison gas comma condolences stop. But what Frances didn't know was that the boys in the candy store who called him a Nazi were right. Nadav had killed Jews too, even if not with his own hands.

How had it happened to him? Nadav wondered as the short end of the rope, at last sliced through, fell to the kitchen floor. When had he become a barbarian?

THE FLOODING is beyond human control. By the time Ellen comes down the basement stairs, the bottom step is already completely submerged, and the water level is rising. Ellen runs back up to pull on plastic snow pants and galoshes, while Jake wades desperately into the waters, gathering the miniature books and dolls and furniture floating on the waves. When she returns, Ellen steps into the ocean, standing across from Jake as they heave the drowning dollhouse out of the flood, holding it high above their heads and bearing it up the basement stairs—Jake silently begging the doorframes to rise, to let the raised dollhouse pass—and then up to the second floor, placing it on the old white-painted desk in Leora's childhood bedroom. Returning to the basement, they close the window again, blocking up the holes in the sealant as best they can with the severed limbs of Star Wars action figures, hoping the aliens will save them. Then it is time to bail.

Ellen and Jake venture out into the storm, armoring themselves in plastic hooded jackets and arming themselves with shovels and massive buckets as they plunge into the backyard ocean. Jake tries to haul out some of the water from the gutter by the basement window as Ellen struggles to dig a small ditch to divert the water away from the house. Both projects are doomed. By the time Jake runs one bucketful of water down into the street, twice that amount has poured back along the wall by the window. Ellen's ditch melts into mud, then into water, as if it had never been dug at all. A moment of eerie peace, shrouded by lightning and thunder, passes as the two of them stare at the melted ditch, the opaque brown waters obscuring who knew what beneath their growing depths. Ellen's shovel has been swallowed by the waves.

"There's nothing we can do. Let's just go into the house and wait," Ellen shouts over the rumbling rain.

They glance at the basement window, and then, wincing against the rain searing their bare cheeks, up at the house. Leora's bedroom window glows yellow out of the dark green storm sky. Through sheaths of pelting rain, Jake can just make out the silhouette of the dollhouse on the desk by the window, and for a brief second during a burst of lightning, he can even see the outlines of its miniature rooms. Then the window vanishes in a rumble of thunder, the whole house blacking into darkness as the power falls dead.

"WOLVES IN the town!"

Perhaps that was the moment, Nadav thought as he secured the rope on the protruding pipe that ran along the ceiling of the little-girl bedroom and positioned the child's white-painted desk chair beneath it, when he first felt himself becoming a barbarian—that dark and horrible winter night while he was thirteen years old, when the cry had gone out from house to house in their town, the bellowing warning freezing each household's blood in turn: "Wolves in the town!"

He was at home at the time, with his family. His was not a normal family, he had come to understand. Normal families had a father, a mother, and as many brothers and sisters as they could handle. But Nadav's family was different. He had no father, no brothers, no sisters— just him and his mother. But they also had other people in their family, in the house where he grew up. There was Hayyim and his wife Sarah, who both seemed about ten years older than his mother, and whom Nadav called Uncle Hayyim and Aunt Sarah, even though they supposedly weren't his real uncle and aunt—just close friends who, his mother had told him, had let the two of them join their family a long time ago, when he was a baby and they were all alone on this side of the ocean. And then there were his five cousins, who supposedly weren't really his cousins—two older girls, one of them married already, two little boys who were quite a bit younger, and one boy, Isaac, who was just a few months older than Nadav. He and Isaac had been together since they were babies, and had done almost everything together, playing together as babies, beginning to learn the alphabet on the very same day, sitting next to each other on the school bench and in the synagogue since they were toddlers. They even looked alike, except for Nadav's blue eyes—they had the same long, thin mouth, the same mop of dark hair, the same handsome profile—so much so that people in the town assumed they were genuine brothers, or at least cousins. But although he occasionally suspected as much himself, as far as Nadav knew they weren't related at all.

That bothered Nadav, when he was thirteen. The family never

treated him any differently, really, but he felt the difference, whether it was there or not. Simple things would make him wonder, like Aunt Sarah passing him the plate of potatoes last at dinner, after nearly all the potatoes were gone. Or Malka, the yet-unmarried older girl who, ever since Nadav had had his growth spurt the summer before, would avoid his eyes as she sat by the stove with her breasts squeezed into her too-small dress, making Nadav wonder whether she was just moody or whether she thought of him as some sort of perverted voyeur. Or the two younger boys, who would babble on and on to Isaac, it seemed, but rarely to him. Isaac never did anything like that, and in Isaac he believed he had a brother. As they sat on the school bench together, or as they walked home with the other boys, he often found himself looking at Isaac—handsome and popular Isaac, always making everyone laugh—and thinking to himself, proudly, That's my brother Isaac. Sometimes just thinking it was enough. But many times, late at night when Nadav lay in his bed staring at the dark ceiling after the lights had been put out, the thought of his brother slipped away into the room's deep shadows. And then Nadav felt as if he were a visitor in a foreign and unfamiliar place, a stranger in the house, in the town, in the whole country, in the whole world.

The moment when they heard the alarm about the wolves in the town, though, was one of those rare moments when Nadav and Isaac were apart. That night, a winter night of deep and early darkness, Nadav had just returned from the study house. Now that they were thirteen, bar mitzvah age, both of them spent many more hours on their religious studies. But Nadav would just as soon have given up his studies altogether. These days he found the ideas he learned to be increasingly unconvincing. He disliked the idea of the "diminishing of generations," for instance, which was supposed to explain why the teachings of rabbis from Talmudic times carried more weight than those of more recent scholars. Each generation, the theory went, was less impressive than the previous one, more removed from a true understanding of the Torah. Nadav wondered if his teacher had just made that one up, to congratulate himself on being older. Or then there was that other lesson, about a man forced to choose between killing another person and being killed himself. "How do you know whose blood is redder?" the text asked, as it declared that the man should submit to death rather than commit murder. "Perhaps the other man's blood is redder than yours." Redder?

What on earth did that mean? Things like that were starting to bother him, and so his mind wandered more and more as he and Isaac, as study partners, pored over the texts. Isaac, meanwhile, had become more and more interested in his studies. Passionate, even. Whenever Nadav's attention drifted off at the study-house table, Isaac would push him and push him, debating into the evening over the meaning of the law. When Nadav couldn't stand it anymore, he would sometimes go home by himself, and Isaac would stay, studying alone. It was one of those nights, when Nadav had left Isaac by himself at the study house, that the cry went out that there were wolves in the town.

Nadav and his family, or what came closest to being his family, were sitting by the stove when they heard the alarm. Aunt Sarah had told him stories before about the hungry pack of wolves that sometimes came out of the nearby forests, ripping through the town with their yawning jaws drooling, howling as they searched for people to tear apart. It hadn't happened for about fifteen years. The town had expanded a bit, driving the wolves far away into the forests. But not far enough.

"Wolves in the town!"

The family stared at each other, their eyes darting around the room as each of them began a private inventory of parents, spouses, siblings, children. Suddenly they all looked up in horror.

Isaac!

"Maybe he'll have the brains to stay where he is," Nadav's mother's voice wavered. "He'll stay in the study house. He'll be safe there. As long as he doesn't try to leave."

There was a small pause before Malka choked. "But what if he's on his way home?" she asked, almost whispering. "It's late already. He'd probably be walking home by now. What if he hasn't heard? You know how he takes his time."

Everyone stared at each other, afraid to vote one way or the other. At last, Aunt Sarah spoke, swallowing until her voice was firm. She turned to face Nadav and clenched her fists.

"Nadav, you can run the fastest," she said without the slightest tremble. "Go, run to the study house and get Isaac."

Nadav stood rooted to his spot by the stove, unable to breathe. The horrible alarm cry ran like cracking icy water through his veins. She was casting him out to the wolves!

Aunt Sarah glared at him, her clenched jaw jutting out in a rage.

When he still didn't move, she screamed: "Go! Now! What are you waiting for, the Messiah? GO!"

Nadav's feet took him to the peg on the wall where he kept his coat, thoughtlessly, brainlessly. He felt the entire family gawking at him, and as he passed his mother's seat, he registered her pleading eyes but decided to ignore them. He wriggled his body, lean and gangly from last summer's growth spurt, into his too-small coat and pulled open the front door. "Be careful, Nadav! Be careful! And hurry!" he heard his mother shout after him. But as Nadav leapt through the doorway, he heard how Sarah slammed the door behind him in case, God forbid, a lone wolf, unsatisfied with her adoptive nephew's flesh, should slip past him into the house to maul her own children. He heard that slamming door as he bounded off into the snow, but he had no time for hurt feelings. Just sheer animal terror. He had been abandoned to the wolves.

Their house was on the far end of the town, and although the town wasn't large, it was spread out more than most; there were many hills and the study house was a long walk from where they lived. Not only that, but Nadav knew that Isaac liked to take a more scenic route home, one that skirted the town's edge closer to the forest, so that he could gaze out at the thick clumps of trees or at the heavy canopy of stars and clouds and think about everything he had learned during the day. Nadav darted to the path that skirted the edge of the town, a path that was completely invisible now in the darkness and snowdrifts, and began running through the thick snow—snow like heavy powder glowing blue in the dark as his eyes adjusted—scanning the snow for footprints in the dim starlight. But the winds were howling across the hills, howling so loud that Nadav wondered whether he was hearing winds or wolves or both, blowing the snow across the surface of the earth with such force that Nadav could actually see the wind moving in waves of blown snow, turning the earth's surface into a wavy ocean or a bank of billowing clouds in the night. There were no footprints anywhere. Nadav twisted his head around as he continued racing toward the study house and saw that even his own footprints had already disappeared. As if he had never existed.

The wind burned Nadav's face as he ran through the night, searing his cheekbones. Thin watery streams leaked out of his nostrils and hardened the skin under his nose into a thin film of ice. He had to squint to see as his eyes began watering, cold tears streaking backward across his temples. He forgot entirely about the threat of the wolves, forgot entirely why he was running. Only his feet remembered where they were running to. He ran and ran, never slowing down even though his body begged him for it, responding to each clutch from his sides and each wheeze from his chest by pushing his legs even harder. He became a wolf himself. After a while he didn't feel anything anymore, not his aching sides, not the pain in his chest, not his racing legs. All he could think of was his brother.

Suddenly, only a few minutes into Nadav's desperate run, the blind blue-white landscape was interrupted by something. At the crest of the next hill, Nadav spotted a shape in the darkness, lying like a fallen log across the invisible path. As he came closer, he could make out against the glowing snow the dark silhouette of a head, a neck, even a slumped-over leg. A jolt of pure horror jabbed him in the back of his own neck. Isaac!

Nadav sprinted up to the top of the hill, but even before he reached the slumping figure the thought flashed through his numbed mind that it might not be Isaac at all. The figure loomed larger and larger as he approached it, and soon it was too big for a thirteen-year-old boy, even a tall one like Isaac. Too thick, too. When he at last reached the top of the hill, he caught his breath as he leaned over the figure, feeling like he was making the kneeling bow from his daily prayers.

It wasn't Isaac. Nadav gasped in relief when he saw that it wasn't. But he gulped the freezing air when he looked again. The man was a peasant. A thick, heavy peasant, clean-shaven and portly with beady blue eyes. Nadav recognized him from his and Isaac's walk to and from the study house. The man used to come to their town every Sunday, when he would go to church and then try his best to sell the pathetic little vegetables he grew on his scrap of hard earth beyond the forest. In the spring and summer, he would sometimes cross paths with Isaac and Nadav, who were often too involved in their own private jokes to notice him lumbering toward them until he was almost on top of them, dragging his giant wheelbarrow behind him as if he were an ox, shouting, "Get the hell out of my way, you shits! Dirty bastards, I'll cut your necks open!" In the winter months he would sometimes come to town looking for work, chopping firewood and hauling logs for old people and widows, and Nadav and Isaac would take pains to avoid him when they spotted him stumbling his way back into the forest, drunk, swinging his ax at his side. He had children, too, this peasant, two boys about Nadav and Isaac's age and two girls, somewhat younger. Nadav had seen the children sometimes on his way to the study house, when they came to town to go to church with their father or to help him or to look for odd jobs. The two brothers were just like their father, coarse and brutal. They made vile gestures when he and Isaac passed, spitting at them and pulling down their own pants to brandish their buttocks in his and Isaac's faces, sometimes even pitching pebbles at the backs of their heads. But the girls were okay, Nadav had always thought. They always seemed to be smiling, running and laughing their heads off as if they couldn't believe how beautiful the whole world was. Once, on the outskirts of the town on Isaac's scenic route, he had even seen one of them naked, her smooth child's body like a boy's, laughing as she jumped into the river on a burning summer day. When he saw her, Nadav had turned away as fast as he could, but he couldn't help thinking about it later as he leaned over his books. The pale spaces between the words on the page fused in his mind with her sunlit skin.

But now her father was lying on his side in the snow, bleeding from his neck. His ax lay beside him with its blade dark, the handle still in his pale hand. His face was frozen in an off-kilter expression of terror, one beady eye bursting open, the other eyelid pulled closed like an awning on a storefront at the end of the day. The body was completely still. Nadav smelled liquor on the corpse and realized the man had probably fallen on his own ax—or had there been some sort of fight? The wind had blown away any footprints. It must have happened recently, though, Nadav reasoned. The wolves hadn't found him yet. The pool of the peasant's blood, soaking the snow, seemed to be spreading and deepening, becoming darker and darker.

The living boy and the dead peasant paused together in the dim starlight. Suddenly and shudderingly, Nadav saw the two of them as if from the outside, as in a photograph, watching himself crouch over the peasant's bleeding wounds. In the distance he heard a howling. Maybe the wind, or maybe the wolves.

This was bullshit, Nadav decided. He couldn't keep hunting for Isaac like this. Suddenly he didn't care about Aunt Sarah or Isaac or any of them. No one was ever going to find Nadav lying in his own blood.

He wasn't very far along on Isaac's route to the study house. But after bending over the peasant's bleeding body lying at his feet, checking once more to be absolutely certain the body wasn't Isaac's in disguise, he straightened up, spun around in the snow, and stumbled over the corpse's arm. Nadav screamed a scream that was eaten alive by the howling winds and began running as fast as he could, faster than he had run before, back toward home, racing down his own invisible tracks.

Isaac could get home by himself, Nadav thought furiously as he pounded through the snow, rehearsing the words he might use to explain it to his family, his sides burning as he gulped the icy air. Isaac would have to be deaf not to have heard the alarm cries. He can run pretty fast, too, you know. Besides, he's staying later and later with the books these days. Maybe this time he'll just stay all night. Let the Torah protect him from the wolves.

It took Nadav much less time to make it home. He raced downhill, panting like an animal, thinking of nothing but wolves, huge roving packs of wolves feasting on human flesh. When he saw his own house in the distance, he ran even faster, forgetting all his excuses, bounding toward the door and pounding on it as if he were waiting at the gates of the world to come. At last his mother let him in.

Nadav leapt into the room, slamming the door tight and bolting it shut behind him. He turned to face his family, all of whom were standing in a semicircle around him. "Back so soon? You've hardly been gone at all! You call that looking?" he heard Aunt Sarah say. He tried to start his excuses, but he couldn't. He was gasping for air.

"Calm down," his mother said, resting her arm on his shoulder, which already came up to her eye level. She pointed into the room. Isaac's younger brothers stepped aside, revealing Isaac himself sitting wrapped in a blanket by the stove. "He took the main route back through town." The family began smiling and laughing, loud laughs of relief that ruffled the air in the cozy room.

Only Sarah refused to laugh. Instead she repeated, shouting: "You call that looking? You gave up on him, you coward! Thank God he decided to take the short way home! He could have been killed! He could have been killed!" Nadav's mother began to defend him, but Sarah refused to hear it, screaming again and again, "He could have been killed!"

Nadav tried to swallow his guilt and ignore her. But when he finally ventured to smile at his brother, he saw Isaac's smile suddenly melt into a look he had never seen before on Isaac's face. It was a look of pure disgust, as if Nadav were the most vile person he had ever laid eyes on in his life. When Nadav saw that face, he was suddenly blinded by the barbarity of what he had done in that moment of spinning away from the corpse in the snow. He had decided that his own blood was redder.

But all that—the peasant's neck, the blood on the snow, the numb revulsion on Isaac's face—all that was nothing, a snowflake on the tundra, a single lost teardrop in the giant salty ocean, compared with what happened between him and Isaac five years later. And then, as he climbed up on the white-painted desk chair in the children's bedroom and slid the noose around his neck, Nadav allowed himself to remember.

IN THE narrow beam of a flashlight, in the haven of Leora's childhood bedroom with its white-painted desk and chair, the half-drowned dolls lay on the dollhouse's second story like gasping refugees washed up after a shipwreck as Jake rubs at the puddles of floodwater on the dollhouse's soggy floorboards, hopelessly, with one of the destroyed dollhouse rugs. The salvaged furniture from the bottom floor is so waterlogged that all of Jake's freshly glued repairs have come undone. The paints, the Spinoza library, and the video collection have been utterly lost. All that remains is the bedroom on the top floor, where the easel stands on dry land. Jake gives the doll wearing the crown another drying wipe with the corner of his own soaked shirt and then gives up, propping her up soaked beside the portrait's frame.

He switches on the light behind the slide painting to give it one last test, thanking God under his breath that he chose a battery-powered light. The painting ignites, and the woman reading her letter bursts into a flash of color that bounces onto the diamond in the crown around the doll's head. Suddenly Jake hears a giant rushing sound coming from downstairs, winds and thunder and great waves of howling rain pouring into the house. Then, just as suddenly, the sounds stop, sucked into silence by a slammed door.

Jake switches off his flashlight and the light from the slide and stands next to the destroyed dollhouse, the unredeemable dollhouse, in the dark, trembling as he hears Leora's voice downstairs, as it laughs and flutters between her parents below, like wind on water. A few moments later, his heart begins to pound along with her feet, as he hears her bounding up the staircase. The door to the room opens.

Leora enters, a flashlight in her hands. The beam moves across the floor, gliding across the room to the bed, stopping just short of Jake's feet. She hasn't noticed him. But she sees, he can tell by the hesitant sliding of the flashlight beam, that something is different in the room. He holds his breath.

Leora's flashlight beam travels along the bottom of the bed, jumps up across the windows, then hovers, slowly, very slowly, toward the desk. The circle of light creeps up, up, up above the drawers of the desk, and suddenly the light strikes it: the dollhouse.

She gasps, then is silent, then gasps again. He hears her starting to sob in the darkness as the beam of light tours the rooms one by one, as if counting them, casting long shadows over the ruins. Suddenly Jake cannot wait anymore.

"Leora," he says, finding her free hand in the dark.

She screams in surprise, then slides the flashlight over to him, finding his hand, his elbow, his ear, his face, and yelps again, and laughs, and kisses him, and laughs again.

"Jake! What are you doing here?"

He takes her hand with its flashlight in his, guiding its light to the doll in the upstairs bedroom, the one standing next to the easel, the one wearing the ring on her forehead. The flashlight beam flickers, jittering along the doll's waist. He reaches with his other hand under the tiny easel and turns on the light behind the slide. The painting glows in the darkness.

Jake turns on his flashlight and points it below Leora's face, trying not to shine it in her eyes. "I tried to fix it, Leora," he says, feeling his voice beginning to shake. "I wanted to fix up the whole house. Really—I bought all these things for it, and I was working on it, I've been working on it all day, and I was planning it for weeks, but then the flood came, and I couldn't—"

But Leora, her face streaked with water, interrupts him, her own flashlight beam moving back to the doll beside the painting. "I like it this way, Jake. It looks more like a real house."

And then she notices the ring.

NINETEEN-SEVENTEEN. Nadav was not yet eighteen years old, and he and Isaac had just been drafted. Nadav was grateful. Tired of the endless track of study with no future in sight other than to become one of the teachers he had grown to revile, Nadav saw in the war an open gate. Isaac felt differently, of course, but there wasn't much anyone could do about it, especially with no money to bribe petty officials or to help them run away. The "brothers" cut their hair, shaved the soft beginnings of their beards, and went off. But the war gate opened wider than Nadav had ever imagined.

What was horrifying wasn't so much the numbers of the dead, the piles of bodies in the bombed-out anthills. Nor was it the proximity to the dead, the friendships forged by months spent breathing on each other in the trenches and then severed by a single shot, nor even the dead themselves, their bodies destroyed in ways that men had never destroyed other men's bodies before—blown to bits, flung over barbed wire, pierced by machine-gun fire, choked by chemicals from poison gas. What was horrifying was the fact that no one, not only not the privates but also, even more horrifyingly, not even the officers or even the generals, had even the most fleeting notion of what was really about to happen on those battlefields. Paging through a book years later in a library in Vienna, Nadav once glanced at a photograph of an elite French battalion being sent off to the war in 1914. They were riding on horseback, carrying swords.

He and Isaac had just enlisted, and much to Nadav's surprise, they had grown apart each day since they had left home, their uniforms in the trenches wrapping and separating them like sheaths of armor. In private, in the few seconds available each day, Isaac still recited his daily prayers, silently, morning, afternoon, and evening. Nadav saw his face, tight-lipped and cold, and knew what he was doing. But he refused to join him.

On that morning, though—the morning Nadav remembered as he climbed up on the white-painted child's chair, taking the rope in his hands—the attack had begun. Isaac and Nadav were positioned along the edge of the outermost trench, firing on orders from a distant blaring commander, separated from their fellow troops by a part of the trench and well beyond anyone's view. Poised with his machine gun, Nadav saw Isaac reaching into his olive green bag out of the corner of his eye, pulling out a small satchel made of black velvet and taking something out of it.

"Isaac, what are you doing?"

During a moment's respite, Isaac had ducked down into the trench, unbuttoned the left sleeve of his fatigues, and pushed it up above his elbow, revealing his pale, hairy arm. He drew his eyebrows together in fierce concentration, positioning the little lacquered box on his biceps and twisting the leather strap around his arm and hand, then placing the other box on his head with its straps encircling his forehead, and finally wrapping the rest of the long strap from his hand three times around his middle finger as he muttered the appropriate biblical verses to himself: "I will betroth you to me forever. . . . I will betroth you to me in righteousness. . . ."

"Isaac, what are you doing?"

Isaac adjusted the circle of leather straps around the top of his head, stretching the leather a bit as he pulled it down much lower and tighter around his head than usual. The black lacquered box sat on his fore-head like a gemstone in a crown. "What does it look like I'm doing?" he spit back.

"You're crazy," Nadav told him. "We're going to have to pull out of here. They're going to have us abandon this trench in the next quarter of an hour, probably even sooner."

"That's why I'm doing it," Isaac answered. The shelling was getting closer. Fully garbed in his tefillin and now beginning to recite the daily morning prayers, Isaac picked up his machine gun and put himself on guard again, still praying.

"How can you aim with that thing on your hand?" Nadav asked.

Isaac paused in his prayers and looked up at Nadav, allowing Nadav's eyes to sink into his before answering:

"How can you aim without it?"

Nadav paused for a second, taken aback as he often used to be when Isaac stunned the people in the study house with a sudden brilliant point. He felt his jaw going slack. But at the sound of another shell hitting nearby, Nadav wrenched his mind back into the trench and rammed his brother's leather-wrapped arm with the butt of his gun, growling, "Isaac, cut the lyrical bullshit, would you? It's not worth it!"

Isaac winced in pain, and Nadav watched him and swallowed. He hadn't meant to really hurt him. But as Isaac's face turned redder and purple veins began bulging beneath the skin of Isaac's forehead, Nadav saw that it wasn't the hit in the arm that had made Isaac wince.

The pressure was building inside Isaac's forehead, his lips shaking.

And then, suddenly, he exploded, shouting, "You think you can just forget about something and it goes away, but you can't, Nadav! That's not the way it works! Even if you think you've forgotten it and gotten rid of it, it never goes away!"

Nadav felt himself growing hot under his fatigues. He swallowed, then shouted, "What the hell are you talking about?"

"You!" Isaac screamed.

Nadav looked at Isaac's face, bursting red under the black leather straps, and screamed back, "You're a goddamn lunatic!"

This time Nadav turned full-face to Isaac and shoved him hard, not expecting him to move much. But to his surprise, Isaac lost his footing and stumbled backward several feet. He staggered to catch his balance again, then tripped in a small pit in the ground, landing on the dwindling ammunition stockpile.

As Isaac fell backward, a crack of sound loud enough to break open the heavens fell between them like a colossal windowpane slamming shut. Nadav himself was blown backward and slammed against the trench wall by the force of the shell that had just exploded. A moment later, desperately trying to escape from the flames of the ignited ammunition pile, Nadav would notice the gashes on his own left arm and feel the screaming pain in his own broken leg. But in that first moment, he looked only at where Isaac had been standing. It seemed to Nadav that God himself had appeared in a cloud, reaching down from the sky to grab Isaac. But when the smoke cleared, Nadav saw Isaac's body on the ground, his legs burning and his neck severed by shrapnel, his dark mop of hair, grown back to its old length in the trenches, soaked with a blast of blood. The lacquered box of the tefillin anointed his forehead with blood. Isaac's blood, Nadav now saw, was redder.

Nadav let the image linger in his mind of Isaac's anointed head, his severed neck, his redder blood. He stood within the image, feeling it, breathing it, frozen and fixed within its frame. Then, in a single leap, he stepped out of the image, kicking the desk chair he was standing on to the floor beneath his hanging feet.

And thus on that drab evening in New Jersey late in 1946, when he was not yet forty-seven years old, Nadav Landsmann took his own life, because no one else would take it.

CHAPTER 10

THE BOOK OF HURRICANE JOB

I.

1. ONCE THERE WAS a man from the land of New Jersey, and William Landsmann was his name, and that man was simple and forthright, and feared God and shunned evil. 2. And William Landsmann lived with his wife in a good house in New Jersey, and his son and his son's wife and his three grandchildren lived nearby, and his possessions included a car, and much clothing, and many blue and white china dishes, and furniture, and many boarding passes, and seven thousand slides of his travels in distant lands. 3. For William Landsmann was wont to wander the earth, and to travel up and down in it, and to find those struggling with God in many lands across many seas. 4. And upon each day when he returned from his journeys, he did bring his film in to be developed, and rendered into slides. 5. And then did William Landsmann cause a light to project the slides upon a screen inside his house, and he did look upon them with the light, and saw that they were good.

6. One day the sons of God presented themselves before the God of heaven and earth, and the adversary came among them. 7. God said to the adversary, "From whence do you come?" And the adversary answered God, and said, "From wandering and roaming across the earth." 8. And God said to the adversary, "Have you taken note of my

servant William Landsmann? There is none like him on earth: a simple and forthright man, who fears God and shuns evil." 9. The adversary answered, "Does William Landsmann fear God for naught? Look,
you have guarded him, and blessed his household and all that he has.
You have blessed his possessions so that they depict the world entire. 10.
But lay your hand upon all that he has, and he shall surely curse you to
your face!" 11. And God said to the adversary, "Behold, all that he has
is in your power, but upon his slides do not put your hand." 12. And the
adversary went out from the presence of God.

13. And so the adversary took from within his power to roll back the
carousel of progress, rolling it many days back, rolling darkness away
before light and light away before darkness, 14. and he appeared in the
time of the grandparents of William Landsmann. 15. And he did afflict
William Landsmann's grandmother with great suffering, such that she
did return to a distant country, 16. and there he smote the mind of
William Landsmann's father with sorrow and loneliness and resistance,
17. and the sorrow and loneliness and resistance bore the father of
William Landsmann into battle, where he met with great torment and
horror by his own hand, which he did raise against his brother, 18. and
when his brother's blood cried out to him from the earth, the father of
William Landsmann heeded it not. 19. And the father of William
Landsmann also heeded not the cry of his wife, and he allowed her to
perish, 20. and thus did William Landsmann's mother perish when
William Landsmann was a young boy, 21. but William Landsmann did
not curse God. 22. And William Landsmann was uprooted from his
native land, and uprooted again. 23. And upon reaching the land of
New Jersey, William Landsmann's father took his life, leaving William
Landsmann alone, with neither mother nor father. 24. And many years
thereafter, the granddaughter of William Landsmann, a young woman,
not yet fully formed, was struck as she walked by the way, and fell, and
died, 25. and the dead girl's parents and brothers journeyed far away, to
California, leaving William Landsmann far behind. 26. And then
William Landsmann's wife was stricken, and her memory slipped away
from her, so that even her husband she barely remembered. 27. But
through all of this William Landsmann did not curse God.

II.

1. Again there was a day when the sons of God came to present themselves before God, and the adversary appeared among them. 2. And God said to the adversary, "From whence do you come?" And the adversary answered God, and said, "From wandering and roaming across the earth." 3. And God said to the adversary, "Have you taken note of my servant William Landsmann? There is none like him on earth: a simple and forthright man, who fears God and shuns evil, 4. and still he holds fast to his integrity, although you did move me against him to destroy him without cause." 5. And the adversary answered God, and said, "That's life! All those whom a man has he will give up for himself. 6. But put forth your hand now, and touch his slides, and he will curse you to your face." 7. And God said to the adversary, "Behold, he is in your hands." 8. So the adversary went forth from the presence of God.

9. And a great hurricane arose and shook the foundations of William Landsmann's house. 10. Behind William Landsmann's house flowed a small stream, emerging from a sewer pipe, 11. and on the day of the great tempest, the stream flooded, and the floodwaters rose, and the floodgates opened, 12. and the waters filled William Landsmann's backyard, and burst through his living room window, 13. and a great wave washed up against the wall of his living room, and took with it the boxes containing the seven thousand slides of distant lands.

14. And the boxes did open upon the waves, and the slides did come loose from their carousels, 15. and each slide did separate from its neighbor, and float transparent on the waters, 16. each broken from its sequence, made meaningless and scattered, 17. country mixed with country, and year mixed with year, 18. none more nor less important than the others, 19. glowing dimly in the green storm-sky light, gently resting on the skin of the water, 20. shining through not pictures, but only the murky deep, 21. thus the slides did float, two by two and seven by seven, out of the window and into the storm, carried far away, through the sewers and out, out, out to the expanse of the ocean, 22. where slowly, ever so slowly, as if feeling time dissolving in the thickness of the water, they drifted down, down, down to the bottom of the sea.

23. Now when William Landsmann's three friends heard of this misfortune that had come upon him, they came every one from his own place: Leora the New Jerseyite, Yehudah the Brooklynite, and Leah the Austro-Hungarianite — 24. for they had made an appointment together to come to mourn with him and comfort him. 25. And when they lifted up their eyes and saw him without his slides, and knew him not, they lifted up their voices and wept, and they rent every one his coat, and sprinkled dust upon their heads toward heaven. 26. And they sat down with him upon the ground for seven days and seven nights, and none spoke a word to him, for they saw that his suffering was very great. 27. After this, William Landsmann opened his mouth, and cursed the day he was born.

III.

1. And William Landsmann spoke, saying:

2. "Perish the day on which I was born,
   Perish the moment my parents met,
   Destroy the instant when his eyes met hers!

3. It would have been better that I were never born
   Than to live to see my images borne on the waves,

4. My life's work shattered, my creations uncreated —
   An entire world discarded down upon the ocean floor!

5. My roaring pours forth like water,
   My anger bursts at the floodgates,

6. And I pour out my wrath into the waters below.

7. Cursed be the God of heaven and earth,
   Who builds up only to destroy;

8. Who builds great cities only to flood them,

9. Who reduces man's empires to dust,
   And casts man's work of life into the heart of the sea!"

IV.

1. Then Leora the New Jerseyite replied, saying:

2. "William Landsmann, I do not wish to speak,
    Yet all the people in your slides could not hold my tongue.
    I do not ask why you curse God, but rather:
    Why do you curse God only now?

3. You curse the day your parents met, and yet
    You did not curse the days they died.

4. You did not curse God upon your mother's death,
    Nor when your father cast you out,
    Nor when two countries did the same.

5. You did not curse God when you found your father's corpse,
    Nor when you buried him in the wilderness, desolate and alone.

6. You did not curse God when you learned your granddaughter lay
dead,
    Nor when your son abandoned you to streets inhabited by ghosts.

7. Yet now your slides are scattered on the waves,
    Images of people you neither loved nor knew,
    Distant strangers now wandering free at last—

8. And for this, for this alone,
    You turn and curse your God?"

V.

1. To this William Landsmann turned red and roared, bellowing before
her:

2. "Woe to you, New Jerseyite, who knowest not the ways
    Of heaven nor of earth, who thinks in terms
    Of 'good' and 'bad,' of 'right' and 'wrong,'

3. With your supermarket ethics! Philosophy of Costco!
    Morality of strip malls; theology of home videos;

4. You who think of unearned suffering only as
     A blow dealt cruelly by the heavens
     And not by people here on earth,

5. You who ask of suffering, 'Where was God?'
     And never 'Where was man?'—

6. You who make of your belief in God
     A Disney World religion!

7. No, you New Jerseyite, you know not
     The ways of men upon this earth.

8. When that young girl, your friend, did die,
     With whom I never shared my tears,
     I sought not God, but you, her friend—
     Yet you chose not to hear.

9. My father's mother left her life behind,
     My father left my mother's life behind,
     And then he left his life behind, and mine.

10. But those decisions, they made! They!
      Not some God who breaks the skies.

11. I cursed not God until today:
      Because in this great world of freedom and of choice,
      Only floods and plagues and hurricanes are still the fault of God."

VI.

1. And then Yehudah the Brooklynite spoke, saying:

2. "Fear not, William Landsmann, all is not lost!
     Restrain your curses, contain your threats!
     God builds a better world for those who wait.

3. Those stricken slides you witnessed as your fate,
     Carried off by water, drowned among the waves,
     Sink not alone into the depths of time:

4. Our God is one who loves to flood the world to cleanse it.

5. One time, when all was lost on earth, God called
   Upon his servant Noah to build an ark,
   To rescue what he could from floods
   That God poured down upon the land
   To turn all land back into sea.

6. Only thus could God save the earth from evil;
   By beginning it anew. For water is
   The only thing on earth that God did not create.

7. When God creates the world, we read:
   'The earth was formless and void,
   And darkness was on the face of the deep'—yes, the deep—
   'And the spirit of God hovered on the face of the water'—yes,
   The water! God never created water,

8. But rather, rules it; in fact, one could say
   That water is a part of God, and he a part of it.

9. In the Bible, water always shows God's power. Read!:

10. 'God sits enthroned upon the flood.'

11. 'The voice of God is upon the waters,
    The God of glory thunders,
    God is upon many waters!'

12. 'Return our captives
    Like streams returning in the desert!'

13. 'Let justice roll like water,
    And righteousness like a mighty stream!'

14. 'The earth is the Lord's and the fullness thereof,
    For he laid its foundations on the seas,
    And established it upon the rivers!'

15. 'Let the oceans roar and the fullness thereof!'

16. 'He turns rock into a lake of water,
    A piece of flint into a fountain of water!'

17. 'He gathers together like a rampart
    The waters of the sea;
    He lays up in storehouses the depths!'

18. 'For the earth shall be filled with the knowledge of God, as the waters cover the sea!'

19. You see, all that's past, William Landsmann,
    All that's past is only prelude.

20. Let it wash, wash, wash away—
    And let life begin anew!"

VII.

1. To this William Landsmann turned red and roared, bellowing before him:

2. "Your justifications flow like water,
    And your self-righteousness like a mighty stream!

3. No, you Brooklynite, you know not
    The ways of God upon this earth.

4. Your God is a God of words, words, words!
    Piles of quotations, chapters of verse:

5. A verse to be born, and a verse to die,
    A verse to kill, and a verse to heal,
    A verse to mourn, and a verse to dance,
    A verse to tear, and a verse to sew,
    A verse to keep, and a verse to cast away—

6. And oh, you do indeed cast verses away!

7. 'God builds new worlds from floods,' you say,
    'By destroying all and beginning new again.'

8. But from that ancient tale of flooding there is one thing you forgot.

9. Open up your book again, and find this missing verse
    Which God proclaims to Noah: 'There shall never be
    Another flood to destroy the earth!'

10. Never again—read it? Never! God does not destroy his world!

11. More evidence, you say? Then turn here, turn here,
    To yet another verse you've cast away.

12. Animals boarded Noah's ark, two by two and seven by seven,
    And from that, you say, the world began anew.

13. But did it not occur to you that God created fish?
    And sea creatures, and seals, and urchins like the boy I was—
    Creatures who have always lived submerged beneath the sea.

14. No 'new world' for them—no, they remained
    Ensconced beneath the ocean's depths,
    Unaware of passing time, sifting sediments
    Of ages past, not knowing of the deluge overhead
    Nor of a world where things can be erased;
    They dive beneath the depths, exploring
    Things cast off so long ago
    By those who thought they were destroying
    What they wanted none to know.

15. No, Yehudah, God does not 'cleanse' the world,
    Nor erase his images from off the earth.

16. Things are preserved, somewhere, somehow,
    And this is not disproved by your ignorance of how.

17. You strive to keep alive all pasts except your own—
    You revive the dead of fiction, but not of fact;
    You memorize the myths, but cast your history in the sea!

18. My slides preserved a world that could be lost,
    And now those slides themselves have disappeared,
    Wrenched from me by the arm of God,
    Whose work of preservation I had hoped to do.

19. No, Yehudah, your God of verse might do this, but not mine—
    Not the God of earth whose storehouses we can find!"

VIII.

1. And then Leah the Austro-Hungarianite spoke, saying:

2. "Please, dear grandson, hold your tongue;
   Your whining makes me sick at heart!

3. Does a wise man answer with windy knowledge,
   And fill his belly with the eastern wind?

4. You wail over pictures as if a city were destroyed,
   Yet I ask a harder question:
   Why wail over anything at all?

5. For tears are wasted, and wailing sucked away
   By the screaming of the winds.

6. I wandered the world all the years of my youth —
   Wandered and wandered, and found no solace in it.

7. I looked to the stars and they were denied me;
   I looked to the rivers and they were sucked dry;
   I traveled from a land of woods to one of iron canyons;
   Cliffs of steel and iron, streets paved with broken dreams.

8. Books tormented me; words gave me no comfort;
   Their letters stuck their serifs out at me
   Like tongues, each speaking evil.

9. I stretched out my hands for someone to catch me
   And they were grabbed and bound together,
   Stitched one finger to another, callused and numbed.

10. I clawed the floor in mourning, I tore my skirt in tears,

11. And when I rose up again, I wandered off once more,
    And cast my past behind me, down to the ocean floor.

12. I wandered farther, farther, farther, across mountains and valleys,
    Until I found an open door and collapsed beside it.

13. Once, I wailed; long ago, I used to rail at heaven,
    But there, in the wilderness, I found my last resort:
    When God does not answer you, stop asking!

14. Were you the first man born?
    Were you created before the hills?

15. I knew, when no more answers came,
   That I should cease to ask, and so should you."

IX.

1. To this William Landsmann turned red and roared, bellowing before
her:

2. "European complacency! Words of worn-out continents!
   Useless, faithless, helpless, hopeless,
   Language of one happy to be buried in the earth!

3. Those who speak like you have lost whole empires
   And protested less than I have for my slides.

4. Content to watch your life roll by, or roll away,
   You cast not just your past but yourself into the sea!

5. I lived that life already, in reverse.

6. As a boy I ceased to question before my mouth had even opened;
   I had barely learned to speak before I sealed my lips.

7. I searched the dictionaries of desire,
   I consulted the archives of despair;

8. I found in them the words to name my grief,

9. But I never expected answers,
   And then I never asked.

10. I wandered silently all these years,
   Asking nothing, and finding nothing in return.

11. For years, so many years, I was you,
   But silence breeds more noise than silence bears!

12. And now I make my own demand
   Upon the God of heaven and of earth:

13. I do not ask you, God, to return my mother,
   Nor my father, nor my years of youth.

14. I do not ask for riches, wisdom, power, life eternal,
    Nor even for justice, or mercy, or love.

15. All I ask for are the images I created of the world.

16. Return my images to me, O God, and I shall return—
    Renew my slides as of old!"

X.

1. Then God answered William Landsmann out of the whirlwind, saying:

2. "Who is this that darkens counsel by words without knowledge?
    Gird up your loins like a man:
    For I will ask, and you will answer me.

3. Where were you when I laid the foundations of the earth?

4. Did you draw the gentle stoop of a too-tall girl
    Who walks the earth with her neck bent forward
    Humbling her head before each day's face?

5. Did you snap a picture of the kick
    Of a tall girl's sister, sharing her bed,
    Who tosses and turns in troubled sleep—
    Or of the kick felt deep within the womb
    Of a tall girl lying in silent fright?

6. Did you photograph a canopy of hanging stars,
    Or the flicker of a flame that eats a rag
    Stuffed into a pipe of gas—
    Or the face of a boy with nostrils charred,
    Sleeping peacefully at last?

7. Did you photograph the loneliness
    Of a child raised in clothes too small,
    In a room too small, in a house too small,
    In a world too small for the smallest corner of his heart,
    The tug of a too-small coat across his thin and growing shoulders,
    Or the soft brush of his mother's lips on his earlobe's edge,

As he turns beneath his blankets, feigning sleep,
Pretending he does not feel the watch she keeps?

8. Did you print the picture of a push of one man against another
In a fire-and-brimstone storm,
Or the sudden trip of a foot in a hole,
That dyed a whole life black?

9. Did your slides include an image of a boy
Who sits before a book each night in silence,
His growing groping fingers searching for a word,
Flipping back and forth between the pages
So as to forget his father's grimace and his mother's darkened face?

10. Will you show your photograph of a tiny bedroom, shared
By father and son, and by the father's corpse,
And by the son who tried his best to drive it from his mind?

11. Where is your picture of a young, young girl,
A girl too young to excavate the storehouses of time,
Or even to explore the closest closets of her mind—
Where is your snapshot of that girl falling down,
Falling, faltering, tumbling to the earth,
On the road, mid-journey, to who she was,
Before reaching who she would never be?

12. Did you snap a picture of sleep's soft talons
That sink into your hands as you sit dozing in your chair,
Arms folded, your head dipping forward as if in prayer,
The sweet deep sleep that summons you first by hand,
Sinking into your flesh until your hands grow numb
And right and left hands melt into the air?

13. Did you photograph the great gallery of dreams
That I hang beneath your eyelids as you sleep?
That great dark curtain that sleep unveils
On the sunken world of past and future—

14. Where are your slides of that gallery of unlived dreams?

15. You eat your meals from blue and white china bowls,
But I eat mine from the blue bowl of summer

And the white bowl of winter,
Each inverted in its turn;

16. You light candles and turn on lights
While I spin the earth and push down its setting sun.

17. You take your pictures of the ocean, of the ripples of its surface,
But have you photographed the fullness thereof—
The centuries of secrets buried at the bottom of the sea?
For there are secrets there, deep secrets—
The past of the world entire, each moment perfectly preserved,
My vast underwater storehouse for every refugee of time.

18. I dare you, William Landsmann, to collect
A gallery of images like mine.
The oceans' roar, and the fullness thereof—

19. These are my images, my universe, my eternity
That I have planted here upon the dry land in your midst.

20. I created you in my image.
I am not created in yours!"

21. And God retreated into the whirlwind.

XI. *The earth & the Lord are the fullness thereof*

1. And William Landsmann rose from his mourning, and left for his next journey, and his wife traveled with him. 2. And he traveled to the land of California, where he went nowhere but to the house of his son, and his son's wife, and his two grandsons, 3. and his camera he brought not.

4. But when he arrived at the house of his son, and his son's wife, and his two grandsons, William Landsmann found redemption— 5. in the form of slides, his own slides, images of his granddaughter, Naomi Landsmann, 6. which William Landsmann's wife, who was sick in the mind but not in the soul, had sent far away to their son in her madness, 7. or perhaps not in madness at all, but in the wisdom, even out of the deepest depths of forgetfulness, of knowing what is worth keeping.

8. May this memory, and each memory created in its image, be a blessing.

CHAPTER 11

A TOURIST IN THE LOST CITY

ATTENTION, ATTENTION!!!!
NEW YORK HAS SUNK INTO THE ATLANTIC!

THE NIGHT before her wedding, Leora had a dream. She dreamt that she had become a deep-sea diver.

It was nighttime in her dream, just as it was outside while she was dreaming: a warm summer night, shuddering with summer-night whispers, moist grass sleeping under a thin mist that hung in front of her parents' house like a veil. Leora's body remained sleeping, tossing uneasily through its very last night in its narrow single bed, but she rose up out of the bed and left her body behind. Not like the way you see it in movies. She didn't turn into a ghostly image of herself, glancing back at her body and smirking as she went off to another world. It was more straightforward than that, as if her body were a sister of hers with whom she had been sharing that narrow bed, and she simply kicked that sister to the side a bit to free herself from the bed, stood up, and walked away, leaving her sister tossing through her violent sleep behind her.

She left her bedroom slowly, treading silently in the dark, leaving the lights out. She walked down the stairs and out the front door into the summer-night mist, wrapped in the vibrations of chirping crickets who were rattling the air as if to scare people back into their houses, to keep intruders out of the deep enchanted summer night. She walked through her neighborhood, then past Jason's parents' house, then past

Naomi's old house, then past Bill Landsmann's house, and then out onto the highway. No one was on the road.

She walked along the highway for a very long time, passing signs beckoning her first toward the towns where her parents grew up, closer to New York City, and then to the ones where her grandparents grew up, even closer, toward that ring of ruined sprawl where her great-grandparents once dropped anchor like Columbus, setting foot for the first time in the New World. She passed these exits, but she didn't take them. Instead she kept walking.

She began walking faster, then even faster, and soon she was jogging, then loping, then running, then sprinting, ignoring each clutch in her sides and never slowing down, sweat pouring across her forehead as she almost suffocated while choking down the thick summer mist — running past burned-out factories and chemical swamps, past rail yards and landfills, past garbage dumps and abandoned buildings, past rotting two-family houses and downed power lines, past unused smokestacks and giant water towers, past empty streets, empty buildings, empty houses, where not a single glowing window illuminated the dark night. Leora kept running and running under the orange highway lights, looking up as the lights raced by in rhythm over her head, like when she was a child and would lie in the backseat of her parents' car, her head banging on the door as she looked up through the side window at the dark heavens, protected from the night's demons by the steady, thumping rhythm of electric streetlights.

And then, during a sudden pause in the lights' rhythm, she stepped off the highway and ran to her destination, not stopping until she had crossed the little park by the water's edge, racing across the pathetic littered meadow until she reached the newly reconstructed promenade. Beyond its railing lay New York Harbor. From the railing, there unfolded before her eyes the southern end of Manhattan, its shining new buildings glowing unearthly colors of orange and green and blue, towering over the harbor's dark unearthly water. Leora had the distinct impression, on that dark summer night, that the city was not anchored to the land, but rather floating, hovering over the face of the waters. Or, more accurately, that the city was only, so to speak, the tip of the iceberg — that something beneath the water's surface, something far larger and weightier and mightier, was supporting it. In front of her, beckoning with a giant torch like a flare at a crime scene, stood the Statue of Liberty.

Leora climbed up on the walkway's railing, balancing for a moment as she looked out at the shining, burning city. As her eyes passed under the Statue of Liberty, she threw herself overboard—diving down, down, down into the waters below, until she reached the very bottom of the sea.

LEORA IS the only person in the world who knows this: There is a city underneath the city of New York.

We are not talking about the subways, or the basements, or the parking garages, or the money vaults, or the underground shopping arcades or the train stations or the sewer systems or the telephone cables or the rat nests. Nor do we mean the organized crime rings or the drug smugglers or the sex merchants or the undercover agents, or the palm-greasing or the deal-breaking or the star-making or the muckraking, or the illegal immigrants or the sweatshop slaves or the children crammed into tiny homes, or the secret interlocking passageways that run between private people's hearts. No, we are talking about a real city, a parallel city whose foundations rest on the bottom of New York Harbor. It is a city made up entirely of things that the people in the world above it have forgotten, all that they have decided, deliberately or otherwise, to cast into the ocean.

Now, you probably already have an image in your mind of what this lost city might look like. You probably imagine people riding those giant-front-wheeled bicycles down streets bustling with bustled women, to the tune of ragtime music. Or maybe you envision trumpeting jazz bands, real-live swing dancers, or speakeasies, or white gangsters. Maybe you're thinking of robber barons wearing monocles while smoking pipes in palatial homes, or scrappy, good-natured newsboys in tweed caps shouting "Extra! Extra!" Or perhaps you've even drawn a mental picture, not yet painted-by-numbers, of billowing sailing ships and men in powdered wigs. But the lost city is no warehouse for nostalgia—not a showcase of the versions of the past that exist only in the present, created out of a mix of thin air and our even thinner ability to see the beauty of the current moment. No, the lost city—and there may well be other lost cities, lurking beneath the Seine or the Yangtze or the Crimean or the Nile or the Baltic or the Ganges or the Amazon or the Danube or the Amsterdam canals, but here we are speaking only of

New York—contains only things that we have truly abandoned, created exclusively out of what we believe to be lost forever.

It is a walled city, this city beneath the city of New York. Its southern wall stands thick and strong, composed of the remains of the wall that once lined Wall Street, the old fortifications built long ago by the settlers of New Amsterdam—back when the greatest sign of a city's strength was what it was capable of keeping out, rather than what it was capable of letting in. As we have said, the lost city is a walled city, but only nominally so. The city is so crowded, so overwhelmingly full, so teeming and screaming and churning and burning with all that we have now forgotten, that it spills out over its walls, the wretched refuse of its teeming shores pushing out in every direction until the walls surrounding its inner core become little more than a technicality. In this underwater sanctuary, however, the huddled masses all breathe free. Its citizens, their bodies remembering the form of a fetus inside a saline womb, breathe through gills in their half-severed necks.

The language spoken here varies from time to time. In the beginning, it was the chirping of birds, vast flocks of birds, sent down below by slash-and-burn farming above. Then, and this has been true for centuries, the lingua franca of this lost city became Manhattan. No, not some metaphorical imaginary language of wealth and poverty and crime and art, but the actual language Manhattan, spoken by the Manhattan tribe of natives who gave up the island a few hundred years ago for sets of beads worth approximately twenty-four dollars. (Some residents of the lost city, the municipality's much-envied elite, wear these beads around their necks.) Of course, other languages are spoken here too. A few hundred citizens speak seventeenth-century Dutch; a dozen or so pride themselves on having mastered Esperanto. And lately, more people are picking up Yiddish.

Outside the walls, the road to the lost city underneath New York is paved with tefillin.

LEORA ENTERED the lost city almost unnoticed. The gatehouses of the city—staffed, she was later informed, by suicides—do not guard the doors very carefully, and the guard on duty when she entered was especially inattentive. The guard, a handsome man in his forties with a graying mustache and bright blue eyes, was engrossed in reading something. From her position, it was hard to tell what it was, but as she drifted up a bit in the water while trying to sneak through the gate, she caught a glimpse of German words—something dense, with footnotes. But then the guard caught her eye and slammed the book shut, covering its title with his arm. "What do you want?" he growled.

She shrank down a bit. Out of the corner of her eye, she saw dozens of people entering through the gate, none of them deigning to show any sort of identification or pass. In the lost city, Leora realized, going in is never a problem. The guards are there to prevent people from going out.

"Just a local map, if you have one," she stuttered.

The guard grumbled a bit, then took out a key and unlocked a drawer of the desk in front of him inside the gatehouse. The drawer burst open, and Leora saw that it was filled with all sorts of papers— typed pages, printed pages, mimeographed pages, handwritten pages in brown ink on yellowing paper. After rummaging for a full five minutes, the guard retrieved a small scroll. Passing the scroll to her through the window, he made an impatient gesture with his hand, growled again, and resumed his reading. Leora hurried through the gate, pausing within the city to unfurl the scroll's waterlogged yellow edges. But once she had opened it, she found that the map was nearly blank, depicting just the contours of the ocean floor—a map only of what used to be. And so she wandered, unable to aim herself anywhere, through the crowded streets.

The streets of the lost city were packed. Contrary to what you might expect, though, there wasn't anything very strange about them, once you got used to the gas streetlamps, the lack of cars, the chatter of the Manhattan language, and the people breathing through gills. In fact, it was almost unnerving how normal it seemed. People were returning from work, hurrying by as if they could think of nothing but the dinner or child or lover waiting at home for them. Some were running errands, shopping for butter churns and sewing machines, while others were window-shopping, debating whether to invest in a reading from the local phrenologist. Still others were just out for a leisurely stroll—young couples holding each other's waists, old couples holding each other's hands, in-between couples piled high with children on their backs. Nothing could have been more normal. Not content with all this normalcy, Leora wandered some more until she discovered the lost city's zoo.

There is a zoo in the lost city, and all of its animals are extinct. The aviary is filled with dodo birds; there are fiberglass cliffs inhabited by saber-toothed tigers. There is a marine exhibit filled with animals Leora couldn't even name—ancient animals, giant scaly things and tiny feathery things and spiky things and slimy things that probably never made it out of the primordial soup. The mastodon show is particularly popular, because at certain times of day, children who come to the lost zoo are allowed to ride the woolly mammoths, grabbing at the behemoths' curly hair in their tight little fists, screaming and crying and begging their parents to take them down. And then, of course, she saw the dinosaurs, their might buried in their loins, their force hidden in the muscles of their bellies. As they jumped and thundered amid the fiberglass hills, they stiffened their tails into tall cedars and the sinews of their thighs knit together, their bones like tubes of bronze, their limbs like bars of iron. But they didn't look much like the dinosaurs you see in pictures and movies. Instead of being covered with scales, they had skin—real skin, almost human, though without hair, soft in some places and callused in others, pulled taut over muscles so that each thunderous step set off a ripple of flesh. And instead of camouflaging themselves in dulled, earthy colors, these dinosaurs were radiant: their skin shone an iridescent blue, fading to indigo, fading to purple, fading to a deep, glowing, unearthly red, the different colors shimmering in turn depending on the motion of the water around them, like tropical fish.

Yet even in the zoo, outside of the exhibits, Leora saw only the ordinary. Children banging on the aquarium's glass, their parents screaming at them in the Manhattan language; younger children feeding the dodo birds; older children throwing coins at the glass, trying to rouse the saber-toothed tiger. The animals, she saw, were castaways. But the people? Ordinary!

Still searching for novelty—though, admittedly, the lost city is not a very good place to find it—she wandered even further into the congested streets until a few helpful citizens directed her to the municipal library, one of the largest buildings in the lost city. She walked up its giant barnacle-covered front stairs, feeling more certain with each slippery step that behind the seaweed-encrusted doors she would at last find her buried treasures.

But to her surprise, although she shouldn't have been surprised, she discovered that most of the works in the library—all, of course, were out of print—were the literary equivalent of trash. Romance novels, yesterday's political thrillers, Cold War espionage tales, pop biographies of people she had never heard of. The how-to section was immense, as was the self-help section. Decades' worth of diet books suggesting that people starve themselves to death, cookbooks whose recipes often called for lard, child-raising books recommending that children not be spared the rod, and books promising people new ways to get rich quick, predicting market peaks and crashes that never materialized. And, of course, thousands of books and pamphlets filled with nothing but outmoded pornography, disappointing drawings of things no longer even considered burlesque. And then there was trash that didn't look familiar: "dime novels," serialized Westerns, almanacs, astrological guides, crop counts carved into pieces of bark.

But that was only the shelved material. Most of the library, Leora discovered, was taken up by archives. Not records of famous people, but of ordinary people, the sort of people whose loose letters and photographs would never have been immortalized in the city above, even by their grandchildren. There were endless piles of love letters, packed by the bundle, letters whose ardor waxed hotter and hotter in each series of correspondence and then inevitably cooled and froze into a bitter final exchange—the sort of letters, Leora thought to herself, that people throw away or burn after receiving the last one. There were application letters for jobs by the thousands, stacked by sender. There were letters from parents to children in summer camps, filled with unheeded advice about poison ivy, and letters from parents to children in military camps, returned to sender, unopened. And then there were the photographs—color, black and white, sepia, all the way back to lithographs, in piles miles high—unlabeled, loose photographs of who knew who, taken who knew where, who knew when, fallen from photo albums, out of context and out of time.

It occurred to Leora, as she flipped through these photographs of people who were beginning to look increasingly familiar, that all her wandering in the lost city thus far had been somewhat beside the point. Dropping the photographs she was holding onto a moldy chrome-lined table and abandoning the stacks of literary trash behind her, she exited the barnacled doors and headed for the lost city hall, to consult the local registers and find out whether she might actually know any of the residents of the lost city.

YES, THE "REGISTERS." There are no phone directories in the lost
city, because telephones have not yet made it here. (Telegrams are
occasionally sent from the lost city to the city above, but the technology
for reception on the other end is lacking.) As Leora walked—or, rather,
swam, or, more precisely, drifted—to the lost city hall, she realized that
she might once more be setting herself up for disappointment. After all,
she had gone to the library with high hopes and had uncovered almost
nothing. It seemed absurd to expect anything more from city hall. But
in the lost city, one quickly finds that it is impossible to dismiss absurd
thoughts—or any thoughts at all, for that matter. There is nowhere left
to dismiss them to.

The clerk at the lost city hall seemed vaguely familiar. He was a
stringy sort of man, young, with a mop of brown hair and a series of
pimples on one side of his mouth. When he spoke, his voice sounded
clear and whole, like a knock on a tree trunk. "Are you looking for
someone in particular?" he asked Leora as he brought out a pile of giant
ledger books, patting the one on top with his hand after he had set them
down. "You realize, we've got hundreds of these back here. They only
cover eras of written language, though. If you're looking for someone
before then, just ask me and I'll see what I can do."

"No, this is fine," she answered quickly, taking the top four books in
the stack. For a moment she wished she had real research to pursue.
But she was only a visitor. A tourist.

Leora sat down and slowly opened the first alphabetical volume. The
pages were gigantic, folio-sized, like an old religious book. Of course,
the entries were all written by hand. She looked up her own name first,
breathing a sigh of relief when she saw that she wasn't listed. Then she
began flipping pages to hunt down Naomi. But on the way to Naomi,
on a whim, she looked up Jason. To her surprise, he was there. And to
her absolute shock, so was she—listed right beside him: "Dr. and Mrs."
He also had a business cross-listing: "See under Physicians, Geriatric
Medicine."

She slammed the book shut.

"Find what you're looking for?" the clerk called from behind the
desk. He was crouching, distracted, beside a large pile of inventory
sheets.

Shrinking back in her seat, Leora stared at the book in front of her as if it were growing uncontrollably, the folio widening and thickening until she could imagine all the listings within it—the boyfriends she hadn't married, the jobs she hadn't taken, the acquaintances she had abandoned, the endless roster of people she hadn't become. And then, beyond that, stood the listings of all the people everyone else hadn't become, all the endless numbers of people who could have been, but weren't. She felt her hand being drawn back toward the book's cover, her fingers edging up over the waterlogged table toward the outdated green leather binding. Then she slammed her hands down and stood up from her seat.

"Yes, thank you for your help," she called to the clerk, her voice self-consciously loud. And she ran out of the room before he had a chance to respond.

WHEN LEORA left the lost city hall, she began to look more closely at the people around her—the people in the streets, yes, but also the people in the windows, some of which were covered with thick curtains, but others of which were glass laid bare, allowing full view of the people behind them. As she looked closer, though, remembering those giant ledgers, she suddenly realized what she was looking at. The people behind the windows, the people in the street, absolutely everyone she had seen in the lost city—they were living through all the things that hadn't happened in the city above, all the choices that hadn't been made, all the lives abandoned, to be lived out only on the forgotten ocean floor. There wasn't only one Naomi in the lost city, Leora realized, but thousands, each a different version of the person she never became. Somewhere in this city, she imagined, she and Jake were married to other people; somewhere else, Wilhelm Landsmann, an old, distinguished gentleman of a modern Vienna, might be in town on a pleasure trip in his retirement. Or perhaps none of them had ever been born, their parents having decided to marry others, or their grandparents having so decided, or their great-grandparents. Among the endless thousands of millions of people who inhabited the lost city, all of these possibilities existed—except for the ones the people above had chosen.

Suddenly she felt, with full force, the immense weight of the millions of gallons of water and abandoned lives on top of her. She fought hard to stay standing, then fell to her knees. The crowds in the street began trampling her underfoot. She covered her face, then rolled under their legs toward an open doorway, narrowly escaping being crushed as she nudged the door closed behind her. She stayed on the ground for a moment, curled into a ball with her face still in her hands. When she regained her composure, she stretched herself out, staggered to stand, and opened her eyes.

She was in a school, a classroom; the sort of classroom she hadn't been in for almost ten years. There was a blackboard, dozens of carved-up school desks and chairs, and a large broken clock on the wall. There were no students there, but in the front of the room, a blank white screen was pulled down, covering part of the blackboard. Toward the back of the room, on a small table, sat a slide projector. It occurred to Leora that students in schools now had probably never used a slide projector before; if a slide projector were to appear in a school again, none of the students would know how to operate it. Fortunately, however, there was someone in the room who could. Seated on a vinyl couch against the room's back wall was Bill Landsmann.

"MR. LANDSMANN?" Leora tried to shout, but her voice failed to carry. There was no way to make herself heard, she discovered, except by whispering. She had never whispered to Bill Landsmann before. "What are you doing here?"

For a moment she regretted her question, turned red, panicked, afraid of what the answer might be. But then Bill Landsmann whispered back, "You shouldn't worry, Leora. I don't live here. Only my slides do—and our friendship, yes?"

Leora began turning redder than the dinosaurs in the lost zoo. Bill Landsmann softened his verdict. "It was too difficult for you, then. I know that," he said. But then he stood up, cleared his throat, and raised his voice. "Who knows what you might have found out about me? Or what I might have found out about you? What do you really know about anyone, other than what they choose to show you?"

She stood motionless in the water. Bill Landsmann leaned forward and switched on the slide projector, and Leora was alarmed by the sudden lion's roar of the projector's fan. Bill Landsmann walked to the side of the room and turned out the lights. The square of white light on the wall fluttered gently in the room's heavy waves.

Bill Landsmann began clicking the slides by, one after another, monotonously, each one shivering with the tension of the water. All of them were blank.

He recited no script. Instead, after the entire slide carousel had been completed, he emptied the machine and held out his hands, filled with the little blank squares, like piles of windows with their blinds drawn.

"These are yours," he said. "You can fill them with whatever you like. But you have to find someone to show them to."

Leora took the slides, each one slipping into her hands like a day not yet lived. Bill Landsmann showed her to the door. She wanted to say something, even if only goodbye, but he didn't find it necessary to speak with her any further. He slammed the door in her face. At first she thought it was an insult. Then she realized it was a blessing, a send-off.

Leora couldn't leave the lost city through its gates, nor did she want to. Instead she sprang off the ocean floor and projected herself upward, pushing hard against centuries of rejected possibilities until she reached the surface, her head bursting out of the saline waters like a newborn child's. The night was fading, caught between darkness and light, leaving the sky a blank, nameless color, an empty canvas. She swam to the water's edge and pulled herself onto dry land, and woke up.

THERE WAS a time when she, too, felt like a tourist in her own life. But those days seem like a long time ago now, like looking into someone else's window.

LANDSMANN FAMILY TREE

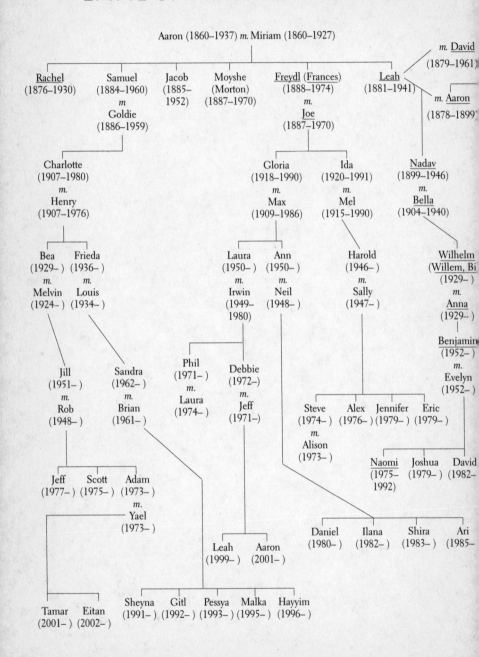

LANDSMANN FAMILY TREE

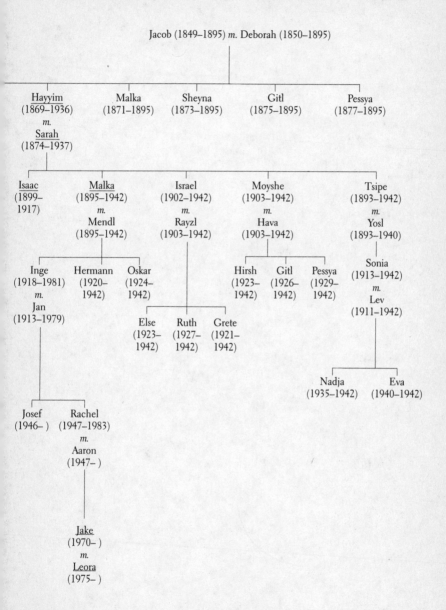

Jacob (1849–1895) *m.* Deborah (1850–1895)

Hayyim (1869–1936) *m.* Sarah (1874–1937) — Malka (1871–1895) — Sheyna (1873–1895) — Gitl (1875–1895) — Pessya (1877–1895)

Isaac (1899–1917) — Malka (1895–1942) *m.* Mendl (1895–1942) — Israel (1902–1942) *m.* Rayzl (1903–1942) — Moyshe (1903–1942) *m.* Hava (1903–1942) — Tsipe (1893–1942) *m.* Yosl (1893–1940)

Inge (1918–1981) *m.* Jan (1913–1979) — Hermann (1920–1942) — Oskar (1924–1942)

Else (1923–1942) — Ruth (1927–1942) — Grete (1921–1942)

Hirsh (1923–1942) — Gitl (1926–1942) — Pessya (1929–1942)

Sonia (1913–1942) *m.* Lev (1911–1942)

Nadja (1935–1942) — Eva (1940–1942)

Josef (1946–) — Rachel (1947–1983) *m.* Aaron (1947–)

Jake (1970–) *m.* Leora (1975–)

Those underlined appear by name in the novel.

ACKNOWLEDGMENTS

I WOULD like to thank Henry Freeman, a world traveler whose stunning slide collection and fortitude in the face of Hurricane Floyd are well known in my home community. I am grateful to him for the initial inspiration for this novel. There are, however, no other similarities between him, or his family, and any of the characters in this book.

I thank the administrators, staff, and researchers of the Lower East Side Tenement Museum in New York City, who assisted me several years ago in preparing an article for *American Heritage* magazine that later inspired a part of this book, and Giulia Miller, who allowed me to read her University College London undergraduate thesis, entitled "Spinoza and the Amsterdam Jewish Community: Who Rejected Whom?" I am also indebted to Dr. Nathan Winter, who provided academic fact-checking on demand (any remaining mistakes are mine alone), and to the many other teachers in my life.

I am grateful to my agent Gary Morris, whose literary and business skills found this book a perfect home, and to my editor Alane Mason, who started reading it before breakfast one morning and did not put it down until she had lavished her attention on every line and led me to make it as good as it could possibly be.

But I am most grateful of all to my "in-house" editors: to my sisters Jordana and Ariel, who cared enough about the characters to think of them as if they were real people; to my brother Zach, because any humor in this book is actually his; to my father, who caught the smallest errors; to my mother, who solved the hardest problems; and to my husband Brendan—my in-house counsel, who never had any doubts.

IN THE IMAGE

Dara Horn

IN THE IMAGE

Dara Horn

"There was a man in the land of Uz named Job. That man was blame-less and upright; he feared God and shunned evil. Seven sons and three daughters were born to him; his possessions were seven thousand sheep, three thousand camels, five hundred yoke of oxen and five hundred she-asses, and a very large household. . . . The LORD said to the Adver-sary, 'Have you noticed My servant Job? There is no one like him on earth, a blameless and upright man who fears God and shuns evil!' The Adversary answered the LORD, 'Does Job not have good reason to fear God? Why, it is You who have fenced him round, him and his house-hold and all that he has. You have blessed his efforts so that his posses-sions spread out in the land. But lay Your hand upon all that he has and he will surely blaspheme You to Your face.' The LORD replied to the Adversary, 'See, all that he has is in your power, only do not lay a hand on him.' "   —Job 1:1–4, 7–13

"Rabbi Levi bar Lachma said Job lived in the days of Moses. . . . But then one could say Job lived in the days of Isaac . . . or one could say in the days of Jacob . . . or one could say in the days of Joseph. . . . A cer-tain rabbi [hearing the dispute] said: Job never lived and was never cre-ated, but was just a parable."   —Talmud (Bava Batra 15a)

"From the start, the forces were unequal: Satan a grand seigneur in heaven, Job mere flesh and blood. And anyway, the contest was unfair. Job, who had lost all his wealth and had been bereaved of his sons and daughters and stricken with loathsome boils, wasn't even aware that it was a contest.

"Because he complained too much, the referee silenced him. So, having accepted this decision, in silence, he defeated his opponent without even realizing it. Therefore his wealth was restored, he was given sons and daughters—new ones, of course—and his grief for the first children was taken away.

"We might imagine that this retribution was the most terrible thing of all. We might imagine that the most terrible thing was Job's ignorance: not understanding whom he had defeated, or even that he had won. But in fact, the most terrible thing of all is that Job never existed and was just a parable."   —Dan Pagis (1930–1986)*

*From Dan Pagis, *The Selected Poetry of Dan Pagis*. Stephen Mitchell, ed. & trans. Copyright 1996, The Regents of the University of California. Courtesy of University of California Press.

DISCUSSION QUESTIONS

1. The novel begins with a description of the main characters, Leora and Bill Landsmann, as "tourists." What makes them tourists, besides their travels? Can one ever stop being a tourist in this sense?

2. Several characters in the novel intentionally change their identities, some by embracing religion, others by rejecting it. What do the different characters—Jason, Leah, and Nadav, among others—gain or lose through these choices? When a person makes the choice to reject or embrace religion at the beginning of the twentieth century, are they making the same choice as a person faced with the same question a hundred years later?

3. While the characters move frequently between Europe and America, the novel ends literally beneath the Statue of Liberty. What kind of picture of America emerges from the novel, from sweatshops to Costco? What opportunities does America offer the characters, and what burdens do those opportunities bring with them?

4. This is a novel of modern Jewish history, but unlike so many novels on this subject, it is emphatically *not* a novel about anti-Semitism, or even about the Holocaust. Instead, the book's tragedies are tragic in the true sense—that is, the characters are generally not innocent victims, but rather bring disaster upon themselves. Does this make the book's many catastrophes easier to understand, or harder? How does this approach change your view of Jewish history?

5. A central theme of the book is the idea of reclamation: ritual objects thrown overboard appear a century later in a junk shop, pieces of coal resurface millennia later as diamonds, a primitive skull is discovered, a neglected dollhouse is restored, and the novel's ending reveals a vast underwater treasury of lost things. In describing diamond formation, Horn writes that "Nothing is ever really lost." But a Jewish new year ceremony consists of symbolically casting one's sins away in order to start a new year. Does it work? Can people be forgiven? If it is true that nothing is ever lost, is that a blessing or a curse?

6. Jake tells Leora that "just because life doesn't work the way you want it to doesn't mean that what happens in the world is completely random. The times when people really do interact with God are exactly those times when life doesn't work out fairly." Is this observation borne out in the novel? In reality?

7. Near the end of the biblical Book of Job, in answer to Job's questions about why he has suffered so undeservedly, God responds by describing the many unfathomable wonders of the world he has created, asking Job if he knows, for example, where the storehouses of snow are kept, or how God sets the boundaries of the sea (see Job chapters 38–41). In "The Book of Hurricane Job" in the novel, God responds to Bill Landsmann's questions by recounting the private moments of the novel's many characters. What kind of limitations of human understanding does this suggest? How much do the characters in the novel really know about one another, and how much do they miss? How much can people ever know about one another?

8. God concludes his words to Bill Landsmann by saying, "I created you in my image. I am not created in yours!" Much of the novel is devoted to images and re-creations: museums figure prominently, paintings appear by Vermeer and Rembrandt, Naomi Landsmann makes copies of famous works of art, photographs take on large significance, miniature enthusiasts create exact replicas of material life, and Bill Landsmann assembles a collection of thousands of slides. When are these images successful, and when do they fail? Are there limitations on human creativity?

9. Speaking of his father, Nadav Landsmann, Bill Landsmann says, "It is often said that we are shaped by our experiences, but I do not believe that's true. . . . I think we are not shaped by our experiences, but by what we do choose—by how we react to our experiences." Do you believe him? For which of the characters in the novel might this be true?

10. The novel borrows language from the story of Cain and Abel to describe the death of Isaac, Nadav's cousin. Is Nadav actually

responsible for Isaac's death? Why does he consider himself to be? Is he responsible for his wife's fate? Which affects him more: his actual experience, or what he makes of it?

11. Besides the Book of Job, there are many references to the Hebrew bible and to Jewish literature scattered throughout the novel. A few of the many examples: in the first chapter, the story of Leora and Bill Landsmann's ascent up East Mountain borrows language from the biblical binding of Isaac in Genesis 22; at the suicide of the aspiring singer Joe Solovey, the novel quotes the Talmud by saying he is "unable to complete his work, but never free to desist from it." Does one need to recognize these allusions, or others like them, in order to appreciate the novel? For the modern reader, are these references another example of how people misread one another? Or are they another example of reclamation?

12. The novel begins with the words, "Accidents of fate are rarely fatal accidents." Which ultimately dominates the novel, free will or fate?

A CONVERSATION WITH DARA HORN

Is your family history comparable to the Landsmanns?

My family history is actually nothing like the Landsmann family history. I am a fourth-generation American. My ancestors came to America from Eastern Europe at the turn of the century (1900, that is, not 2000!). If anything, my family's experience is reflected in that of the character named Freydl/Frances, who happily settles into life in New Jersey without looking back. I invented this particular family history in part because I wanted to demonstrate the difference America made in the lives of so many European Jews who were lucky enough to come here as early as my family did, and the many ways in which America, despite being older politically than most of the countries in Europe, really remains a vast new world.

I wrote this book while living in England—I had won a scholarship from Harvard to spend a year at Cambridge University, where I did a master's degree—and I think it shows in the novel that I was a little homesick for America while I was writing it. I specifically remember coming back to my student residence there from a shopping trip to what I considered a rather limited European-style supermarket in Cambridge and then sitting down to write the scene that takes place in Costco, an American chain superstore that carries every possible product you could ever dream of in absolutely absurd quantities. (It is a real store, incidentally, a national chain that exists from New York to Hawaii, and the description of it is true to life.) Europeans tend to look at things like this as nothing but silly materialism, but while I was living in England I missed the sheer exuberance of it—not the idea that you could have anything you wanted, but the idea that you could actually *want* anything you wanted, that no idea was too unconventional or too absurd. I wanted to show America as a new world of possibilities, where you can become whatever you want to become (as characters like Jason/Yehudah and Freydl/Frances do), and what that choice really means—both the exuberance and the burdens of that freedom.

I should say here that while the story of the Landsmann family is purely my invention, the historical details are accurate down to the square footage of the apartments (I'll get into this later). I should also say that even though my family is thoroughly American, I have traveled a tremendous amount (much like Bill Landsmann in the novel), to about forty or so countries around the world. I don't have a slide collection, though.

Do you come from a family of believers?

My family is Jewish and ascribes to the American Conservative movement in Judaism (which is right in the middle of the religious spectrum between orthodox and reform). We are, as you put it, a "believing" family in that I was raised to believe in God, to value the sanctity of life, and to take seriously the teachings of the Torah—which involves both being educated in and often wrestling with the tradition. While I can't claim to observe every ritual, my religion is the path by which I reach my understanding of the world.

Is the story of the tefillin in New York Harbor true?

The story of the tefillin at the bottom of New York Harbor is, as far as I can tell, true. I first heard this story from a classmate at Harvard College, who told of how his great-grandfather saw people throwing their tefillin overboard on the ship that first brought him to New York. I was very struck by this story and thought it was unique to my classmate's family. However, I then mentioned it to others and soon found that among Jews of a certain generation in America (those now in their sixties or seventies), this story is something that everyone seems to know—I would start telling them the story, and they would quickly supply the ending. Of course, this might mean that the story is simply a popular legend. But then I discovered an interesting piece of evidence. While I haven't seen it myself, I am told that in a museum in Nova Scotia in Canada, there is an exhibit featuring "A set of phylacteries [tefillin] removed from the floor of the Atlantic." That clinched it for me. (I did not, however, have the experience of seeing them in a junk shop!)

Other historical details?

I tried very hard in this novel to ensure that the details were historically accurate. This was of course hardest in the story that takes place in the 1890s. However, I had several sources against which to check my facts. A few years ago I wrote a story for a magazine about the Lower East Side Tenement Museum, a museum in New York City located in a restored tenement building that demonstrates how turn-of-the-century immigrant populations lived in this neighborhood of New York, which at the time was a large center for Eastern European Jewish immigrants. All the details about Leah's family's living conditions—the square footage of the apartment, the gas lighting, the sink (but without running water), the use of the living room as an extra bedroom, the boarders, other material details—come largely from the research this museum has done into material life at the time.

As a person familiar with Yiddish sources, I also knew a lot about this period from articles, novels, and other sources written about this neighborhood at the time period—the situation of Jewish garment workers at the time is familiar to any student of Yiddish literature.

Also, there was at the time a very popular advice column called "A Bintel Brief" (A Bundle of Letters) in the largest New York Yiddish newspaper, parts of which have been published in English translation in book form. I read these letters and was incredibly moved by them, and many other details of this particular chapter come from there. For example, one letter describes how factory owners would "fix" the clocks in the factories by turning back the hands on the clock so that people would work longer than they were being paid to work. The tension between the old world religious life and the new world is also of course reflected in these letters. One letter is written by a man who divorced his wife and then decides he wants to remarry her, but he cannot because he is a cohen and now his wife is divorced! I drew on these details as well as other information I have through Yiddish literature in reconstructing this time and place.

Other items in the book are also historically accurate. The character Leah, for example, the child of a woman who was raped, is sixteen–seventeen years old in 1898 because there were pogroms in Yelizavetgrad and surrounding towns in Ukraine south of Kiev in the spring of 1881, during which many Jewish women were raped. Like Nadav and Isaac, many Jews were drafted into the Austro-Hungarian Army during World War I. There was a Montessori School in Amsterdam in the 1930s and 1940s which did expel its Jewish students when the Nuremberg Laws went into effect in Holland (one of these students was Anne Frank). I consulted maps of Amsterdam from this period and discovered that there were dozens of chocolate and candy factories, so Willem walks by a lot of them as he strolls through the city. The Carousel of Progress Ride is a real ride in Disney World, and it really was transplanted from the New York World's Fair of the 1960s. Even a more recent detail is true: in 1999, there was in fact an early hominid skull that turned up in a gift shop in New York! I'm sure there are historical errors and even more historical stretches, but I did try to ensure the accuracy of the work.

How would you yourself weigh the story: is it primarily a new book of Job, or a specific sort of coming-of-age novel?

I'm not so excited about "coming of age." On the other hand, I also don't see this book solely as a rewriting of the Book of Job. While the Book of Job is the most obvious reference, the book is in fact saturated with references to various parts of the Hebrew bible and rabbinic literature.

In studying modern Hebrew literature, I became intrigued by the way that modern Hebrew and Yiddish literature, particularly the work of the early modern Hebrew and Yiddish writers, almost constantly refers to the Hebrew bible and commentaries on the bible, even while challenging the religious tradition. This is particularly easy to do in Hebrew, because of the language's long history and the echoes tied to almost every word. I wondered whether it was possible to create this sort of literature—using biblically anchored language within a secular text—in English. At first I thought it would be awkward to include biblical allusions in an English book. However, I soon realized that most English readers are familiar with biblical literature only in archaic translations. This made it possible to create a work in English that could be read on several levels without overburdening the language. I wanted to create a different style for American Jewish literature, one more connected to the Jewish literary tradition of constant reference to ancient text.

As for Job: When I was twelve years old, I became a Torah reader for the children's congregation in my synagogue, which made me very familiar with, and fascinated by, the text of the Hebrew bible. In college I majored in literature and focused on Hebrew literature, and I soon became intrigued by the Book of Job. This book is, of course, one of the most compelling and confusing books in the bible, and for that reason, I believe, it also has some of the most beautiful poetry ever written in any language.

What intrigued me most, though, was what I saw as the ultimate question of the book of Job. The book asks the question that so many people ask themselves: Why do bad things happen to good people? But as I read the book again and again, I decided that this question was misleading. To me, the central question of the Book of Job isn't that common question—which, after all, can't really be answered and isn't answered at all in the book of Job—but rather: Are people "good" to begin with, or are they shaped by their experiences? What makes "bad things" important isn't whether they happen to you or to someone else, because that's not your decision. What makes them important is the part that is your decision: what you do with them once they've happened. It is a commonplace to say that people are shaped by their experiences. But that implies that you can't control who you become, since these experiences are left to accidents of fate.

This premise—that the most fundamental aspects of your own life are left to chance—is the subject of many books and movies of varying quality. What I hoped to do, in this novel, was to present a different idea. People are not shaped by their experiences, which they cannot choose, but rather by something they do control: they are shaped by what they make of their experiences. I also wanted to write a book that believed in happiness, that showed that happiness was possible, even in a world dead set against it. Happiness, I believe, is not something that one finds, but rather something that one makes.

In this sense, I suppose, it is a "coming of age" story, but one that has very little to do with age and very much to do with taking responsibility for one's own life and choices. That's something that can happen at any age. It doesn't happen in a moment, but over a lifetime.

SUGGESTED FURTHER READING

The Book of Job
See especially Chapters 1, 2, and 3; Chapter 38:1–30; Chapter 42:1–6, 12–13, 16–17 (*Tanakh, A New Translation of the Holy Scriptures According to the Traditional Hebrew Text* [Philadelphia: Jewish Publication Society, 1985]).

I. L. Peretz, "The Dead Town" (1895)
English translation available in *A Treasury of Yiddish Stories*, ed. Irving Howe and Eliezer Greenberg (New York: Penguin, 1990).
   In this short story by the classic Yiddish writer, a traveler meets a man on the road who claims to live in a place called "the dead town," a place that can't be found on any map—a town where most of the inhabitants are already dead, but none of the living residents have noticed.

Nachman of Bratslav, "The Seven Beggars" (early nineteenth century)
English translation available in *The Tales: Nahman of Bratslav*, ed. Arnold Band (New York: Paulist Press, 1978).

This complicated mystical tale by a Hassidic luminary tells the story of two children, abandoned in a forest, who are rescued by seven beggars. Years later, when the children marry, the seven beggars reappear at their wedding, each bringing a story with him. One beggar's story takes place in a pair of countries where no one is able to sleep.

Travels of Benjamin of Tudela (twelfth century)
English translation available as *The World of Benjamin of Tudela: A Medieval Mediterranean Travelogue*, ed. Sandra Benjamin, trans. A. Asher (Madison: Fairleigh Dickinson University Press, 1995).
> This medieval travelogue recounts the voyages of a Jewish merchant who made a point of visiting and documenting Jewish communities throughout the medieval world.

S. Y. Abramovitch, *Travels of Benjamin the Third* (1878)
English translation available in *Tales of Mendele the Book Peddler*, ed. Dan Miron and Ken Frieden (New York: Schocken Books, 1996).
> This comic novel by the classic Yiddish writer, set in a small Russian Jewish town, tells of a modern-day traveling Benjamin—an idiot who barely makes it around the block.

Sholem Aleichem, *Yosele Solovey* (1889)
English translation available as *The Nightingale, or, The Saga of Yosele Solovey the Cantor*, trans. Aliza Shervin (New York: Putnam, 1985).
> This novel by the best-known Yiddish writer is about a prodigy cantor named Yosele Solovey ("Yosele" is the Yiddish equivalent of "Joe"; "Solovey" means "nightingale") whose professional success quickly leads him to personal ruin.

A Bintel Brief: Sixty Years of Letters from the Lower East Side to the Jewish Daily Forward, ed. Isaac Metzger (New York: Schocken Books, 1990).
> Published in book form in English translation, this volume is a collection of letters first printed at the turn of the last century in the advice column of the most popular American Yiddish newspaper. Written by people desperate for help in their new country, the letters reveal the particular problems Jewish immigrants faced in their new home—as well as many problems that never grow old.

S. Y. Agnon, *A Guest for the Night* (1939)
English translation available, trans. Misha Louvich (New York: Schocken Books, 1968).

> This Hebrew novel, written by a Nobel laureate, describes a visit to a devastated Jewish town in Poland fifteen years after World War I. In one scene, a wounded Jewish veteran recalls being in a trench during a battle and seeing an arm wrapped in tefillin, severed from its body.

Hayyim Nachman Bialik, *Random Harvest* (1923)
English translation available in *Random Harvest: The Novellas of* Bialik, trans. David Patterson and Ezra Spicehandler (Boulder, Colo.: Westview Press, 1999).

> This autobiographical novel by the most acclaimed modern Hebrew poet describes the life of an orphaned Jewish boy in rural Ukraine. In one scene, the narrator recounts how wolves occasionally entered his village.

H. Leivick, *The Wolf* (1920)
English translation available in *American Yiddish Poetry: A Bilingual Anthology*, ed. Benjamin and Barbara Harshav (Berkeley: University of California Press, 1986).

> This long poem by an American Yiddish poet describes the destruction of an Eastern European Jewish town during World War I. A rabbi, the sole survivor of a massacre of the town's Jews, escapes to the woods, where he is transformed into a wolf.

Yankev Glatshteyn, "The Crown" (1956)
> This American Yiddish modernist master published many volumes of poetry. His collection *Fun Mayn Gantser Mi* ("From All My Toil") contains the following poem:

The Crown

This song in my voice that chants, with proper cantillation,
the melody of memory, the haunting humming,
this crown, shot through with silver, that you see on my head,
where did it come from?
Where?

With a wild prank,
with boyish will,
some forty years ago,
through a portal of the ship,
I sent my tefillin out on the waters.
Like cast-off bread, the tefillin's crown came back.
After many years, the soaked crown swam back.

A silver crown.

Like an unhatched egg,
God's sorrow lay before my father's threshold,
when, with a heavy heart, a half-dried wineskin,
I set out on the roads.
Severed, forlorn and tattered,
I began my wandering
through the terrifying wilderness of our century.

O, forty thorns of my century.

A God-seeker, I tapped blindly with my staff
and skillfully avoided the quorum in the synagogue.
As for my parents, made in God's image,
I more than once encountered them on the roads.
Your Jewish head is naked and bare,
I heard them say.

Your Jewish head, child.

O, leave your bread on the water,
The straps that bind you,
Throw them into the deepest abyss.
Throw! What kind of meaning do they have, anyway?
Many days from now, you will find them.

You will have to find them.

Now my parents have been rewarded.
My head is crowned.

With ancient gray Jewishness.

(translated from the Yiddish by Dara Horn)